POWER OF THE MOON

Power of the Moon series book 1

TINA CARREIRO

Time and Tide Books
www.timeandtidepublishing.com

Time and Tide Publishing, LLC
7040 Seminole Pratt Whitney Rd. Suite 25-109
Loxahatchee, FL 33470

Copyright © 2011 Tina Carreiro
Second Edition 2012

www.timeandtidepublishing.com

Cover by Tincar Creations

Library of Congress Control Number: 2014937850

ISBN-13: 978-0-9856576-0-4
ISBN-13: 978-0-9856576-1-1 (ebook)

10   0   9   8 5   6   5   7   6   0   X

ACKNOWLEDGEMENTS

My heartfelt thanks go out to Cindy, and Erin. Thank you for taking time out of your lives to read my rough drafts and provide me with direct and honest input. Asia and Sheryl—you rock!

To my mom, you read everything I hand you and the excitement that lights up your face only makes me type faster. Thank you for saving my creative work from school and instilling the idea that I can do anything I set my mind to. This is a result of you not hiding the romance books when I was little.

To Dawn, thank you for being there, every day, exactly when I needed a writing buddy. You have been a tremendous help and a great friend, for not only letting me bounce ideas off you but you also love my Mia. Your reassurances kept me on solid ground.

To the West Family—Joe, Emily and Alex. I can't thank you enough for taking me under your wing and sharing your years of editing and publishing knowledge with me. From the oldest to the youngest West, you have helped mold my baby into something great. Thanks for coming to my rescue

To Jodi, thanks for being my editing life-line, picking me up when I felt discouraged, and giving me the reassuring boost that kept me going. Caramel Macchiatos all around!

To Amanda, thank you for your keen eyes and incredible patience. And for not simply brushing me off when I asked you to recheck my baby for errors.

My husband, Matt, you are the love of my life, my leading man, best friend, and soul mate. I knew I had something great if I pulled your emotions into a romance novel, which is something you normally wouldn't read. Thank you for your constant encouragement, patience, laughter, and inspiration. I couldn't ask for a better critique than the one you gave me.

DEDICATION

To Matthew and Samantha, who are my best creations and my husband, Matt, who is my greatest adventure.

~ *"Tempus Vitam Regit"*

ONE

*K*nowing when someone was going to die was something Mia had grown accustomed to, and she had just spotted another dead man walking.

Shit... not Art. She focused on him as he rambled through the gas station parking lot, hoping he'd come inside as he usually did. Now that she knew his fate, it weighed heavily on her heart, and she had an unusual urge to dig deeper. Uncrossing her legs, she hopped off the counter and tore her gaze from Art to focus on the approaching customer.

"Hello... MEE-ah." He drew out her name in a taunting gesture. Just what she needed—Russell.

It was times like these she hated working at the gas station. "You know it's pronounced MY-ah, jerk."

She snatched the bag of chips and scanned the barcode.

"Hey! Watch it. You almost touched me, freak. Keep your hands off," Russell said, as he shoved his thick tongue under his upper lip and sucked.

Mia ignored him. After all, she was a freak. Russell had been driving it into her head since elementary school. And at twenty-seven, it didn't really bother her anymore.

Mia giggled as a tiny surge of energy washed over her.

Standing next to Russell was the apparition of an old woman with white hair. The ghost was flicking at his ear with her finger, tormenting him to no satisfaction. Mia knew he couldn't feel a thing.

Russell looked around the empty store, then followed Mia's gaze to the vacant spot next to him. "You truly are fucked up, aren't you, freak?"

Mia looked at the old woman, then back to Russell. "Oh, piss off, Russ. Your grandma's just a little disappointed in you, that's all."

"Shut up! My grandma's dead. Give me my stuff... freak." Grabbing the bag, he hurried out the door.

Whether Mia liked it or not, she was like a walking cable box rigged with steal-a-vision, her mind picked up everything, especially the dead.

Disgusted by Russell's teasing, Mia tugged off her nametag and threw the cheap piece of plastic in the cash drawer.

Working the graveyard shift had its perks—people ignored her most of the time, and she preferred it that way. The actions of others had caused her to wrap herself in protective layers, blocking emotion, love, and trust. With two jobs, Mia didn't have time to notice her lack of friends or social life.

She focused on Art as he made his way to the door, his aura was becoming more defined as he approached. The halo of color reflecting life's energy was something most people couldn't see. Mia could. To her, people were like walking mood rings, and the ones who came in late at night mostly had lustful auras. Not that she knew a lot about lust. She had made the mistake of trusting a couple of men in the past—boys really. It wasn't that she didn't want someone. It was just difficult. As if the images she picked up from her so-called boyfriends weren't enough, she was also a conductor of negative ones, and those played repeatedly in her mind like a movie preview, making intimacy a nightmare.

When she dreamed, vivid images of death haunted her, and as much as she tried to block them, they still managed to work their way through. This made spooning impossible. Her solution: no touching, especially men. For five years now, these rules had worked well. Highly emotional situations were something she stayed away from, and she was skilled at avoiding them most of the time.

"How're you doing tonight, Art?" Mia grabbed a pack of Marlboro Reds from the cigarette rack, never taking her eyes off him as he approached.

"Oh, fair to middlin'," he slurred. Art's tanned skin made his empty, blue eyes shine like sapphires. Gray streaked the brown hair framing his face in a messy just-out-of-bed look. A long, brown belt fastened into its last hole kept his baggy pants from falling off his skinny frame. Deep wrinkles and dark, rough patches on his face were evidence of lots of sun and alcohol.

Mia took a deep breath and slid the pack toward Art. She had to break her rules if she wanted to find out why death had marked him. Her fingers brushed over his knuckles, and a small current of electricity rolled over her skin as familiar images flooded her mind—the same images she had witnessed before during accidental touches and the same images consuming Art, making him the man he was.

The argument he'd had with his wife replayed in her mind. That fatal night unfolded as Art drove away in anger, ruffled by news of an unexpected baby. Art had wanted more for their child, a better life than he had growing up, and wasn't prepared. When Art realized he was wrong, he rushed back to his wife with a tiny shirt that read *I Love Mommy*. On his way back, a teenage driver ran a red light, T-boning another car and ejecting the driver. The teenager's car spun and came straight toward Art's, smashing into the front bumper. When

Art had gotten out of his vehicle, he focused on the ejected driver's crumpled body lying in the middle of the intersection, recognizing every delicate feature.

His wife.

Art knelt, and held his wife's limp body. As she took her last breath. His life ended with hers. He'd never forget the note they found at his house that night. She was coming to find him, to make everything right. He blamed himself for her death and he'd never recovered from the pain of losing his wife and child.

Holding back tears, Mia yanked her hand away and avoided his eyes. She scanned his light-blue aura which was fading into a whitish, silver color. *Shit.* If she could just get past the death of his wife, maybe she could find out what was wrong and help.

With a touch of irritation, she looked at the computer as it beeped and noted the gas pump number in use. It severed her concentration on Art. She looked up just as the chime on the door went off.

Wanting to keep him close, she nodded toward the refreshment counter. "Art, go get some coffee and a snack. It's on me."

"Thank you, darlin'."

While Art was getting his snack, a man ripped straight out of GQ magazine entered the store. The man moved so smoothly, Mia swore he was gliding. He wore his light brown hair close on the sides and flattened on top, except for the front, which spiked up and curled back in a loop. Muscles rippled beneath a tight, black shirt, and his legs were as firm as tree trunks.

He walked straight to Art, and the old man's frail frame cowered from the man. Mia felt negative energy fill the room. She focused on GQ's lips, picking up the conversation from their motion.

I don't think so. Shooting daggers at the threatening man, Mia's protective nature surfaced. She hit the panic button behind the counter and grabbed the Louisville Slugger her boss kept hidden. Seconds later, she stood in front of the two men with the bat in hand.

"Art, are you okay?" Mia raked her eyes over his trembling body.

"Mind your business, girl." GQ's menacing voice rolled through the air, jump-starting her pulse. Mia's nerves crept into her throat, forming a lump she tried to swallow so not to show fear. *Never let 'em see ya sweat.* The words of her grandmother echoed in her head. *If you think they can beat you, they will.* The advice of dead loved ones always came at the strangest times.

"Why don't you pick on someone your own size?" Mia tightened her fingers around the bat as she raised it and narrowed her eyes.

"Am I your size?"

The deep, chilling voice filled the air behind her, and she turned. The doorway framed the man, his bulk took up the entire entrance. With his mullet style, sandy-blond hair and muscles stretching the fabric of his clothes, he looked like he was late for a wrestling match. The hem of his black, leather duster hung just below his knees, and dark sunglasses wrapped his face. When he removed them, his eyes seemed to glow from within.

Must be a night out for the freaks, but those are cool contacts.

"Woman, move aside." His voice sent a powerful burst of energy toward her, and though Mia's heart skipped a beat, she stood her ground.

Move aside? Her inner rebel stood up, and she shouted, "No!"

As she stared at him, his aura materialized. Mia had seen many auras in her life, but never one like his. Metallic silver embedded into the blackness of his aura, and a bright white formed the outer crest. It was beautiful, but she had no idea what it meant. Black wasn't good, she knew that, but the metallic shimmer throughout was a mystery. She made a mental note to Google it later.

Mia's face relaxed. Her head tilted to the side as she gazed at his aura—it was mesmerizing.

"Woman!" His tone was firm, but his expression bewildered as she continued to stare at him. Lowering his head like a bull ready to charge, his stare intensified as if he were trying to speak to her with his mind. When he narrowed his eyes, the white glow increased, and a reddish tint took form.

A wave of dizziness instantly hit, and her stomach became queasy. She wanted to lie down. When her knee slightly buckled, she clenched her teeth, narrowed her eyes, and glared back at him. Her fatigue faded as she pulled on her inner strength, intensifying her gaze. Glowing Eyes' aura twitched like an interrupted cable signal. *What the...?* With an intent stare and a raised brow, she smirked. "Are we going to do this all night?"

With wide-eyes, his head snapped up, and his lips parted in shock as he looked past her to GQ.

Okay, I'm officially weirded out now. What in the hell just happened? Mia's thoughts raced, trying to piece things together.

Glowing Eyes twitched his head at GQ, shifting his gaze back to Mia. GQ grabbed her from behind, pinning her arms to her sides causing her to drop the bat.

A sharp sound followed by a hiss came from behind her, and it rolled inside her ears, bringing all the hairs on her skin to attention.

With his lips pulled into a tight line, Glowing Eyes glared at GQ, shook his head no, and focused on Art.

"Art, come," he ordered.

Mia's eyebrows drew together as Art went past her, his aura twitching and small spaces appearing throughout its crest. It became dimmer the closer he got to Glowing Eyes whose own aura grew brighter with every step Art took.

"Art, you disobeyed me. Now, you will be punished. Go to the car."

Mia spoke before her brain could stop her. "Over my dead body. I'm not going to let you take a helpless man out of here." The faint sound of sirens echoed in the distance as she struggled in GQ's grip.

"Oh please, Master. She would taste so sweet." GQ's voice sent shivers through her. She glanced up at the security mirror. His lips were pulled back, revealing two sharp, pointed teeth and his eyes glazed over like a starving man being handed a steak. *Fangs?*

The sirens grew louder as they approached. GQ bent down and raked his teeth across her neck, nicking her skin.

"No!" Glowing Eyes' stern voice drew GQ from the love affair he was having with Mia's neck. His movements froze, leaving his mouth still, but allowing his gaze to trail over to Glowing Eyes who shook his head. "Leave her. We must go. Now!"

Before letting her go, GQ flattened his tongue on her shoulder and slowly licked his way up to her ear.

She swayed forward as he released her, clutching her stomach to ease the sickness swirling in its pit. She knew for certain GQ wanted to kill her and eat her, but she wasn't sure in which order.

Seconds later, an officer walked in with his gun drawn. Mia stood frozen as he walked toward her. "Ma'am, are you alone in here?" His voice sounded muffled in her mind.

"Yes," Mia squeaked out.

"Ma'am! Are. You. All right?" the officer shouted, indicating this wasn't the first time he had asked the question.

"I'm sorry. Yeah-yes... I'm okay." She shook her head, trying to make sense of what she'd just witnessed.

"Ma'am, were you robbed?" the officer asked while sliding his gun back into its holster.

"No, sir." Suddenly, she snapped out of the daze and grabbed his arm. "Holy shit! A man—Art—was just taken against his will."

"Was he physically taken?"

"Well, no, but..."

"So, he just walked out?"

"Uh... no, he was forced to walk out..."

She watched the officer's face as he took down her statement, shaking his head. When she said the man had glowing eyes, his expression changed, and his pen came to a stop.

Great, he thinks I'm a whack job.

She continued until he held his hand up at the fang part.

"Ma'am, will you excuse me, please?" He walked over to his partner who had helped himself to a cup of coffee, and spoke in a low voice. When he rolled his eyes, Mia folded her arms across her chest.

Yep, they think I'm a whack job.

The officer taking her statement squeezed the radio mic on his shoulder. "Can you go to a clear channel?" he asked, walking further away.

Mia's comfort level lessened drastically as bits of the conversation reached her.

"Yeah. Glowing eyes and fangs, 10-4." Releasing the mic, he walked back to her. "Ma'am, I'm sorry, but there isn't much I can do about the guy you claim was taken from here. If he walked out of the building on his own, then he wasn't forced. He left of his own free will. I can take a report on your assault. You said the man grabbed you from behind?" The officer tapped the back of his pen on the pad and waited for her response. She was just about to respond when his radio beeped with a long tone, followed by a strong voice calling out a code.

"Shit, it's the sheriff." The officer's eyes widened, and he grabbed his radio so fast, he fumbled to keep it in his grip. His partner snapped to attention and came to stand by him. "Yes, sir, I'm still 10-12 with the victim." Mia listened as the sheriff informed him that someone would come out tomorrow evening to take her statement.

"Can't they come out tonight? It's almost five A.M., and I don't want to relive this again tomorrow."

"Ma'am, they're sending someone from a special unit. That unit works the night shift which is ending soon. Sorry."

"Fine." Mia sighed.

As they left, the officer slid his notepad back into his pocket, looked over his shoulder, and commented to his partner, "I love it when they call out a detective—no paperwork for us."

TWO

*B*reathing a sigh of relief, Mia wearily unlocked the door to her studio apartment. She dragged herself in, closed and locked the door behind her, and took a moment to rest her eyes and lean her shoulder against the wooden frame.

She loved her apartment. Hardwood covered every inch of the floor, accented by large, beautiful throw rugs. She felt comfortable here—more comfortable than she felt anywhere else. It was one of the few places she didn't feel like a complete freak. At home, she could be herself.

She walked to the window and pulled the curtains shut, letting darkness fill the room. Light was the last thing she wanted when she was in bed.

Her king-size canopy bed was centered on a large area rug. Sheer white swags flowed from the top and hung to tie at each post. Only a few pictures adorned the walls, and she didn't have many knickknacks around. Previously owned items still had energies attached to them, and she didn't need, or want, the distraction.

She fell on the bed, exhausted. As always, she hoped to get some much-needed rest, and yet, the *peaceful* sleep she'd hoped for never came.

Her mind drifted into a familiar dream. The rhythmic sound of drums beat in her head, drowning out the cries of a baby...

She was weightless, and the scene around her moved rapidly. As she gazed up, she saw the moon. Its glow began to transform into the man with the glowing eyes. Soon the events of her night took over, replaying within her dream. Art stepped in front of the man, and then everything faded except for Art.

Mia felt the heat from a fire as thick smoke filled the air and her senses. She searched for Art through its suffocating layers. Soon the crackle of the fire became louder, and the heat intensified. Through the haze in the distance, she found him. Fire covered his body, but he was alive. When she ran toward him, a wall of flames engulfed her, and the glowing eyes appeared once more.

Mia jolted awake, drenched in sweat. She hated these dreams—dreams she knew meant *something*—dreams she couldn't tell anyone about without having the crazy label stamped on her forehead.

From her nightstand, she retrieved her journal and wrote down every detail she could recall. She was hoping to write more about the drums constantly beating, moving her forward toward *something*.

The recurring dreams started the eve of her twenty-seventh birthday and came every night after. She tried to inch the dream onward to find out more, but it often stopped at the same spot—with the moon bright in the sky, and the sound of a baby.

Who was the baby? And why was it crying?

Not wanting to get up and face the day, she snuggled into the blanket and stared at the ceiling. Her Siamese cat jumped onto the bed, kneading the pillow by her face. He lowered his head, butting it against hers as she scratched between his ears until he fell and flipped to his back.

"You hungry, baby?" Mia stretched along with the cat. Trying to get motivated, she sighed, cursing herself for being lazy. If she had gotten up earlier, she could have researched the strange aura from last night. Now she only had enough time to shower, eat, and feed the cat before going to work. She also needed to check on Art—she knew something was wrong.

***

Mia had barely made it into the gas station before Shannon gave her the run-down of what needed restocking and what was already on order.

"Which one of you messed with my surveillance system?" Stan yelled from the back office. They blankly stared at their short, cranky boss as he walked toward them.

"What's the matter with the system, Stan?" Mia yelled back.

"The tape is missing. That's what the matter is—which one of you messed with it? I'm docking your pay for the price of the tape if I don't get it back," he said, shaking a stubby finger. Not only was he a constant complainer, but he was also extremely cheap.

"No one messed with it, you miserable ass," Shannon spat back, her face twisting in disgust.

"Then where's my tape, Shannon?"

"The police came in after Mia left and took it."

"Police? Why would the police want the surveillance tape?" His face turned a shade of puce before his eyebrows dipped into an angry 'v.'

"Would someone mind telling me what happened in my own damned store? Seems like something I should know about, doesn't it?"

Shannon looked at Mia, but she just rolled her eyes and walked toward the register, stashing her purse and coat on a shelf underneath.

"There was an... *incident*... here last night." Shannon cocked her eyebrow and looked toward Mia.

"What kind of incident?" Noticing the way Shannon kept staring at her, Stan's focus went to her as well. "Is there something you want to tell us, Mia?" He crossed his arms and waited.

"No, it was... nothing. And it won't cost you any money, Stan," she said in a childish manner.

"Well good! If it does, it'll come out of your pay! The next time the police come to my store, I had better know about it. They'd better bring my tape back. Shannon, clock out! You're five minutes past your shift, and I'm not paying you to sit here and chit-chat." He grumbled under his breath as he walked back to his office.

"That man really needs a good blowjob," Shannon said, grabbing her belongings. "I guess if you want to tell me what happened, Mia, you will. Till then, I ain't gonna bother you about it,"

"Really, it was nothing, but thanks for your concern." Mia turned away and started counting the cigarettes on the rack. It was the only inventory they took the entire night. Stan was paranoid about people stealing them. Thank God he didn't ask them to count the Reese's Peanut Butter Cups, or Mia would be in trouble.

Several times throughout her shift, she checked the clock. It was odd—normally several regulars stopped by. But not tonight. The night was dead, not even the cops had shown up.

At two-fifteen, she counted eight candy wrappers and one twenty ounce soda that had fallen prey to her. At three, she gave in. Art, who usually came in a few times a night, still hadn't shown. If her vision was right, she knew something would happen to him sooner or later. She only hoped she wasn't too late.

Mia stepped from behind the counter and hung the "Back in Thirty Minutes" sign before locking the door. Luckily for her, the police hadn't been there yet, and the surveillance tape was still in their possession, so Stan wouldn't find out. If he did, she'd definitely lose her job.

A few minutes later, she was in her car and on the road. It wasn't far to Art's place, and within moments she'd pulled into a wooded area just off a long footpath. She immediately smelled the smoke when she opened her car door.

Her psyche started to twitch, unease swirling in the pit of her stomach as her pulse raced. She knew exactly what she was going to find. She'd already seen it.

Racing from the car down the dirt pathway and toward the smoke, she saw a faint light. It appeared through the mass of tiny pine trees ahead of her. She should get back in the car and run away like she usually did, but something urged her forward into the thick trees.

She came to a clearing. Her eyes darted around, catching her surroundings. The smoke was too intense—it burned her eyes and throat. She put her hand up to cover her nose when the smell overwhelmed her. That was when her eyes landed on what had made the flames—Art's body.

He had the appearance of an overcooked marshmallow, scorched clothes hanging from his small, lanky frame. And though his ruptured skin was charred beyond recognition, she knew it was him.

Close beside him was the cardboard structure he slept beneath, a few sheets tied to it as makeshift curtains. *How did the fire stay in this little area?* She looked around, trying to find signs of charred trees anywhere else. Nothing. It didn't make sense. Tears pooled in her eyes. She was too late to save him.

"Excuse me."

Startled by the deep voice behind her, she jerked into a whirl. A figure stood in a spot that had been empty a moment ago. Her hand went to her chest, and she took a defensive stance.

"What are you doing here?" the figure asked.

A strange inflection danced in the voice, and it made her ears tingle. It was calm and soothing with a massive amount of energy flowing from it, carrying strength and power. She instantly felt pulled to it. She tried to focus on the man's face, but the smoke burned her eyes, and it was too dark. The only thing she could clearly make out was the shiny badge reflecting light from a few remaining flames.

"I'm sorry. I didn't mean to trespass on your crime scene."

"Thank you, but this isn't a crime scene. It seems to be an accident."

"I hardly think it was an accident, officer."

"Why would you say that?"

"The fire, the way it was contained." Disappointed in herself for not finding Art in time, she let her anger surface. "Have you identified that man?"

"Do you think you know him?" He stared at her.

"Yes, I know him. His name is Art." She wanted him to confirm what she had already known, but, more importantly, she longed to hear his voice again. For some odd reason, it calmed her. *Why is he staring at me like I have two heads though, like he's trying to unlock a secret code?*

"I'm sorry, but I can't tell you that until we notify his next of kin."

Mia's expression fell. She went there to find Art, was too late, saw this horrible scene, and now Mr. By-The-Book couldn't confirm the identity of the dead man. Shaking her head, she let out a frustrated sigh. "Well, isn't that just wonderful. I have to go."

"No, what you have to do is explain to me what you're doing out here, in the woods, with a dead man."

"You know what? I think I've had enough of people telling me what to do in the past few days! Excuse me." She pushed past him, her anger rising. She should have listened to her dream and gone with her instinct. Who knows—maybe she could've saved Art. Discouraged, she knew she had to leave this scene behind her. Fast. Her pace quickened. Soon her strides became long, and she ran.

Minutes later, she was in her car and hitting the gas. Her vision blurred as tears welled in her eyes, and she tilted the rearview mirror to wipe them away. *Damn.* Blue lights. Sighing, she pulled over, taking deep breaths as she teetered on the edge of a meltdown.

The streetlights illuminated the area, giving it a picturesque glow. Despite what had happened to Art, it was a beautiful night. The moon hung bright, and the stars covered the sky, their light dimmed only by a thin veil of smog.

She watched the officer dismount his motorcycle and remove his helmet. His thick, dark brown hair almost looked black as it shimmered in the light. Mia had an instant urge to run her fingers through it.

He walked toward the car with smooth strides. With the window down, she could hear the sound of his boots on the asphalt, clicking along as he walked. The air thinned as he came closer. From the moment he'd taken off his helmet, Mia had felt his eyes on her.

She stared at the boots traveling up his legs to hug the top of his calves. His pants were tucked inside and clung to his thighs, accentuating his muscles. His gun belt and the leather strap that ran diagonally across his chest, shined with a polished glow.

As he approached her window, nerves circled in her stomach. She kept her eyes forward, hands on the steering wheel.

"May I see your license, please?" His voice was smooth and sounded familiar.

"Yes, sir," Mia said as she leaned over the passenger seat and fumbled with her purse. A second later, she produced her license.

"What's your name?"

"Mia." She raised an eyebrow and wondered why he'd ask for her name when he had her license in his hand.

"Let's try this again. What is your name?" The authority in his voice deepened.

"I said, Mia. It's right there in your hands," she said with more attitude than she'd intended.

His head snapped up, eyes narrowing as they locked with hers. "Step out of the car, please." He opened the door, leaving his hand to rest on the top.

She grazed his arm as she slid out, causing instant bumps to travel over her body. She tried to mentally shake the feeling by resting against the car. As she leaned back, she lifted her gaze slowly from his boots to his eyes, not missing an inch. *Oh. My. God. Save a horse, ride a cowboy.*

Her eyes moved over his strong, chiseled face and a set of full lips made for kissing. He looked at her, his intense stare framed by thick, long lashes. Her gaze locked with his, and she lost herself in their deep brown abyss.

"I want you to tell me your name again, and this time, your real name." His voice calmly swept over her.

She dropped her eyes before she embarrassed herself by drooling, and suddenly remembered her real name was on her license. "I-I forgot my real name was on my license. I'm sorry. I don't go by that name."

"Do you hate it so much that you can't even say it?"

"It's Miakoda, and yes, I hate it." She lifted her eyes back to his, and then wondered how many people looked at him every day and never realized he had a tiny black spec mixed with the gorgeous brown.

He stepped forward. "It's a shame to hate such a beautiful name." His eyes caressed her face.

"Well, I've never met anyone who thought it was beautiful. Everyone thinks my parents were either drunk or high when they named me."

"It is beautiful and a powerful name. Do you know what it means?"

Of course she did. Who gets a fucked-up name like that and doesn't research it? She shook her head "no."

He leaned forward slightly, as if he had a secret to tell. His closeness seemed to suck the oxygen out of the air, and she breathed deeply as his scent wrapped around her. Resting his hand on the car, he leaned into her. "Miakoda means 'power of the moon.'"

His voice was perfect, seductive, and it drew her right in. When her name poured over his lips, she fell in love with it. It had never sounded so beautiful—sexy, even. It was arousing.

"Why do you keep staring at me like that?"

"Like what?" He flicked his gaze over her.

"Like you're confused and I don't know—hungry."

"There's something about you, beyond your beauty." His forehead wrinkled. "I can't put my finger on it."

Her lips parted, and her nipples tightened as they pressed against her shirt. His eyes darted to her breasts. *Oh, God, he knows. How does he know?*

When he slid his gaze back to hers, he seemed just as enthralled as she was. Her body began to bow into his as if he willed it forward.

Suddenly, he straightened and took a step back. The instant connection, she was sure they'd both felt, left him looking bewildered. He seemed to harden himself, shaking it off and snapped back into cop mode.

"Mia, why did you run from me when I asked you what you were doing back in the woods?"

"I thought I recognized your voice... I'm sorry for running from you, but Art was kind of a friend."

"I'm sorry about your friend, but that doesn't explain why you ran from me." He was staring at her like *that* again.

"You said it wasn't a crime, but an accident, and that upset me." She raised her eyes to his so he'd know she was serious. "Art's death was no accident. Someone killed him. I think I know who it was."

"Would you like to tell me how you know this?"

"No, you're just going to laugh at me, or think I'm nuts, like the two officers last night." She looked away, embarrassed by what she knew she'd have to tell him, and knowing once she did, he'd never look at her like this again.

"Do you work at Stan's gas station down the street?"

"Yes. How do you know that?"

"I was supposed to meet you earlier, but the call came in about your friend Art. I had to handle it first."

He leaned forward and opened her car door, the air between them charged with electricity. Their attention was drawn to the streetlight as it flickered. His suspicious eyes darted back to hers. "Let's get you back to work. We can talk more inside."

"Okay," Mia readily agreed. Though, she probably would've done the same thing if he'd said, "Let's go rob a bank together."

She struggled to keep her eyes forward as she continuously shifted her view to the mirrors, watching him. He stopped talking into his shoulder mic, and then suddenly he was at her window. "Mia. Wait. I'm sorry. I'm needed back at the scene with your friend's body. I'll come back tomorrow to take your statement."

"Ok. I'll see you tomorrow." Mia watched him as he made the U-turn. He looked magnificent, strong, powerful. *Yummy.* Disappointment washed over her as he vanished from her sight.

She pulled into the station and parked. Looking around the lot, she found it empty. *Just like me,* she thought as she went back inside to finish her double shift. Feeling lonelier than she had before, she pulled out the cleaning supplies from the back office to keep her busy. How could she feel this way about someone she doesn't know? Was she that hard up? Maybe five years had been too long?

Overtired and slaphappy, Mia's eyelids grew heavy as she placed the mop against the counter, the inviting smell of coffee calling to her. Taking a sip, she leaned back, letting her eyes wander. *Damn. Shannon never cleans anything.* After wiping her finger over the top of the filthy soda fountain, she shook her head in disgust and began sponging it down. As her foot bumped the garbage can underneath, her gaze fell upon a piece of trash beside it. Mia reached down and grabbed the red object. She froze. Chills raced through her arms and legs and crept up her spine. Art. It was Art's pack of Marlboro Reds.

She inched the pack open. Five cigarettes and a rolled up piece of paper stared back at her. Thinking it may be a clue from last night, she pulled the paper out. Engulfed by a massive wave of negative energy, the visions swarmed her, and she dropped to her knees.

Slowly, an arm comes into view as someone hands Art the Marlboros. His face. I need to see his face...

Beep...

The 'gas pump in use' alert yanked her from the trance.

Her mouth watered, and she fought the sick feeling in the pit of her stomach as nausea took form. Failing miserably, she grabbed the trashcan and vomited. What was happening to her? Her visions had never been this strong. Her sensitivity to things had increased, too, in the last couple of months, and she wasn't sure how to handle them.

Mia shoved the rolled up paper and pack of Reds into her pocket and wiped her mouth with a napkin. Thankful for pay-at-the-pump customers, she watched the car drive away.

THREE

*M*ia dropped her belongings on the floor as soon
as she walked into her apartment. The smoke from the
woods tangled with the smell of the cop's cologne and
lingered in her hair. As much as she hated losing his
scent, she had to wash off the smell of burning flesh.

Standing under the stream of water, she closed her
eyes and rested her palms on the tile, the warm water
beating on her face. Instantly, the cop appeared in her
mind. She felt him as if he were in the shower with her,
his hands on her skin, sliding over her breasts. Every
inch of her ached with need.

Her eyes snapped open. *What is happening to me?*
Normally, Mia didn't have sexual urges. She might as
well be a nun, having no interest or desire to be
touched. Grabbing the knobs, she turned the
temperature to cold and quickly finished washing,
fighting the urge to pleasure herself.

Walking to her dresser, Mia pulled out her
nightclothes. She preferred comfort over sexy any day
of the week. Her white, cotton boy shorts and light-blue
tank caressed her skin as she wiggled in bed, warm and
cozy.

Imagining the cop in bed with her was easy since she
couldn't keep the images out of her mind. Her thoughts
kept shifting back to the shower, thinking of how he'd
feel wet and soapy against her skin. She needed a
distraction that would drive him from her thoughts, so
she picked up a book off the nightstand. After a few

minutes of pure irritation, she tossed the book to the end of the bed.

"Fuck." Everything reminded her of him.

Giving up, she pulled the covers over her head and within minutes, she fell asleep.

Before long, he was there in her dreams, dominating them, as if he had always been around. Different fantasies played out, yet they all ended with the same outcome—a powerful climax.

She slept fitfully, the dreams plaguing her throughout the night.

She leaned back, her body shimmering with the faint light from the moon as he whispered her name. She looked into his eyes, her climax building, but suddenly their deep brown beauty was gone. They quickly transformed into the cold, glowing eyes she had come to know too well. Four terrifying words came in a demonic whisper: "I'm coming for you."

Startled, she shot straight up, scrubbed her eyes, and then grabbed the clock, focusing on the red digital numbers. She was shocked that she'd slept, even fitfully, for seven hours. Normally, she had to exhaust her mind to get a good night's sleep. Taking a few deep breaths, she stood and headed to the kitchen.

She patted her rumbling stomach and tied her knee-length robe as she stared into the empty cabinets. They reminded her how lonely she was. Although, she did a good job of fooling herself into believing she wasn't lonely. She had suppressed emotion for so long she had felt dead inside—until the cop. Now, she suddenly felt as if the world were moving. She knew it was silly— she'd only just met him.

She grabbed the Honey Nut Cheerios from the cabinet and had just turned to get the milk from the refrigerator when someone knocked on her door.

She jerked her head toward the sound. No one visited her. She glanced at the clock. Six-thirty p.m.

Her heart skipped a beat when she peered through the peephole.

It's him! Here, at my apartment! Her mind raced. Her eyes darted frantically around the room.

Is it clean enough? Do I have anything weird laying out? Am I clean? She sniffed herself for confirmation.

He knocked again. "Mia, it's Detective Barnett, from last night. Are you available?"

Was I available? If he only knew how available I was...

Tiny sparks of electricity danced inside her as she unlocked the door, a process in itself. Two deadbolts, a chain, and a regular thumb lock.

"Hi, umm... Detective Barnett, was it?" Her words stumbled out. *Great time for my tongue to stop working. I sound like an idiot.* She tried to focus.

"Yes, it is. Detective Cole Barnett." His smile melted her heart.

"What are you doing here? I mean, how did you know where to find me?"

He grinned. "I'm a good detective, Mia."

She opened the door and walked away so he could enter. She peeked at him over her shoulder as he stood in the entranceway, tracing the length of his body.

"Well, Detective, do you usually find what you're looking for?" She'd never flirted before, nor had anyone flirted with her. She liked it! It made her insides glow.

His face abandoned all expression. "No, sometimes we search our entire existence for something, though we may never find it." His voice held a sound of yearning, and Mia felt a sense of sorrow until the corners of his mouth pulled up into a smile.

She turned to face him, forcing her gaze to meet his dangerous, soul-melting eyes. "I hope you find what you're looking for, Detective."

"Oh, let's just say I have renewed hope."

Cole thought he'd imagined the pull her closeness had invoked within him last night, but that wasn't the case. He felt the same reaction now, the same pull. He could feel her excitement when he was near, and as he stared into her stunning blue eyes, he felt the pull again. He couldn't wait to get to her apartment, and now that he was there, he fought the urge to hold her and take her lips. No woman had ever done this to him before. *I must have her. I have to taste her to be sure.*

"Are you coming in, or would you like to stay out in the hallway and talk?"

"I haven't been invited in, yet."

"Detective, won't you please come in and interrogate me? I mean..." Redness tinged her cheeks, and she pulled her gaze away from his. He laughed deep and loud.

"I'm sorry, I didn't mean to—"

"Say that out loud? And yes, I would love to." He stepped inside, pausing to survey the apartment. His eyes came to rest on the table in the kitchen. "I've interrupted your meal. Should I come back?"

"No, that's okay. Besides, you look so excited that I invited you in, I wouldn't have the heart to send you packing." She put the milk on the table. "Would you like something?"

"Yes, I would. Could you please go put some clothes on?" He boldly looked her over.

Mia looked down at her loosened robe, giving him a peek at her panties and bare belly. She pulled it together with a panicked expression. "I'm sorry."

"Don't be sorry. I just don't think I can get any work done if you're dressed like that."

"Excuse me." She quickly walked over to the bathroom area.

"That's a beautiful shade of red on your cheeks." He watched her silhouette as she dropped her robe.

"Glad you like it," she muttered, "It's probably going to stay that way, especially since the only thing separating you from my naked body is a thin six-by-twelve wooden room divider."

If she only knew he could hear her. Smell her. And there was that pull again. He felt connected, in tune with her. Cole didn't have to turn around to know she was watching him as he stood by her bed. He felt her. He imagined laying her on the bed, gliding his fingers down her stomach, and sliding them into the panties she had innocently displayed for him. He spoke with his back to her. "Is this your mother in the picture?"

"Yes, it is."

"You look like her."

"Can I ask you to do something for *me* now?"

"What can I do for you, Mia?" He arched a brow.

"Move away from my bed, please."

He slowly walked toward her. "Does that bother you—me being so close to your bed?" He inched closer to her.

"Just as much as my clothing bothered you, Detective."

He could tell she was nervous, playing right back with him. Desire filled the air. Mia sucked in a breath, held it, and kept her eyes safely on his chest. He came to a stop inches from her, his shirt brushed hers as he stepped to the side and walked past.

The chair moaned as he slid it across the wood floor. She looked back at him.

"Breathe, Mia" He smiled when she complied. Taking a deep breath, she turned. Cole stood at the kitchen table, hands resting on top of the pulled out chair. "Come finish your meal, and I can talk to you over here. Is that okay?"

She nodded as her hand slid over the top of the chair, closing in on his. The air charged and electricity arched between them, snapping in the air.

"Ouch!"

Cole grabbed her hand, circling his thumb on top of her soft skin. Something inside of him shifted at the slightest amount of her pain; a protective feeling emerged. "Are you okay?" he asked, his tone laced with concern.

She pulled her hand from his, nodding as she sat. Cole watched her finger trace circles on the polished tabletop, mimicking the way he had stroked her hand.

"Is this what you usually eat for dinner?" He glanced down at his watch as he sat in the chair next to her.

"I eat whatever seems good to me. I'm bored with food lately. After you have the same thing over and over again, eating isn't satisfying. You just do it because you need the nourishment."

"I know exactly how you feel." He grabbed a pad from his top pocket. "Do you mind if I ask you some questions?" He placed his pen on the table and waited for her response.

Mia's cat jumped up to bat at the pen, then arched his back and hissed. Cole didn't flinch, but eyed him curiously.

"I'm sorry. He usually doesn't do that. Bela, get down!" She placed him on the floor as his fur stood at attention.

"He? Bela?"

"I named him after Bela Lugosi." She bent down to scratch Bela between his ears. "Do you know who that is?"

"Yes." He leaned back, sliding down in the chair. "Which of his characters do you like the most?"

Mia exhaled sharply. "Dracula of course. Isn't that everyone's?"

With an ironic smile, Cole picked up his pad and pen from the table, and chuckled.

"I'm sorry. Did I... miss something?"

His eyes darted back to hers. "No." The radio on his belt emitted a tone. "Excuse me, Mia." He stood to make his way to the living room and turned back for his pad and pen just as Mia was getting up. She jumped when his chest brushed against hers.

"I forgot to get my pad and pen." He leaned over to collect them, the closeness of her body setting him on fire. And from the red color spreading over her skin, she was burning from it too. She quickly stepped back and tumbled over the chair. The bowl flew through the air behind her, landing in the sink with style. Mia's landing however, was not so lucky.

He laughed heartily. "Mia, did I do something to make you afraid of me?" Cole knelt in front of her, gently cradling her neck and back as he slowly lifted her into a sitting position.

Mia scrunched her face and rubbed her head where it had connected with the floor. "I'm not afraid of you—it's your touch. I don't like to be touched."

"Isn't that a shame." He smiled and stood. "Are you okay? Does it hurt?"

"I'm okay. The pain went away the moment you placed your hand on me." Her brow creased.

"Ah, see, touching isn't so bad." He held out his hand to her. "I got a call. I have to attend to an incident at the beach. We'll try this again, tomorrow." When she slid her fingers across his palm, an electric current radiated from their connection, slithering through his limbs in a constant hum. He pulled hard, and she landed against his chest. A strand of blonde hair fell to rest against her crimson-colored cheekbone. The urge to kiss her overwhelmed him. As if it had a mind of its own, his hand glided to the small of her back.

Her gaze fixed on his. Again, her body bowed toward him. "Thank you, Detective. I'm looking forward to seeing you tomorrow." Her tone was trance-like.

Her closeness was killing him, and his feelings caused him to break the rules. Like right now—touching a victim of a crime while on duty. He should pull away, but all he could think about was bringing her closer. She smelled so damn good. No perfume, just her scent, and a faint aroma of fruit from her hair. He could eat her alive, right here, right now. He reached his hand up to sweep the stray hair from her face and tuck it behind her ear, but quickly snatched it back. This wasn't like him. He took a step back. "And I look forward to seeing you, Mia. Off duty."

Cole's sexy smile was full of anticipation.

***

Oh, yeehaw! Her insides screamed as she closed the door behind him. Lost in thought as the scent of Cole lingered in the room, the phone went unnoticed until the answering machine picked up and pulled her out of her daze. She snatched the phone from its cradle.

"Hey, Cyn. How's my BFF?" She jumped on the couch and tucked the phone under her chin.

"Hey, Mia. It's time for girl's night out. You in?"

"Yeah, I'd love to come. Tell me when and where."

Girl's night out was something they tried to do at least once a month. Cynthia spent most of her time with her boyfriend, Kevin. Mia was envious. She desperately wanted to feel a deep connection with someone—someone who could reach out and embrace her soul. Sadly, she felt she was holding out for something that didn't exist for someone like her. They'd have to embrace her weirdness, too, and that would never happen.

"Let's meet at the usual place, usual time."

"Sounds good to me. Oh, and I have to tell you about the guy I met. I know you're busy, so call me back later and we can catch up."

Mia ended the call, twirling the phone in her lap by its antenna, wishing she could go back to bed. Bela jumped up and purred loudly, lulling her into a catnap with him.

As her eyes jumped into a REM state, the sound of drums began to beat...

She floated along and stared at the moon, passing the same tree she'd passed a million times before. A baby began to cry. She pushed further along, until at last a new sound arose.

Deep, rhythmic chanting filled the air.

She jumped, startled awake as the last beat of the drums slammed down with a force that echoed in her mind. Mia headed straight for the shower. Her shift started at ten, and now she was running late. Trying to shake the dream from her mind, she rubbed her fingers over the tile.

She loved the bathroom. The walk-in shower had Southwestern style bricks on the outside and a neutral sand colored tile on the inside. The large, multi-head spout made her feel as if she was bathing in the rain, just like the ones seen on "Most Luxurious Spas" on the HGTV channel. It's what had sold her on the apartment.

Patting her hair dry, she froze as she stared at the discarded pants she'd worn last night. She forgot to tell Cole about Art's pack of Reds.

Fear tugged at her, afraid of what she would see when she touched the pack again. She tried hard to block everything except the note. Breathing deeply, she reached down and quickly withdrew the pack. The smell of tobacco rose to her sensitive nose as she pulled the note from inside. Unrolling it slowly, the letters revealed themselves like movie credits. "Three girls."

What the hell is that supposed to mean? Now she felt bad for blocking the images. She thought the note would hold more information. She didn't expect it to say, "Hey, the guy in the red shirt killed me, and here's his name and address." But come on... *three girls?*

She stuffed the note back inside, pulled on a pair of jeans and a tank, and then shoved the pack of Reds into her pocket.

She couldn't wait to share the note with Cole.

FOUR

*M*ia put her purse behind the counter, and turned to Shannon who strummed her fingers on the counter. "You know Stan was still in a pissy mood today over that damn tape."

"And hello to you, too, Shannon."

"Yeah, go call your friend, and see if he'll bring it back. Since I have to see Stan more than you do, I'd appreciate it if you'd get him off my ass."

"What friend would you like me to call?"

"That gorgeous hunk-of-a-man that came in here earlier, that's who. I'm sure you know the one—he was sporting a gun and a badge. I'll tell you what, he can arrest me anytime." Shannon laughed as she looked at Mia.

Cole's image flashed through her mind, and she felt the heat crawl into her cheeks. Normally, she wasn't the gossipy type, but damn, she had to tell someone. "He *is* attractive... What did he say? You told him where I lived?"

"Look at your eyes all lit up with excitement."

"Shush. Just tell me."

"No one told him. He talked to Stan, and you know how he feels about cops."

"He wasn't rude to him, was he?"

"Why? Would that bother you?"

"Yes, it would. He's a cop, and it would be disrespectful. You shouldn't be rude to anyone because of their profession." Just like the people that came into the station, Mia thought. They threw money at her as if she were a servant.

"Well, well. There's your man now, Mia. Look!" Shannon leaned over and turned up the TV sitting on the counter.

The ten o'clock news was broadcasting live coverage of a homicide, and Cole was in the background bent over a body bag lying on the beach. *Oh, God.* She placed her palm on her stomach. What a terrible person she was to feel this excited about seeing him when there was a dead body in front of him.

"Yeah, that's him—" Mia's words hung in midair, her last choking out and stopping her speech.

Like a foggy daydream, the vision came.

The image flickers underwater; a girl's head thrashes side-to-side, as she fights for her life. The surf is tainted red as the girl struggles against the set of strong arms pushing her down. At the base of her skull, two large thumbs held her under, and it isn't long before the struggling stops. Tiny bubbles drifted up from the girl's mouth, the last bit of air freed from her lungs. Long black hair envelops her face, floating freely around her as her wide eyes—frozen with fright—stare directly at Mia.

"Mia. Mia!" Shannon snapped her fingers in front of Mia's eyes, then shook her by the shoulders. "Help you do what?" She stared at Mia. "You were screaming 'Help me', but your words were, like, gurgling out." Shannon scrunched her face, puzzled.

"Turn off the news, Shannon." Mia struggled with waves of emotion. Her nose burned on the inside, as if stung by water, and her body trembled. They're coming on stronger, Mia thought with one last shiver.

"Girl, you just freaked the hell out of me. That was strange. I'm out of here. Don't forget to tell handsome you want that tape." Shannon grabbed her belongings

33

and snagged her purse on the corner of the door handle as she fled.

***

It was five in the morning when Mia finally stopped moving. Trying to occupy her mind, she had cleaned the entire station. Twice. She sighed in relief—only one hour left. Sitting behind the counter, she propped her feet up.

A car glided into the parking lot and stopped next to the window where Mia sat. The passenger side window descended, inch by inch, revealing the most gorgeous face she'd ever seen.

Cole's deep, brown eyes locked with hers, and for a second, she thought they glowed. A smile that could melt steel appeared on his face and made her heart pound so hard it echoed in her ears.

When she smiled back, he shifted in his seat as if uncomfortable, his fingers were tracing the steering wheel, and his tongue slid out to wet his lips. Mia leaned toward the window and pressed the speaker button. "What can I get for you, Detective?"

He reached for the mic and then his voice came over the car's P.A. system. "Come closer to me, Mia—on this side, please." He tapped the windowsill with his hand.

She stood and walked outside, pausing between the headlights. Fire ran over her flesh as she cocked her head toward him, meeting his heated gaze with a bewitching grin. As she stared, she noticed his grip tighten on the wheel. She continued to his side of the window, yearning to feel his skin as she slid her fingers across the smooth metal of the car and squatted down by his door. Overlapping her hands on the windowsill, she rested her chin on the top of them and let her eyes trail up to his.

"I can't stay," he said, softly.

"Why did you come, then?" Mia felt comfortable in his presence, unlike the tension she'd felt in the presence of other men.

"My shift is ending. I wanted your face to be the last thing I saw tonight." His voice was sincere as his soft eyes caressed her face.

Mia's heart melted with every word. *Can this be happening? He has to be toying with me. There is no way someone like him could be interested in me. No way. Maybe he just wants "it" and figures I'm simple enough not to cause problems when he doesn't call back. He's good. Very smooth with his words. I need to remember myself. No men. No touching. Safe. Shake him off, Mia!* Her internal struggle caused her to look away from his stare.

"Oh, before I forget" —she took the pack of Reds from her pocket and handed them to him—"these were Art's. I found them last night on the floor. There's a note inside."

Rubbing his thumb across her knuckles, he took the pack and placed it in a hard, black briefcase on the passenger seat.

"Aren't you going to look at the note?" she asked, still tingling from his touch.

"I've seen enough for one night." As gentle as silk slides on skin, he brushed his hand against her cheek. "I really have to go now, but I'll see you tomorrow."

Lost in thought as he drove away, Mia walked back into the store. She wanted to ask him about the girl on the beach and talk more about Art. She wanted to ask him what his favorite color was, and if he liked chocolate or vanilla. She wanted to hear his voice say something, anything to her. As much as she struggled with herself, she knew he made her feel different. He stirred something within her that had lain dormant for a very long time.

FIVE

*M*ia's days usually melted into each other, but now, she looked forward to a new one. Cole filled her dreams once again after the drums subsided, and she hoped to see him again tonight. Her dream lover. That's what she'd decided to nickname him because she'd been doing things with him in her dreams that would earn her a high-five from a call girl.

9:55 p.m. I'm early. She sighed, trying to drown out Shannon, who had started yapping as soon as Mia opened the door.

"Hey, did you pass that accident when you came in?" Excitement exploded onto Shannon's face.

"No, I ran errands and drove a different way in." Mia shoved her belongings under the counter.

"Well, look. It's all over the news." She pointed to the TV.

A crowd gathered around an accident. The camera panned to the police cars parked on the side of the road with their blue lights flashing.

Mia's heart skipped a beat, the sight of them stirring her excitement. *Cole.* She didn't know why she knew he was there, but she did. "Turn it up, Shannon." Mia flicked her hand in the air to hurry her along.

The news reporter cleared his throat, and then spoke with all the theatrics of William Shatner. "This is still under investigation, and all lanes have been closed. Behind me, you see the crowd growing... that's because the body covered on the ground may be the sister of a local gang member. According to people here at the scene, she's an illegal immigrant and was allegedly killed by a rival gang. The police think it may be a hit and run—not gang-related. We will reveal more to you throughout the night. Chip, back to you."

Mia gripped the counter. The pit of her stomach tightened into a ball as images flashed through her mind. *The girl under the tarp appeared, but she was not dead. Blood streaked her face and continued to roll down her shoulder, covering a small tattoo of a ladybug on her chest. Tiny branches tore at her calves as she ran through the woods. Sheer terror shot through her as something grabbed her from behind, slammed her into a tree, and shattered her beyond repair. Her body folded into itself slowly, sliding down the tree until she slumped to the ground—her face frozen in time with a mask of fear.*

"Hey, psycho! Snap out of it." Shannon snapped her fingers in front of Mia's face.

"Shannon, I've got to go. I'll be right back." Mia turned and headed toward the door.

"Oh, no you don't, Mia! Get back here, my shift is done. I'm not waiting for you to get back!"

Mia shouted over her shoulder as she walked out the door, "Do what you have to. If you can't wait, lock the door behind you."

Mia had no clue what she was doing. It felt as if some mystical force was driving her. In the past, she had always run from her visions, but now something pulled her into them. The excitement built inside as she drove.

People congested the area, making it impossible for cars to pass, so Mia parked down the street. She took in her surroundings as she approached the scene, and, just as the news had reported, gangs were definitely present. Rival gangs stood on opposite sides of police tape in a silent standoff. The yellow tape attached to each police car formed a barricade to keep the crowd back.

Mia grabbed her stomach. Everyone around her projected an aura of anger and hate. The negative energy grew stronger with every step she took.

Pushing her way through the crowd to the front of the scene, her eyes fell upon Cole, causing her skin to tingle and her pulse to quicken.

Pressed and polished, he was perfect. Not one hair on his head was out of place. She couldn't help it—her eyes slowly devoured his backside while he talked with another officer. *Damn, he looks good.* The desire to kiss him grew, and she touched her lips as if that would trick her mind into thinking she did what it asked.

She accidentally nudged the guy next to her. "Sorry."

"Hey, bitch. Watch where you're going." The man spoke with a thick Spanish accent.

Mia glanced at him, and then let his comment slide off as she refocused on the scene.

Mia noticed a sudden change in Cole's posture. His body stiffened, his muscles tightened under his shirt, and then he lifted his head. In an instant, he snapped it around and locked his gaze with hers. His jaw clenched, and his brows drew into a mixture of confusion and anger.

And then she felt it, whatever it was. Her lips parted, and she breathed in the hot, humid Florida air. She could physically *feel* him, and he knew it, judging by the expression on his face.

Whoa. What was that?

His intense gaze pushed her back a step. He rose, and mouthed a word she didn't have to hear, she felt it. *"Mine!"* He turned his head and stared at the man standing next to her.

"Did you hear me, *puta*?" The man grabbed her forearm, twisting her arm back.

"Take your hands off of me!" Mia's words echoed through the crowd. An uneasy feeling lifted into the night air, and excited images of violence grew stronger in her mind. The gang members were waiting for someone to start the riot they craved, and Mia had just given them the green light.

"What're you gonna do, puta?"

"You shouldn't worry about what I'm going to do..." Mia said, smiling up at him, taking joy in watching his expression change to puzzlement. "You should be more concerned about what *he's* going to do." She tilted her head toward Cole as he grabbed the man's hand from her arm, and in one quick swoop, her assailant was easily put on the ground.

Cole looked up at her with narrowed eyes, and she felt his projected anger as he called out over his shoulder, "Paco!" An officer immediately came to his side. "Can you take care of this for me?" Cole stood, jerking the gang member to his feet as if he were a rag doll. "This crowd is going to blow. Tell the sheriff we need to get crowd control here." He nodded toward the sheriff as Paco took the gang member and left.

Cole snapped his attention back to Mia. He gripped the underside of her bicep and tightened his hold. Lifting her by the arm, he walked her away from the crowd. When they reached a patrol car, he deposited her against it.

Mia glared at him, rubbing her bicep as she spoke. "Thanks for releasing me from your cop grip. You were hurting my arm."

"What are you doing here? This is no place for you."

"I had a visi... I had to see... Wait. The last I checked, I was old enough to make my own decisions." Mia clenched her teeth.

Cole grabbed her arm and pulled her to him, a storm brewing in his eyes as he stared down at her. "You may be old enough to make bad decisions—"

"Is there a problem here, Detective?" A southern voice sounded behind them. The approaching man wore similar clothing as the other detectives, with a badge clipped to his waistband. He stood about 5'8", which put him two inches above Mia's height. His mustache and hair were jet black and neatly trimmed, and his big blue eyes lit up his pale face.

"No, John-Sheriff, there's no problem," Cole replied, never taking his eyes off Mia.

"Sure looks like there's a problem to me, Barnett. I've been looking for you. This crowd is going to break at any minute, and there's going to be bloodshed. Normally, I'd have you stick around, but you don't look like you can handle it this time."

"*I* can't handle it? I'm the most controlled cop you have."

"Cole, leave. I haven't, um... eaten, so I'm taking off myself." He patted Cole on the shoulder. "Go take care of that other incident we need to investigate." John nodded at Mia then left.

"Do you think you can take your hand off me, now?" Mia glared at Cole, who'd barely moved since the sheriff arrived.

Instantly he lessened his grip, "I'm sorry for losing my temper. I don't want to see you hurt, and this is a bad place for you to be. I... need to protect you."

"Why?"

"I... It's my job."

"Thanks for your concern, but I can handle myself." She ripped her arm from his grip, pushed past him and fled.

Mia felt a surge of strong energy, more powerful than she'd ever felt, and it was right behind her. Her pace quickened—she didn't want him touching her again. Her anger brewed, but she knew if he touched her, she would instantly forgive him.

Looking over her shoulder, she yelled, "Stop following me!"

"I just want to help you to your car."

His voice called to her body, which wanted to stop, but her mind pushed her forward.

"I don't need your help." Mia's words hung in the air as she tripped over a traffic cone, falling ass over feet.

A melody of laughter poured from him.

"I'm so glad I can be your source of entertainment." Rubbing her backside, she glared at him.

"If you'd stop running from me, you'd stop falling." Cole held out his hand to her.

As Mia eyed the masculine veins on his outreached hand, she envisioned it gliding up her stomach to cup her breast, then quickly shook the image from her head.

Get a grip on yourself, Mia. "No thanks." She picked herself up and slapped her hands on her jeans to dust off her backside.

"Let me see you safely to your car." His eyes flicked over her.

"Fine." She turned on her heel, and they walked in silence. She scowled at him in protest when he grabbed the handle to her car door.

Smirking, Cole shook his head in the slightest of movements and removed his hand.

Wanting to get away quickly, she didn't bother with her seatbelt, which was always the first thing she did before driving.

***

When Mia pulled into the gas station, it wasn't a surprise Shannon's car was gone. Mia walked toward the entrance, pulling her keys from her pocket, but paused at the door when a car pulled in.

Cole.

Her nerves tugged as she fumbled with the key and tried to fit it into the lock—the same lock she'd opened a million times before had now become impossible, and she dropped the keys. As she reached down to pick them up, Cole's hand slid over the top of hers. She froze.

I'm going to hyperventilate, she thought as she tried to control her breathing. Her hand shook as she tried the lock again. A jolt went through her body as Cole's hand slid down her forearm and over her wrist to steady her hand.

"Miakoda, let me help you." His gentle voice stroked her as his arm rested on hers. His body barely touched her backside, but it was enough to send her into a tremble. They inserted the key together. Unlocking the door, Cole leaned forward to grab the handle.

Mia didn't dare move at the risk of touching more of him. Her mind scolded her as the entire length of his body pressed against hers. She should have moved. She felt his arousal slowly growing against her flesh. Leaning back, she rested against him, his closeness feeling so right.

Cole stilled, and a small deep grunt came from within him.

Captivated by his closeness, Mia didn't see the car on the opposite side pull in or hear the chime of the pump.

"Miakoda," he whispered. "You have to go inside."

"Why?" she asked in a dreamy voice.

"You have a customer."

"Oh! Uhm, thank you. Are you coming in?"

"No, I think I'll need a minute."

"I know what you mean." Mia moved away from the comfort of his body. "So,... will I see you in a few?"

"Yes, and I will see you," he said in a devilish tone.

As she stepped inside, she quickly glanced back. The flirtatious grin on his face made her heart flutter.

Mia helped the customer on pump eight while she checked the answering machine. Good. No messages. She was praying she wouldn't get in trouble for leaving the station unattended. She ran to the bathroom and checked herself in the mirror. Her cheeks were flushed and her eyes glossy.

What is wrong with me? Really, it's not like I haven't been around a man before. Yet, she knew the difference. He was different—intoxicating. Maybe the five years of abstinence had amplified her sex drive.

Her joy faded with the chime of the door. She remembered why Cole had come and that she'd have to tell him about the men from the other night. She definitely didn't want to tell him about her freakiness. Oh, yeah, and she sees dead people. She didn't want to lose the way he looked at her—how he looked *at* her, and not *through* her.

Cole leaned against the front counter, drinking from a black container. Her simplicity made her angelic, and the sight of her ignited his soul. This feeling was new to him. No one had ever had this effect on him, and the cat and mouse game she played with him earlier had left him aroused. He wanted to be near her, and his hands wanted to explore her body. The pads of his fingers yearned to learn every fine line in her skin. He wondered if she knew how beautiful she was. No make-up, jeans, sneakers and she was the sexiest thing he had ever seen. All it took was one look, and she had him hook, line, and sinker.

His eyes never left her as she walked around the counter. He kept a safe distance and followed.

He noticed a change in her mood. "Is there something wrong, Mia?"

"No. I just... I just want to get this over with." She threw her chin up and avoided his eyes.

He knew she was lying, but sensing her discomfort, moved on. "Okay, let's get this over with, and then we both can go home and take a cold shower."

Her face instantly relaxed, and Cole loved that her smile was only for him.

"Tell me what happened the other night." He pulled a pad and a pen from his top pocket as Mia recapped the story, but he didn't start writing anything until she described the glowing contacts.

"Are you writing down that I'm crazy?" she asked with a nervous expression.

"No, Mia. This is the first time you've told me anything of interest, beside the fact you were going to take on a guy with a baseball bat." He peered up at her as he wrote his notes and smiled. "Continue."

"Then me and the big guy had a stare-off, and I guess I won, based off his reaction."

Cole's pen came to a halt. Jerking his head up, he stared at her.

"Great. Déjà vu."

"What do you mean, you won?"

"I noticed something strange happening to his... I mean, he just looked upset. You know, that I didn't back down."

With an arched brow, he studied her. She was nervous, and she was still lying to him. He'd get the truth out of her later. "Tell me about the other guy." Leaning back on the counter, he relaxed. Crossing one leg over the other, the tip of his boot came to rest on the floor.

Mia tilted her head and stared at him. "How do you do that?"

"Do what?"

"You relax when I tense." She narrowed her eyes and looked at him, deeper than before. "It's like you can read me or something."

Feeling her probing eyes, he hardened his gaze. "Maybe I'm just a good detective." He raised a brow as she continued to stare as if he held secrets to the universe. "What are you trying to see, Mia?"

She shook her head, confused. "There's nothing. I mean, nothing. I'm sorry." She pinched the bridge of her nose, "GQ. Right. Okay."

She began telling him about GQ, but suddenly stopped and focused on her shoes.

"Why are you afraid to tell me what happened?" He kept his voice calm, soothing.

"I want to tell you. I know that would make you happy but..." Taking a deep breath, Mia blurted, "I'm-afraid-you're-going-to-think-I'm-crazy-weird-and-I'll-never-see-you-again."

"Mia, I need to find out what happened. Please, trust me."

She rubbed her arm and shifted against the counter. "After GQ said 'Master, please. She would taste so sweet', he raked what *I* think were fangs along the base of my neck."

Cole froze.

"See, just like the first officer." She gaped as the pen snapped in his hand.

He felt rage within him. Someone had touched what was his, frightened her, and put his mouth on her. The thought of her being hurt tugged at the core of his anger.

"Can you identify them?" His words bit out between clenched teeth. "Could you pick them out, if you were to see them again?"

"Well, yeah, I could pick out an aura like that, I... I mean they looked unique to me, so I could probably identify them." She looked back and forth between Cole, the overhead lights, and neon signs.

Cole followed her gaze. "What is it?"

"Nothing, I guess. I thought your eyes started glowing, but it must have been a glare." She looked up again and then shook her head.

"I have to go. My shift is ending. I'll talk to you again tomorrow." He smiled. "Then, I'll find out what you're hiding from me." He placed his card on the counter and walked toward the door. "You call me *immediately* if you need me, or if they come in here again. Do you understand?"

"I won't be here tomorrow. I work at my other job," she said, picking up his card.

"Where is that?"

"Your card says you're a Special Ops Detective. What were you doing on a motorcycle the other night?"

"I am many things, Mia. To answer your question, I'm certified on the motorcycle, and when they need an extra man for a detail, I gladly volunteer. I love motorcycles. It's like riding a horse with wheels that goes very fast." He turned and leaned toward her across the counter. "Not many people would have picked up on that. You're very observant. Where can I find you tomorrow?"

"You're the detective—you figure it out." Her smile made her eyes shine. Cole leaned further across the counter. His gaze flicked from her lips to her eyes. Heat crawl into her cheeks, and her lips trembled.

"It would be my pleasure, Mia." He peeled himself away from her, inclining his head before he spoke. "Until tomorrow."

SIX

*M*ia didn't sleep well. Something about the two girls didn't sit right with her, but surely, they'd figure everything out in an autopsy. That's what happens on TV, right? People die, it's a mystery, and then forensics figures it all out in an hour show like Hawaii-five O.

After taking a quick shower, she slapped on some mascara, grabbed some food, and was out the door on her way to her second job.

Mia pulled her car into the Horizon Gardens Funeral Home parking lot. She had worked there for a couple years and loved it. Cal, her boss, had called her in advance to let her know about a viewing tonight, and a couple of new bodies that were brought in. Since there was a service being held, business attire was mandatory. She smoothed the front of her black dress pants and flung her jacket over her shoulder. Straightening the line of buttons on her blue blouse, Mia walked toward the building in uncomfortable heels. Skirts weren't her thing, so the suit would have to do. Working a service was uncommon for her, unless they were short on help. Mostly, she worked in the back, preparing the ashes for families, assisting with cremations, and keeping the paperwork in order for the embalming. Occasionally, she'd do the corpse's makeup, if needed.

Jerry Storm greeted Mia as she walked through the back door. He was an older man in his mid-forties with grey streaked through his black hair. He normally cracked jokes constantly, but he looked serious.

"Hey, Jerry. What's going on?"

"Mia, I wanted to meet you at the door, to tell you... We have Art. They delivered him last night, and he's in the cooler. Are you going to be all right?"

The concern on Jerry's face surprised Mia and warmed her heart. "Yes, Jerry. I'll be okay. I've worked here long enough to know a body is just the shell of the person who passed. But thank you for telling me."

"Alrighty then." He noticeably relaxed. "Let's get to work. We have four on ice, two on the table, and one on the barbecue," he said, his usual demeanor returning.

The funeral home lingo had bothered Mia when she first started, but she realized this was how they coped with their jobs. If you couldn't find humor, it would get to you.

When the funeral home closed, Mia vacuumed the viewing room, then rolled Mr. Roberts' coffin to the back. She took one last look before turning away and pressed the collar of his jacket down. *We did a great job on him.* He looked distinguished in his old war uniform. She had placed his grandfather's cavalry sword in his hand and rested it against his shoulder. It was the final touch to make sure he'd looked perfect for his family.

Usually the bodies aren't moved when a two-day viewing is scheduled, but Mr. Roberts' room was needed for another viewing tomorrow. They had to play musical bodies in the morning, as Jerry would say.

Mia's stomach growled as she grabbed her lunch/dinner and went outside to find her favorite spot in the cemetery, but first she made sure to lock the door since she was the only one working late.

The mild night air brushed over her skin, and the clear sky revealed a full moon surrounded by stars. Sitting on a concrete bench under a beautiful oak tree, Mia was surrounded by Mr. Williams, who died in 1920, Mrs. Cramer, who died in 1971, and Joey, who died in the early 1900's. Joey was believed to be three years old, but they hadn't kept good records back then. A couple feet away sat two beautiful slabs of concrete standing about four feet high, one on each side of the bench, with inspirational verses carved into them.

Mia opened her sandwich wrapper and spread the waxed paper out on the bench along with her chips and soda. Leaning back against the tree, she stretched out her legs and relaxed.

"Mr. Williams, Mrs. Cramer, Joey—how is everyone tonight?" She took a bite of her sandwich and stared at the stone plates around her. "Mrs. Cramer, I read in the paper the other day that they finally put up barricades where your car accident happened. It took thirty-seven years, but they're there now. Your husband was there and placed a heart shaped sign in the ground with your name on it. I had no idea he was a police officer."

"Do they ever answer you back?" a smooth, deep voice asked from behind her. Mia closed her eyes at the sound of Cole's voice—he soothed her all the way down to her toes. Normally, she would've been embarrassed if someone caught her talking to no one, but she wasn't.

"No, not yet," she replied, a smile on her face.

Cole moved in front of her.

"Do you usually sneak up on people, Detective?" She raised her eyes to meet his.

"Do you usually talk to the dead?" he challenged with a wicked grin.

"Why, yes, I do. I prefer the dead over the living."

With a fervent gaze, he knelt in front of her. "That's good to know. I'll remember that."

Cole wore jeans that fit snugly and accented all the right places, with a white, long sleeve, button down shirt neatly tucked into them, and black boots polished to a shine. His eyes heated her entire body with a signature look that she felt was only for her. Mia jumped up from the bench. She was sure her panties were going to fall to the ground, willed there by his commanding stare alone. If she didn't break away from his gaze, she'd be having sex on top of Mrs. Cramer in no time.

"Is there something wrong?" He rose to stand in front of her.

"Cole"—she swallowed a lump as he stepped closer to her—"I've made some bad choices in the past and have some... hang-ups. I've been abstinent for five years, and there are reasons why I'm alone. With just a look, you do things to me that no one has ever done before." Mia paused, staring at his serious expression as if he hung onto her every word. She dropped her gaze to his shoulders. "It scares me. I don't think I can trust myself around you."

"So you choose to run?" Cole grabbed her chin between his fingers, forcing her to meet his stare.

A reflection of light caught her eye, and she tilted her head down toward the source. A badge was hooked on Cole's belt, and light bounced off the shiny surface. Next to his metal shield was a gun and handcuffs—blue handcuffs—not the standard silver colored ones. The simple distraction allowed her mind to shift and change the subject. "Are you here on business?"

"Yes, Mia. I need to find out what you're hiding from me and why." He stepped back, stiffening at her avoidance and looked her over as if trying to break a secret code.

"What do you mean, Detective?" She lifted her chin with an innocent tone.

He moved quickly toward her, almost gliding, pushing her back into the tree. "Tell me why the man with the glowing eyes was upset by your stare-off."

His aggressiveness should have frightened her. Instead, it was turning her on. Heat poured over her cheeks. "Cole, I'm going to tell you something, and you need to promise me you won't run away or think I'm crazy. Promise me you'll keep an open mind, that I'll see you after tonight," she pleaded with him.

"Miakoda, please, trust me." He leaned into her, pressing her against the tree.

Her breathing became heavy. "I won't be able to speak if you don't back away from me."

"You can't run if I have you pinned."

She fought to block the images slipping into her mind from his closeness. His cheek rested against hers, and her fingers itched to touch him. "Cole, I'll tell you, but you have to move away from me. Please?"

"I'll back off when you start talking." His lips trailed down her neck.

If I knew being interrogated was like this, I would have been a criminal. Mia found her voice and recounted the stare-off with Glowing Eyes. As promised, Cole backed away. She told him everything, hoping and praying it wouldn't change anything.

"What do you see when you look at my aura?"

She tilted her head and stared at him. "It's beautiful. It has an outer color of blue that fades to pink, with a touch of light red"—she grinned—"which is lust."

"Anything else? Focus on me, Mia."

His serious tone took Mia by surprise, and she focused on him again. Her lips parted, and she sucked in a breath as a metallic crest began to appear around his aura.

"Mia, I'm going to look at you like he did. If you start to feel weak, I want you to do the same thing you did to him, okay?"

"Okay."

Cole lifted her chin. "Mia, your life may depend on this. Please, trust me." He stepped back to gaze into her eyes and, with a hardened look, their stare-off began. His eyes darkened.

Instantly, she felt weak, and her stomach churned. Mia stood her ground. Lowering her head, she pulled her energy up from below and glared back at him.

In an instant, his aura twitched. He stared harder with determination creasing his forehead.

When Mia returned his increased effort with more power, she felt energy circling like never before.

His eyes widened then returned with reinforced focus letting Mia know he felt the same electric spike in the air she had.

Mia felt strong, but grew tired of the game. "Cole, can we stop now?"

In a moment of déjà-vu, Cole's head snapped up with his eyes wide. "Did you not feel anything when I looked at you?"

"That's a loaded question, Cole. I always feel something when you look at me—I have since the first time we met."

"Please, I know you don't fully understand, but I'll explain everything to you later. Did you feel weak at all? Did you feel like you had to obey me?" Agitation laced his voice.

"Obey?" That was what Glowing Eyes had said to Art. His aura was metallic, too.

Mia's mind clouded with thoughts as she pieced things together. A vision snapped into her head of a man walking through the graveyard—her graveyard. She closed her eyes, shutting Cole out to get a better feel of the vision. As the man continued through the cemetery, Mia could read the names on the stones he passed. This was the strongest vision she'd ever had. It was clear, like watching HDTV.

"Mia?"

When she opened her eyes, Cole's head turned, looking out into the distance.

"Cole, do you sense him, too?"

"Did you see someone when you closed your eyes?"

Mia's fear tugged at her. She looked at his eyes, now completely dark, yet a glow formed behind his beautiful irises like a candle in a window.

She swallowed hard and answered, "Yes." *What the hell is going on?*

"I can sense him, but I don't know exactly where he is. Can you see where?" Cole's voice was calm but firm. "Show me, Mia, show me what you've got."

She closed her eyes, reaching out with her mind until the aura of energy materialized. *Bingo!* Her eyes snapped open. "Mrs. Stewart. He's a couple yards to the north of us by a statue of an angel. He just passed over Mrs. Stewart's grave. She died in 1983."

Cole's mouth parted with a look of astonishment, then a grin wrinkled the corner of his mouth.

"You think I'm weird, don't you?"

"No, Miakoda. I think you're extraordinary. I think you're a rare beauty, and you have no idea the power you possess. Go back inside, my love. Don't open the door to anyone but me."

She walked briskly back to the building as Cole went in the other direction. *Wait, did he just call me his love?*

Mia stopped dead in her tracks. A man rested on the backside of the building. He lifted himself off the wall and walked toward her. *Oh shit, I was so focused on the man moving through the graveyard, I didn't sense this guy at all. Yo, dead people. You're supposed to help me see everything.*

"I'm sorry, Sir, but the graveyard is closed. You'll have to come back tomorrow to visit your loved ones." Her voice was shaky. She heard a sound in the distance where Cole had gone but kept her eyes focused on the man in front of her. He looked ragged, rough—like a criminal.

"I'm not here to visit any loved ones. I'm here to give this place another permanent resident." His voice was ice cold as he pulled a gun from behind his jacket. Mia felt an intense energy force, and the surrounding air suddenly charged with electricity. She turned her head to look behind her. Cole was coming across the field of graves. *He's too far away to save me.*

The man raised his gun, pulled the hammer back, and took aim. Her heart beat wildly in her chest as the man pulled the trigger. She caught a flash from the corner of her eye, and then Cole stood in front of her. He fell to one knee without making a sound, then slowly stood. The man fired again. Cole swayed back taking the second hit in his left shoulder.

"Now, it's my turn." Cole's voice rumbled like thunder. The man's eyes widened with a fear that sent chills down Mia's spine, then turned and ran toward the graveyard, not once looking back.

Cole fell to his knees, blood saturating his white shirt like red wine spilling on a white tablecloth. Mia bent down in front of him, and his eyes came up to meet hers as she ripped open his shirt. There were two bullet holes pouring blood—one in his top left shoulder, the other in the middle of his chest.

"You're not wearing a vest?" Anger and fear knotted at the pit of her stomach. "I'm going to get your radio and call for help." She leapt to her feet and his hand grabbed hers.

"No! Mia, you can't call for help."

"What?! You want me to sit here and watch you die?"

"I'm in a special unit. This is the job I've chosen, and you can't call for help." His strained voice gave away his pain, but he calmly pulled out his phone. She watched him, stunned at his behavior. Blood still poured from his wounds, and he dialed the phone unfazed by it, as if it was normal. Cole reached for Mia, pulling her down in front of him. He slung his arm over her shoulder, resting it there for balance.

"Sheriff, I've been injured," he said calmly, as if telling him the time of day. "Two silver bullets, special ones." Cole paused, listening. "Yes, sir, I won't let him get away."

Mia gaped. *Are you kidding me? His boss is more concerned about the guy getting away? What an asshole.*

"Yes, sir. I have her here with me." Cole nodded his head at the phone in response. "I know enough to tell you she needs to be protected, and we may have rogues in our area. Call me later." Cole's arm dropped to the ground, and the phone rolled out of his hand to rest in the grass. "I'm sorry for what I'm about to ask, but I need your help, Mia. Don't run from me." His eyes searched hers for understanding. "If these were normal bullets, even normal silver bullets, I would have been okay, but these are special silver bullets, and I can't get them out on my own. I'm lucky they didn't pierce my heart, or I wouldn't be looking at you right now." His eyes were waiting for a response.

Fear started at Mia's toes and climbed up her body until it rolled out as a laugh. "Why, are you a werewolf?" She forced her lips into a smile and swallowed hard.

"No, Mia. I'm a vampire."

She jumped to her feet and backed away. He fell back, sitting on his legs and looked up at her. "Jesus, Mia. Don't look at me like that, with fear in your eyes. That hurts more than the bullets." His unsure eyes saddened, and his face paled. "You're afraid of me, and I need you. More than you'll ever know." He sighed as she shook her head in disbelief. "I promised you that I'd keep an open mind, and wouldn't run away from *you*,"

Cole said, reminding her of her earlier plea for acceptance. "I won't hurt you, Miakoda. Please." He held his hand out, his eyes imploring her.

Her heart throbbed, and her soul pulled her closer as their eyes met. She put her hand on his, once again feeling the tiny pricks of electricity running through her body from the contact.

He slowly closed his hand around hers and pulled her down to kneel in front of him. Still on his knees, he straightened and slid one hand to the small of her back, the other sliding up to grasp her neck. Cole pulled her to him. Bending down, he brushed his lips across hers, gently kissing her.

When he pulled back, she didn't move, her eyes stayed closed as she burned the kiss into her memory. She felt his body tremble and opened her eyes, noting the reflection of pain in his. "What do you need me to do, Cole?"

"Take the bullets out before my body closes around them."

"How?"

"You have to find something and dig them out."

Are you fucking kidding me? She remembered her keys and patted her pocket, searching for her small Swiss Army knife. Pulling them out, she stared at the knife. *Which tool would be best to use?* Since it was the knife's small version, it didn't have all the tools that came with the standard size. *Damn, the tweezers would have come in handy.* Mia giggled as she held back a touch of hysteria. The corkscrew was definitely not a good choice. It would have to be the knife.

"Cole, this is going to hurt."

"Not any worse than the silver burning me." He clenched his teeth as he spoke. "I'm getting weaker. Hurry."

Mia straddled one of his knees and tightened her thighs around his leg, pausing before putting the knife into the middle of his chest. "How do I know how far to go in?"

"Put your finger in first to see how deep the bullet went in." He stared down at her, but she didn't move—all she could do was blink. "Mia, I'm losing a lot of blood. Please."

Her eyes never left his as she slid her pinky into the bullet hole. Halfway down the length of her finger, she felt the metal. She looked down at the knife. Tilting her head, she brought her gaze back to his, and tears stung her eyes.

Cole bent and gently kissed her forehead.

Mia took a deep breath and put the knife in the hole of his chest as he winced. She worked the bullet closer to the surface until it was visible. She tugged, but it was stuck and began to suck back into the hole. *This was insane. I'm going to buy the large size army knife after today. I really could use a pair of tweezers...*

"Cole, it's stuck."

"Get. It. Out."

She wiggled the knife more, using both hands to help dislodge the bullet. The blood oozed out, coating her fingers, making the bullet slippery as she tried to pinch its tip.

"Lean back." She pushed him backward, holding the bullet to one side of the hole with the knife. Without thinking, she leaned down and bit the end of the bullet with her teeth. The taste of iron filled her mouth as she worked the knife together with her teeth—tugging and pulling to extract the bullet. Blood trickled down her throat as the bullet popped free. She felt strange, alive. Leaning back, she locked eyes with Cole. A glow lit behind the deep brown of his irises. Tilting her head, she slid the bullet out from between her lips, the jagged metal cutting into her flesh before it dropped to her hand.

The bullet had mushroomed from hitting a bone in Cole's chest. The pattern of the mushroom was unlike any Mia had ever seen. It flared out like a large flower and had ripped through Cole's flesh. If he were human, he wouldn't have survived it.

"Would you like to keep this for evidence?" She grinned, trying to make light of the situation. Cole didn't answer, but she saw the amusement in his eyes. He simply nodded toward the other bullet in his shoulder.

Mia leaned forward, straightening on her knees to reach the other bullet lodged just below his collarbone. She inserted her pinky. This time, feeling like a pro as she judged the depth of the bullet. *This one is deep.* She withdrew the full length of her pinky and began working the knife in the hole.

"Cole, you need to straighten back up for this one."

Sliding his arm around her for support, he watched her intently as she focused on her task. When the bullet was insight, Mia leaned forward, and grabbed the bullet with her teeth.

Cole winced and trembled, and then Mia felt something else. She released the bullet from her teeth, holding it in place with the knife. She didn't dare look at him, but she felt his eyes burning into her.

"Are you aroused?" she asked.

"You have no idea..." His voice was deep with a seductive promise, and laced with hunger.

Mixed feelings swirled around her head. This was too much—way too much, but her body didn't care what the hell her head said and responded. She visualized his arousal, and her pulse raced. *Stop that, and get the bullet out of his body.* She pulled her focus back to the bullet, but a part of her she didn't know existed came to life as the evidence of his arousal pressed against her belly. And this time, she let her lips brush the surface of his flesh before she wrapped her mouth around the jagged bullet and bit down.

His shaft jumped at the touch of her lips, a shudder running through his body as a small grunt came from deep within. "My love, you are playing with a fire that you do not fully understand." His arm, resting around her lower back, tightened. "There are times I may not be able to control myself. I am injured, and I need to feed—this would be one of those times."

Mia's mind registered his words, but her body wanted him. The bullet slipped into her mouth, his blood trickling down the back of her throat once again. She dropped the bullet onto the ground. Her body was in overdrive. *What is happening to me?* Mia struggled with the urge to slide her hand down the front of his jeans and rub the stiffness pressing against her. Her tongue jetted out, licking just below the wound. When she heard a familiar, unforgettable sound coming from Cole's mouth, Mia tilted her head up and met with a set of eyes glazed over with hunger—the same craving she'd seen in GQ's eyes the other night.

Cole's mouth opened. His tongue slowly slid out, licking an elongated fang. Mia swallowed the lump in her throat, and she was now certain the weird noise she'd heard was the sound of fangs sliding out. A tremble rolled over her body as she stared into the eyes of Cole's primal being. With mounting fear, Mia tore her eyes from his gaze. She gaped.

The holes were closing, and tiny fragments of silver popped out from his flesh as his body rejected them. In one sudden movement, she was flung onto her back. Cole's body pinned her to the ground, and his lips came down upon hers, hard, cutting the skin. He took her lip into his mouth, sucking and moaning as drops of blood from the tiny cut dotted his tongue.

"Oh, God. I'm sorry, please, don't kill me." She pushed on his shoulders, but he didn't budge. His whole body had hardened. Mia quickly realized she might be in trouble, and she'd have better luck flipping over a truck.

Mia struggled beneath him, but it only intensified the excitement in his eyes. Releasing her lip, Cole stared down at her with cold, black eyes that had completely changed to predator—Cole was gone.

"It's been a long time, but I still love when my prey fights back." He lifted his chin and dropped his head back, peering down at her as if trying to find a good spot to park his teeth.

"Cole, please. Please don't bite me," Mia pleaded as her fear ticked faster. She stopped squirming, grabbed his face, placing a hand on each side of his perfectly smooth cheeks, and tilted his head until he met her gaze. With all the strength she could summon, she stared into his eyes. Her energy surged with power—raw power, as if she had captured a bolt of lightning. "Cole! Please, hear me... You have to go catch the bad guys."

His aura twitched as she spoke, and he instantly loosened his grip. He stood with ease, briefly staring into her eyes before vanishing with a speed she had never seen.

Mia sat up, breathless and frightened. She flinched as screams echoed from the darkness of the graveyard. The top of a large tree began to shake, and the screams increased. Leaping to her feet, she ran to the back door of the funeral home, tripping once on the way. *Damn dress shoes. This is why women in horror films are mauled first.*

She reached the door and with haste, slid the key into the heavy-duty lock. After jerking on the large handle, Mia wedged her body through the open crack and slammed it behind her. She leaned her back against the door and slid down until she hit the floor. The coolness of the metal penetrated her skin as she cradled her knees and sobbed.

After five minutes, she buried all her emotions deep inside, suppressing them as she'd done all her life. A second later, she sprang to her feet as the room echoed with the sound of knocking.

SEVEN

*M*ia's heart pounded fast, causing her neck to pulse with its beat. She grabbed the phone by the door, immediately releasing it as negative energy stung her and images swirled in her mind. *Shit.* The phone was dead. She didn't need to put it to her ear to confirm the vandalism her vision had shown her.

"Mia, open the door." Cole's voice was low and demanding.

Ignoring his request, her eyes darted around the room. She was still trying to shake the images as she looked for something to use for protection.

"I can feel you through the door. I know you're standing there."

He can do that? I wonder if he can see me flip him off. "Go away!"

"I need to come inside. I won't hurt you. Open the door." His tone was laced with agitation.

"That's what you said before, and then you tried to eat me!" she screamed, hitting the door with her palm.

"To be fair, I did warn you. I'm sorry if I frightened you. I won't eat you. I promise. I'm full."

He was serious. Her face scrunched in disgust.

"Mia, if you don't open the door, I will rip it off the hinges. I need to come in, now!"

I can't believe this is happening. This. Is. Real. "Hold on." She ran to the closest viewing room and found what she was looking for. Climbing on a casket, she grabbed the large cross off the wall, then ran back to the door to let Cole in. Her heart pounded harder, echoing in her ears as she rested her hand on the door. She forced herself to turn the lock. The room flipped, and her vision blurred as the blood racing through her system made her dizzy.

Cole's commanding voice sounded through the door. "Stop!" She stilled her hand on the door lock. "Miakoda, calm yourself, breathe because I'm going to need you when I come inside."

"Stop calling me that!" She blew a puff of air upward, blowing her hair off her forehead. "What do you need me to do?"

"Open the door."

She inched the door open, shielding herself behind the security of its steel, and took in the sight of him. His shirt hung from his body, torn like rags, exposing his taut, muscular physique. The jeans she had admired earlier were ripped in several places, and blood covered them. She didn't dare meet his eyes.

Cole reached behind him grabbing something as he walked past her.

Slapping her hand over her mouth, Mia gasped as he dragged two bodies behind him—dead bodies, streaking the floor with blood like a paintbrush needing more paint.

He dropped them, turned, then walked toward her.

"Stay away from me."

He ignored Mia's demand and continued toward her.

Pulling the large cross from behind her back, she held it out. Her voice rose. "Keep away from me!" Fear caused her to squint until her eyes were little slits.

Cole stared down at her and ripped the cross from her hands. "Don't be naïve, Mia. The same things that worked on your Dracula are not going to work on a real vampire, at least not all of them." Looking down at the cross, he laughed before he threw it to the floor. He walked to the door, slammed it, and turned back to face her. "Miakoda, what did you plan to do with the cross?" His eyes lit with amusement.

"Well if it didn't cause you to burst into flames, it was big enough to hit you with. And stop calling me that." Before this evening, she had loved anything that came out of his mouth. Now, she just felt like a fool.

With incredible speed, he pressed against her before she could move, brushing his lips against her ear. "You are the only thing that will make me burst into flames." Lust rolled out on his voice, making each syllable he uttered pure sex. "What would you like me to call you?"

Mia's body fought for power over her mind, dreamily thinking that if she could have him before he killed her, that wasn't so bad. Right?

"Just call me Mia, okay?"

He glided his lips across her skin, barely touching its surface. "I can call you either name," he breathed. "I like both. Do you know what Mia means?"

She shook her head, her eyes fixed on his.

"It means *mine*." His words rumbled out in a tone that made it clear he was staking his claim.

She shivered, her nipples growing stiff under her shirt.

He watched her stare past the bodies on the floor to the blood soaking into the cement. Then, there it was.

"Cole, please get off of me." She shoved him back. "I'll help you, and then you need to go."

He searched her eyes. "Why? Your body tells me different. Yet, you put your wall up so quickly. Look how tight your jaw is set"—he smoothed a finger over her face—"how tiring that inner struggle must be."

"Stop. I'm upset with you and... It's not fair that you can do that—read me." She turned away from his stare. "What do you need me to do?"

"I need you to fire up the ovens so I can throw these two guys in."

"Are you frigging kidding me?" Her jaw dropped. "I can't do that! I'll be fired. Besides, don't you have to report this?" Her eyes darted to Cole's phone, the ring filling the small room.

His eyes never left her as he spoke. "I have both of them." Cole poked one of the bodies with his boot. "Luckily, I'm at a funeral home, and can dispose of them here. They were after Mia—she needs protection. Make sure there's a day man for tomorrow, I'll take the nights." He nodded. "Yeah, I'll touch base with you later." His eyes held hers as he shut the phone.

"This is beyond you getting fired. Do you understand these men came to kill you?" He kicked the two bodies. "They're bad men, Mia, and I have a feeling that more will come for you." He paused and rested his hands on his hips "You're upset with me, but I don't have time for human emotion nor do I have time to sugarcoat the situation. I won't apologies for my *deal with it* approach."

She glared at him.

"Okay, you're not upset, you're really, really angry with me."

She nodded. "Not for your directness. I hate when people beat around the bush, but I am mad at you for other things." Walking over to the oven, she pushed the button. "Give it a couple minutes to heat up. It gets to 1600 degrees fast."

Mia moved to a cabinet on the opposite side of the room and pulled out a heat reflective, aluminized apron, and tied it around her waist. She pulled a pair of gloves from the apron's pocket, slid them on, and turned to walk back to the oven.

Cole grinned as he watched her every move.

Her nostrils flared. "I'm glad I can be a constant source of entertainment for you. Would you like me to juggle a couple of urns?"

"You're very cute when you're mad. I can't help but smile."

Mia clenched her teeth and took a calming breath. "We can get started. I'll go grab a couple cardboard containers to put the bodies in."

"There's no need for that. I'm going to throw them in at the same time." Cole bent down and easily picked up the two bodies.

Mia flung herself in front of the oven door. "You can't do that! The law requires that only one person be cremated at a time."

Cole's laugh came out fast and loud as he tilted his head, staring at her to move aside. Mia didn't move until his jaw twitched—she wasn't going to win this one.

Stepping away from the door, she cleared her throat. "Do you know if the bodies have any pacemakers or anything else inside them that might explode at a high temperature?" Her tone was serious, businesslike, but her hand trembled as she opened the door.

"See what I mean—you're cute. In a situation like this, you think about things most people would forget in a state of panic." He smiled with a look of admiration as he deposited the bodies onto the rack and pushed it toward the flames. The rack stopped as the dead man's hand wedged between the rack and the door.

"See, this is why we needed the container," Mia said, tilting her chin up in triumph.

"No, that would have been a waste of time."

"No, the box would've prevented body parts from getting stuck." She grabbed the hand that was stuck and pulled, trying to free it. As she yanked, her face reddened and her jaw tightened. The lights in the room flickered.

Cole jerked his head toward the ceiling, closing his eyes briefly. When he returned his gaze to Mia, the caution in his eyes moments ago had disappeared.

"Let me do it." Cole reached for the hand.

"No. I can handle it."

Snap!

"Oh, great! I broke his hand. How many crimes am I going to commit with you tonight, Cole?" Her voice cut the air like a knife.

Cole's brows drew together. "What are you talking about, Mia?"

"It's against the law to mutilate the body of a corpse. Breaking bones is a form of mutilation; now I've mutilated his body."

"No, *I* mutilated his body. You simply cracked his wrist," Cole calmly stated. He closed the oven door and turned toward her, challenging her fixed gaze.

"Do you have something you want to say to me, Mia?" His jaw ticked, waiting for a response. Dropping her eyes, she walked away. He flashed past her with supernatural speed to block her escape. "Stop running from me, and speak to me."

Anger shot out of Mia like a bottle rocket, and she shoved him back. Cole's fangs popped, and his eyes widened. "No human has ever dared to push me, and if they had, I'd have torn their neck from their body. Say what's on your mind."

"You want it, here it is: If I need to be protected, it won't be by you. After tonight, I don't want to see you again. You-you made me show you my secret. I felt like a freak! I'm so pissed off at you that I want to make your aura twitch! You're a... a vampire. That's something that needs to be brought up right away, Cole." She deepened her voice to an imitating low tone. "'I'm looking forward to seeing you off duty, Mia'—and I bite." Waving her hands in the air, she continued. "'Your face is the last thing I wanted to see tonight'— and I bite." Tears pooled in her eyes. "I was starting to trust you and... you bite, and you're dead. Dead, Cole."

She turned away from him. "I'm going to get a mop from the embalming room and start cleaning up the mess." She didn't look back as the door closed behind her.

Cole's hearing was so sensitive, he heard her tears hit the concrete floor. He stared at the door for what seemed like hours, motionless, his mind trying desperately to keep him from going after her.

He didn't intend to make her feel "had." The need to tell her about his secret had brewed inside of him from the moment he'd looked into her eyes. He'd never wanted to tell anyone more than he wanted to tell her. Cole had attempted it before, telling a human what he was, and the result was wiping another memory clean. He never found *the one,* but he found women that filled the emptiness inside him, ones he could tolerate. Cole gave up trying to find someone to share his life with decades ago and threw himself into his work, which became his obsession, until Mia walked into his life. It was like he was back to where he started, struggling to bury the beast within, like a newly made vampire. He prided himself on his control—control others didn't possess—control he had mastered. Cole hated to feel unbalanced and shook his head to clear his thoughts, dislodging Mia from his mind. *Work. Focus.*

EIGHT

*M*ia stood in a room that reeked of embalming fluid. She walked over to the cabinets lining the back wall and retrieved the cleaning supplies, pausing as the sound of the back door filtered into the room. Her lips parted in disbelief. *He's leaving?* She shrugged. She'd have to clean everything herself. It'd be easier that way anyhow, since she wouldn't have to look at Cole anymore. As soon as she finished her thought, sadness filled her. It was then she realized how attached she was to him so quickly. *Why?*

She jerked her head toward the door, vacantly staring at Cole as he walked through it, filling the room with his presence.

He walked past her, dropped a duffle bag on the table, and studied her with a guarded expression. "I need to wash, and change, then I'll help you clean. I have to burn these clothes as well." He tugged at his torn shirt and undressed as if she wasn't in the room.

Her eyes traced the contour of his bare chest, his muscles rippling with each of his movements. Next, he removed his blood-soaked boots and started unbuckling his jeans. Mia realized she was staring. Her eyes met his, and she felt the heat crawl past her cheeks and settle into her ears. "I'm sorry. I'll give you some privacy." Grabbing the mop, Mia walked toward the door.

"You can stay if you want, my love."

Without acknowledging his words, she let the door close behind her. Tears rolled down her cheeks, burning her skin as they silently fell to the floor. Her thoughts paralyzed her. He'd hurt her. Did he even care? Was she being irrational? She stared down at the bloodstained floor realizing the mess wouldn't be there if the men hadn't come to kill her. Cole scared the hell out of her, and he'd tried to kill her, but he'd also saved her life. Regardless, there was no way it could ever work with him—no way. *Cut the ties now.*

Cole entered the room, opened the door to the oven, and threw his clothes in with no regard for Mia's two attackers who were still cremating inside. While his back was turned, Mia glanced at the fresh pair of jeans hugging his body. His black boots shined with a perfected polish, and his dark blue shirt fit snug against his broad chest. A gun fit onto his belt, and two pairs of handcuffs completed the equipment he carried.

Mia's pulse raced at the sight of him. She couldn't control it, and it irritated her, especially since she knew he could feel it when it happened. "Cole, I'm sorry for snapping at you. It seems you bring out the worst in me. I still don't want to see you on a personal level, but I shouldn't be rude to you. You saved my life, and I'm thankful." She brought her eyes up to meet his.

"I know what you mean. I find it a struggle to control myself around you, too, Mia. It not only bothers me, but embarrasses me as well. I have worked hard for one hundred and twenty-nine years to master my control. I'm proud of that. I'm a powerful vampire—more powerful than most in this area. Then you came along and have tested me. Do you know how hard it was for me not to feed from you? Once I tasted the tiny drop of blood from your lips, it took everything I had to pull myself back. If it wasn't for your strength... I don't know what would have happened."

After dipping the mop into the water, Mia began mopping. If she kept busy and averted her eyes away from his, it was easier to talk. "Why is that? Sex? You were aroused and pressing against me —do you drink from everyone you have sex with?"

"No. But they usually go hand–in–hand. It's much better when it happens that way. Drinking blood from a human is exciting and very arousing. If you happen to be having sex first and get to feed during..." His tone turned to longing as it trailed off into a memory. "That's the best feeling a vampire can experience."

"You drink blood from a human every night? You just chase someone down and kill them?" She stopped mopping to meet his eyes, watching for a lie.

"No, Mia." Cole smiled, his eyes held her with adoration. "Yes, I drink blood every night, but I don't hunt and kill people. I do miss the hunt, though—it can be very arousing."

"Where do you get the blood from then?" She rested her hands on the top of the mop handle.

"I can't tell you. I'm sorry. I have to protect my kind."

She nodded in acceptance. "Okay. How much blood do you need until you're... full?" Mia put the mop back in the bucket, swirling it as the water tinted red.

"I'm older. I don't need much, but, like you, I can overeat. If you taste good, I'll want more than needed." His smile turned into a dangerous grin.

Searching for a new topic, Mia turned her back to him, mopping over the same spot she had just cleaned. "You're one hundred and twenty-nine?"

"No, I'm one hundred and sixty-three. I have been a vampire for one hundred and twenty-nine years." Cole stepped closer. "I love answering your questions, Mia."

"Why?"

"It gives me hope." He shrugged. When their eyes met, there was that look, and Mia felt the urge to hear everything about him.

A loud bang shattered the silence of the room. They turned and looked behind them, then Mia glanced up at Cole. "What was that? I hope nothing is blowing up from inside the oven. You did check all their pockets and take their watches off, right?"

Before he had a chance to answer, the noise came again, louder. Mia dropped the mop and walked quickly toward the embalming room where the sound came from.

Cole bowed his chest. "That's my girl. She walks toward danger instead of running from it—unless it's toward me, of course," he muttered.

"That's because you bite. Oh, and I don't need super vampire hearing to hear you muttering behind me."

Before she reached the door, Cole blocked the entrance. "Let me go first."

The banging continued. When they realized where the noise was coming from, they turned toward it in unison. Standing together, they gaped at the freezer.

"Mia, who is in there?" Cole's voice hardened and his eyes began to glow.

"Uhm... we have, Mrs. Claxton, a friend of the owners, a Jane Doe and..." As her wide eyes snapped toward Cole, Mia's voice caught in her throat. "Art!"

Cole placed his arm across Mia's chest, pushing her back behind him. "This is not good."

"What do you mean 'this is not good'? What happened to 'I'm a powerful vampire'?"

The banging increased, and the metal door bowed out with each blow. Mia heard the chilling sounds from inside the cooler. A body bag rubbing against the concrete floor. Carts holding corpses clanging together as someone—*Art?*—thrashed around. A vinyl bag ripping, then gushing sounds, like someone was eating watermelon. It all made her stomach queasy.

"Cole, what was that?" The fear climbed up into her throat, choking it off into a whisper.

"Art is awakening as a vampire. I can only assume that he's very, very hungry. Most new vampires are after they've awakened. They need to feed right away, but the cold blood from the dead bodies in there will not satisfy him."

Art's feet scuffed along the concrete floor as he started to move around the cooler.

"Cole, what do we do?"

Cole walked to the cooler and leaned against the door, putting his hand on the handle.

"Mia, you stay over there. Back all the way up against that casket."

She looked behind her at the casket, then slowly followed his line of sight directly back to the cooler door. Her eyes widened in disbelief as she glared. "You're going to use me as bait!"

"Why is it so hard for you to trust me?"

"Mia? Is that you?" Art's voice grated through the cooler door in an eerie growl.

Her eyes darted to Cole's, searching for what to do next.

Slowly, he shook his head.

"I know that's you out there. I can smell your blood. It wasn't supposed to happen this way. You have to help me. I was supposed to go on to my wife and baby." He slammed his fist against the door. "This can't happen. I have lived long enough in pain. Let me die so I can love again."

Art's words pulled at her heart. She couldn't ignore the pain in his tone. "Art, I'm so sorry..." Her voice cracked as her tears fell.

Cole looked at her as he leaned against the door. "You really need to pull yourself together, Mia. You're no good to anyone like this. You need to calm down."

Calm Down? Did he just tell me to calm down? Everyone has certain words that make them snap, and "calm down" was Mia's. He'd just pushed her red button. "You are a heartless ass, Cole. Everything that's happened tonight is completely out of the norm for me, and you have the audacity to tell me to *calm—*"

With a loud bang, the cooler door flew off its hinges, slamming against the wall with Cole behind it.

Art went straight for Mia. His body still appeared burnt with pieces of new skin exposed as it healed itself. Wrapping his hands around Mia's neck, he lifted her off the ground and slammed her into the coffin behind her. Her feet dangled above the cement floor as her hand came up and grabbed the arm holding her throat. Mia scrambled against Mr. Roberts' chest, desperately trying to gain her balance while Art pushed her further inside the casket. Every time she picked up her hand to fight, she fell further back. Dying in a coffin was not on her top-five-ways-I-want-to-die list. Everything was happening so fast, and she tried to stop her mind from spinning. *Think, Mia...* Her hand slipped off Mr. Roberts' chest, and landed against cold metal.

Art's body suddenly lifted off the ground, and he released her throat. Cole backed him away from her, tossing him to his knees as Art fought back. He was no match for Cole.

Mia watched Cole skillfully unsnap the leather handcuff case next to the pair of blue handcuffs hanging from his belt. In one smooth motion, Cole put the cuff around Art's wrist. Art screamed as smoke billowed up from his skin, and he slouched as the silver cuffs wilted his strength.

"Mia, please. My wife is waiting." Fighting with everything he had left, Art's desperate voice called to her. Mia stared at the burning flesh around his wrist, and her mind clicked into action. She grabbed Mr. Roberts' sword from the coffin.

Cole's eyes snapped to hers. "Mia. No!"

She slammed the sword into Art's chest, piercing his heart. Blood spewed from the wound like a water line bursting, covering her. Mia watched in horror as various body parts melted, exploded, or quickly decayed as if part of a week-old corpse. Staring at the mass of blood on the floor, Mia gasped for air, then looked away to focus on her breathing.

From his kneeling position in front of what was left of Art, Cole's eyes came up to hers. For a moment, Mia thought she saw a small hint of admiration, but it quickly faded. He was not happy.

Well, screw him. "Was that calm enough for you?" Mia said with all the sarcasm she could muster.

"You shouldn't have done that." He stood, glaring at her.

"Why? You think I should have let him live in pain—for eternity. No one should have to live like that."

Cole was in her face before she could blink. "Some people *do* live in pain, Mia, every day, but we pull ourselves together and try to move on. Art was weak! You didn't have the right to do that. We needed him." The hardness began to fade from his face as he searched her eyes. "There's blood on your lips." He dipped his head toward them.

"What?"

His gaze darted from her mouth to her eyes, then his jaw set in a tight line, and he looked away. "He could have answered some questions for us about the man with the glowing eyes."

Behind his deep brown gaze, Mia saw a reflection of pain, and thought about his words. Like a burning ember placed in the snow, her temper subsided. "I'm sorry, I didn't think of that."

"Of course you didn't. You let your emotions take over and lead you." The muscle in his jaw twitched.

With an exasperating sigh, she shook her head. "Well, at least I have emotions, so excuse me." She walked past him. "Me and my *emotions* need to start cleaning." After she surveyed the damages, she turned to face him. "I'm definitely fired. Thanks again for a lovely evening."

Cole stared at her through narrowed eyes, but didn't respond.

Frustrating woman.

Cole pulled his phone from his pocket and pushed a button. "Sheriff. We need a cleanup crew. We also have an unauthorized re-birth." He picked up his bloodied handcuffs from the floor and placed them on the metal table. "And I also need a door to a cooler. Hold on and I'll get you the number." Cole walked directly to the cooler's model information.

"How am I going to get all this blood out?" Cole heard Mia murmuring to herself as she pulled her saturated shirt away from her skin. "I can't wait to get home and lock myself away from everyone. Especially—"

In an instant, he stood in front of Mia, looking down at her while he finished telling the sheriff the specifics of the evening. Her eyes told him a different story than her words. Something held her back from him, and his arms ached to hold her, comfort her, until she felt safe in his presence. He slid the phone back in his pocket, and lifted her chin with his finger.

"I don't know what circumstances occurred in your life for you to build such a strong brick wall around your heart, but I do intend to tear it down. I know you feel me, as I can feel you. I *do* have emotions, Mia, and you've provoked every one of them since I've met you. I'm sorry I lack basic human sentiments. I don't care about the weak or the evil, but I'm intrigued with your passion for life and baffled with your willingness to find the good in everyone. But evil will prevail if you keep thinking like this. There are some that are evil, with no good inside them." He stroked her cheek with his thumb. "I want you to look back at the day we met until now, and you'll see I haven't laid one brick on that wall around your heart. Please, stop treating me as if I did."

Mia swayed forward as she stared at him with a captivated gaze. Her brows dipped, and the depths of her blue eyes swirled with turmoil. The knock from outside of the room broke their stare. "Cole. I. You could really hurt me. Please." She took his hand away from her face and moved toward the door.

If only she knew. He took in a breath he didn't need, then whooshed past her out of the room to answer the door. Mia followed, keeping her distance as he talked to the sheriff.

"You need to go home now," Cole said as he eyed her appearance. "We'll handle everything here."

* * *

Mia wasn't in the mood to argue. Blood covered her from head to toe, and she desperately wanted a shower.

As she moved toward the exit, Cole grabbed her hand. "Come in the back with me. Let me wash you first. You don't want to leave here looking like that, and I'm sure you want to get the blood and entrails off."

It was crazy how he could read her mind. She pulled her hand away from his as if it shocked her. His jaw tightened at her actions. Mia walked to the back as he followed close behind. Another officer came in, dropped a change of clothes on the table, then left.

"Take your clothes off, and I can wash you down." Cole's face held no expression.

"Absolutely not! I can do it myself. You can go outside and guard the door." She waved her hands in the air to shoo him away.

"You're never going to get all of this off by yourself. Stop being stubborn, and let me help, or I can get one of the female detectives outside. Either way, someone is going to help you, so make a decision." He gave her a stern look, folding his arms and challenging her with his stance.

Damn him. "Okay, but I'm not taking off my panties." Cole shifted his position. A grunt sounded in his chest, and he stared at her. "Stop looking at me like *that.*" With her back to him, she stripped down.

"This may be harder than I thought." Cole grabbed the embalming room hose and held it over her shoulders. The water ran over Mia's body, hugging every curve and she shivered from its cool touch.

As she ran her fingers over her flesh, ridding it of blood, she laughed to herself. The sheriff was right—it was convenient they were at a funeral home since it had the necessities for a cover up.

She stared at the concrete floor as the water and blood mixed and swirled around the drain. Cole raked his fingers through her hair, loosening the strands to free the blood and flesh that were stuck. Goosebumps blanketed her skin as his fingers tugged at the strands, and the water ran free over her shoulders to stream across her breasts.

This was the furthest she'd been with a man in a long time.

She looked at her toes and saw bubbles running over them as Cole massaged her head. "You brought shampoo?"

"How else do you expect to get a new vampire's goo out of your hair? Some can be very messy. The older ones just shrivel, aging rapidly." Mia sensed his smile.

"Are you always prepared?"

He spun her around to face him. Mia's hands snapped to her breasts, shielding them from his eyes as he looked down at her with his fangs out.

"No. I wasn't prepared for you." He bent down to kiss her.

"Don't." She turned her head. "This is why I said I didn't want to do this. You're taking advantage of the situation."

She was damaged and didn't want unneeded emotions or memories stirred up. Grabbing the towel from the embalming table, she wrapped it around her. A quick shiver ran through her as distant memories filtered through her mind. She hardened herself and emotionally shut down.

"Mia, I'm sorry. You're right." He ran his hand through his hair.

Leaving her clothes behind, Mia bolted out the door.

"Where are you going?"

She didn't answer. When she came into the other room, five people stopped what they were doing and stared.

"If you all will excuse me." She walked toward the exit, stopping at the shelf next to the door to retrieve her purse—mindfully holding up the towel.

"Mia. Stop!" Cole demanded as she opened the door.

"You stay away from me, Detective Barnett."

Snickers and crash-and-burn whistles filled the room as she walked outside. She came to a halt halfway to her car and locked eyes with Cole, resting against the driver's door, relaxed and poised.

"Get off my car, Cole, and please stay away from me."
She was agitated, but she knew if he tried to kiss her
again, she would fall victim to it.

"Are you going to drive home in a towel? You know
that's police property?"

Cole's toying grin and casual tone raked her nerves.
Mia didn't know if she wanted to hit him or throw him
to the ground and ravish him. What she *did* know was
he made her blood boil.

She ripped the towel from her body and faced him.
Her bare breasts rewarded his heated gaze as her
nipples grew taut in the cool night air.

Mia threw the towel toward him, and he stumbled
back when he caught it.

"Here, Detective. I believe this is your property. The
towel, that is—not me." For the first time since they
met, Cole was speechless, his lips parted in disbelief.

Mia took advantage of his stunned silence and
jumped into the car, leaving a trail of dust and gravel
behind her as she fled.

NINE

*P*ulled from a deep sleep by the rapping on the door, Mia slid the clock on her nightstand closer. *Who could be knocking at eight a.m.?* She shoved her arms in the sleeves of her robe as she walked toward the intrusion.

As soon as she neared it, a voice called out from the other side. "Mia Starr? This is Detective Gonela. I just wanted to let you know I'll be out here guarding your door."

Leaving the safety chain attached, Mia cracked the door and inspected the good-looking man standing outside. A very tall, broad-shouldered Hispanic stared back at her with eyes as black as coal.

"Good morning, Detective Gonela. I'm sorry, why are you here?" She wiped her sleepy eyes.

"I can't disclose the exact reason, ma'am. Just know I'm here to look after you." He smiled. His Spanish accent more defined as they spoke.

"Do you know *who* could disclose the exact reason?" Everyone had secrets involving her life, but she wasn't allowed in on them? She was getting annoyed, to say the least.

"That would be Detective Barnett or the sheriff, ma'am."

Mia rolled her eyes. She didn't know the sheriff, and she really didn't want to speak to Cole. "Thanks. You want a cup of coffee or something?" She felt weird leaving him in the hallway, not that anyone would see him. Mia was the only tenant living above the three mom-and-pop businesses in the triplex.

"No. But thanks for the offer." Gonela tipped his head and winked. Mia stared back at him. She swore his black eyes flashed gold. She quickly scanned his orange-colored aura, indicating he was friendly. The aura was basic except for the exceptionally bright bands running through its crest like Cole's and the men from the gas station. Not metallic, though.

"If you change your mind, let me know." She smiled and shut the door, her mind in a jumble. Why did Cole suddenly feel she was so important and needed protection? What kind of danger was she in?

Mia quickly raced through her morning routine. Once dressed, she sat on the couch. She tried to piece everything together. Like her dreams, she considered writing everything down—map it out or something.

Bela jumped in her lap, rubbing his head on her open palm. His ears suddenly flattened. Jumping down, he walked to the door and sniffed the air. His fur instantly stood, and a deep, low meow challenged what he felt was a threat.

"Bela. Get over here. It's just a policeman. He's here to protect us." Bela turned as if he understood, tail twitching in the air before he disappeared to his favorite spot under the bed.

Mia wrote down the events of the night before, trying to make sense of them, but her mind kept drifting to Cole. She was still angry with herself for letting her guard down and allowing Cole to get to her the way he did. She felt like a fool, and although she wanted to be angry with him, a part of her was hungry for him.

It was noon before she moved from the couch to soothe her growling stomach. She was still lost in thought as she poured a bowl of cereal. "I know one thing I need to find out. How to kill a vampire." She

looked at Bela who was staring at her. "What? I know
I'm talking to myself, but I'm only certifiable if I talk
back." She poured Bela's food and then grabbed her
bowl. "Now, if someone is trying to kill me, and that
someone is a vampire, then I need to protect myself."
Her mind scrolled through everything she knew so far.
"Not much, since vampires aren't supposed to exist."
She sorted through the things she'd read, and compared
them to what she knew as fact. The only thing she knew
for certain was silver had an immobilizing effect.

With that in mind, she picked up the phone. "Hey,
Mom. Do you still have all that old silver of
Grandma's?"

Mia's mom had kept many things when her grandma
passed away a couple of years ago. Things no one else
cared about, like postcards and handkerchiefs she'd
blown her nose in—clean, of course, but it still grossed
Mia out. Her mom also kept the last thing her
grandmother had been knitting, the needle still stuck
into place. It was as if her mom was waiting for
grandma to come back and finish it.

"Of course, I have it." Her mother's voice was tired.

"Is there a lot of silverware and serving stuff?"

"It's every silver piece your grandma had. She
wanted you to have it, anyway. It's here if you need it,
still in the box she packed it in."

"I'm going out with Cynthia tonight. Can I stop by
tomorrow and grab it?"

"That's fine, Miakoda. Oh, sorry... *Mia*."

"Okay, Mama, I'll see you then." She hung up the
phone. Excitement set in as she thought about her girl's
night out with Cynthia. She needed a break from the
weirdness in her life, and her mind needed a break from
Cole.

Mia walked to the door and cracked it. "Detective
Gonela?"

"Yes." His response came quickly.

Mia felt secure knowing he was standing right there, as promised. She slid the chain off and opened the door. His shoulder rested against the wall as he stared at her with a relaxed and confident expression.

"I'm going out later. Do you have to follow me?"

He glided his gaze over her frame before focusing on her eyes. "Yes, ma'am. Do you need to go to the grocery store?"

She arched an eyebrow. "No. I'm going to a night club with a friend tonight."

Pushing himself off the wall, Gonela looked down at her with disapproval. "I don't think that's a good idea, ma'am. Detective Barnett said you should stay out of sight and not draw any attention to yourself." His tone changed to full-blown cop mode.

"Really? Is that what he said?" Her eyes narrowed, and she shot daggers—daggers meant for Cole. Just the mention of his name made her blood run hot.

"Yes, he did."

"You're saying I can't go out with my friend? Is that right?" Mia's temper rose with every word.

"No. I said it wasn't a good idea. It may put us both in danger."

"Well, you can stay here, and I'll go. I'm sure whoever Cole is guarding me from can kill me here just as well as they can kill me in a nightclub. I'll be leaving at five." She closed the door before he could respond. Her face burned with anger. Mia wasn't normally rude, and she knew he was just doing his job, but the need to get out and give her mind a rest won over the need to be polite. There was no way she was staying home tonight.

Usually, Mia dressed down. That changed with the attire she picked out for the club. She wore a little black dress that screamed "Look at me!" with its snug top, flared bottom, and chiffon overlay. It looked beautiful when she twirled. A cute little pair of black, strappy sandals with a small heel completed her look. Mia never wore much makeup—she put mascara on, as usual, and rolled lipstick lightly over her lips. A dab of perfume was the final touch before walking out the door at five p.m. sharp.

Gonela's eyes rolled over her as she locked the door to her apartment. "Would you like to tell me where you're going—to make it easier on me. Or are you going to try to lose me?" His tone held an edge of agitation.

Mia couldn't blame him for being annoyed with her. He should be. "I'm going by the Lake Worth beach. Go up to the top, and there is a night club there called—"

"Hurricanes."

"Oh, have you been there?"

"No, but I've arrested people that go there." He grinned.

"Are you trying to piss me off?"

"By the color in your face, you're already there. Besides, I was just adding a point to my scorecard." He marked the air with his finger.

***

Mia sighed when she reached the rusty iron gates at the bottom of the stairs. Tired and annoyed, she had no desire to struggle with the dilapidated structure. Since she'd moved in she'd battled with them in a tug-of-war every time she wanted to enter or leave her apartment. Placing her palm on the iron, Mia pushed. The gate flew open as if it were cardboard, catching her by surprise. She missed her routine step to the side, and her heel caught in the sidewalk crack, causing her to stumble forward into her car. She rolled her eyes and opened the door. Once concealed inside, her thoughts took over. Why was she so mad? Sure, she felt deceived, but it was more than that. She really liked Cole. She shuddered at the image of his fangs. Her phone vibrated, and she shook her head at the display. *Can't Cynthia just call me? Does it always have to be a text?* Darting her eyes back and forth between her phone and the road, she typed "30 minutes."

Mia loved Hurricanes. It used to be an old casino, but had been converted into a themed nightclub. Tonight's theme was 'Double Shots.' Double shots of music and double shots of liquor was just what she needed.

Mia didn't usually drink much. Growing up surrounded by alcoholics did that to a person. But she wanted Cole out of her head, even if it was only for a night, and this was the only way she knew how to do it.

Once parked, Mia ignored her tail and walked alongside the beach on the walkway. The ocean waves lapped at the sand as the moonlight danced softly on the tiny ripples of water. She breathed in the salty air, and serenity washed over her.

When Mia entered the club, her eyes instantly found Cynthia who greeted her with big hug.

"You don't know how bad I needed this night," Mia said.

"Who you telling?" Cynthia gave her a knowing smile. She had been with her boyfriend Kevin for a couple of years now. He was the man of her dreams, with a head full of dreadlocks and a body that looked like it was chiseled from stone.

Mia hooked her arm through Cynthia's. "I need to take it slow tonight, or I may be done quickly." They walked toward the bar.

The nightclub was on the second floor and looked typical—nothing special setting it apart except the beautiful view. The club faced the beach and had windows traveling down its entire front giving a perfect view of the ocean.

Detective Gonela leaned against the bar, eyeing Mia as she sat on the stool next to him. She glanced at him, silencing him with her eyes. Reading her expression, Gonela nodded—apparently understanding her need for him to be discreet.

Once Mia figured everything out, she would tell Cynthia, but not now. Not tonight.

"Hey, Cyn. Hey, Mia," the bartender said, tossing two beverage napkins on the counter in front of them.

"Hi, Stewy," they said in unison.

"Cynthia—Heineken and a shot? Mia—Coors Light?"

"I think I'll have a shot right away," Mia said before he turned.

Both Cynthia and Stewy's head snapped around.

Mia darted her eyes back and forth between them. "What?"

Cynthia shook her head. "Don't you give me that *what.* Okay, what's up? You never have shots this early in the night, and you're dressed to hurt someone, girl." Cynthia placed her hand on her hip and glared at her.

Mia quickly glanced at everyone, especially Gonela who seemed to be hanging on to every word, before returning her gaze back to Cynthia.

"I don't want to talk about it right now, Cyn, okay?"

"Okay, but you *will* fill me in later."

"Yes." One of the things Mia loved about Cynthia was she knew when to back off, and when to pry.

When the DJ's voice came over the speakers, both girls smiled. He was a friend of Cynthia's boyfriend, which meant their songs would play first. They wrote their requests down on a bar napkin, and Cynthia delivered it to the DJ. When she came back, they counted to three, downed the first shot, and chased it with beer.

The music began, and Cynthia jumped off the barstool. "Ha! My song is first. I love this song!"

They counted to three and did the second shot. "Come on, let's dance!" Cynthia grabbed Mia's hand and pulled her to the dance floor.

Mia never left her drink unattended, afraid someone would put something in it, but with Stewy watching their stuff, she felt confident nothing would happen to it. Besides, Detective Gonela had her back too.

Hip Hop wasn't Mia's thing, but her BFF liked it, and since Cynthia danced to her songs, she only felt it was right to return the favor. Mia could move to this music, but not like Cynthia could. When she moved, it was like watching waves in the ocean. Mia loved watching her dance, but more so she loved watching the men watch her dance. When she started swaying, she grabbed their attention, and like a snake charmer, she had the males captivated.

When the song ended, they ran back to the bar for another set of shots. Already feeling the effects, Mia giggled. This was why she usually waited until later into the night to do shots. Detective Gonela closed his phone as Mia approached the bar.

Mia glanced over at Cynthia who was busy talking to Stewy and then back to Gonela. "Can I buy you a drink, Detective?" Mia asked.

"No, and I can see by your expression you're halfway to mindless. You should slow down yourself. You need to keep a clear head, ma'am, but I guess no one is going to tell you what to do." He gave her another disapproving look.

She narrowed her eyes at him. Since her brain was on a lunch break, she had no response. Grabbing another shot, Mia raised her glass to the detective and downed it. Cynthia's second song thumped loudly in the room. Grabbing Mia by the arm, Cynthia pulled her from the chair and set her in motion toward the dance floor. Mia bumped into chairs and tables, the alcohol taking over and leading the way. She stopped dancing— she could feel the liquor slithering through her veins, impairing her body and basic thought patterns.

When the song ended and Mia took a step toward the bar, Cynthia grabbed her arm. "Hold up, Mia. You want to tell me about this guy? You're hot tonight, and out to damage yourself. I can tell he's what's bothering you."

"I don't want to talk about it." Mia walked toward the bar, and Cynthia was right behind her, nagging her as they reached it.

"No, you need to talk about it. Stop *running!*" The more Mia ignored her, the louder Cynthia's voice became. "Wow. This guy is really under your skin."

"I don't want to talk about it." Mia grabbed her beer, holding it to her lips as she glanced at Detective Gonela. She froze.

Cole stood in his place. He was so close, she felt the heat from her body bouncing off him. He rested an elbow on the bar, one boot on the foot rail, and watched her intently as she finally moved to sip her beer.

She wasn't prepared for this. Cynthia's voice filtered into her hazy mind as she watched Cole. "Mia, did he do something bad to you? I've never seen you like this over a man."

"Cyn. *Shut. It.*"

"No, don't tell me to shut up when I'm trying to help. You're afraid. You really like this guy, and you won't allow yourself to fall because of your fucked-up past experiences."

"Cyn, please. Not now," Mia pleaded again, glancing at Cole who was listening intently. Although his eyes held hers, his face was empty of any emotion.

"You're going to talk. I think you might love him or something with the way you're acting. You must have had an instant connection with him. Mia, this is what you've been waiting for. You always said the moment you look into a man's eyes and his soul reaches out and touches you, he will own you forever."

Mia dropped her head onto her arms in defeat and then straightened, taking a step back. Cole and Cynthia's eyes connected.

"Cynthia, this is Cole. Cole, this is my best friend, Cynthia. Now that you have met, you can talk amongst yourselves."

Cynthia wiggled her fingers in the air, and Cole returned the greeting with a simple nod. Cynthia flicked her gaze quickly over Cole, picked up her drink, and tapped it against Mia's in approval.

Time to step away from the alcohol, Mia thought as her head spun.

Cole's lips curved into the slightest smile. "You smell incredible. What are you wearing?" His tone was calm and smooth.

"Silver." Mia met his gaze, which was a mistake. His eyes melted her as his laugh rolled over her.

She couldn't handle him with alcohol in her system. Saved by her double shot and requested songs, Mia ran to the dance floor as Def Leppard's "Pour Some Sugar on Me," pounded the speakers. She moved her body in ways that called to all males within a five-mile radius, which was unusual for her.

Cynthia came to stand beside her. "I don't know how to handle you when you're acting like this," she yelled over the music.

"Just dance with me." Mia gave her a quick hug.

"Can I say one more thing?" Cynthia asked. "He is friggin' hot, and that badge and gun... Oh my, I see your problem."

They laughed as they danced. Cynthia didn't know the half of Mia's problems, but she could pick out her main one—Cole. Mia's eyes roamed back to him against her will. He stood so still almost in a trance-like state, though his eyes followed her everywhere. It heated her up, making her want to run to him.

When the song ended, everyone left the dance floor except for Mia. She knew her second request was coming, and she could already feel the song before it began. Her eyes moved to Cole.

The DJ sounded over the speaker. "This goes out to the pretty lady of the night—Mia. 'Love Bites.'"

Cynthia grabbed Mia's shoulders. "I can't dance with you to this shit. I'll meet you back at the bar."

Mia stood in the middle of the dance floor, alone with her thoughts, and her fears. She started to sway to the music as it ran through her body. It soothed her in her alcohol-induced state. Her hips drew an invisible swirl as she bent her knees and swayed. She closed her eyes and saw Cole, then she opened her eyes and saw Cole. She couldn't escape him.

A hand grabbed her arm and turned her. "I've been watching you all night, babe," the man said. Mia vaguely recognized him from earlier when he had been in the corner drinking with friends.

A large hand came down on his, ripping it off Mia's arm. "And I have been watching *you*." Cole's voice was threatening as he looked into the man's eyes.

"It's okay—he's my bodyguard." Mia removed Cole's hand from the man and began pushing Cole backward off the dance floor. His face hardened with every step. She glanced up at Cole, then turned and walked back over to dance floor, holding her arms out to the man waiting for her.

As the music ran through her, she felt Cole, not the guy she was dancing with. *What am I doing?* She tried to clear her head and let the music soothe as it filtered through her. She lipped the song as he spun her. "I don't want to touch you too much baby, because making love to you might drive me crazy." Her grip slipped, and she landed against a hard chest. Looking up, she swayed and locked eyes with Cole.

"It may drive us both crazy." His voice was confident and deep. The air thinned, and Mia couldn't catch her breath. Her fingers rubbed against Cole's shirt as she stared up at him.

Her dance partner grabbed her arm and pulled her away. "Dude, you're starting to piss me off. I'm dancing with her."

A light began to shine in the back of Cole's eyes, and Mia heard his fangs slide out. *Oh, shit.* Mia shook her head trying to drain the alcohol from her brain.

"Your dance is over. Why don't you, and your hair gel, go back over to your boyfriends and have a drink before I rip your head from your neck?" Cole glared down at him, and to Mia's surprise, the guy's ego jumped to challenge.

He was no bigger than Mia was, but the effects of the alcohol must have made him feel ten feet tall. "I will wipe the floor with you, asshole!" He poked a finger into Cole's chest.

"Okay, that's enough." Mia was desperately trying to sober up, quickly. "Go cool off." Looking up at Cole, she pushed his chest, and he didn't budge. His eyes where fixated on the man.

"I want to rip him apart." The glow in his eyes intensified.

"Detective, you're on duty. Go cool off." Mia knew he was very devoted to his job, and he would never disgrace his badge. Mia didn't want to be the cause of him doing so either. Cole looked down at Mia, and the glow subsided. He quickly turned and walked away.

Mia faced her dance partner. "Thanks for the dance, but we're done here."

She looked over her shoulder and caught Cole's eyes, a smile twitched at his lips. As Mia turned to leave, the man grabbed her arm, hard, and pulled her to him. He slid his hands down, grabbed her bottom, and squeezed. Cole paused at the door and looked over.

"Come on, baby. I've got a red Porsche outside that I would love to ride you in."

Cole started to move toward them, but before he got the chance to act, Mia squatted, stretched her leg out, and swept the guy's feet out from under him as ladylike as she could in a dress. She had him on the ground before he knew what was happening. "Now that's just rude! Didn't your mama ever tell you to keep your hands to yourself? You'll never get a good woman that way."

The man picked himself off the floor and called her a few names before stumbling back to his table.

Mia began to unravel, and if someone pulled her string any further, she would completely fall apart. She walked to the bar where Cynthia had been watching.

"I was in the bathroom, so I must've missed some of the action. Are you okay?" she asked.

"Can we just go? I've had enough for the night." All the joy drained out of her. She knew everyone was right—she needed to face the things she harbored deep inside sooner or later, and in her current state, she felt like tonight might be a good time.

As they collected their things to leave, a loud noise from outside shook the windows of the club. The music stopped, and it grew silent. It sounded like a semi truck plowed into the building. Everyone ran to the windows to find the source of the noise.

A man screamed, "Dude, my Porsche! Someone hit my car!" The crowd started moving toward the door like a herd of cattle. Mia was pushed out into the roadway with everyone else. Out in the sand on the beach, sat a red Porsche almost bent in half and completely trashed. Mia stared in awe—she knew what had demolished the Porsche. *The strength it must have taken to destroy a car with your bare hands...* Her head spun, and the approaching sirens made it throb. She felt Cole as she walked the sidewalk along the shore. He was out there somewhere. The crowd gathered around the car, and she could hear the different explanations of what may have happened to the Porsche.

Looking past the crowd, out past the car, her eyes scanned the shoreline and fell upon Cole. He was further out by the water. He knelt down in the sand, slightly bent forward with his arm resting on his knee. She watched him as he looked out into the water, the shine from the moon covering him like a blanket. *What have I done to him?*

Cynthia tapped her on the shoulder as she closed her cell phone. "Mia, I need to leave. Let me drive you home, and we'll come back tomorrow for your car."

"I'll be fine." Sadness seeped into Mia's tone.

"No, you won't. I've never seen you this bad before—you're not driving." Cynthia reached for the keys clutched in Mia's hand.

Mia knew better than to drive in her condition, but she wasn't going to ruin Cynthia's night by allowing her to watch the breakdown she felt coming. Cynthia needed to go home to her boyfriend and have fun.

"Cyn, you're not getting my keys, and you're not driving me home." Mia flung them behind her. Now she'd spend the rest of the night on the beach, sobering up and looking for her keys in the sand. Mia waited to hear the keys land, focusing on the noise so she'd have an idea where to start searching. She heard them hit something solid and swung around to see where they had landed. *Crap!*

Cole's hand was in the air with her keys in his fist. She'd have said *good catch* if she hadn't felt like stomping her feet like a child. He walked to them with Mia's keychain looped around his finger. "I have her. I'll see her safely home." He stared at Cynthia.

"You know, I think that's a great idea. Be careful though. She's like a wild horse—hard to break." Cynthia smiled and gave Mia a hug, then left her standing beside Cole, alone.

Mia stumbled, and Cole caught her. He grabbed her arm and walked her to his car in the same under-the-arm, cop grip he loved to use on her. He propped her up against the vehicle while he opened the passenger door.

"That hurt. You don't have to be so rough." Mia rubbed the visible fingerprints on her skin.

"The way you were acting in there, I didn't think you cared too much about how people treated your body." His voice struggled to keep a calm tone.

Her jaw dropped. "How dare you. You have no idea what I've been through in life. I don't even let people touch my body, and—"

"You let him touch it." He pointed toward the Porsche. "Get in the car."

"I don't think I should ride with you." Mia's pulse quickened at his tone and fear surfaced. She flicked her gaze toward the Porsche, a reminder of what Cole was capable of if he lost his temper. Mia didn't want to end up like the Porsche and she didn't want to throw up in Cole's car, either, because eventually that was coming. He pressed his body against hers, squishing her into the metal of the car and glared down at her.

"Get in the damn car, now!" he said, between clenched teeth. Mia obeyed. Cole slammed the door then sat in the driver's seat before her mind registered he'd moved. Her stomach churned and her eyes lost focus. Everything in front of her flipped repeatedly like a movie stuck on the same frame.

"Put your seatbelt on," he ordered.

"No." She fought the urge to throw up. The seatbelt's restraint wouldn't be wise. Her mouth watered, and she continuously swallowed. In vampire speed, Cole opened her door, and pressed one knee between her legs. He grabbed the seatbelt and leaned into her to fasten it. Mia felt a stronger urge and she put her hands around Cole's neck, pulling him to her. Mia brushed her lips across his and kissed him passionately. Cole's hands dove into her hair as he deepened the kiss. With a low grunt, he pulled away.

"Not like this." His lips curled, exposing his fangs, and he blew out a calming breath.

Jerking her hands away from his neck, Cole placed them in her lap.

His rejection stung. With everything else that had happened between them her natural instinct was to hurt him back.

Cole stared at her. She turned her head to the side and slowly brushed her hair back with the tips of her fingers exposing her neck. She watched him with a slanted gaze.

His eyes began to glow as they darkened. He watched the vein pulsing just beneath her skin. His fangs grew longer to tighten his jaw.

"Would you like a drink? It's laced with rum." Her tone was ice cold. She could have said 'fuck you' and it would have had the same effect.

Cole clicked the seatbelt into its latch. Without taking his eyes off her, he slid his hand behind her head, making a fist around her hair. His fangs grew longer, and he watched her swallow hard at the sight of them.

She was playing with him, and he didn't like it. If this were anyone else, he would have drained her already. He yanked Mia's head back.

Her eyes widened as he inched closer, the pulse in her neck beating wildly. He wanted to taste her; the pace of her rapid heartbeat would cause the blood to flow easily. Cole brushed his lips on her skin and paused over the throbbing vein. It beat against his lips—calling to him, taunting him. The vampire within urged him forward. He closed his eyes imagining the taste of her, the feel of the warm, velvety texture as it slid down his throat. *Mine.*

His fangs barely touched her skin, and a small whimper escaped her throat. Cole raked them upward, leaving a small red trail that marked the skin up to her ear. Another whimper escaped her lips. He could take her right now. His groin had grown so hard it ached inside his pants and throbbed just as hard as the pulse in her neck.

Cole tightened his grip on her hair, and she squeezed her eyes shut. "Look at me, Mia." When he was sure she focused on him, he loosened his grip. "Don't ever tease a vampire." He gently kissed her lips. "I don't want you this way."

He was back in the driver's seat before she could blink.

Mia rolled her window down and sucked in a staggered breath. She looked frightened, nervous, and he watched her struggle with both emotions. She laughed, but her expression remained dejected. "What kind of vampire are you, or man, for that matter?" Tilting her head, she looked at him. "I thought vampires liked blood and sex?"

His grip tightened on the steering wheel—any tighter and it would have snapped under the pressure.

"They do." John's voice cracked out like a whip. He stood beside Mia's window with his arms crossed over his chest. When Mia jerked her head toward him, John added, "A lesser man, and weaker vampire, would've ripped your throat out and drained every last drop of blood from your pretty little body" He leaned into the window, and the look he gave Mia caused her to retreat into the seat.

Cole knew John was on his side but the need to defend Mia, to protect her, swirled inside him.

"Have some respect, young lady. Stop acting like a child. From what Cole says, we need you and I can't for the life of me see why." John glanced at Cole then turned his narrowed gaze back to Mia. "You're letting your fear make you weak, and this isn't a game. Cole, get the lady home and report back in a while."

Mia grabbed John's arm. "If I have to be guarded, can't someone else do it?"

John chuckled. "Not if you want to live."

"Oh, no. Not now!" Mia finger's turned white where they gripped the sheriff's arm. With her free hand, she seized Cole's forearm. "No, no... Please."

TEN

A familiar feeling started to swirl in the pit of her stomach.

"What's wrong with her? Is she going to be sick?" Mia could hear the sheriff, but his voice had become muffled.

"She's in the ocean." Mia squeezed her eyes shut as the vision started.

"Who's in the ocean? Cole, how much has she had to drink?"

"Mia, where is she?" Cole's calm voice soothed her.

When the next image hit, she dug her fingers into his skin, and felt him jump from the pressure. "She's straight out from where you were kneeling. Not too far out from the pier." Mia opened her eyes.

Cole stroked her hand that lay on his arm with a feather touch. With rapid breaths, Mia retreated back into the seat. Her muscles tightened and trembled.

Cole looked at the sheriff. "John, have you experienced anything like this? What do we do?"

John shrugged. "Haven't a clue."

Mia's eyes slammed shut, and she watched in horror as the dark chambers of her mind replayed the girl's murder. She shook her head from side-to-side.

"No... It was a vampire. He ripped chunks of flesh from her body. Oh, God. The blood. It's everywhere." Mia swallowed hard before continuing. "She's screaming and screaming, but he won't stop—it excites him when she screams." Her eyes flew open. She tugged at the sheriff's arm as she looked up at him. "You have to look at her body carefully. The fish have been eating at her for days, and you're not going to be able to tell she was attacked. Look at the other two girls too. Closely."

"What two girls?"

Mia was unable to answer. She pushed the door as hard as she could, and John wisely moved out of her way. She threw up everything she had in her. A napkin appeared in front of her face, and she took it from Cole's hand. Wiping her mouth, she leaned back into the seat. Stomach acid still burned her throat, and silent tears began to run down her cheeks. Her vision was blurred, but she could make out the sheriff's figure at Cole's window and the sound of their muffled voices.

"Looks like I'm going fishing tonight."

"You need me to come back and help?"

"Naw, get her home. Bring her in tomorrow. I see how valuable she is to us now, and I want her tested on the other stuff you told me about." He leaned down into the window. "I don't want anyone to get their hands on her. Understood?"

Cole nodded. John tapped the metal roof and walked away.

"They're going to get their hands on me, aren't they?" Mia lifted her heavy lids to meet his gaze.

"I'll be damned if anyone ever touches you, but me." He tightened his grip on the wheel, and his jaw ticked. "No one will hurt you, Mia."

Her lids fell, and she felt the vibration of the car engine underneath her. As her stomach settled, she drifted to sleep.

***

The next time she opened her eyes, Cole was laying her down on her bed. She felt his hand on her knee, then he slowly glided it down to her ankle. His fingers stroked her skin as he removed her strappy sandal. He treated the other leg the same, as if he was learning her flesh, sliding his hands down her calf until he found her sandal and removed it. He tugged on her arms, pulling her up until she slumped against him. Her head rested on his shoulder as he knelt down on one knee. His hands rested on her outer thighs, one on each leg. Slowly, his fingers moved up her skin, sliding her dress from underneath her. Mia's mind was in a fog, she just couldn't send the signals to the rest of her body to move away from him. Her lips rested on his neck as she put her hand on his arm.

"No. Please, don't," she said, just managing to speak.

"Don't worry, I won't." His hands continued moving up her frame as he slid her dress over her head and skillfully unsnapped her bra. "I want to, but not like this." He lay the dress down and pushed her slightly back until she was looking into his eyes. His hands came to rest on her shoulders, and he slid the straps of her bra down her arms as he spoke. "If you want me, you'll have to come to me. I don't play games, Mia." He grabbed her nightshirt, and she lifted her arms for him. He never glanced at her breasts, though she wanted him to. She never wanted anyone to look at her, but she *needed* him to, and the thought was unsettling.

He slipped her nightshirt over her head and scooped her into his arms. Cole lay her gently down on the pillow and pulled the covers up. He gazed down at her. "Can I ask you something?"

She wanted to say "No." She knew alcohol worked like a truth serum, and she was afraid of what he was going to ask. She swallowed hard, faced her fear, and nodded her head.

"Why do you guard your heart the way you do? Why haven't you let a man get close to you? Did someone hurt you that deeply?"

He'd just pulled the last thread that was holding her together. Tears pooled in her eyes. "Because men do nothing but hurt you mentally and physically. They touch you when they aren't supposed to, and they take without asking. Daddies leave, boyfriends and husbands cheat—Lies, that's all they are—lies."

He sat down on her bed, and she turned her back to him, rolling her body into a protective ball. She spoke in a whisper that only a vampire could hear. "You want me to face it? I'll face it. You want me to see the awful pictures in my mind that I try to block out to make me feel normal—to give me peace? To face the things that frighten me and have scarred me for life?"

"We all have scars, Mia. They are supposed to make you stronger, not paralyze you."

"All my boyfriends have cheated on me after promising me the world to get what they wanted. The worst part is, I could see them cheating in my dreams. What will I see if I look inside you, Cole? Will I see the same? I've never had a man be respectful or honest with me, even you. You deceived me. You dropped a big bomb on me, one that has shattered my reality." A shudder rocked her body. "You bite, and I was..." *No. No.* She couldn't go there—it was too dark of a memory. She tightened her eyes to flush out the images. He would never know that scar. It was the deepest one she carried. "I have a good system to protect myself from the world. I don't want any more pain. Now, can you go, please?"

Mia felt him rise from the bed, and then heard the sliding glass door open to the balcony. Looking over at the front door, she could see all the locks were secure, and the balcony was vacant. Cole had gone. She lay down on her pillow, the room still spinning, her loneliness consuming her, and she cried. Everything that had happened in the past, her life almost ending, but most of all, Cole kneeling on the beach, collided and consumed her mind. She hated herself for how she had made Cole feel. For the first time, she felt lost in her king size bed. Mia felt laid open, her emotions bared as she sobbed and set her pain free.

When her body eased down and no more tears would come, she looked over at the clock. She had cried for an hour straight. She heard a noise from the balcony and lifted her head off the pillow. It was Cole. He sat in a chair on the balcony with a slightly bent leg resting on the railing, and the other on the ground. He tilted the chair back, balancing it on its back legs.

Mia stumbled out of bed and went to the sliding glass door separating them. She looked down at her toes, realizing he must have seen her lose control. She hated the thought because she knew how Cole felt about weak people.

His gaze met hers, dark eyes swirling with a pain she didn't understand. His elbow rested on his knee, and a black container dangled between two fingers. Cole swirled the canister, took a drink, and then stood to face her.

They were inches apart, separated by glass. His face was expressionless as his gaze bore into hers. His jaw ticked, and Mia lowered her head. She was sorry for the way she'd acted at the nightclub and the way she'd made him feel.

When she looked up, Cole was gone.

ELEVEN

Who the hell was knocking this early? Mia rolled out of bed and put on her robe. Her balance was still unsteady.

The familiar voice called out from the other side as she approached. "Good Morning, Miss Starr. It's Detective Gonela. I'm here to watch over you. Are you going anywhere today?"

She opened all the locks, except the chain, and cracked open the door. "Not until later—around six." The detective looked at her, and his eyes scanned her up and down.

"No work today?" he asked with a grin.

"I'm calling in sick."

"I thought so. I'll be here if you need me." He nodded his head, and she closed the door. She walked over to the phone and called in sick at the gas station. She was glad she wasn't scheduled at the funeral home.

She shuffled across the floor to the kitchen for some water. Her eyes noticed a piece of paper on the table wrapped around something. She got a glass of water, never taking her eyes off the piece of paper. She sat down and, as she unrolled it, a piece of a red rock fell out and bounced onto the table.

She picked up the rock in one hand and rolled its jagged shape between her fingers, then read the words on the paper. She couldn't help but drop a couple of tears, staining the paper where they fell. She read it again, trying to file it into memory.

Here is the first piece of brick we chipped from the wall around your heart last night.
Cole.

She gave the rock a closer look and began to smile. The man paid attention to detail. It was an actual piece of red brick. She did feel better. She had told him things she had never told anyone else, and it'd felt good.

Her thoughts returned to his eyes when he was on the balcony. He looked so sad, so empty. She remembered he'd said something about being able to feel her because of the blood she swallowed. *Was he feeling me?* She didn't see how it was possible because it wasn't even a lot of blood.

She decided to jump in the shower and wash the drunk off her skin, then she wanted to do some research about vampires on the computer.

After she scrubbed the alcohol stink from her body, she stood in front of the computer, sipping her coffee. She sat down and Googled "swallowing vampire blood." She couldn't believe all the results that appeared. What could she trust to be true?

She read all the information she could, absorbing it, not knowing where reality stopped and role-playing games began. When she looked up from her computer, she noticed hours had passed. Her brain was jumbled with information overload. Some of the stuff was way off the charts with weird sex acts and cults that drank human blood. Mia would have to go to the source for her answers. She knew if she asked Cole questions about himself, he would be honest.

She powered down the computer and readied to leave. She always felt closer to her roots when she went to her mom's house, so she dressed accordingly—a pair of jeans, a simple dark blue shirt, and a pair of black cowboy boots. It was already going on six when she slid her keys in her pocket and opened the door.

Detective Gonela was waiting on the other side. "My shift is over, Mia. I am leaving now."

"Okay. Thank you, Detective." As she reached the iron gate at the bottom of her stairwell, she thought about something she had read on the Internet. It said that vampire blood makes you stronger. She wondered if that was why she opened the gate so easily last night. She put her hand on the gate and pulled, and it flew open once again. It had to be true.

She reached down to unlock the car door, stilled, and took a deep breath. Her heart beat faster. "I can feel you when you're close. Is it because I swallowed your blood?"

Cole stood behind her. She felt the energy from his body wrap around her.

"Partially. Are you going somewhere?" His voice soothed her.

"I have to go to my mom's house. Are you following me tonight?" She held still, key poised in front of the lock.

"Yes." He put his hand on hers and turned her toward him. "Will you let me drive you?"

She stared at his chest. "I guess it would be easier for you that way."

"What do *you* want, Mia?" Cole put his hand under her chin and lifted her face to look at him.

"I want to ride with you. And if you don't mind, I'd like to ask you some questions on the way."

"I would like that. Can I ask *you* some questions?" He flashed a smile that made the world tip as he nodded toward the car behind hers.

After giving him directions to her mom's house, she walked to the passenger side. His hand came over hers, opening the door for her.

A man had never opened a door for her before. The slightest touch of his hand sent bites of electricity up her arm. She wondered if he felt it, too. She didn't know how to act, so she just stood there.

"Is something wrong, Mia?"

"No, I... I've never had the door opened for me before."

"Never?" His brows dipped.

"No." She realized she was staring as if star-struck and quickly shook her head. He was already behind the steering wheel when she sat and reached for the seat belt. His speed was something she had to get used to—it was freaky.

"Thanks for not fighting me on the seatbelt," he said, smirking as he turned the key in the ignition.

The memory of last night came back to her. She felt the heat creep into her cheeks, and she lowered her head. "Cole, I'm sorry for my behavior last night. Especially what I did to you in the car—you know, when I showed you my neck and..." She looked at her fidgeting hands in her lap. He made her nervous. She heard his fangs slide out and snapped her gaze to his.

"Sorry. I was thinking about what I could have done to you under different circumstances."

Her pulse raced. She wiped her hands on her jeans, trying to dry the sweat from her palms. He looked at her and opened his mouth. She watched as his fangs slid back and disappeared.

"Mia, slow your pulse. I can feel your blood rushing through your veins. I can't help the urges you provoke in me. Please, don't be nervous around me." He turned the directional signal on and made a left. "Do you remember what I told you when you were on your bed last night?"

Another embarrassing memory, her face turned bright red, and she felt the heat roll into her ears. "When you undressed me?"

He looked at her, a tiny glow illuminating the back of his eyes. "Now, I'm trying really hard to keep my fangs in for you. Don't make me visualize it. And, yes, that would be the moment I was referring to."

"You said you were done with me, so I shouldn't worry." She looked at him, and he stared at her, expressionless. "Could you please watch the road?"

He quickly pulled over, placing the car in park. "No, Mia. That is not what I meant. I'm not even close to being done with you. I crave you like I crave blood." He ran his fingers through his hair. "You're confused right now, and I'm in the middle of that confusion. I don't want to cause you any more pain. If you want me, you will give yourself to me."

Mia's inner struggle continued—the fight between what her body wanted, what her head told her, and what her heart felt.

"Now"—he drove back onto the road—"what about those questions? Maybe I'll match you question-for-question."

She sighed heavily. "Okay, but nothing too personal." His laughter was music to her ears.

"I will try, my love. You first."

"Tell me about your blood I swallowed. That's why I can feel you, right?"

He glanced at her. A sexy grin stretched across his face. "The effects differ depending on how old the vampire is. With older vampires, only a little blood is required to feel the effects. You didn't swallow much of my blood. It will wear off quickly. The first time you drink blood from a vampire, you'll be able to feel that vampire's influence." He paused and chuckled. "Don't look so alarmed, you'd have to drink the blood consistently to keep a strong connection, unless you're the vampire's chosen mate—his bride. Then the rules are different." He glanced at Mia. "My turn." His tone was light. "Do you always research everything?"

"Yes, I love researching things. I wanted to be a cop, once."

"Really? Why didn't you?" Cole arched a brow.

"My... abilities made the dream impossible, and there's too much politics in your line of work. The bad guys have the upper-hand because of all the rules set by the courts and politicians."

Cole chuckled. "I know what you mean." He inclined his head indicating it was her turn.

"Did your blood make me stronger?" She slid down in her seat, relaxing more with each word.

"Yes, and it will have your sex drive working overtime." His eyes scanned her as he spoke.

A burst of laughter flew out of her mouth, and she clamped her hand over it. "I don't think I need your blood for that. After not getting any for almost five years, it's been working overtime. And you on top of me in the graveyard was the first time..." *Shit*. Was she willingly talking about sex with him? Over sharing, she thought and straightened in the seat, staring down at her lap once again.

Cole closed his hand over hers. "I'm sorry for advancing on you like that."

Mia slid her hand from under his and quickly changed the subject. Cole had a knack for making her lose her concentration. "I read that you have the capability to make people do what you want, or erase their minds when you need them to forget something. Is that true?" Mia pointed. "You have to make a left at the light." She shifted in her seat toward him. "If it's true, have you done that to me?"

Cole's jaw twitched. He studied her as if he knew the direction of her question. His expression held a look of disheartenment. "I'm sorry to disappoint you, but I have not. When I pressed you against the tree, you responded to me out of your own desire." A dangerously sexy smile waited for a response.

She quickly looked out the window, away from that look. "Have you tried to control me?" She laced her fingers together in her lap and met his gaze.

"Yes, I have. When I asked you to stare at me, the way you stared at the man at the gas station. And then again inside the funeral home." He rubbed his palm up and down his bicep. "I saw the pain and fear I caused you. I wanted to take that away and make you forget the night. I didn't like the way you looked at me, Mia. I was going to tell you I was a vampire. I wanted to ease you into it. I had no control over what happened that night."

"It didn't work? Or have you made me do something I don't know about?"

"No, it didn't work. This is why I think the man from the gas station wants to kill you. I could get into your mind, but it would take time, and it would make me weak. Your mind is much stronger, more complex than other human's. It's easier to kill you, than to be weakened by you. You would leave a younger vampire weak for a day, and a stronger one would be vulnerable for a couple of hours. Hence, you are a danger—a true threat to vampires. The vampire you had a run in with thinks you know something. He knows you saw Art leave with him, and Art is now dead." He stroked the top of her hand with his thumb. "You have power, Mia, which I don't think you fully understand, and it leaves you vulnerable. I will not let anything happen to you. I am a man of my word."

His words were honest and direct, but Mia wondered how Cole could keep her from being killed. If other vampires wanted her dead, he couldn't possibly protect her from all of them.

"It's the end house down on the right." She pointed her finger to where they needed to go. Embarrassment washed over her as they pulled into the drive. She hadn't been able to help her mom clean up the place since her brother went missing.

Mia grew up around rednecks, and her mom's yard was a reflection of this culture. Her nephew's little motorized vehicles were up on cinder blocks next to the racing car half-painted in primer gray, which also sat on blocks. Chickens roamed free in the yard, and the potbelly pig came running toward the car as they pulled in. The tires crackled over the mixture of grease and shell-rock in the driveway. Car parts and trash riddled the yard. At one time, six people lived in the house, and Mia's mom was the only one who cleaned. That takes its toll on a person. No one had seen Mia's brother in years, which left her mom out here alone, but her mom liked it that way. It finally gave her some much-needed peace.

Cole was at Mia's door before the motor fully shut off. She stepped out, and he stared at her with loving eyes.

"You look very nice, today," he said.

"Oh? I'm not dressed as nice as I was last night, but thank you."

Cole slid his left arm around her waist, moved her to the side, and shut the door. Even though his skin was a little cool, her flesh burned wherever he touched.

His gaze roamed her eyes. "No, you look much better today. I like you in jeans, and those boots really look nice on you."

Mia leaned into him, wanting to taste his mouth as the allure of his lips called to her.

"Hey, Mia, come in the back way. I'm cleaning, you can't get in the front door," Mia's mom yelled from the house, breaking the trance she was in.

But she didn't take her eyes off of Cole. "Did you do that? Make me want to kiss you?"

"No, that was you." His voice was low with a seductive pull. "I'll never try to control you. You *will* give yourself to me."

Oh, baby, would I. No, Mia, bad. A deadly, vampire relationship will not work. Mia stared into the depths of his brown eyes and searched for the answers to life, the answers to make this thing work between them. She found peace in them—they made her want to let go of her fears, her worries, and the rest of her pain from the past.

She could never fully be with him though, and she knew the reality of that. She'd never been able to be intimate with anyone. She always tensed or imagined she was somewhere else. It was her mind's defense system, and it kept her from thinking or seeing any unwanted presences. Now, on top of that, she would have to worry about him biting her.

"Cole, I don't think I can ever—"

"It's not the time to talk about this. I have other places I need to take you, so let's finish your visit here. I want to talk about this more later."

"That sounds good." Mia turned to walk toward the house. "Come on in." He didn't budge. "Aren't you coming?"

"No, I'll stay here so it's not awkward for you." His eyes held a hint of wariness.

"Nonsense." Mia jumped at her mom's approach from behind her. "Mia, you need to learn to relax. I've been telling you that for years, and you never listen to me," she said, looking toward Cole.

"Mom, this is Cole. Cole, this is my mom, Sharon." Her mom's head tilted and she stared.

Cole shifted his feet.

"I see you're an officer. Has my daughter done something wrong?"

Cole cleared his throat. "No, ma'am. I'm protecting her."

Her eyes widened, and then she tightened her lips and nodded her head in understanding. "Well, I haven't seen your kind around here in a while..."

"She means the police. When my brother lived here, the police were here a lot," Mia said, giggling nervously, trying to break the tension that no one else seemed to feel but her.

Sharon turned to walk back to the house, pausing at Mia's words. She looked back over her shoulder. "No, I don't, Mia. He has two sets of handcuffs, and that blue pair dangling out of his belt tells me he is something more than a cop, or human for that matter. Geez, you'd think I dropped you on your head when you were young. Cole, you are welcome in my home. Please, come in."

Cole smiled as he walked past Mia to follow her mom. Mia stood still with her mouth hanging open. This was so like her mother. She loved the element of surprise and used it often. When Mia was ten, her mom stood in her doorway at bedtime, and instead of saying goodnight like a normal mother, she said, "Hey, do you ever feel like you're being watched when no one is around? Well, if you do, don't worry. It's just a ghost. The guy who owned the house before us, died on the couch. He's harmless. Goodnight, now." Mia could strangle her sometimes.

"Mia Lynn, don't stand there with your mouth open—you're gonna catch flies. Come on, now."

Mia entered the kitchen, pulled out the chair next to Cole, and sat. She was still stunned, but Cole was amused at the whole situation.

"I'll get you both something to drink," Sharon said.

When Mia heard the familiar sound of the refrigerator creaking opened, she glanced at Cole. "Hey, Mom, Cole can't..."

Sharon came back into the room with a diet soda for Mia and handed Cole a black container.

"Here ya go, Cole. It's not fresh. It's about four weeks old, but it's never been frozen, so it should still have all the good stuff in it. I already twisted it for you so the heat packs have been activated."

Cole's smile reached his eyes and lit with a hint of delight. "Thank you, ma'am."

"Now, that is polite, but I'll have none of that ma'am stuff. It makes me feel old. Please, call me Sharon."

Cole nodded while Mia sat silently in shock, shaking her head in disbelief.

"Mia, lighten up," her mom said, sitting back in the chair.

"Where did you get that? Does that have...? It has, *blood,* in it?"

"Well, what did you think he'd be drinking—apple juice? I got it from a friend. He comes around every once in a while to, ya know, visit." A grin stretched across her reddened face.

"Mom! Please!"

A big, deep, glorious laugh rumbled out of Cole, his cheeks expanded, and he quickly covered his mouth to keep the liquid from spewing out.

Mia glared at him.

"Oh, Mia, get over it. Just because you don't have sex doesn't mean I can't."

She wanted to strangle her mother as she twisted her fingers nervously. Next, she fully expected her mom to pull out pictures of her when she was little, naked in the tub or on the toilet.

"Okay, can we stop? I'm going up in the attic to get the box down." Mia stood. "Is it marked?"

"I'll come help you." Cole stood to follow her.

"Thank you, but I got it. Please, stay here." Mia didn't know what would be worse—her handing him a box of silver from the attic, or letting him stay behind to talk with her mother. As she reached the attic, she stopped and smiled. She just realized that her mother was actually smiling at a man she brought over. She had hated every person Mia had ever brought to meet her.

She retrieved the box quickly, left it by the back door, and headed into the kitchen. "Cole, can I have the keys to the car? I need to put the box in the trunk." He turned to her. Their eyes connected, and instantly her insides started to glow.

"I'll get it for you." He started to stand, and she quickly placed her hand on his shoulder, holding him in his seat.

"Thank you, again, but I can do it." His eyes narrowed in suspicion as he handed her the keys.

Mia carried the box to the car. She'd never seen a trunk so immaculate. It was full of police things, but there was more than enough room for the box due to the obsessive organization of the items.

If she took too long, Cole would be by her side in a minute to help, and she couldn't have him touching the box. She wasn't sure if the silver would have an effect on him or not, and now wasn't the time to find out. She'd research it later.

Rushing back into the kitchen with labored breaths, she sat back down beside Cole. His drink sat in front of him. Out of impulse, she reached over and grabbed it, tracing her fingers along the spiral symbol on the front of the black container.

"What does this symbol mean?"

He looked up, his eyes lovingly caressing her face. "No one has ever taken interest in my container, much less touched it."

"I'm sorry. You don't have to answer the question."

"Don't be sorry. It just... It gives me hope." He smiled with a shy expression, showing a vulnerability she hadn't noticed before. "It's the symbol of life."

She looked back down, her eyes transfixed on the container.

"You want to know how it works?"

He could already read her very well. She wasn't sure if she liked that or not. "Yes. There are three parts to it?" She tilted the container sideways as she studied it.

"It looks like it has three separate parts, but the top and the bottom are used to break the heat packs that surround the cylinder holding the blood. You twist the top and the bottom like this, and it breaks the heat packs, and they start warming the blood." He put a hand on the bottom and the top of the container and twisted it like a waiter with a double-ended pepper grinder.

Mia took the container back out of his hands, "That's cool. Who came up with something like that?"

Mia looked at him. She'd never seen him breathe like that before. She watched his chest rise and fall a couple times, as if he needed a calming breath. When she met his gaze, the look he gave her was of complete wonder.

"Yep, she's a rare one, Cole. You thought she'd say 'Ew, gross!' and get up and run, didn't ya?" Sharon asked.

"I was hoping she wouldn't." His phone rang. "If you ladies would excuse me, I have to take this call." He flipped open the phone and walked into the other room.

"Miakoda Starr, he's the one."

"Mom, don't start. Please." Mia rolled her eyes at her.

"Lower your voice. Vampires have very good hearing." Her mom stared at her from across the table. "Now, you listen to me, Miakoda. If you think you're the only one in this world who's been hurt, you're wrong. I know your scars are deep because of everything you have seen, and everything that's happened to you, but you have to cut it loose and live." Mia's mom was never the type to beat around the bush. She was blunt and to the point.

"You don't think I know that? I'm trying! You don't understand how..." Tears welled as she struggled with her words.

Sharon grabbed her hand, stroking the top for comfort. "Yes, Mia, I do understand. *Things* happened in my life, too, and if you let those things consume you, they win."

Mia looked into her mom's eyes as they filled with tears. "You never told me that before." Mia's mind was running. Although she hadn't told her mom half of what had happened in her life.

"Some things you have to work through on your own and figure them out."

"Like finding out vampires are real? You think you could have told me that?" Mia's lips pulled into a smile, her tears receded, and she laughed. Laughter through tears was the best kind of medicine in her opinion, and she let the feeling wash over her.

"Now, would you have believed me if I did. Or would you just think I was crazy like you usually do?" Sharon let go of her hand and leaned back in the chair.

"I would have thought you were crazy because you are." Laughter rolled out of them as Cole walked back into the room.

He looked at the two of them, concern on his face. "Is everything okay? Do the two of you need privacy?" His expression looked pained, and Mia noted his hand as he moved it toward her, then pulled it back, tucking it into his pocket.

"No, we're okay. Just hashing through some old wounds," Sharon said.

The pain in Cole's eyes stabbed Mia's heart. When he searched her fixed gaze, she knew he understood what they were talking about. "I'm sorry to break up all the fun, but we have to get going." Cole smiled at Sharon as he spoke.

"Cole, I suspect you're protecting my little girl from vampires." He nodded in agreement. "You keep her safe, you hear? If you can throw a lasso around her and tie her down, make her relax, you might have a chance. Oh, and watch that temper of hers." Sharon giggled as she watched Mia's cheeks turn red.

"May I ask you why you think she may be interested?"

Oh, please don't answer that, Mom. Mia chanted.

Cole stared at Mia while he waited for Sharon's answer.

"Because you've touched her soul. I can see it when she looks at you. She's just a stubborn ass and won't let anyone close enough to her. But you mark my words— you are what she's been waiting for her entire life." Sharon pointed her finger at him to make her point.

"Okay! Well, it has been fun as usual, Mom. I'll come back soon—when I'm ready for more embarrassment." Mia gave her mom a hug before leaving.

Cole walked around to the passenger side to open the door for her. He paused at the trunk, and his eyes narrowed and locked onto hers as he walked up. He leaned forward, pressing his body against hers as he put the key in the door. His lips brushed her ear, and her body tingled in response. "I have to watch you every minute, don't I?"

"What do you mean?" She found the air thin while he was close to her.

"You filled my trunk with silver. What are you up to, my little rebel?" He pulled his head back and gazed into her eyes, his smile holding her captive as he stroked her jawbone with his thumb.

Sharon yelled at them from her doorway. "Mia, we need to talk some more, about your gifts. They're growing stronger, and there are some things you need to know before all hell breaks loose. Oh, and about that other thing we talked about—follow the signs, they'll show you he's the one."

Mia blinked and Cole was standing in front of her mom. She watched as the redness crept into her mom's cheeks as Cole spoke to her, charming his way into her heart, no doubt. He placed a kiss on her hand, and then was back in the car with the engine started before Mia got her seatbelt on.

She felt her own cheeks flush as she marveled at his speed. She wondered what else he could do with that speed. "Where to, my bodyguard?" Mia allowed herself to relax in his presence, leaning back into the seat.

"Our first stop is the funeral home. Can we continue our question game?" He flashed a heart-melting smile.

Mia returned the smile. "Sure, if that will make you happy."

"You make me happy, Mia," Cole said, a tiny glow emerging in the back of his eyes.

TWELVE

*A*s Cole pulled into the funeral home, Mia straightened her spine, and he felt the tension radiate from her body.

Her eyes scanned the area. She took note of Jerry's car, which sat alone in the parking lot. Cole watched her as she searched the perimeter, tilting her head to focus on the dumpster that rested against the side of the building. She didn't miss an inch of the area.

A smile twitched under the surface of his lips. Mia scanned the lot like a predator—just like he did.

Cole's admiring eyes held her as they walked in silence to the back door. She was alert as she surveyed her surroundings. He knocked on the door, never taking his attention off her. His unfulfilled urge to hold Mia when he found her crying at her mother's house resurfaced. He wanted to fix whatever haunted her, and it burned inside him. It killed him that she was so tormented.

Mia turned toward the sound of the knock. His hand twitched to touch her hair as blonde strands circled her neck; his lips tingled, remembering the feel of her skin underneath them. Unable to resist the feel of her, he raised his hand to touch her cheek. "Damn," Cole cursed under his breath as the door opened.

"Hey, Mia... Detective. It's nice to see you again," Jerry said as he stood back to let them inside.

Mia's nerves swirled inside her stomach. They were back at the scene of the crime. She glanced over her shoulder at Cole, who gave her a reassuring nod. Mia scanned the room, and searched for the tiniest thing to be out of place, but the room was spotless. How in the hell did they clean up so fast?

"Jerry, I think I left something in the embalming room the other night. I'll be right back." Mia left quickly before anyone could respond. Her mouth fell open as she entered the embalming room. Its pristine shine was impressive, not one hint of vampire entrails anywhere. She walked to the freezer, inspecting it closely. She ran her finger over the metal, searching for its imperfections.

A soft gasp escaped her as the tip of her finger slopped down with the metal. They didn't only replace the door, they duplicated the embedded dents and scratches in the old one.

"Did you find what you were looking for?" Cole's cool voice sent shivers through Mia's body.

"Cole, this is amazing. How did they do all of this in one night?" Mia asked, pausing as Jerry walked into the room.

The old man looked around and smiled. "Mia, I don't know how much caffeine you had the other night, but this place looks great. You even cremated Art for me. I know that must have been tough. Thank you so much for helping. I don't feel so backed up now." Jerry smiled, and for the first time since Mia had known him, he seemed relaxed.

Mia glanced at Cole. He nodded, and a tinge of excitement built inside her as she looked into his eyes. Secrets—they shared something dangerous.

"Well, I'm going, Mia. You have the keys. When the detective is done, please lock up. I'm so glad they didn't steal anything when they broke in the other night. We just had to repair the phone line they cut. Anyway, I'm out of here. Detective, I hope you catch the thieves. Thanks again, Mia." Jerry sighed, exhausted. He made an attempt to wave, but his hand only made it to his waist before he walked out.

Cole waited long enough to be sure Jerry was gone, then he nodded toward the door. "Follow me. I have to meet someone outside."

"Why do you look like that? Is something wrong?" Mia followed, hoping he would elaborate on the visitor, but he said nothing. She turned and locked the door behind them.

"No. I need to tell you something; explain some things to you. I want to prepare you for... stuff."

"Stuff? Who are you waiting for?" When she removed the key from the deadbolt, Cole reached down, and cupped her hands with his and searched her eyes.

"Things are going to start happening around you that you aren't going to fully understand. I'm not always going to have the time to explain them to you right away, but I will explain them. Miakoda, I ask that you please trust me."

A white van with police markings pulled into the back parking lot. Cole pulled his hands from Mia's and stiffened his posture as a person emerged from the van and walked toward them.

As the figure came closer, the light from the building exposed a female. Mia's eyes flicked over her body. You could barely see her waist, especially if you focused on her large breasts. Black hair caressed the woman's hips as she swayed toward them, stopping inches in front of Cole.

"Rosetta, thanks for coming. You look lovely as usual," Cole said with a charming smile.

Mia took in Rosetta's beautiful features, petite, hourglass figure and narrowed her eyes.

Rosetta responded with a lively grin. "Thank you, and you're looking deliciously dead as usual," she replied with a wink.

Mia pulled her shoulders back, straightening her posture. *I'm not sure I like her.* A quick scan of Rosetta's weird aura showed no metallic impression— not a vampire. *It's beautiful though, and why wouldn't it be? Look at her.* Rosetta's aura had bands of gold on the outside ring, brighter than normal, but not as bright as the vampire's.

Mia's blood started to heat, and she narrowed her eyes. *The woman can't have a beautiful aura and be beautiful. That's just not fair. She is way too close to my vampire.*

Mia caught herself, and smiled. *Did I just say "my?"*

Cole looked at Mia, momentarily confused, and then his lips pulled into a satisfied grin. He felt her pulse quicken; she knew he did from the wicked gleam in his eyes. *Damn him.* Mia took a deep breath to regain control of her pulse.

"Mia, this is Rosetta Vega. She's our Special Ops Crime Scene Analyst." Cole didn't remove his gaze from Mia as he spoke.

Rosetta's cute, petite laugh rippled through the air. "Is that what you're calling me these days, or is she a newbie?" Rosetta said in a playful tone.

"I left you something in a tree, a couple yards out. Why don't you get to work while I explain some things to Mia." Cole's tone held a tinge of a warning and his face tightened.

"I'm sorry. I didn't mean any disrespect. It's been a long drive, and I'm a little overtired. Mia, it's nice to meet you." Rosetta turned and walked in the direction Cole indicated.

"Mia, I need you to sit in the car," Cole said, his voice strong and laced with authority. He had snapped into full cop mode.

"Why? That's ridiculous. I don't see why I need to sit in a stuffy car. I won't get in anyone's way." Her face pinched in disapproval.

"Mia, get in the car." She opened her mouth to offer more protest, but his phone interrupted. He glared at her. "I need to get you in the car." His annoyance was evident as he answered the call. "Yes, the tracker is here, Sheriff," Cole replied into the phone. "No, she just got started."

A sound shattered the air, and every hair on Mia's body rose to attention. She searched the area with wide eyes, and her pulse beat so quickly it pounded against her neck.

"Sheriff, I need to call you back." Cole snapped the phone shut, grabbed Mia by the arm, and walked quickly to the car. "Why must you always argue with me?" he asked, his pace quickening.

"What the hell was that? Was that an animal? The only time I've ever heard a sound like that was on the Discovery channel." A wave of energy blew across the air, and her heart jumped in her chest.

Cole didn't answer. He focused on getting the key in the car door and then quickly shoved her in. Shutting the door, he glared at her through the window. "Stay in the car, and keep the windows up. Do you understand?"

His jaw tightened as he met her defiant eyes. She hated when he talked to her like a child. He definitely didn't deserve an answer. She narrowed her eyes at him and crossed her arms over her chest before she looked away. Cole walked a couple feet away from the car. The light from the building barely touched the spot where he stood, but the moonlight lit the area well enough to make out their surroundings.

"It's too late to search for a more concealed location so, let's get this over with." He spoke into the night, but loud enough for Mia to hear him. He stood very still. After a couple minutes, he knelt, resting his forearm on his bent knee. Mia followed Cole's line of sight out into the distance. Her mouth dropped open and she blinked a couple times as she watched the scene before her. Emerging out of the darkness was the most beautiful animal she had ever seen. The leopard walked up to Cole, and laid its head on his shoulder. He scratched behind its ears. Mia watched in awe—it was as if they were talking to each other without words. The leopard turned and then motioned its head for Cole to follow. He quickly glanced back toward Mia, then followed the animal into the graveyard.

After a half hour, the car filled with stale air making it hard to breathe. Mia was getting tired, and she wiggled uncomfortably as she tried to nap. This whole situation was nuts. Out of boredom, she tapped her fingers on the dashboard as she looked out the window.

Cole was out there, Rosetta was out there, there was a leopard loose in the graveyard, and she was stuck in the car. This wasn't nuts, this was bullshit.

She stepped out of the car, grabbed the keys to the funeral home from her pocket and walked to the door, looking around with every step. She still hadn't recovered from the night before, and exhaustion was setting in. It was only going on nine, and she felt completely drained.

Once safely inside the funeral home, she went to her favorite hiding spot, and in no time at all, she drifted off for a nap.

Her dreams took over quickly, and the drums began to beat in her head, louder than they'd ever been. She pushed the dream, urging it to go further. She had to know—was she supposed to save the baby that cries?

The moon shone down on her, and the chanting echoed through the night as she was carried along. The pace was becoming faster, and faster. Her body jerked around. Now she could see more than the sky and the tops of the trees. She was staring at a large, male Indian standing in her path. The Indian's form began to change into Cole as if her mind wouldn't let her gaze upon another male. This time she had gone further in the dream. Now, what does it mean?

Beautiful dreams of Cole began, locked in his loving embrace. He placed passionate kisses on her skin, then the dream turned dark, and Cole turned on her, biting a chunk from her skin like the girl in the ocean. She fought, trying hard to awaken from the dream before she saw anymore. She felt his hands pushing down on her shoulders, holding her down...

"Mia. Mia!" Cole's voice jerked her from the dream.

Her eyes flew open. Her screams shattered the silent room as Cole shook her, his hands on her shoulders.

"It's me, Mia. It's me." His voice was soft, gentle. He smiled down at her. "Am I the cause of your screams, or are you screaming because you just woke up in a coffin?"

"I was screaming because of you! I was having a bad dream with you in it... And there is nothing wrong with this coffin. This is my favorite one. It's not cold like the others made of metal. Look at the detail in this wood. It's beautiful." She looked up into his eyes after leaning out over the edge of the coffin and pointed out the detail in the wood. "You think I'm weird." Mia's words came out more as a confirmation than a question.

Cole slid his arms underneath her and scooped her out of the coffin, holding her close to him. "No, I think you're right. I have this exact model at home. You're welcome to sleep in it anytime."

She wiggled in his arms as the images from her dream came back to haunt her. His face hardened, and he slowly released her from his strong hold. Mia couldn't help it—she was frightened. A sudden chill blew by her, and she hugged herself for warmth. Cole reached his hand toward hers, and she jerked away out of impulse.

His eyes narrowed as he stepped closer. "I don't have the patience for this. Every time I feel like I've gained an inch, you take back a mile." His voice was low as he tried to gain control of himself. "What did your dreams tell you?"

Mia swallowed hard and tried to get the lump down that had caught in her throat. "Nothing. Let's go. Didn't you say we had a couple of places to go?" She pushed down her fear, breathed deep, and drew up the courage to move past him. She moved faster than she intended. Her fear brewed inside, bubbling over as she reached the door.

She looked behind her as the door swung open for one last glimpse of him before she shut him out. She turned and leaned back against the closed door. Closing her eyes, she tried desperately to control her fear before he came after her.

"Why do you do that?"

Mia jumped, flinging her eyes open as Cole put his hands on the door, one on each side of her head. He was so fast she never saw him pass her. Her heart beat wildly inside her chest. Part of her wanted to run, the other part desperately fought to stand her ground. *Don't fear him.*

"Cole, please..." Familiar pools of water formed in her eyes. She turned her head away from him. *Don't show weakness.* Her face brushed his hand laying beside her on the door.

"Your tears burn me worse than silver. Please, tell me—" Cole's words fell short as she put her hands on his chest and pushed him back. She felt a massive wave of energy engulf her as Cole's anger built. She saw the frustration she caused within him. She felt trapped, caged, and her fear mounted.

He grabbed her head with both hands and walked her back until she was pinned against the door. His eyes began to glow as he brought his face closer to hers. She felt the intensity in his eyes, felt the pull on her mind. Her eyes widened.

"You... You lied... Again! You said you would never try to control me, and that's what you're doing right now!" She stared back at him, challenging his power. She knew she was no match for him, and he would eventually win.

"You test me too much, Mia. What do I have to do to get you to trust me?"

"Trust you? You're doing something you said you wouldn't do, and you want me to trust you?" She spoke with bitterness as every untrustworthy male she'd ever known entered her thoughts.

Cole slid his hand down her throat. She felt his thumb trace the large vein tapping wildly against her skin while his other hand slid to the back of her head and closed around her hair.

"You don't leave me with many options." His voice was low, powerful, and his scare meter went up.

"You have options. You said most vampires wouldn't waste their time trying to control me, you said they would rather—" Her voice caught in her throat when she realized what she was saying. Cole's face tightened, his jaw ticked as his eyes burned into her.

"Kill you," he concluded, and that was all it took for her fear to jump right out of her.

She turned her head, her lips running across the arm holding the back of her head, and she bit down, hard. A sound of pain escaped his chest, his eyes went wide with shock, and he stepped back giving her enough room to bolt toward the graveyard.

The ground was wet and slippery from the sprinklers, and she fought for traction as she ran. Mia broke one of the rules of what not to do when running from your killer—never look behind you.

As she looked back, her foot caught on a brass flower vase sticking out of the ground, and she toppled over it, holding her hands in front of her to break her fall. Her head grazed the tombstone as she hit the ground, and blood poured from the wound. She instantly felt light-headed.

"Now, see what you've done to yourself." Cole stood over her. She looked over her shoulder at him and started to crawl away. Her hands dug into the grass as her knees slipped in its wetness. Cole grabbed her leg. "Mia, stop!"

THIRTEEN

*L*ike a frightened rabbit, Mia looked lost to her fear.
With her jaw set tight, she kicked at him, and he could
tell her mind had already made up its own version of
what was about to happen. Cole grabbed both of her
ankles, yanked her toward him, and flipped her over
onto her back. He sat on her midsection. She continued
to kick her legs and strike out at him with her fists.

"Mia, stop," he said as he grabbed her arms and held
them down into the grass, then laid his body flat on top
of her, pinning her to the ground. "When you're calm,
I'll get off."

She still struggled against him. He grabbed her face,
and before she could strike him with the hand he freed,
he grabbed it and quickly tucked it under his chest.

"Mia, look at me." His breathing was heavy, and his
voice became a low growl. He was on the edge of losing
his control. She represented temptation, and it stroked
the vampire within to take her every time she denied
him. He could easily have her anytime he wanted—
that's what others did—but he not only wanted her to
want him, he needed her to want him.

When she looked at him, he knew from her
expression and hurried breaths what she was seeing.
His fangs were extended and his eyes had gone black.
He was sure the tiny glow he felt inside made its way to
his hungry eyes that held hers as her rapid pulse pushed
blood from the cut on her head.

"Don't ever run from me again, or anyone like me.
The chase, the hunt, it's too great a pleasure for a

vampire. The next time, I may not be able to control myself, and I know other vampires won't care to control themselves. They'll rip you to shreds, Mia. Do you understand?" His voice was raw with need and concern. His fangs ached with the need to feel her skin wrap around them.

She shook her head, her chest heaved with each deep inhale.

Cole closed his eyes and breathed in. "You're bleeding. I can smell it," he said as he turned her head to the side and inspected the cut. The dark red liquid ran down the side of her face, glistening as the moon's beam hit the stream. The hunger grew within him, and he battled against his beast. *Take her. Here, now.* He returned his eyes to hers.

"You sure know how to test me, Mia. Are you trying to push me over the edge?" He let out a long breath. "What did your dreams show you, Mia? What did I do to frighten you like this?"

She wiggled beneath him, froze, and then her lips parted. "Oh, my. You're—"

"Very hard. Don't change the subject. Your dreams?"

"You attacked me and bit chunks out of me like the girl in the ocean. Like the other vampire," she replied, shaky and without inflection.

Her words cut him, and he looked away from her. "I'm a vampire, Mia, but I'm not like the others you've seen. Just as there are bad humans, there are bad vampires. It pains me that you fear me—I'm sorry if I don't handle it well. Maybe your mother is right—I may have to tie you down to make you relax around me. I will not harm you." *I can't harm what I love.*

He wrapped his arms around her and rose to his feet without bending his knees. "My blood can heel and my saliva has a coagulant in it. If you let me, I can stop your bleeding." His eyes pleaded with her. He wanted to prove he wasn't going to hurt her.

"Please, don't bite me." She searched his eyes, for what, he wasn't sure. Reassurance?

"When you give yourself to me, completely, I will bite you. Until then, my love, I will only nibble on you." He smiled, and her expression changed as if his words had melted her fears. She shifted, a flush ran over her skin, and he noted the confusion on her face at her own arousal.

"I think I have done enough damage for one night. I don't want to get you all worked up again. I'm sorry, Cole. There's a first aid kit back in the building."

He cupped her face with his hands, stroking her cheek with his thumb. "If you feel that you have caused me so much trouble, then the least you can do is let me taste you." He bent down and placed a kiss on her lips.

When she closed her eyes, he gently rubbed his lips against hers, and felt her pulse increase. A shallow moan escaped his throat. The blood from her cut beaded and poured faster from the wound, running down her cheek and over Cole's thumb. He stared at the blood, transfixed as it glistened in the moonlight. Lifting her chin, he watched as the blood continued its journey, rolling down the contour of her jaw, then trailing down the length of her neck to pool in its valley. It rippled as her pulse pounded against her neck. Immense pleasure rolled through his body as he watched the blood sliver down, close to her jugular.

His fangs slid out, the vampire emerging from within. He pushed his desires down and pressed harder against her body trying to replace one urge with another. His tongue flicked over his fang. *Torture. This was pure torture.* "It's been so long since I've tasted blood directly from the source." A hint of longing went unchecked in his tone. He leaned further down, his lips dangerously close to the blood trailing down her neck. Any further and he would lose her forever. He wanted her vein. It called to him. *Must bite.* He battled his thoughts.

He could feel her conflict as she struggled to trust him. Her shaky hand slid under his arm and held on to the back of his shoulder. "If it's been so long, how do you know you can control yourself?"

"Because Mia, I want more from you than just one taste." Tilting her head back more, he slowly moved his lips over her chin.

She looked in his eyes. "I..." She opened her mouth to speak again but nothing came out. She briefly looked away from him as if she searched for the right words to say. "I know you're not a man to be pitied so please don't think I'm patronizing you. I fear you, but I need you to stop the bleeding, please. I'm starting to feel light-headed, and I'm not sure if it's because you're close to me, or that I'm losing blood."

He breathed in the aroma of her blood. She nodded her head, and he knew she understood the silence of his stare. He bent down, fixated on the end of the blood trail. Slowly, he opened his mouth, and his tongue lapped the pool of blood that lay in the trench of her neck. He slid his tongue over her skin, pausing on her jugular vein, beating wildly under his tongue. His shaft throbbed with need as he continued to lick his way up the blood trail to the source pumping the liquid.

Pleasure tingled through his body. He tightened his grip around her, sounds of pleasure escaping from his throat as he lightly kissed her temple. The wound was just above his lips. He tilted her head and gazed into her eyes. A shy smile met his pleasure-filled face as he licked his blood stained lips. She pressed her legs together, and he felt her body's temperature rise. A quick inhale of her scent confirmed it—she was aroused.

"Mia, I'm going to cut my tongue and put my mouth around the wound, sealing it, so your blood will clot."

She stared at him, with a lost look in her eyes and her mouth slightly opened. He held her tightly to him. "Are you bracing me or bracing yourself for this, because I feel like I'm being squeezed by a python."

He didn't answer. He placed his mouth around the wound, and she jumped from the contact. His lips surrounded the cut as his tongue traced its length. The tip of his fangs pressed into her skin and her body instantly tightened. Her breaths came quicker, and he could taste the salt from the sweat beading on her forehead. He held her tighter—his body trembled as a wave of pleasure passed through him. He wanted more of her, and he struggled with his hunger as he felt her go rigid underneath him. He had to stop. His mouth stayed on the wound savoring her taste. More, he wanted more.

His phone sounded dull in his mind. With each ring, it pulled him further back into a state of consciousness—away from the euphoria her blood and body stirred within him. For the first time, Cole was agitated with the interruption of his work. He stepped back, and flipped open the phone. His eyes held hers as he spoke briefly, then returned the annoying device to his pocket.

"We're late." He slid his hands into her front pockets and pulled her against his body. "Thanks for the snack. Let's go clean you up some more. The bleeding has already started to clot." He glided his fingers down her arm until he found her hand, and locked his fingers around hers as they walked in silence back to the car.

Once inside, Cole reached over and popped open the well-organized glove box. He moved a carton of latex gloves, and pulled out a container of antibacterial wipes. He cleaned her face, gently, as if she were a priceless piece of crystal.

"Can I ask you a question?" he asked in a soft voice as he finished his last wipe down her neck.

"Are you starting our game again?" She glanced at him as he turned to start the car.

"We can if you'd like, but my question is nothing to be toyed with." He pulled the car out of the parking lot, briefly looking at her before he spoke. "I have waited a very long time to find my match—my soul mate—and I can feel your soul call to me, even when I'm not with you. Tell me you don't feel it. Tell me that the keen senses I have perfected all these years are wrong." *Tell me you are not my bride.*

Cole lacked most human emotion, but for some reason he felt anxious, and his hands gripped the steering wheel as he waited for her to respond.

Mia breathed deeply, sweat beaded on her palms. She knew if she lied, he would know, and he deserved better than that. *He deserves better than me.*

She wiped her palms on her jeans and took a deep breath, trying to hold back her emotions. She searched her heart, then dug down deeper into the bottom of her soul. She couldn't hide it from him any more than she could hide it from herself, and it was time to face it— admit it to both of them. Cole had a knack for making her face things she desperately tried to avoid.

"I felt it the first time our eyes met, in the woods, even though I couldn't see you in the dark... I felt you," she responded with a shaky voice. Looking out the window, she avoided his gaze. Things were moving too fast. She felt as if she couldn't breathe. She was still coping with the realization that vampires were real, and now he wanted her to cope with a relationship... with a vampire. Did true love move at this pace?

He reached over and slid his fingers across her palm before he grasped her hand.

Mia's lips parted, the sensation of his touch inducing tiny pricks of electricity to dance over her skin. It was as if an invisible field was between their hands, and when they entwined their fingers, it pushed it through, causing waves of energy to move through her.

"If you feel it, why do you fight me so much?"

She wiggled in her seat, uncomfortable with the answer. "Because you deserve someone that you can be yourself with, someone that will give you everything your heart desires. And I don't think I could ever let you drink from me. The thought scares the hell out of me, Cole. Not only that, I've never been able to be with a man, you know, *intimately*, and not tense up. I usually visualize myself somewhere else so they can at least enjoy themselves. Not that they cared I wasn't having any fun." She stared at their hands as she continued. "It's just... you shouldn't waste your time on me," she said in a soft tone.

Cole looked at her, a devilish grin pulling at his lips. "You didn't seem that tense when I was licking blood off you in the graveyard," his husky voice probed further.

"You didn't hear a word I just said, did you?" Her eyes flew to his, and she stared at him in disbelief.

Laughter spilled from his lips. "I heard every word you said, my love. But those excuses you've given yourself all these years to protect your heart from others won't work on me. You just gave me my answer, and I don't have to feed from you—"

She held out her hand. She knew he was lying. "Oh, yes. You. Do. You told me yourself that sex and drinking blood go hand-in-hand. Why would you cheat yourself like that?"

Cole looked at her, the back of his eyes flickered with a soft glow. "Because I want you, and only you."

Mia opened her mouth to protest, but only choked out a sound as her body lunged forward, the seatbelt grabbing at her chest and holding her tight to the seat as the impact from the car behind them rippled through the car's metal.

Cole pulled the car to the side of the road and looked over Mia's body, assessing it for damage. He reached for the door handle, glancing back at her before stepping out of the car.

Mia recognized that look—he gave it to her often. It was his "stay here" look. She glanced in the rear-view mirror as he walked toward the back of the car. A familiar feeling tightened in the pit of her stomach. She clenched her hands into tight fists, her nails digging into her palms as a wave of negative energy hit her like thick fog. *Where is it coming from? Can't he sense something is wrong?*

She jumped out of the car. "Cole, stop! Something's not right." He stopped instantly, but kept his focus on the two men emerging from the van. Something passed Mia, knocking her back into the car at such a fast speed she couldn't see what hit her. Noises filled the air outside.

Mia only knew of one thing that moved that fast, and that was Cole. She lay back on the seat, pulled open the glove box and frantically searched for the trunk release button. As she pressed the button, something grabbed her legs and dragged her from the car.

"Oh, good. You opened the trunk. Now I've got a place to put ya so I can bring you back to the boss." The man grasped Mia's shirt collar and dragged her to the back of the car.

Cole's body leaned against the front of the van. Two men—one on each side of him—held small, silver chains that wrapped around his wrists.

Mia's gut clenched. This was her fault. If she would've stayed in the car... She'd caused him to lose his focus. That was how they got a jump on him. She scanned the men's auras—normal, if that's what you'd call it. Hate and greed filled their souls. A light-orange ring circled the outside of their auras, telling her they weren't that bright.

She wasn't so lucky with the man that held her. He wasn't normal. He was a vampire. The same metallic tint as the others speckled his aura. It was dim though, much lighter than the rest of the vampires she had seen. Maybe he wasn't as powerful as the others.

As the vampire pushed Mia backward into the trunk, she glanced at Cole. Her shoulders hit the box she had placed there earlier, and her mind started to spin. She desperately tried to keep her thoughts together. *What to do first? Try to save Cole, reach in the box and find something to hit this guy with, or die?* Her adrenaline kicked in. Blood raced through her veins with excitement. She should be afraid, but for some strange, warped reason, she thought she could take this vampire.

"Get in," the vampire said and pushed her further inside the trunk. The corner of the box stabbed her in the back.

Mia stared at him. Everything about him was short; his hair, his height and his fangs. She continued to size him up. He looked young, maybe early twenties.

She wondered if fangs grew as vampires aged. Maybe he doesn't know how to make them come out yet. "Wait, aren't you hungry?" she asked, matter-of-factly.

She quickly peeked at Cole. His head snapped up and wide eyes stared back at her in disbelief. The silver that wrapped his arms like a tight vine was burning his skin, and smoke slivered into the air as he fought against the chain.

With a clenched jaw, he tilted his head up, his gaze was filled with mounting rage at her reckless words. It was like watching the Incredible Hulk fight the beast inside, but instead of keeping him in, it appeared Cole wanted to go green. Suddenly, he stilled. Slumping a bit, he breathed deep with his eyes closed.

She had to act now. Her hand slid into the box and she fumbled around, searching for something to use as a weapon. When the vampire looked into her eyes, a brief victory washed over her. Her question definitely threw him off his game.

He stared at her, stunned, considering what she said. "Yes, I'm very hungry. But I was told to bring you back *untouched*." His voice laced over with need.

Mia's fingers walked over a knife inside the box. She gripped it tightly as she began to laugh—half from nerves, and half to push his buttons. "Oh, you have a master? What are you, like an Igor or something?" Her condescending tone did the trick—he was instantly pissed.

The back of his hand slammed against her face, cutting her lip, and Mia wiped it with the back of her hand. Her eyes trailed up to Cole.

Cole's eyes bored into the back of the vampire. He pulled on the chains as the two men snickered, watching the vampire wrap his hands around Mia's throat.

"I am going to rip your throat out," he sneered. His voice was hoarse and alarming.

He lifted Mia off the ground, and her thoughts became fearfully clear. She remembered something Cole told her. The pressure on her throat intensified as

Igor squeezed. Laughter rattled out from her closing windpipe, and she desperately tried to form words.

"Oh, please, Igor. You probably can't even control me with your mind. You're an assistant!" Her eyes narrowed at him, waiting for him to challenge her. *Come on. Take the bait.* Her mind was running on pure adrenaline.

The two men holding Cole egged Igor on.

Cole stopped struggling, pain settled on his face, and he peered at the chains as they burned through another layer of skin.

Mia breathed in as Igor stared down into her eyes. She felt the pull of his mind as it reached in, trying to strip her of her control. She focused and quickly stood.

Igor stumbled back, his eyes widened in bewilderment.

They stood face-to-face in a showdown. It was high noon, just like in one of her favorite western movies. She saw his aura twitch, and she took a step forward. Locked into her gaze, Igor took a step back, and she wasn't letting him go. Mia's power surged as his diminished. His aura twitched again, and spaces formed around the bands of color. *Got him!* She smiled inwardly.

Mia took another step forward. Igor stepped back. An uneasy feeling filled the air as the men holding Cole stared at her with worried expressions. She didn't know how she would handle the two men and the vampire. She didn't think that far ahead and prayed they wouldn't move.

Mia continued to push the vampire back until Cole was almost at arm's reach. She stopped. *Now what?* Her mind froze.

She needed to help Cole, but couldn't break the connection with the vampire, and the men began to shift restlessly. One of the men slid his hand inside his jacket, and an image of his intent flashed through Mia's mind. He was going for a silver stake. It wasn't big, but it was enough to kill a vampire.

She slowly moved her hand, pointing to the guy to the right as she kept her eyes bored into Igor's.

"You stake him, and I will kill you after he's dead. And if you run, I will hunt you down," she said, her calm voice a façade to the true fear running through her.

The man paused for a moment, then dropped the stake on the ground. They had no idea what Mia was, or what she was capable of doing to them. She tried to steady herself as she began to shake.

"Drop the chains, and I'll let you live!" her powerful voice commanded, and to her disbelief, they did what she asked. Bluffing was not her best quality. A surge of victory swept over her as the chains dropped to the ground.

When the men turned to run, Cole grabbed them, forcing them to the ground. He held them there while he regained his strength. Afraid to let him go, Mia focused on Igor. Suddenly, she remembered something else Cole said. *You can weaken a younger vampire for an entire day.* She needed the silver chains by Cole's feet. She broke her gaze.

Igor dropped to his knees, and Mia fell with him. Leaning forward, she quickly grabbed the chains and wrapped them around his wrists. He slumped to the ground with a catatonic look upon his face.

The man to Cole's right reached for the stake, and Mia quickly kicked it out of his hand.

Cole jerked his head toward the commotion. When he saw what she had done, his eyes glowed with a mixture of emotions she couldn't begin to sift through.

Mia watched the man on the left tremble as Cole's fangs elongated, and his face slightly changed as he let his beast peek out. She took a step away from Cole. He looked scary as hell, and the man on the left began to babble. He pleaded as Cole stared down at him.

The man turned his fear-filled eyes to Mia. "You-you said if we dropped the chains, you would let us live."

Cole turned toward Mia, his lips pulled back and his fangs fully extended.

He. Is. Pissed. She shook her head as she stared at the shell of a man in Cole's grasp. This is exactly what she'd been talking about—the criminals always getting the upper-hand. This man assisted in almost killing her and Cole tonight. He will go to jail and be out in two days to do something like this again. She took a deep breath, internally struggling with her moral fibers. She stepped closer to them and searched the man's hate-filled aura. Images of things he'd done flashed through her mind. She grabbed the man's face, making him look at her. She felt Cole's eyes clinging to her, analyzing her actions.

"I said *I* would let you live. He's a different story"—she tilted her head toward Cole—"he's hungry, and you are a bad man." Her tone held no compassion.

Mia turned quickly, walked to the trunk of the car, dropped the silver knife back into the box, and then slammed the trunk shut. She moved fast. Once inside the car, the screams from the men chilled her to the bone. She locked the door and clasped her arms around her head. Mia didn't want to hear, see, or think about what Cole was doing.

Minutes later, Mia heard sirens in the distance growing louder. Soon a protective circle of police cars surrounded her. Blue lights illuminated the area. She reached up, adjusted the rear view mirror to inspect her throbbing face. *Shit. That's going to leave a bruise.* The swollen area on her cheek was getting worse.

The tap on the window caused her to jump. She rolled it down.

"Ma'am, Detective Barnett thought you might need an ice pack and some water." The uniformed officer handed her the items as he spoke.

"Thank you." Mia left the window cracked and let the cool night air circulate the staleness inside the car. Leaning back into the seat, she placed the ice pack on her face.

She cracked open the water bottle, placed it against her parched lips and enjoyed the cool sensation of the water as it traveled down her body to rest in her stomach. It was the best water she'd ever tasted. She frowned as she realized she was sensitive to everything now.

The sight in front of her caused her to choke on the water. Two officers walked by with the men from the van and put them into the back of a police car. He didn't kill them, she thought in surprise.

A vampire cop walked by next and placed the vampire criminal into the back of a utility truck with heavy-duty steel sides. When the doors opened, she could see shiny, silver metal. *How many cops here are vampires?* She scanned the area, looking closely at the auras around her. There were six other vampires right outside the car, capable of killing her before she could blink. She pondered how many people knew about them. Her acknowledgment came from a place beyond reality. She looked closer, noticing most of them had two sets of handcuffs, like Cole.

Cole's voice passed through the open crack in the window. It tingled in her ears, and her body instantly reacted, making her nipples tighten beneath her shirt. He leaned against the car as he spoke with the sheriff before unlocking the door. Her breath caught in her throat. *Get a grip, Mia, he is just a man—an overly gorgeous, powerful man who is dead, wants to bite you and drink your blood. Could be worse—he could be a zombie that wants to eat your brains.* She giggled to herself as her thoughts ran wild, wondering if he would always have this effect on her.

The sheriff slid into the driver's seat, cocking his body toward her. He silently studied her for a minute, then rubbed the back of his neck as he spoke.

"You're very brave, Mia. You had me worried the other night with your actions at the beach, but it seems like you've pulled your shit together. I have asked Cole to bring you in. He can explain to you what that means." His eyes came up to study her face. "We need you right now, and you need us. You're now under our protection. I have arranged for you to be off work for a couple days. We've dealt with your bosses, and we'll compensate you for your time. I'll talk with you some more back at the station."

He moved toward the door, then paused. "Thank you for helping Cole tonight. He's very upset that you were hurt. Mia, he's not only my best detective, he's a very old friend. If you need anything, please ask me." He nodded in appreciation.

She was learning this form of vampire communication. They didn't communicate like humans. There were definitely no hugs or high-fives, just simple nods and other small gestures with their bodies. Mia opened her mouth to respond, but he was already out of the car.

Cole stood alone by the door, his hand resting on the handle as if he wasn't sure if he wanted to open it. Minutes passed before he slid into the driver's seat and turned the engine over in silence.

Mia grabbed her seatbelt and winced in pain as she brought it across her chest. She grabbed her side. Cole quickly grabbed the belt from her hand and snapped it into place for her. His eyes locked with hers as the silence thickened in the car. He gripped the steering wheel tightly as he pulled away from the scene.

FOURTEEN

Cole pulled the key from the ignition. He ran his hand through his hair, opened his mouth to say something, then closed it. Mia jumped when he appeared at her window. She glanced back at the driver seat to confirm he'd left. He opened the door and held out his hand. When she slid her hand into his, he let out a sigh of relief. As they walked in silence, she couldn't help but wonder what was wrong.

Mia took in her surroundings. The police headquarters was bigger than she expected. From the road, it looked like giant steps cascaded up toward the sky, but now that she was closer, she could see the building closest to the road was a single-layer building. The one behind it was a six-story building painted in two-tone neutral colors with a twelve-story building behind that.

Cole passed several people who said 'Hi', and he simply nodded with his face drawn tight as he walked passed them. Mia looked back at them, but they didn't give him a second look. Were they accustomed to his detached demeanor? Was he always like this?

He walked into an empty room, pulled Mia in with him, then closed and locked the door. An examination table sat in the corner of the room and a bathroom on the opposite side.

Cole's silence tugged at Mia's nerves, making her uneasy. He lifted her onto the examining table, then walked over to the cabinets across the room and began searching through them. Not finding what he was looking for, he turned his attention to the drawers. A few seconds later, he withdrew a large icepack and placed it on the counter. Mia studied him, trying to read his face as he gathered more items, but he cloaked his emotions well. He placed the supplies onto the table next to her, reached for her shirt, and pulled it over her head. She didn't protest. His silence was telling her something.

Cole lightly traced the bruise on her side with his fingers. The bruise covered the area from her hipbone to the bottom of her shoulder blade. Mia winced in pain from his touch. His eyes darted to hers and in them, she saw a reflection of her pain. He gently held the ice pack to the bruised area on her side while his other hand inspected the rest of her body—turning her arms, looking at her neck, then tilting her forward to inspect her back.

"Cole, I'm okay. I'm just a little bruised," she said, softly.

His face masked with concern as he repositioned the icepack.

Her heart swelled. No one had ever taken care of her before. But his silence was tormenting her. "You didn't kill them."

"No, I didn't," he said, then looked away from her, staring at the wall as if he were examining its imperfections.

Mia glided her fingers across his cheek and turned his head toward her.

"Did you feed on them?" she asked. Cole pulled her hand away from his face, avoiding her eyes.

He was trying so hard to show her that he wasn't something she should fear—and this had to happen. "Yes, I did." His voice was low and deep, rattling up from his chest.

She stared at him. *What did I do to make him so angry that he can't even look at me?* The realization that she cared what he thought settled into her mind. Her eyes glistened with tears. "Are you mad at me, because I got out of the car?"

Cole snapped his gaze to hers. He pulled her off the table and stared down at her. "No, I'm not mad at you. Please, don't cry, Miakoda. I'm angry with myself—I almost lost you." The back of his hand brushed her bruised face. "I... the thought of never touching you again, it's too much."

"But if I hadn't gotten out of the car, you wouldn't have been distracted, and those two men wouldn't have gotten the jump on you. All of this is my fault. I'm sorry." Her emotions let go, and tears rolled down her cheeks.

Cole's lips came down onto hers, drowning out her sobs. "You saved my life. Mia, you were incredibly brave." His voice turned velvety as he leaned down and kissed her again.

His lips felt good, and made all her worries melt away. She deepened the kiss as the excitement of the night rolled back into her mind, and the effects of the adrenaline rush tingled inside her.

His breathing became rapid along with hers. He moaned against her lips, then suddenly pulled away, his lips curling to expose his fangs.

Mia's body was on fire as she locked into his heated gaze. This can get out of hand quick, she thought as she straightened her posture and picked something else to look at. "I can see what you mean about vampires being excited with the chase and the hunt," she said, quickly changing the subject.

"Is that where the passion came from in your kiss? Did what happened earlier excite you, my little rebel?"

Cole smiled, knowing what excited him—she did. He needed to feel every inch of her body, taste her wetness, her blood, and stroke her nipples until she screamed his name in ecstasy. He pressed against her as he waited for her response.

"It did a little. I was surprised, though, that you didn't kill them."

His lips came down on hers, hard, with no regard for her bruises, and she melted into him. He pressed against her, harder, and she whimpered a cry of pain. He relaxed his grip, and trailed kisses along the bruise that surfaced on her face, gently brushing his lips across her skin until they reached her ear, sending her body into an uncontrollable shiver.

"I was surprised you gave me the okay to kill them." He breathed against her ear.

"I'm struggling with the way I feel, but they deserve what they got. You should've seen the things they've done, Cole. Awful things—they deserved to die. What kind of person does that make me, that I feel that way?"

Cole couldn't think to answer Mia because the thought of her accepting him for what he was, and allowing him to kill those men, made his shaft grow with excitement. He pressed his thickness against her leg. Mia swallowed hard, and her habitual protective shield began to roll up like a force field, almost as if her internal body yelled, "Scotty, shields up!" The feeling was almost palpable. With his hands roaming freely, she stiffened under his touch, pulling herself up straight.

Reading her signals, his hands stilled, flexing with a need against her skin. A tormented sigh blew over his lips as he visualized throwing Mia on the table and burying himself deep inside her. The eagerness for her wetness to soothe him, for her muscles to wrap tightly around his cock and stroke him until he came throbbed below his waist. Cole pulled away, shook the images from his mind and thought about something to shrink his loins.

He lightly kissed her lips as he brushed her hair off her shoulders with his fingers. Cole wanted to tell her everything, and he would always be honest with her. Mia would be his soon, and he didn't want anything between them. Taking a deep breath, he tilted his head and captured her gaze. "Not to disappoint you, my love, I did kill one of them. When you were pushed into the car, you didn't see the third man with the homemade silver net. The two guys in front of the van were the distraction. If you hadn't gotten out of the car and stopped me... I was one-step away from the net. While you were shoved into the car, I got the third guy. The other two guys grabbed me when the vampire that passed you knocked me to the ground. That's when they wrapped the silver around my wrists." Cole searched her eyes as he spoke.

Mia grabbed his hands, turning them over, examining his wrists and forearms. She stroked her thumb over his wrist where marks should have been from where the chains burned his flesh. There were no marks; everything had healed.

She didn't run. Cole found this very satisfying.

The knock at the door caused Mia to jump. Grabbing her shirt with a panicked look, she slid it over her head.

The sheriff entered the room and suspiciously looked around before his eyes rested on Mia. "Cole, you're on duty—remember that. We have a lot to do, and I need to talk to Mia. Pull it together, and let's get going."

"Sheriff, I'm sorry—do you think we can do this tomorrow? I have had enough for one night, it's already after midnight, and I'm really tired."

"Well then, stop fooling around, and let's get going. You can leave when I'm done with you." His look was hard, but a hint of a smile pulled at his lips before he walked out.

Cole shifted his stance, he stared at her, unable to keep his feelings at bay, a grim look upon his face. "I'm about to bring you into my world. You're going to see some things that will not agree with the reality you feel safe in. I'm on duty. I can't comfort you the way I would like if something upsets you, but I will be next to you the whole time." Cole squared his shoulders and stood tall. "It's not just about being a law man, Mia. I'm also a vampire, and we are held at the highest regard. I can't show any weakness, and they will eat you alive if *you* show yours." He nodded, then gestured for her to move in front of him.

They walked down a hallway to an open space, a desk and an office sat off to the side. The walls were bare, making the place look lifeless and cold.

The sheriff stepped out of an office. "Cole, I need to see you. Mia, have a seat." He pointed to the chairs against the wall.

Cole entered the office, closing the door behind him. The sheriff rubbed the back of his neck and stared at him. "Cole, we need her, maybe more than we know right now. I want Al to test her. I may want her in all the way."

Cole's expression hardened as he stepped closer to the sheriff. "No. She's not ready for something like this. You'll put her in danger."

"Back down. She's already in danger, and this isn't your call. We'll do what we can to protect her. Cole, she stared down two vampires—her days are numbered if that gets out." He ran his fingers through his hair, blew out a puff of air and continued. "You know as well as I do, vampires won't like the fact that she can pick them out of a crowd, and if she can see us, what else can she see?"

"I will *not* allow this! She will run from—"

"You? She'll run from you? Is that what this is about, Cole?"

"She doesn't even know what she's capable of, John. If you start throwing things at her, she's going to run. Yes, from me. And far away from all of this." Cole stepped closer. "She is mine. I cannot allow that to happen."

"In all the years I've known you, I've never seen you struggle like this. It's getting harder for you to conceal this... battle inside of you." His eyes widened. "Are you saying what I think you're saying? She's your bride?" His voice rose in surprise.

Cole's body responded to the sound of the word. "You know I hate the term *bride*, but yes, I think she is my match. I feel different when I'm with her. I tasted her blood, and I felt my own stirring to life."

John wiped his mouth. His eyes dilated, and his fangs slid out. A shudder washed over him. "Did your heart beat?" He stepped closer to Cole, an eager expression on his face.

Cole looked away and studied the wood grain on the desk. "No, but I haven't fed from her yet. She's afraid of me, and it kills me, John." A painful knot formed inside him.

"How can you be sure?"

"Because I feel the connection. We're similar creatures. I don't understand it or how it's possible that we like the same things, right down to the hand-carved, details etched into a wooden coffin"—Cole shoved his fingers through his hair and stared at John—"and I'm sure I'll kill anyone that tries to hurt her." Cole's muscles tensed at the thought of losing her. Once she sees things in his world, she might run from him again, and this time she wouldn't look back. The thought pained him immeasurably. He should grab her and run—take her away from all of this. *Protect what's mine.* The possibility of his fears becoming reality had his mind contemplating. How long could he hide her? If their secret got out, the world would be in chaos—law and order disrupted. This was what he stood for—to protect. Not just her, but all humans.

John put a hand on Cole's shoulder and squeezed. "I feel for you, partner. We go way back. I know the pain you've endured. I know what makes your soul void from any type of emotion, because we're a lot alike. And I can see the torment in your eyes, the struggle to protect what you feel is yours. However, I have to keep the peace between the lore creatures and the humans—so do you."

"Cole, we have evolved with humanity, and we are the guardians over the humans. This is our job. This is how we survive, so we can peacefully coexist. I don't think you give Mia enough credit. She's strong. I'm putting you in charge of bringing her strength forward. Pull it together—this is the only way to protect her, and you know it."

Cole's lips tightened into a thin line. Anger burned in his eyes and he avoided John's stare. With nothing left to say, Cole walked out.

* * *

In the waiting room, Mia sat back in the chair and thumbed through the magazines on the table. They were mostly men's but the girly ones never interested her anyway—the ones that told her why she should hate men. Mia knew why she disliked men, and she didn't need to take a test in a magazine to see if she should leave the one she was with. She liked looking at the beauty tips, of course, but she was sure tips on how not to get bitten by your date wouldn't be in the advice column.

Her fingers came across a magazine on house designs. The front depicted the featured house which was a beautiful log cabin. Mia opened the magazine to the article and took in a sharp breath as she gazed at the beauty. It was her dream to live in a place like this. The wood seemed cozy and warm. She ran her fingers over the fold out.

"What has your pulse so excited? Since I wasn't in the room, I'm curious."

Mia jumped, startled by Cole's unannounced closeness. She was beginning to think he got some sort of pleasure from sneaking up on her. "Nothing."

"It can't be nothing. I've been watching those beautiful blue eyes scan the magazine, and now you're transfixed on something. It has you completely relaxed."

"It's something I don't think I'll ever have." She spoke in dreamy despair. "But I'm in awe of its beauty."

Cole reached down and grasped the magazine between two fingers. His eyes never left hers as he slowly pulled the magazine from her hands. The corners of his mouth showed the slightest indication of a smile. "I know how that feels," he said as he looked down at the picture. His eyes sparkled when they returned to her face. "We have similar taste."

The sheriff walked past them, shuffling papers in his hand. As he passed through the door, he looked back over his shoulder. "I'll meet you two in the M.E's office. Barnett, remember what I said."

Mia stood up and wiped her palms on her jeans. *Okay. I'm being brought into "his world."* Nerves tugged at her. Mia inhaled deeply, then puffed her cheeks out to exhale. She tried hard to keep her breathing under control so Cole wouldn't notice her elevated pulse.

"How far is the Medical Examiner's office?" she asked as they walked into the hallway, side-by-side like co-workers. Mia glanced at Cole. His demeanor had changed. He drew his posture into a straight line, and his face was emptied of any emotion. *He's in cop mode.*

"It's not that far. The victims—the ones you dreamed about—are there. We want you to look at them."

Mia abruptly stopped. All the blood drained from her face. "What? Why?"

"We thought you might pick something up, or tell us more about why you said we should look at them closely. The M.E. hasn't picked up anything unusual." He put his hand on her shoulder and nudged her forward.

She looked at him, puzzled. "When did I ever say that?"

"In my car at the beach, right before you vomited."

Mia wrinkled her forehead trying to grab the memory from her mind. "Oh, God, I did say that. I-I didn't want anyone to know." Her stomach clenched, and her nerves started to climb higher into her chest. "Cole, I don't want to do this. I've never tried to use this thing on purpose. It just comes to me. What if I'm wrong?" She swallowed the lump in her throat.

Cole stopped and looked around before placing his hands on her shoulders. "What if you're right? It's not going to hurt to try." As tender as his voice was, it didn't stop the tears burning in her eyes.

This... thing had teased her, her whole life, popping up at the most inappropriate times, and sometimes embarrassing her. Now they want her to show people what she sees, what haunts her dreams, in public? "I really don't want to do this."

"Mia, we have dead victims here, and someone is trying to kill you. This isn't a game. It's not about who may think you're weird. We need your help." His tone thickened, and his face hardened.

Mia narrowed her eyes at him before she turned on her heels, her pace quickening. She was pissed. "You know I have issues with this. There is no need to make me feel like shit about it. I'm not a child. I know this isn't a game." She opened the door in front of her with a shove and walked through, then turned around to face Cole. "You know what, Detective? I'll do this, but I'm not doing it for you! I'm doing it for those girls. So don't worry about my feelings or the fact that I'm weird—" Mia grabbed his forearm. The tug in the pit of her stomach intensified.

She felt Cole's muscles tighten as she dug her nails into his flesh. The intense feeling brought her to her knees. Whistles and vulgar slurs came at her from everywhere.

"Hey, baby, wooohooo! Hey, Officer, can we get some of that for good behavior?" a prisoner yelled.

The negative energy overwhelmed her, and the room started to spiral. She focused on Cole's legs to keep her balance, and then felt his hand cup under her arm. He started to kneel, then straightened his stance and let out a frustrated groan. "Mia, I can't... you're no good like this. Stand up before they pick out your weakness. You need to learn to control your anger and this *thing* you have." He tugged on her arm, "Mia, look at me. Look into my eyes. Focus on me." His voice gave her the momentary diversion she needed.

Cole was right, she knew he was but didn't know how to control it—that was always the problem. She took a deep breath. *Fuck. Not working.* "I think I'm gonna puke," she mumbled as she placed her hands on her knees and swallowed the extra saliva entering her mouth.

"Mia, block it out, and pull yourself together."

"You're an ass—heartless—once again." She looked up and met his piercing eyes.

"You need to calm down." Cole held back a grin, purposely pushing her red button. He watched as fire flashed in her eyes and built within her. She was breathtaking, stunning. *Mine.*

He jerked his head toward the ceiling. The lights flickered throughout the cellblock. *That's odd.* His senses were on high alert.

"And you need to piss off. Which way do we need to go? I want to get this over with and go home, then you can go back to whatever dirt pile you crawled out of."

The tiniest hint of a grin pulled hard on the edge of his lips, and he fought the urge to break out into a full smile. *That's my girl.* She was pure fire when angry. An inferno he would gladly walk into, just to press his lips against hers. His fangs inched out at seeing her like this. Fighting hard for control, he pushed the carnal urge back down.

FIFTEEN

*W*hen Mia turned away from him, she took in her surroundings. Several levels of jail cells reached up to the ceiling where they stood. There was nothing warm about the place. The gray paint was old with various patches chipping off the wall. It was dead looking. It gave off a cold, empty feeling, just like the many eyes that were staring at her.

The air thinned, and a sense of claustrophobia began to creep up on her. Everything seemed so confined. Bad men were everywhere. Some were playing basketball, others—cards, but all of them had one thing in common. They were criminals.

Cole grabbed the underside of her upper arm. Picking her up off the floor, he moved her along with his cop grip. "We need privacy. Now." His steps were urgent as they walked the entire length of the cellblock. When they reached the elevator at the end, Cole pushed the button, and the doors opened.

Once inside, Mia realized she hadn't gotten any feelings or visions since the moment Cole had said, "Calm down." She filed that away in her memory since she was trying to learn how to control the feelings, and everything else in her life at the same time.

When the elevator door closed, Cole turned to her. A savage light came into his eyes as if someone flipped his switch to "on." His lips came down onto hers, hard and hungry. He devoured her mouth demanding a response.

There was something to this feeling. It was a mix of danger and excitement, and it ignited a fire inside her that she wasn't ready to extinguish. She was starting to crave it. Mia felt as if he was going to push her through the elevator wall, and knowing his strength, he could probably do it. When the elevator bell rang, he released her from his grip, pulling his lips away, leaving her flesh burning. Breathless, she gazed at Cole and drank him in, swallowing a lump at the sight of his fangs. His eyes darkened with desire, and the fabric of his clothes stretched under his taut muscles. Mia lost herself in the depths of his deep brown gaze, staring at the tiny black speck by his left pupil. It captivated her, like an imperfection in a diamond. It was her speck—she claimed it like an undiscovered star.

"Now, how do you expect me to control my anger when you can't control your urges? You're not a very good teacher, Detective."

His lips curled, and he straightened his posture. With an arched brow and a flirtatious grin, he responded, "As I told you before, you make it hard for me to control myself."

"And you make it hard for me to control my anger." She lifted her chin, and they exchanged a back-to-work look.

As she passed Cole walking out of the elevator, he bent down and whispered in her ear. "I don't sleep in the dirt."

His low seductive voice rolled around in her ear causing her body to shiver. She smirked. "Where are we?" Mia shook herself, mentally trying to jump back into reality and out of the land of lust. These feelings were so unlike her.

"This is the section where the high level criminals are kept. Most of them here are on death row." He placed a hand on the small of her back and moved her forward through the L-shaped cellblock. Mia shifted her eyes to the men in the cells; evil filled their hearts. She blew out a burst of air.

"Death row. That's a joke."

"What do you mean?" he asked as they reached the last cell. Cole searched his clothes and pulled a security key from his pocket, swiping it across the pad to open the door in front of them.

"Death row is a joke, that's what I mean. This guy for example," —she turned away from the door and faced the cell that was behind them— "gets to choose how he dies. He gets a nice peaceful death by lethal injection. Do you think his victims had a choice how they died? Do you think the woman he strangled and stabbed, then raped had a choice? How about her little girl? He suffocated her with a pillow first and hid her body so she wouldn't see what he had done. Do you think she had a choice?" Mia's voice grew louder as she spoke.

The man rose from his bed and looked at her with surprise. She stared into his cold eyes. "Ooh... I'm sorry. They didn't know about the little girl. They never found her, did they? Well, they will now." Mia stared him down, taking a step closer to his cell, anger built inside of her. "She's here, and she's not going to let you get away with it. Her name is Emily. Do you remember her?" Mia gave a reassuring look to the apparition next to her.

The man lunged his hand through the bars, grabbing the hem of her shirt. Cole quickly snatched Mia out of his grasp and met her eyes with a look of understanding. "They get theirs, Mia, don't worry."

Right, she thought with disgust, and pulled his arm off her.

A red light lit above the cell and rotated inside its dome. As the alert-light swirled around the room, casting its glow over her, Cole swung her around and pressed her back against the security door.

He fumbled in his jacket until he pulled out the key. As the cell door slid open, it squeaked on its neglected tracks. "Fuck. Too late." He stood stock still in front of her as a wall of protection. Cole's fangs slid out, and an excited glow crept into his eyes.

Mia watched him, her breath became rapid as the nervous energy repelled out of the holding cells and wrapped around her. *Something's coming.* A nervous realization washed over her as Cole rested his hands on the door, one on each side of her head. His lips pulled back exposing his fangs. *He knows what's coming.*

"Mia, I can't open this door when the cells are open. Stand still, and don't move." Concern laced his voice, chilling her to the core.

The heavy door leading into the cellblock swung open and hit the wall as if it was as light as a saloon door. Something flew by Mia leaving a trail of color like a shooting star. Terrifying screams were followed by a voice that chilled her to the bone.

"No. Stop.... Please! Just kill me... please, let me die."

A shiver of panic ran through Mia until she looked into Cole's eyes. The screaming continued along with the sounds of a growling beast. She stared at Cole, taking refuge in his gaze and blocked out the sounds. There was a final plea for death that gurgled out, then silence. The glow from the flashing red light stopped, and the cell door squeaked until it was back into its locked position.

"Barnett, I didn't see you there. Dude, I'm sorry. Were you feeding? I didn't jump your dinner, did I?" the uniformed officer asked as Cole stood back, revealing Mia's body. "Nice. Looks like you're eating gourmet tonight." He wiped the blood from his lips with the back of his hand.

"No, she is helping us out—sheriff's orders."

162

The vampire took a step back. "Are you the woman that did that to the vampire in the holding cell?"

Mia met his eyes, his face was still covered in blood, and he didn't seem to care. This was natural to them. *Gross.* She glanced at Cole. His face held a look of apprehension, and she understood his expression. She avoided the vampire's question all together.

"Is he dead?" She pointed to the man in the cell lying on the floor. Blood soaked his shirt and dripped from his neck into a red pool on the cement floor. The vampire looked at the cell and snickered as he turned back to her.

"Naw, he wishes. It's against policy to kill them. We just drain them until they're unconscious. He'll feel like shit for a couple days, and then we can feed from him again. I'm going for another artery next time," he said as casually as someone would say they wanted to king size their fries.

Conflict and nausea gnawed at Mia. This was too much for her to process in one night. She needed out of this tiny space and away from the blood. "Sorry for interrupting your meal." She looked at Cole, but couldn't fully meet his eyes. *He's one of them.* She grabbed the key card from his hand, and held it in front of the security scanner releasing the door. She walked through, not waiting for Cole. There was only one door to the right, Mia headed toward it, fast.

Cole's hand gently slid under her arm. "Mia, stop. Turn around, and look at me."

She tugged her arm from his grasp. "I can't look at you."

He placed her against the wall and cupped her face with his hands. "This is what I feared. You're really shaken. Look at me, please," he whispered.

Tears stung her eyes as she met his. Conflict burned in her heart, seared by her scarred past. "You do that?

Is that what you meant by 'they get theirs'? Is that how you feed, how you bite? Violent, like that?" Her eyes clouded with tears. She needed a break, time to think. It was all too much.

"I have not fed on death row in a very long time, but yes, I have fed like this. This is not how I feed every day. Being a vampire cop takes more restraint than anything you could imagine. Sometimes urges are too great. This is how we release our anger, our frustrations, and our desire to kill the criminals we deal with day in and day out." His eyes urged her to understand, but she couldn't grasp everything that had happened. "You said it wasn't fair that the criminals got to choose how they die, and that a peaceful death was unjust. Has that changed?"

"No, it hasn't. Cole, that was one of the most horrific things I've ever witnessed, and you've done that." She reached up and removed his hand from her face.

Cole's body straightened, his face hardening as his jaw clenched down. His tone was harsh as he ground his teeth. "Is that what you can't accept? You think *I'm* the animal, and not him? Not the criminal?"

The pain in his eyes resurfaced, tugging at her heart. Deep down, it was satisfying to know the criminals got theirs, but she didn't know how to feel about Cole. She averted her eyes as she spoke. "Can we just go? I'm getting really tired."

He clenched his teeth, making his jaw tick before he grabbed the door handle in front of them and motioned her to walk through the door. His eyes burned holes into her as she walked past him.

Mia didn't think she could fear him any more than she already did, but as she went past him, her body clung to the wall. She heard his fangs snap out, fast like a switchblade. She didn't dare look at him; she could feel his anger.

Cold, gloomy walls surrounded them in the hallway. Doors were on each side, and one at the very end. Mia walked to the first door and stopped. She wasn't going to ask him which door to open. She wasn't going to ask him anything for that matter. She cursed her pulse for giving her emotions away, she knew he felt it, and it had been elevated since death row with no ease in its pace.

Cole flew by her in vampire speed to the door at the end of the hall. Opening it, he glared at her as she walked toward him. He took a step forward, forcing her to brush past him and inhaled deeply as she passed. When he grabbed her arm, she stilled. Her heart pounded against her chest.

"What took you two so long? Mia, come with me," the sheriff said.

Cole released her arm.

Mia sighed in relief but still couldn't look at Cole. She felt his presence though, it vibrated through her with such force she knew Cole was about to explode.

"Cole, what's the matter with you? You haven't been right for days. I think you need to take a walk over to death row. Listen... I know it's been a couple, well, more like eighty years since you fed there, but I think you need to go release some aggression. You're like a time bomb lately, and I don't need someone as strong as you blowing a fuse."

"No thanks. You know that's not my way," Cole replied through clenched teeth.

John jerked his head back, his brows drawn in confusion. He shifted his gaze between the two of them then his face relaxed, and his expression changed as if a light bulb dangled above his head. "I see. Cole, I don't want to do this, but if you're struggling with something, I'm going to put another detective on as lead." He chuckled to himself.

Cole's eyes widened as he met the sheriff's. "You've never had to do that before—why now? Why would you say that?"

The sheriff looked at Mia, and Cole followed his line of sight. "Because I haven't seen you tested like this in over one hundred years, my friend. You fed off those two men earlier, and I can still see the bloodlust in your eyes. It looks like you're being provoked by this little lady. Go take a break!" His tone was stern.

"No, thank you. I don't need a break. This is my job." Cole's jaw twitched in defiance.

The sheriff took a deep breath, then sighed. "I'm not asking, I'm telling. The break isn't from your job, it's from her. We'll see you in a few minutes." With that, the sheriff took the back of her arm in the now familiar cop grip and walked her to the far side of the room to yet another door.

I feel like I'm in the matrix. I'm never getting out of here on my own, that's for sure. Where is Neo when you need him?

SIXTEEN

*M*ia stopped as she entered the room. The cool air raked over her skin, chilling it, coaxing tiny bumps to rise on her flesh. The white walls had faded to a dull cream with chips of paint randomly missing. Stainless steel tables were scattered around the room, and the smell of bleach overwhelmed her senses.

Mia glanced at the outline of lifeless bodies inside of black bags, hidden under white sheets. Reality slowly seeped into her mind. As she turned, she focused on a female corpse, exposed and inanimate, lying on the table. She could feel others present in the room as she shifted her focus to the slender man in front of her. He picked up a pale arm and examined the skin on the corpse. He had blue eyes inset within his oval face with ordinary features but his aura told Mia he wasn't an ordinary human. He was a vampire. The first she had seen with very little hair.

She scanned the other two auras in the room. Vampires. When she finished scanning the drop dead gorgeous one, he winked at her. The other was round in the gut, but nice-looking. He appeared much older than all the vampires she had seen up until now. *Great. I'm surrounded by heartless, blood-suckers. I hope I don't get a paper cut.*

The sheriff placed a hand on her shoulder, walking her over to what she assumed was the M.E., and then his eyes skimmed over everyone. "Okay, I've briefed all of you on what I'm trying to do here. I don't know if it's going to work." He gently squeezed Mia's shoulder. "I don't know what Mia is capable of, but we're going to give it shot." His face hardened. "Nothing leaves this room or there'll be consequences. Does everyone understand?"

They nodded in compliance, and then they looked at Mia. She felt their excitement, but didn't understand it. Her hands started to sweat, and unease twisted in her gut. Cole was the only person she had completely confided in. He knew she felt uncomfortable even talking about this. Now she had to show someone what she could see and feel.

The M.E. leaned across the table, extending his hand over the dead body. "You look a little nervous. My name is Tom. Why don't you come closer to the body, and see if that helps."

Mia nodded, taking a step closer to the table. Her hands started to shake, and she looked over her shoulder at the sheriff. "I-I don't know how to do this. What do you want me to do?" They stared at her. "I've never done anything like this before."

A loud, cocky laugh erupted from the drop dead gorgeous detective. "It's working well so far, sheriff."

The sheriff snapped his head toward him, giving him a look of warning before taking Mia's arm. He walked her closer to the corpse.

She looked down at the lifeless body, encouraging her mind to see something useful. So far, she could only see the cold and colorless skin. They had already removed some of the dead girl's organs, and her chest cavity was open, displaying the remaining ones. Her forehead had a lengthwise cut across it, and her skull was exposed with her skin peeled back over her like a mask. Dead bodies were nothing out of the ordinary for Mia, but seeing them like this was.

"When do you usually see things?" She heard the sheriff's voice, but couldn't pull her eyes away from the body. She stared past the metal tool holding the ribcage open, her gaze fixated on the inside of the chest cavity where meaty flesh, muscle, and ribs were on display. It should've completely grossed her out. It would for a normal person. Instead, it filled her mind with questions. She wondered what they took out first, if they found any clues, how much lungs weighed.

"Mia, I asked you a question."

She turned toward him. "I'm sorry. Umm... well, I usually dream about them, but lately I've noticed some different ways that they're coming to me—like the other night. Mainly, it happens when bad energy is around me. The most intense visions are coming through if something provokes intense feelings. Then, the images start pouring through me."

The door opened, and the sheriff's eyes strayed from Mia to acknowledge Cole coming through the entrance. She felt him before she heard the sound of his boots on the concrete floor. She closed her eyes and took a deep breath as he drew closer and closer to her. Her body sensed his nearness, and she reached behind her, grabbing the examining table to, steady herself.

"Yum. Someone's blood is soaring."

Mia opened her eyes to find the source of the comment. It was the gorgeous detective. His eyes narrowed at her, and his fangs popped as he licked his lips.

Cole moved in front of her, creating a wall and blocking the other detective's view of her. She trailed her eyes up from his waist to rest on his handsome face. Cole tilted his head down, and peered at her with a look that could make a nun sin. It jump-started her pulse to a rapid beat. Her breathing became gasps. The familiar feeling in the pit of her stomach knotted her gut, and the lights inside her head started flashing.

The visions were coming.

She turned away from Cole, and gripped the table. The pads of her fingers pushed against the cold steel turning her knuckles white. Cole move closer, and her hands flew to her head—the feeling was too intense. She felt as if she was picking up every dead body in the room at once, and was sure blood would trickle from her ears at any minute.

"Do you see anything?" the sheriff asked.

"Yes. It's too much. I see them all. I can't make sense out of them. It's too much." There was a flicker of panic to her voice.

"Looks like we found the source of her intense feelings." The voice of the gorgeous detective teased once again.

"Quiet!" the sheriff ordered.

Mia felt Cole's hand on her shoulder, and she shuddered under his touch. Half of her felt frightened of him, the other half wanted to lean and relax into his chest.

All at once, voices entered her head. Each wanting to be heard, but she could only make out one. "Mia, slow your pulse. Breathe."

She started to focus as he kneaded her shoulder. She saw the dead girl on the table flash in her mind and her head twitched as if to follow the vision. "She's running from something."

"Well, we know it wasn't from the Buick that hit her." The gorgeous detective chuckled. Mia's thoughts stumbled at the comment. He was obviously full of himself. On the other hand, maybe the chemicals from the excessive amount of hair gel he used seeped through his skin, and damaged his brain.

"Russo, one more interruption, and you're out. Do you understand?" The sheriff's tone was venomous.

Mia refocused. "She wasn't hit by a car." She heard restless movements all around her when she spoke.

"She was chased, and then attacked." Her lashes flew up. She turned around wide-eyed and looked at each one of them except Cole. "She was killed by a vampire."

They stiffened, looking at one another with an unspoken understanding. When she turned back around, Tom was staring at her with a twisted face. She suspected it was because he had come to a different conclusion regarding the girl's death.

"That's impossible. There are no marks on her. She's not drained, and the damage she sustained was from the car hitting her." His voice held a hint of animosity.

They looked back to Mia. "It is possible, Tom. He chased her, jumped on her, and had sex with her while he fed from her until she passed out. After he woke her, he cut his upper thigh by his... his genitals"—she blushed as she pointed between her legs to help translate her words—"and made her drink his blood while he did"—she placed her hands behind her back, not about to make *that* hand gesture—"something... sexual to himself. She healed, he licked the bite marks and then chased her again, this time he slammed her into a tree. Two other men took the body and placed it into the street to make it look like a hit and run."

She looked around the room with a curious expression. "Did you check her blood? Can you tell the difference between vampire blood and human blood?" Breathing with confidence now, she threw her shoulders back and tilted her chin up.

Everyone looked back at Tom. "Yes, you can, and no, I didn't have a need to check her blood, but I will do that now." Tom bowed his head, he seemed embarrassed he had grown indolent.

"Wait. We're going to take the word of the corpse whisperer over there instead of Tom's?" Russo blurted out.

"Russo, shut it! Tom, I want the blood work back before dawn. All of you remember—everything stays in this room. I don't want you talking to anyone, including your fellow officers. Mia, come over here, and look at this one." The sheriff pointed to the table across the room where the indentations of a body lay under a white sheet.

As Mia walked toward it, she could feel Russo's eyes watching her, and then he flashed in front of her. He leaned an elbow on the table and his gaze undressed her. "Hey, Mia, why don't you help me take a little bite out of crime later on?"

Before she could open her mouth to protest his repulsive behavior, Cole zipped by, knocking her into the sheriff. He grabbed Russo by the throat and lifted him off the ground. Moving past the table, Cole slammed the other vampire into the back wall. The drywall buckled and crumbled over Russo's head forming a visible indention. Cole's fangs jolted out as rage flicked in his eyes.

Mia's transfixed gaze drank in every muscle in his body as it went taut. He was a vision of power, and strength, and she couldn't help but be aroused.

Cole's voice came out like thunder shaking the surrounding air. "You or anyone else touches her, and I will kill you. That is something you can take out of this room—tell everyone, especially your fellow officers."

Mia felt a whoosh of wind as the sheriff passed her to stand by the two men.

"Cole, put him down," the sheriff said in a calm, but firm tone.

Mia had seen that look in Cole's eyes once before, and she knew he was almost gone beyond reason. He tightened his grip around Russo's neck, and a small rumble escaped from his throat.

The sheriff's voice was firmer, more urgent. "Cole, you're much older than him. There is no way he could beat you. You win. Put him down."

Cole still did not move.

Mia couldn't watch him rip Russo's throat out, even though he would be much more appealing if he wasn't able to speak. She took in a deep breath, relaxing her body. Again, she breathed deep, making it known that she was breathing. She could tell he could feel her breathing, relaxing, as if he were inside her skin, by the way his muscles loosened. Remembering what Cole said about weakness and it being looked down on, despised, she spoke. "Cole, it seems that I can do this better when you're standing next to me. Can we all get back over here and finish this? I want to go home."

Cole instantly released his grip and turned toward her. He took a couple of steps, and then Russo opened his mouth again.

"Damn, Cole, I don't see any marks on her. Why don't you mark your territory, then I would've known she was yours."

Cole jerked his head back to Russo. He stepped toward him and then paused as the sheriff grabbed Russo by the throat and buried him deeper into the wall, giving Cole a grin. "Learn when to keep your mouth shut, Russo. More importantly, learn to respect your elders." He turned away from Russo and motioned behind him with his thumb as he talked. "Tom, call maintenance and have them fix the wall before morning."

The sheriff walked over to Mia and whipped the white sheet off the corpse on the table. "As I recall, you want to go home. Cole, get over here, and stand by the lady."

Mia looked at the sheriff. He was difficult to figure out. He was obviously a smart man, and she could see a little of the relationship between him and Cole. It went much deeper than a mere friendship.

Cole stood behind her. Once she felt his presence and the warmth from her body bouncing off him, she focused on the corpse in front of her. The condition of the girl's body was grotesque. Being in water a couple of days had taken its toll on her skin, which had severely wrinkled, and in some places seemed slimy.

As soon as Mia squeezed her eyes shut, her body jerked at the first flash of light in her mind's eye, but this time, she controlled it. She maneuvered through the clips in her mind, picking out the essential details, playing them slowly, as if she pushed a button on a remote control. She opened her eyes and looked at the sheriff. "This one pretty much happened the same way. He attacked her, had sex and fed from her until she passed out. He gave her vampire blood and licked her marks to heal them. After, he held her down in water by the back of her head until she drowned. The same two men threw her off the Lake Worth pier." Mia followed everyone's gaze back to Tom who still stood by the first body extracting blood. *Poor Tom.*

Tom looked up from his task, staring back at them. "What? Yes, she drowned, but there are no signs of a struggle. There are no bruises around her neck from someone forcefully holding her down. If what you say is true, Mia, and she was given vampire blood, then she would have had more strength to fight back." Tom's lips pulled back into a tight smirk, as if he just laid down a royal flush.

Everyone looked back to Mia.

"She was only given enough blood to heal the marks, and she did fight. She clawed at him with her nails, but you wouldn't know that because the fish have chewed away her fingers. The vampire who did this"—Mia pointed to the lifeless body on the table—"used his two thumbs to hold her down. He placed his thumbs high up on the back of her skull. He knew what he was doing, and he didn't think you'd check there."

This was starting to feel like a tennis match as everyone's head snapped back to Tom.

"Tom, did you check the base of her skull?" The sheriff's face masked with disappointment.

"No, I didn't, yet." In a flash, Tom was in front of Mia. He tilted the corpse onto its side. Mia's hand went to her mouth as the skin on her arm slid down, like the green slime she had played with as a child, and threatened to slide off the bones.

The sheriff took the woman's hair and gently pulled it up. She had thick curly black locks making it hard to see, but as everyone leaned in to get a better look, they could see the presence of the bruises—two of them, one on each side of her skull.

"Tom, can you get a sample of her blood, too?" Cole's voice was so close to Mia's ear, she flinched and everyone stared at her when her pulse jumped.

"Okay, Mia. One more, and that will be the last of the three girls." The sheriff placed his hand on her shoulder and tilted his head toward the other table.

Her mind was trying to tell her something. She took a couple of steps as the sheriff's words rolled around in her head, then stopped. "Wait! What did you just say?"

Everyone's eyes were back on her, except for Russo. He had pulled himself out of the wall earlier and was standing as far away from her as possible. He didn't even try to look at her.

"I said there is one more."

"No, no. After that." Mia waved her hand in the air, swooshing away the wrong words.

"That will be the last of the three girls." His brows knitted. "I don't know what you've got, Mia but your blood is soaring with excitement."

"Three girls. That's it! Cole, did you read Art's note? The one I gave you? The one I found in the cigarette pack?" Her words rushed out as her brain clicked on the memory.

Everyone turned to Cole.

"No, I didn't. I haven't gotten around to it yet."

The sheriff threw his hands in the air and looked around the room at his men. "What am I working with? A bunch of fucking rookies?" He lifted his hand and shook an accusing finger. "Tom, you should have looked at that blood when I told you to look at all the bodies closely. Cole, you have been a lawman for almost one hundred and forty-six years, and you don't look at a note that is part of a crime?" His nostrils flared, then his fangs shot out. Mia stepped back as he continued to take most of his frustrations out on Cole. "Cole, you're slipping. Get rid of the distraction, and screw your head back on." He turned to Mia next. "Mia, get over there to the last corpse, and let's get this over with. I am paying you for this, so consider yourself my employee, and you are subject to an ass chewing if necessary."

She walked over to the corpse in silence. The sheriff grabbed her arm from behind, glaring at the rest of them. They all stayed back. Mia took note again as they seemed to silently communicate without words. It was starting to freak her out.

The sheriff pulled her closer to him, leaning down with a deadly stare, his teeth clenched as his words came out in a whisper for her ears only. "And another thing, Mia. Don't play with him. He's known more pain than you'll ever know in your human existence. If you don't want him, tell him." Releasing his grip on her arm he added, "Not that he'll listen to you when you do."

She took a step back, bumping into to something, she looked up and gazed at Cole. His face was hard, his eyes empty. It almost looked as if he were in some sort of trance. He briefly looked into her eyes, then over at the sheriff again. They talked without words, and Cole nodded.

Mia moved closer to the last table. The sheriff removed the white sheet from the body and Mia's hands flew to her mouth in horror. This was the worst of the three. A wave of bad energy, powerful energy, came from the corpse and knocked her back into Cole. She reached back and grabbed his shirt, twisting the material in her hand as she turned away from the table. The visions were horrible, haunting. Desperately, she searched for her voice to tell them what she saw. Her knees went weak, and she reached her other hand out and wrapped Cole's shirt into her fist, trying to stay on her feet. Mia took comfort as he slipped his hands under her arms for support.

"Can you tell us anything?" The sheriff's voice broke through the violence rolling around in her head.

The girl's death was on instant replay in her mind. Her breathing became rapid as she ran beside the girl in her vision. "She's running... No, don't look behind you. Run! Run! He's got her. It looks like the same woods as the other two." Mia jumped and gripped Cole's shirt tighter, holding on for dear life, watching the vampire savagely sink his teeth into his victim. Tears broke through her clenched eyes. "He bit her. He's ripping her pants off and he's taking her." She couldn't open her eyes. She was trapped inside the intense vision. She could hear fangs popping all around her from inside the room.

"Can you see who it is? Can you describe him?" the sheriff asked.

"He's-he's... Oh, God. He just ripped a chunk out of her shoulder, and now her side." She buried her face into Cole's chest, and her body trembled. Cole kept his grip on her arms, holding her up more than he knew.

Her sobs were uncontrollable as the tears poured down her face. "His hair is dark, a little longer than shoulder length—" She yanked on Cole's arms. "I have to stop. I don't want to see anymore, I don't—"

"No, Mia. Just a little more." The sheriff pressed.

Her blood soared through her veins, and her heart pounded against her chest. Mia's body jerked again as the next image flashed through her mind, and she reluctantly continued. "He's... ripping into her flesh, and he's... What the fuck is that? He's changing. He's mauling her like a... Oh, sweet Jesus. He's turned into a... hairy, wolf thing." Fear jumped straight out of her body, and she felt the blood drain from her face. Her eyes flew open, and she released Cole's shirt, backing away from him so fast she almost tipped the corpse over.

Cole stepped closer to her as she slid down the table. Feeling her way across the cold steel, she wanted away from him fast. Her eyes were wide, and she was borderline frantic.

"He changed! You guys can really do that? Do you change, Cole? Can you change?"

Her hands came across a desk and Cole grabbed for her arm just as she slid up onto it. She pulled her legs up and pushed herself back, sliding on papers as her hands desperately tried to get traction. She pushed hard with her heels and hit the wall.

"Mia, please. It's okay." Cole tried to comfort her in front of the other vampires.

"No. No, it's not okay, Cole! Can you change?"

"Mia, we're the good guys. All vampires have a special trait, a special power," the sheriff said.

That's not comforting. Mia's mind locked on that thought.

Cole's eyes darkened, and he held out his hand for her.

She flinched as if it were fire. He put his hand down by his side, and in a whisper, he said, "Mia, please. This is not helping anyone. Come down off the table."

"No, that doesn't answer my question. Do you change?" She shook her head, the pain and fear evident in her voice.

He reached for her again, and she pushed back more into the wall, knocking over a large lab vial. Water splashed onto her pants and Cole's shirt. His face tightened. He grabbed her and pulled her off the table into his arms.

"Enough!" The growl rolled up from his throat, vibrating every bone in her body. She squirmed in his iron grip, but realized it was useless. His arms encircled her, holding her tight. Even though she feared him, she took comfort in his arms and cursed the conflict within her.

"You do change. That's why you won't tell me. You become that horrible beast I saw rip that girl to shreds." She buried her head in his chest and cried.

The only thing Mia could hear was her sobs and his breathing. *Wait. He's breathing.* Mystified at the breaths that had fallen into a human-like rhythm, her gaze darted to Cole's and froze. Blood danced at the edge of his lashes, threatening to overflow.

"If you two are done..." The sheriff's tone was nothing less than impatient.

Mia stared into Cole's eyes, her breathing still rapid, as she watched the Master of Control harness his emotions. The pool of blood from his left eye slipped back into his tear duct, but the other wasn't as obedient. It was going to fall.

"Cole. Let's go. We have work to do." The sheriff's voice snapped her out of her daze.

He can't turn around like this, she thought, and she wasn't going to let him, especially in front of Russo.

She may fear him, may not want a relationship with him, but she knew he made her feel something—she just hadn't put it all together yet. She wouldn't be able to live with herself if others saw Cole in his moment of weakness. Even if she was scared shitless, he was reacting to her fear, and this was her fault.

"Cole, I. I'm sorry. I splashed water all over your face," she lied. Turning in his arms, she looked at the table behind them and searched for something to wipe his eyes with, but it was empty.

"Here, I have some rags. We know how Cole is about his clothes," Tom said as he started moving toward them.

Mia reached down, fast, and ripped the bottom of her shirt making it into a ragged half-shirt.

She moved a shaky hand up, pressing the fabric over the red, shimmering liquid in his right eye just as Tom reached them.

"I said I had rags." Tom looked at her strangely.

"I'm sorry. I didn't hear you. I'm human—I don't have super, vampire hearing like you do." She forced an uneasy smile. Cole put his hand over hers and nodded. His eyes held an expression of thanks. She slid her hand out from under his, and he closed his eyes as her fingers brushed his face. "Make sure you wipe the other side in case some splashed over there, too."

He wiped again, then dropped his hand to his waist. There wasn't a trace of red anywhere on his face, but it was on the torn piece of shirt.

"Can I have my shirt back?" She held out her hand, and Cole looked down at the material he palmed, noting the bloodstains. He knew as well as she did, if someone saw the shirt, they would know. He handed it to her with full trust in his eyes, and she shoved it deep into her pocket.

His eyes held a mixture of emotions that he quickly suppressed. His jaw twitched, and he snapped back into cop mode. Turning from her, he walked away, leaving a void.

"Mia, when you're done with your human emotions, get your ass over here." The sheriff turned his head toward a chair. "Tom, call down and get us some food. I think Mia's visions have got us all a little riled. Cole and I only need one. Get Russo and Cramer two. Oh, and bring Mia some water."

Not moving, she gaped at the shredded corpse. Despite her distance, she could see where the creatures from the sea and lore had devoured her. The white sheet popped in the air as it flowed down back over the body. In a daze, Mia brought her eyes to Cole's as he released the cover. With the slightest twitch, his head inclined as if to say, "Let me take this image away for you."

Mia was trying to understand this unspoken, secret body language between vampires, and now she found herself doing it. She didn't speak, but gave Cole a smile of appreciation for what he had done.

"What do you need from me, Sheriff?"

The door opened, and Russo rushed over to the girl standing in the entrance. He took the black containers and the water from her arms, and shut the door behind her. The others hurried over, grabbing the containers from his arms, leaving him with two black containers and water. He looked down at the water and then to Cole.

"Cole, can you take this water, please?"

Mia glanced at them. They acted like they were starved for blood, and she couldn't believe the change in Russo after the little incident with Cole.

Cole walked over, and snatched the water from Russo's arms. Cole glared until Russo lowered his head in submission.

Cole turned, setting the water on the empty table closest to Mia. His eyes barely grazed her as she walked over and took it. Mia didn't realize how parched she was until the cool water ran down her throat. She glanced at them over her bottle. Russo had already finished both containers, Cramer was on his second, and the sheriff and Cole had just opened theirs. Cole and the sheriff must be older, she thought, remembering Cole had said older vampires need little blood.

"Mia." The sheriff twitched his fingers in the air. "Come here, so we can go over some details in Cramer's notes."

"Can I just stand over here, away from all of you?" She gulped when his head bowed, and his eyes became slits. "No disrespect, sir."

"No, you can't. Get over here. If we were going to kill you, we would have already done it. I realize this is all new to you, Mia, and that's why I've been patient, but don't push it." His eyes stayed on her as she took the chair Cole had motioned for her to sit in. Cole stood behind her.

"Cramer, you ready?" the sheriff asked.

"Wait. Cramer?" Mia's forehead wrinkled in memory.

"Yes." The detective looked at Mia, puzzled.

"Did you have a wife that died in a car accident in 1971?" You would think with all his extra weight, he couldn't move that fast, but he was in front of her on one knee before she realized he moved. His eyes filled with sadness.

"How did you know that? How?" He gripped her leg, and she felt Cole stiffen behind her. She caught an exchanged look between Cole and the sheriff.

Mia crossed the line of weirdness a while ago, so nothing she said in front of them from now on could make her feel any weirder. "I know you'll think this is odd, but I have dinner with her almost every night. Her resting place is by my favorite spot at the funeral home. I just told her the other night that they put up the barricade where her car accident happened."

"Alleged, car accident. She had bite marks on her." Cramer stood, tension washed across his face.

"And they weren't from you?"

"I wasn't a vampire then."

"You loved her. I can see that. I'm sorry for your loss."

"Mia. You can tell me what happened, can't you?" His grip tightened on her knee. "Have you talked to her? Can you do that? I need to know. I need to bring her killer to justice." His eyes began to glow. "You can talk to the dead, right?"

"She's talking to *you*, isn't she, Cramer?" the sheriff asked and cleared his throat. "Let's get back to work."

Cramer's face hardened, and he nodded to them. The nodding thing is just not good enough for something like this, she thought as she reached out, grabbing his hand. He tilted his head and looked at her touch.

"I promise I'll try to find out what happened."

Cramer brought her hand to his lips, breathing in deeply as he gently laid a kiss upon her skin before taking out a pad and pen from his pocket. Tom lifted himself onto the empty table next to her, and Cole stood behind her. Russo stayed clear across the room.

"Mia, you said it looked like they were all in the same patch of woods?" the sheriff began. Leaning back, he folded his arms in front of him.

"Yes."

"Tell me what else you saw that was a commonality between them."

"Well, I can tell you they were all gathered by the same man. They went willingly, and there was a sense that once their bodies were found, no one would care much. Is that true? Is there something about them that would make people not care about them?"

"Detectives, what do you think?" The sheriff eyed his men.

She felt Cole's hands leave the chair as he spoke. His voice sent waves of electricity through her. "They were all illegals. Someone knew we had many unidentified illegal immigrants washing up on the beach. They knew we wouldn't look at the bodies too much, assuming they'd drowned. The one with the car was an illegal also—a relative to one of our local gang members." Cole's voice deepened as he continued. "Who said this was a car accident? I don't recall seeing a car at the scene. Russo, you were lead—where was the car?"

"We didn't have a vehicle. We had two witnesses that said they saw a Buick run her over." Russo moved a step closer to the group.

Mia laughed unexpectedly, and everyone looked at her.

"Something you want to share, Mia?" the sheriff asked with an arched brow.

"Yeah, find the two guys that claimed to be witnesses. They were probably the ones that dumped the body. They didn't come off as being bright in the visions. Hell, they are probably driving around in a Buick." The sheriff smiled at her in a way a father smiles at his child that accomplished something, and it warmed her.

"Well, let's wrap this up for tonight, and let Mia get home. We've got three dead girls and one killer so—"

Mia cleared her throat. "I'm sorry for interrupting, sheriff, but you have three dead girls and three killers.

None of the vampires were the same." Their expressions instantly changed.

"Oh, shit," the sheriff muttered. "Well, at least we think we have one of them. Cramer, call over to Sector 13, and find out where Victor Tino is. Last we heard, he went to Italy. He fits Mia's description of a shifting vampire. Everyone report back to me tomorrow. Mia, Cole—you two, come with me." They followed him through the far door, leaving everyone else behind. Once inside, he turned to them.

"Mia, I want to show you something, only because I have taken a liking to you, and I hope we can come to an understanding. We need each other. You're sharp, and you look at things others don't, with or without your special trait." He wiped his mouth with his hand as he continued. "Cole, you're one of my oldest and dearest friends. We watch each other's back. I've never kept anything from you, and you have extended me the same courtesy. I wanted you here because I want you to see and hear everything that I'm going to say to her. Walk this way."

They walked in silence into the next room. In front of them was a section of two-sided glass. A man in a prison uniform sat in a chair on the other side. Mia scanned the room. It appeared to be an infirmary. Two nurses stood next to the man, one taking his blood.

They moved on, passing through another room that descended with a set of stairs. The sound of machines grew louder as they continued walking. The sheriff lifted a curtain that covered a glass window and tilted his head toward it.

Mia watched the machines as they took familiar black canisters and packed them with bags of blood. They slid down a conveyer belt to another machine that fitted the heat packs.

As she watched the machines, a female worker walked by with her lips tightly wrapped around a straw protruding out of an IV bag. Mia looked closer. She recognized her as one of the nurses from the room they had just passed through. "This is how you get your blood? From the prisoners?" Mia asked as she stared through the glass.

The sheriff smiled, watching her look at the machine like she was memorizing every gear that turned within it. "Yes. No blood is to be taken from a law-abiding citizen without permission or just cause. We have laws, Mia. Cole and I have been upholding the law for a very long time."

"Does every vampire have this as a food option?"

"No, not every vampire can be trusted. This is mostly for law enforcement," Cole answered.

"Why not give it to them all?"

"Job security. Vampires still have bills and taxes, Mia." The sheriff chuckled. "Plus, we wouldn't have enough for supply and demand for everyone."

"Others are allowed to attack and feed from humans?" Her tone held a touch of anger, the visions from before still dancing in her mind.

"No. They can only legally feed from a giving source. Some humans know about us, and some enjoy it, Mia." The sheriff's smile lit a glow in his eyes, and Mia pulled back at his excitement.

"Do the prisoners know what you're doing?"

"No, we test them twice a month for diseases, and take a couple pints of blood in the process. We know the individuals who keep clean and the ones who have bad blood. We rotate the donors so we don't harm them by taking too much."

Mia was trying to grasp the new information. The sheriff was telling her the process as carefree as someone telling her how to stock a shelf at a grocery store. "Sheriff, why are you telling me this? Isn't this sacred?" Again, she found a look of sincerity in his eyes.

"Mia, my name is John Carr. Please, call me John when we're not working. To answer your question, yes. This is very sacred. No other human citizen knows about this. I will trust that you will keep it with you."

"Why did you tell me then? I don't want this knowledge. How do you hide it from everyone else?" She took a deep breath. Thoughts of what might happen to her if she didn't keep quiet played in her mind.

"First off, we're the government. We can hide anything. Stick with us long enough, earn my trust, and maybe you'll meet Jimmy Hoffa. Second, I'm telling you this because you have pushed Cole to his breaking point. He obviously feels strongly about you, and you have seen some things tonight that have frightened you. I want you to know that we're all not like what you've seen."

She took in every word John had said. Frightened was an understatement. She wanted to know things and had a ton of questions.

"Do you... Do you all feed from humans like the man on death row and in my visions?" She held her breath waiting for the response.

"No, those are two completely different feedings that you witnessed. Besides, I think Cole has been to death row maybe twice since I've known him. And he would never kill the innocent, Mia. Besides, he only likes to feed from women—he gets aroused too much when he feeds from the vein, and he doesn't want to be near a man when that happens."

She blushed, remembering how big Cole's arousal felt when he pressed it against her body. Her pulse jumped and Cole moved forward with a knowing grin. *Damn it.*

"All right, John, that's enough about my arousal. If she has questions about that, she can ask me."

"But you won't answer my questions. Do you change?" His smile faded, and he remained silent. "If you won't tell me, will you allow John to tell me?" she asked, looking back at John. "Does he change?"

"That's not for me to tell you, Mia. A vampire's power is a personal thing. I want the two of you to stay away from each other, emotionally and sexually until we can get this case solved. Understood?"

"Is John older than you, Cole? I mean, do you have to do what he says?" She turned to back to John. "Are you his master?"

An unexpected burst of laughter came from John. He smacked Cole on the shoulder and laughed harder. Cole's body stiffened at his teasing.

"Mia, you're cute. You aren't afraid to ask anything, are you? Yes, I'm older and stronger, but no, I'm not his master. The only tie a vampire has is to his maker, his sire, but even that has an out. If you don't have a maker anymore, then you can be claimed by another vampire for protection and such. Our world is kind of like *The Godfather*. We have an understanding to respect our elders, or there will be consequences." He glanced at Cole. "Yes, he has to do what I say, but I suspect there are some things that'll make him break an order." He chuckled as he glanced over at Cole again. "Cole, bring her to Sector 13 tomorrow. I want to do some tests on her, see what she's got. Mia, I have some more questions for you. I'll see you both tomorrow."

Mia blinked, and he was gone, leaving her standing alone with Cole. Unable to speak, she froze, and her pulse started to beat rapidly. Cole glided past her to the door behind them. She followed him up a set of stairs, directly out into the parking lot, grateful she didn't have to walk through the matrix with him.

They drove in silence, and she found herself nodding off. When her eyes fluttered open, Cole was tucking her into bed.

"Thanks, but I can't sleep in these clothes. I'm going to take a quick shower first." The heat surfaced in her cheeks as she brought her eyes to his. The thought of him being there while she was naked in the shower started the tingling sensation between her thighs. Then her mind clicked on an image of him as a vampire-wolf. A shudder ran through her, and she looked away from him.

His muscles tensed at her reaction. He quickly turned from her and walked over to the couch. "You take your shower. I'll stay until my shift is over," he said in a deflated tone.

Mia nodded in vampire fashion. Since he was staying, she needed to find something more appropriate to wear after her shower. She searched through her drawer, but never having been put in this situation before, she realized she had nothing appropriate. Grabbing her usual tank and panties, Mia headed toward the shower, and chanced a quick glance at him before she went behind the divider. His eyes were on her, caressing her skin as she disappeared behind it.

She was relieved to wash the smell of the night's events off her body. Her mind did a medical check— ribs, face, kidneys. All seemed fine, just a little bruised. Mia turned toward the water. The stream beat on her nipples, instantly they hardened to painful points. She imagined Cole's lips around them and tilted her head back, arching herself toward the water. *What would it feel like to have his mouth on me?* A soft, unchecked moan drifted out of her. Mia jerked her head straight, and jumped away from the water. *Jesus. What the hell is wrong with me?*

Mia seldom thought about sex. Now she couldn't stop thinking about it. She quickly finished washing, being extra careful not to let her hands linger anywhere. She pulled on her wrap to cover her tank and panties before stepping out from behind the divider.

"Better?"

She trailed her eyes over him and froze on his knowing grin. *Oh, God. He knows I was thinking of him.* Cole was deadly in more ways than he knew. He was drop dead gorgeous, confident, and the essence of power. She took a deep breath. "Yes, thank you. You look tired, Cole." Although she thought vampires weren't supposed to get tired, maybe he was stressed or something. According to the sheriff, it was her fault.

"Well, I've had a rough night." He gazed at her with an accusatory look and leaned against the sliding glass doors by the balcony. She followed his hand down as he adjusted his jeans.

"Oh, Jesus." She covered her eyes. "I'm sorry. I didn't know you were—"

"As I said, I've had a rough night. Your shower was just icing on the cake. The thought of the water gliding over your naked body." He rubbed his hand over his mouth. "It's not only your blood—I want to taste every inch of your flesh. And your soft moan only my ears could hear, did this." He pointed to the hard bulge in his pants. "I was imagining my hands gliding over your breasts, washing you with the scented soap I can smell on your skin. It's on my to do list."

"I... I..." She couldn't find the words.

"I am a man, Mia. You excite me. Yes, I'm hard. No need to struggle for something to say but before you go to bed, I want you to know that it took every ounce of strength I had not to comfort you tonight. Seeing you cry as you did the other night... I could feel your pain,

Mia. It shot through me like daggers of ice. Then you looked at me like *I* was a monster. Yes. I'm exhausted."

"It's all too much, too fast. I never wanted to cause you grief, I'm only trying to be honest. I've been through some... things in my life that I'm not ready to share with anyone. Maybe this isn't a good idea, you being here. If you got hurt because you were tired, because of me, I'd feel awful. You scare the hell out of me, but I don't want you to get hurt."

"Well, if it will make you happy, I'll close my eyes once you're in bed."

Climbing under the sheets, she pulled the covers up to her shoulders. Once safely hidden from his eyes, she wiggled out of her wrap. She felt the heat of his stare, but was too tired to be scared or embarrassed. She turned on her back and quickly drifted off into a sweet, naughty dream.

Cole's gaze stroked her entire body as he walked toward her. Slowly, like a predator, he latched onto her eyes, holding them captive. He unbuttoned his shirt and pushed it past his shoulders, exposing his masculine chest. As the fabric slid off his arms, his muscles twitched. She wanted to trace her fingers over every muscle in his body, and she could feel her fingers gliding over the bumps on his stomach.

She wanted him closer, needed him closer. He placed a knee on the bed, but held his distance. His image began to fade, and she fought to keep the dream going. "No, not yet. Please, come to me. Please, Cole. Come to me." The urge to have him built within her. She wanted him. She needed him.

She felt her hand drifting into the wetness her dream had created, and her eyes fluttered open at her touch. With wide eyes she jerked her head back into the pillow. Cole hovered above her, and she was looking directly at him. His eyes were closed, and his arms were folded in front of him. She opened her mouth to scream.

Cole's eyes snapped open at the sound of her inhaled breath. His hand flew over her mouth, and he fell from his levitated state, covering her body with his and trapping her arms.

His eyes searched around in confusion. "What just happened?" His gaze flicked down as she jerked beneath him, but he still kept his senses sharp and his keen eyes surveyed the room. His features relaxed and he looked down again as Mia tugged harder on her hand trapped between her legs. Cole rolled over to his side and rested against her body.

"What were you dreaming about?" His voice was low, and his mouth curved into a devilish smile.

"Wouldn't you like to know?"

"Oh, yes. I would. Because I think I missed something fun."

"Well, it's none of your business," she answered, quickly.

"I need to figure out how I got over here. I closed my eyes over there." He inclined his head toward the sliding glass doors. "Now I'm on top of you in your bed. Not that it's a bad place to be, but I need to know what you were dreaming. Was I coming to protect you?"

She turned her head away from his probing eyes. Her mind struggled to formulate a confession. "No, you weren't."

"There's a nervous edge in your voice, and your heart is pounding, Mia. If I wasn't coming to protect you, then what were you dreaming about?" His eyebrow arched, mischievously.

Persistent, as usual—he was a master of interrogation. She slowly turned toward him. Even in the dark, his eyes were inviting. His expression changed the minute her eyes locked with his. He knew.

"You, Cole. I was dreaming of you. I called to you. I wanted you to come to me." She searched his face and waited for the smile of victory he usually gave, but it didn't come.

"Interesting. I think you should have a talk with your mother, and tell her about this." He began to roll off the bed, and she grabbed his arm. He turned to her.

"Cole, I have to know—do you change?" Her eyes were wide, and she knew her face had scrunched into an agonizing expression, bracing herself for his answer.

He stood and tucked the blankets around her body, gently brushing her cheek with the back of his hand. "What would it change if I answered? Can you answer that?"

She shook her head.

Cole walked away from her and grabbed his radio off the couch. He looked back. "I need to go now. My relief is already here. I'll see you tomorrow. And next time, will you consider me as an alternative to self-satisfaction?" His lips curved into wicked grin.

Mia shook her head. "You're impossible. Goodnight, Detective." She turned her back to him as he made his leave.

SEVENTEEN

*M*ia awoke to the smell of coffee. The scent filled her senses, pulling her to a conscious state. She took a deep breath and stretched. The dull ache in her body reminded her of last night. The steam from the coffee maker hissed.

Mmm... coffee. She jolted upright, her eyes darting around the room. *Wait. Who made coffee?* She pulled the covers up to her neck.

"Hello? Is anyone here?" She jumped at the knock on the door.

"Miss Starr, it's Detective Gonela. Is everything okay?"

She heard the voice through the door and hurried over to it, cracking it just enough to peek.

"Have you been in my apartment, Detective?"

"No. Is everything okay?" he asked, looking alert and ready to break down the door if needed.

Mia looked behind her and inspected the room. Her eyes fell upon a note that was wedged between the salt and peppershaker on the table.

"Yep, everything's okay. Thank you." She shut the door, went straight for the note, and stared down at it. *Coffee first.* As she filled her mug with caffeine, her eyes strayed to her discarded clothes on the floor. She sat her mug on the counter and went to the scattered clothes. It drove her crazy to see things out of place.

When she picked up her jeans, she noticed a lump in the pocket. She pulled out the torn piece of shirt from last night, and the tip of her fingers grazed across something hard. Fumbling around inside the pocket, she closed her fingers around the object and pulled out a small piece of red rock. She rolled the piece of brick between her fingers, smiling at its rough edges. *When did he put this in my pocket?* A lot happened last night, but she couldn't place when he'd slipped it in.

She hurried over to the note. Her eyes scanned the paper. *"You need to be at this address downtown at seven p.m. You can't miss the building—it's twenty-one stories with dark, tinted windows. It's known as The Darth Vader building. Go to the eighteenth floor and give your name at the receptionist desk. Wait for me. I'll be there. I left something in your pocket last night when we were in the graveyard. You gave me your trust—remember that. Cole."*

She sat down on the couch sipping her coffee as she dialed her mom's number.

"Mom, I need to talk to you. In person. Something weird happened last night."

"Something different, other than your day-to-day weirdness?" her mother asked, laughing into the phone.

Mia sighed. "Yes, Mother. Something very *unusual*."

"I see. I'll be there tomorrow. I'll stop by on the way to the doctor's."

"Great, I'll have your favorite coffee creamer ready." She was excited. Even if she knew the conversation would be weird, she missed her mom.

"Mia, you're not going to like what I'm gonna tell you." Her mom's taunting tone only confirmed that she was taking joy in this already.

"Mom, it can't be any worse than what's going on right now." Mia held the phone away from her ear as her mom's laughter vibrated the speaker.

"Mia, it can always be worse. I'll see you tomorrow."

She tapped her finger on the phone. There was something else she had to do today. The silver. *Oh, crap.* She'd forgotten the box in Cole's trunk, but she could still call her friend Bernie about what she had planned.

Bernie was a big, civil war reenactment geek and during events at the South Florida fair, he was the village blacksmith—a very talented one, too. She hung up the phone with him after assuring him she didn't need him to make jewelry, and explained the list of items she wanted made out of the silver after it was melted down. She would drop everything off tomorrow.

Mia looked into her closet. Cole didn't say how to dress for the meeting. She decided on a pair of jeans, a white top, and a pair of black boots. She clipped half of her hair back behind her ears, leaving the rest flowing down her back. Before leaving, she quickly tossed a black blazer over her one shoulder.

Detective Gonela was already in his car. She motioned for him to follow her, then realized how silly that was, knowing he'd follow her regardless.

Cole was right. You couldn't miss the building. Compared to the other structures, it looked dark and ominous—something Batman would use as a hideout. The entire structure looked as if it were made of black glass, and in between each floor was a strip of red that circled the building.

It was just as magnificent on the inside as it was on the out. She glanced at the buttons inside the elevator as the man beside her pushed his floor number.

"You look lost..."

"No. I... ahh... forgot something." She quickly jumped out of the elevator and bumped into Detective Gonela.

"I bet you're confused. Sorry. I tried to catch you before you got into the elevator. Let's take this one over here." He tilted his head toward the open elevator on the other side.

"There is no eighteenth floor. How am I supposed to push something that doesn't exist? Look. It skips eighteen and goes right to twenty-one."

"Mia, you have to stop thinking things don't exist. Everything is a possibility." He chuckled through his warm smile and took out a little fob that was on his key chain. He held the fob next to where the button for floor eighteen should have been. When the fob was in front of the missing number, the space began to glow red, and the elevator jerked into motion. So did her nerves.

If this door opened and Tommy Lee Jones was on the other side, she was going to freak the fuck out.

"Miss Starr, once the doors open you'll see a reception desk. Go over to the desk, give them your name, and then have a seat and wait for Cole. You can't get into any rooms unless you're escorted." He grinned as the doors shut.

"Thank you, Detective." Her mind was spinning with speculation. Mia had no clue what to expect. Excitement mixed with her nerves, and the adrenaline began to pump. She craved this feeling and the adventure was really doing it for her. It sure as hell beat working at Stan's gas station. The funeral home was different because she found the place interesting, but not on this level.

She walked straight ahead to the receptionist's desk. The black marble floor reflected the images from above like a mirror. The tile continued up the walls and sparkled as she walked past. The only thing in the room was the desk and a long bench that sat to the side of it. There were no doors or windows.

Two girls sat behind the chest-high desk, one standing as she approached.

"Hi. You must be Miss Starr. Please, have a seat." Her tone was polite. She looked to be in her early twenties with long brown hair and to much makeup.

"Thanks," Mia said as she sat on the bench.

The second girl stood to pull something off the counter, and Mia glanced at her. She was much prettier than girl number one, with black shimmering hair that swayed past her shoulders, full lips lightly painted, as was the rest of her face, and man-made breasts. The size didn't seem natural for her small frame. *Jesus.* Mia giggled. *If she was in a plane crash, she could use her breasts as a flotation device.*

Mia picked up a magazine, trying to drown out their chatter. They caught up on TV shows, and what they were watching tonight, then it got interesting. They started talking about a man.

Now Mia understood why Shannon liked gossip so much. This was getting juicy. Mia turned toward their voices.

"Oh, God. That man makes me melt just by looking at me—he is so damn good-looking." They laughed and giggled as they continued to talk.

"I know what you mean, girl. You know, I heard he once gave a girl an orgasm *just by looking at her*. And making love to him is maddening."

"No way!"

Mia was hanging onto every word.

"He's still single, too. I would love to make that man happy. Watch—I'm going see if I can get him to hug me this time."

"What time did you say Cole was coming in? I want to go freshen up before he gets here."

Mia stopped breathing, her chest tightening. He doesn't belong to her; she shouldn't be jealous. But she was. Her knee began to bounce which was one of many nervous ticks that she had. She didn't like these girls.

The brown-haired girl ran into a small hallway behind the desk emerging a couple of minutes later, smelling like a prostitute. Mia honestly didn't think she could apply any more makeup, but she did. *Does she think men like that? Wait. Do they?* She wondered if Cole liked that.

Mia's jealously flared as they continued the conversation. She couldn't concentrate on what they were saying. All she could think of was ripping the shiny black hair out of the woman's head. The elevator dinged and out walked their king. *Will they come around the counter and bow at his feet?*

His eyes met hers, and his lips curled into a gorgeous smile. Then they diverted from her to the two bimbos behind the counter.

"Hi, Detective Barnett," they said in unison.

They must be attached at the brain. Mia put her hand on her leg to stop it from bouncing. Her face tightened as the jealously boiled inside, and she couldn't stop the heat from creeping into her face. Cole paused when he reached her. *Fuck, he knows.* He turned his head and gave her a knowing grin, which made her temper even hotter. *Ass!*

"Well, good evening, ladies. Don't the two of you look lovely this evening?" He approached the desk, playing them...and her.

Cole's body reacted as soon as he felt Mia's blood soaring. He'd thought about her all night—mostly about her hand wiggling between them. Cole longed to feel a woman underneath him, and last night set him on fire. It would have been easy to slip his hand under hers and help her relieve her sexual needs. Mia needed it just as much as he did, and no matter what she said, he would be the one to give her that release. Cole couldn't help but play this up. Mia did feel something for him, and if this was the only way he could bring it out of her, then he was going to use it to his full advantage.

The black-haired girl batted her lashes so fast she was at risk of losing an eye. She leaned far over the counter toward him, enough for him to see her store-bought chest.

"Oh, Detective. I've missed you. You haven't been here in a while. Can I come around for a hug?" She moved off the counter, and Cole stepped back. Before he could answer, he felt the jealousy shoot out of Mia like a bottle rocket, and she was on her feet.

"You most certainly cannot." She gave them a hostile glare.

The girl stopped dead in her tracks, shooting daggers at Mia as she spoke. "And, why not?"

Cole stared at Mia, waiting for her answer with a grin. *Say it. Because I'm yours, and you don't want her touching me.*

"Because... he's on duty, and this is a place of business. He's not here to have your fake boobs flopping all over him." The girl jumped back as if Mia's words slapped her, and she retreated behind the desk. Mia turned her gaze back to Cole, "Can we go? I don't want to be here all day while you try to get a date."

He raised an eyebrow as he tilted his head, looking into her eyes. "Oh, I don't think I was trying, but since you're in a hurry—right this way, Miss Starr." He gestured with his hand to walk to the other side of the room.

"Shall I throw rose petals at your feet?" she said with a British accent, while glaring back at him. His smile broadened. "I hate your perpetual calm manner. There's no door here. Would you like me to walk through the wall?" Her voice was still inflamed.

He reached out and pushed a tiny tile that blended into the wall, causing it to slide open, and then put his hand on her back, following her through the opening.

"You need to learn how to control all that emotion. Like I said before, you need an outlet." He smiled as they walked over to the table sitting in the middle of the room.

The room was simple, but because of the variety of equipment scattered around, Mia couldn't tell if it was a test lab, or used for meetings. Cole pulled out a chair and motioned for Mia to sit down. Her temper was still hot. With a defiant glare, she shook her head.

"Why do you have to be so difficult? I need you to relax. Please, sit down." His tone never wavered from calm.

She slammed herself down into the chair, simultaneously crossing her arms and legs. Cole's eyes narrowed. He bent down to whisper in her ear. "All that heat in your blood is getting me excited. As for that little incident out in the waiting room—now you know how I felt at the night club."

She leaned her head back until their eyes met, the memory of how she acted that night coming back to her. "You're right, but I'm sure she doesn't have a Porsche I can demolish. How am I supposed to calm myself down as you did?" As soon as the words left her lips, she wanted to press a button to recall the message. She was instantly reminded that you shouldn't ask a question if you didn't want the answer to it.

He was so close that she felt her breath bounce off his face. He brushed his lips over hers, and she tightly wrapped her fingers around the arms of the chair, her skin tingled from the sensation.

Cole closed his eyes and moved his lips to her cheek, brushing them lightly over her skin.

Fire and passion replaced her anger. Mia didn't move as he continued his gentle motion, moving back to her lips. Her hand twitched as her brain told it to grab the back of his head and bring him down to her mouth, hard. Images of Cole sinking his fangs into her skin, an untamed look in his eyes, flashed through her mind. She couldn't tell if it was a vision formed from fear, or a forewarning. Her whole body tensed.

Cole's eyelids popped open. His expression held the knowledge that something inside her sex drive malfunctioned, and he had lost her once more. His hands gripped the chair, as his tongue darted out to lick his fang. Mia watched his eyes move to her neck and then with an internal grunt, he pushed himself off the chair and backed away from her.

"Did that help any?" His seductive voice rolled in her ears.

Mia straightened herself in the chair and tried to regain her composure. If she opened her mouth to speak, her words would fall out in an incomprehensible order. All she could do was smile in response.

The door on the other side of the room opened, and Mia was glad to see another person. She couldn't trust herself to be alone with Cole. Her body would give in to him eventually. Would he be disappointed soon after? Could she give him what he needed? The man who entered the room brushed his hands down his lab coat. Mia stood to greet him. He had at least five inches on her, with a medium build. His black hair was neatly cut on the sides, and missing on top.

"Hello, Cole. And you must be Miakoda Starr. My name is Alfred." He extended his hand, giving Mia's a warm shake.

"Hi, Al. You can call me Mia." She quickly scanned him—human, a brilliant one, too, but very sad.

Cole sat in a chair to the right of Mia, and Al seated himself in front of her. He put a pad on the table and leaned forward, clasping his hands together and entwining his fingers. His voice reminded her of a counselor—soft and even.

"Mia, I'm going to ask you some questions. We want to get an understanding of what you can do. Please start from the beginning, and tell me about the auras and the visions." He sat back, sliding the pad and pen off the desk and resting it in his lap.

"I don't know what to tell you. Where do you want me to begin?" Her tone camouflaged her nerves.

Al leaned forward, putting his forearms on the table. "Mia, you stared down a vampire. *Two* vampires. We know the one that tried to kidnap you was a fledgling, so his powers weren't that strong. We don't know anything about the one from your workplace, but if he was stronger than the fledgling, then you have a very powerful mind. We need to find out how powerful." Al leaned back and concentrated on Mia.

Mia's throat was suddenly dry. Her hands were starting to sweat. She palmed her jeans, a nervous trait she suspected Cole had come to recognize. She glanced at him, catching his stare. *Why did he watch her like he did, studying her, and why did they need to know all of this?* Her mind needed a diversion.

"I'm sorry—what's a fledgling?"

Al looked at Cole before he spoke, and Cole nodded. "A fledgling is a newly made vampire."

A breathy sound came from Mia's nose. "I wish that was in their vampire aura, because that would help me a lot. Maybe it was... The fledgling was dimmer than the others."

Cole's body went rigid at her words and Al shot straight out of his chair. He stared at her with wide eyes.

"What... what do you mean by that? Can you see them? I mean, could you pick a vampire out of a crowd?" His voice was unsteady. He swallowed hard as he waited for her response.

She looked at Cole. He was leaning forward, waiting for her answer. His forehead wrinkled with worry.

Mia's pulse took off like a jet. She had slipped, and she knew it. She never wanted anyone to know this. She abruptly stood, and Cole's hand quickly clamped over hers. "You're not running. Sit."

"I don't want to do this." Her voice rang with panic.

His thumb stroked the top of her hand. "I will protect you, Mia. Always."

Al cleared his throat. "Mia, can you see them? This is very important."

Mia fell back into the chair, cursing herself for her mistake. She put her elbows on her knees and then put her face into her hands. She was a dumbass for slipping. Taking a deep breath, she looked at Al. "Yes, I can see them."

Cole's hands tightened around the arms of the chair, and the wood creaked under his strength.

Al's face went through several expressions: ecstatic, frightened, worried. He looked over at Cole. "Cole, the chair. Please, you are about to break it. You know it's hard for me to get any new equipment around here."

"Al, this does not leave this room. Understood?" Cole leaned forward. His eyes seemed to jab Al as he backed away from him.

"Yes, Cole. Of course." Sweat beaded on Al's temple. He removed a handkerchief. Dabbing his forehead, he sat down and grabbed his pen. He looked over at Cole who was shaking his head and he immediately put the pad down. He took a deep breath before continuing.

"Mia, have you picked up any images from the vampires?"

"No, I don't think so." She scrunched her face as she tried to remember if she had.

Cole looked instantly relieved. Al's eyes went between the both of them again.

"Have you tried? Did you see anything when either of the vampires grabbed you?" Al shifted his feet and dabbed his forehead with his handkerchief. He was starting to make her feel uneasy.

She rubbed her palms on her jeans, back and forth until Cole's hand went over hers. Mia looked into his eyes and took a deep calming breath. "The only time I've tried to see any images was in the graveyard, with Cole, and recently in the morgue. Other than that, they just sort of pop in."

Al placed his pen on the table, his elbows rested on the chair, and he clasped his fingers in front of him. "Well, let's do a test then. Mia, please stand. Cole, I'm going to need your assistance since you are the only vampire in the room."

Shit. Not good. Her mind scattered. Her body had a restraining order on Cole, because when she was near him, it betrayed her.

Al grabbed his pad from the table and walked over to stand in front of them. "Mia, you said the visions or images were stronger with contact, right? I want you to look into Cole's eyes and touch him. Let's see if we get anything." Al's tone lifted with excitement.

Crap! Mia turned to face Cole. *Just breathe.* She trailed her eyes up his frame and then settled into his deep brown gaze like a warm blanket. She instantly relaxed. God, how she wanted him.

"Mia, I need you to touch him." Al's voice guided her as he spoke.

"No. I don't want to touch him." Her voice sounded foreign as she fell deeper into Cole's eyes.

Her lids slid shut as Cole's hands glided into hers.

"Yes, you do," he whispered. "I know what you're really feeling. You can't hide the speed of your blood rushing through your veins every time I'm near you."

Mia's body jerked as the images quickly grabbed her.

"Mia, tell me what you see," Al said in a soft voice.

She was lost—lost in a dreamy state of mind. This was different from any vision she'd had before. She felt a sense of tranquility as the images continued.

There she was, lying on her canopy bed. Panties were the only thing covering her body. The glow from the moon illuminated the room, casting a blue glow over her bare skin. The white, sheer swags were pulled back and tied to the post with beautiful ribbons. Big, white, fluffy pillows elevated her body as she lay back on the bed. She felt completely relaxed. A pearl drop of blood ran down her neck like a bead of sweat on a hot summer day. It continued its journey down her skin and over her collarbone, trailing over the top of her breast. As the drop continued rolling down between her breasts, her hand slid down over her stomach and then to her thigh. Cole appeared at the end of the bed, his muscles bounced as he moved slowly toward her like a predator. The tinted glow from the moonlight lit his masculine chest like an object on display. He placed his knee on the bed, and his hand reached over to caress her inner thigh. It gave in to his soft touch and fell to the side, inviting him in. His eyes glowed with desire. His fangs jutted out, and she was unafraid. She knew they were about to be buried into her flesh. The anticipation of the bite drove her to madness. She was wet and ready.

"Mia, do you see anything?" Al's voice broke the vision, and Mia snatched her hands away from Cole. She turned toward Al, her face full of heat. Al took one look at her, and she knew he could tell where the visions went. "I'll take that as a yes. No need to answer. Cole, what were you thinking of?"

"If I left the flood lights on at my house." Cole turned his gaze to Mia as he answered, and she glared back at him.

"You were not."

"Why? Did you see something different?" Cole's expression scrunched with a puzzled look.

Her eyes narrowed at him. He was toying with her. *Wasn't he? Or was the vision all my doing?* She tried to swallow, but the dryness in her throat had increased.

"Al, can I get something to drink? Water or something, please?"

"Yes, Al. She does look a little... flushed. Get her some water, quickly, please. If I had something she could drink, I would give it to her right now." Cole's gaze heated as he looked at her.

Al pushed a couple of buttons on the desk phone, then hung up. He looked back at them. His eyebrows drew together at their demeanor, then he grabbed the pad of paper and sat down. "Since the two of you have come up with different images, I'm going to mark this test down as inconclusive for now."

Mia was still lost in thought as Al went to retrieve the drinks from the receptionist. She wasn't sure of herself. She didn't feel like the images came from her, but she could be wrong. She glanced at Cole who had sat down and relaxed back into the chair, stretching his legs out, crossing them at the ankles.

She sat down and took a sip of water as Al continued. Not only was she thirsty, but her body was still on fire. The visions were so intense she couldn't stop glancing at Cole's lap.

"Mia, have you ever heard of telekinesis?" Al cracked the cap on a bottle of water. "Few vampires have had this ability. For a human to have it...well, it's unheard of."

"I think so. That's like the movie, Carrie, right? Where she can move things with her mind?" She felt naïve when Al chuckled.

"Yes, that would be correct. Have you... ever moved anything without touching it?"

Cole looked at her, the excitement evident in his eyes. He waited for her to answer Al's question. Sadness filled her—she was going to disappoint him. She didn't have any vampire, super powers to make him proud.

"Nope, sorry. I haven't. I don't think my mind is that powerful. Do you, Al?" Curiosity lifted her brows.

"Mia, I don't think you realize how much mind power it takes to stare down a vampire. I want to try a couple of tests, but first you need to know that telekinesis requires a very high level of concentration."

Better ask Cole to leave then, her mind interjected.

"You need to focus, and you need to learn how to relax. You need to believe that the object will move. Those are the steps: Focus, believe, and then move the object." Al nodded on the last word as to mark his point.

"You make it sound so easy. Have you ever met anybody with this ability?" Mia leaned forward, getting wrapped in Al's fascination on the subject.

"No, I haven't. But I have always wanted to study someone who had it."

The door in the back of the room opened. A man walked in accompanied by a woman who was Mia's height. She had curves in all the right places on her thin frame, and her sun-kissed skin accentuated her light-brown eyes. The ends of her dark hair flared up and bounced on her shoulders as she walked into the room with confidence, brushing down the jacket to her pressed black suit.

Mia scanned them quickly. The woman was a vamp, but the man was not. He walked to the table and laid a stack of papers in front of Mia while the woman took a seat next to Cole.

Al stood and snapped his fingers in the air. "Oh, Mia, I almost forgot. I need to get a couple vials of blood from you."

Mia's eyes widened with panic. Her palms instantly became hot and damp. "Why?" Her voice trembled. She didn't wait for an answer. "I'd rather not. I have... a needle phobia." *A anything puncturing my skin phobia would be more accurate.*

"Mia, I have to. I won't hurt you. You can trust me."

Cole shook his head and placed a hand over his mouth as Mia took her battle stance against Al. "She would rather be strapped with meat and jump into a lion pit before she trusted someone." A tiny sound escaped Cole's nostrils at the thought.

"What?" Mia asked in an agitated tone.

"Hold off on the blood for a minute, Al."

The man who placed the papers on the desk laid a pen on the stack and pushed it toward Mia.

"Miss Starr, I'm Agent Kent with the FBI, Division 13. We monitor and protect all paranormal activity."

Mia slapped her hand to her mouth as uncontrollable laughter rolled out of her. "You're kidding me, right? Like The Men in Black?" Agent Kent wasn't amused, but Mia couldn't control her laughter.

"Has she been screened for drugs?" Kent asked.

"The next thing you're going to tell me is that aliens exist." Her laughter came to a halt. "Wait. Do they?"

Agent Kent's face remained expressionless. His lips drew to a tight, thin line as he spoke. "I'm not at liberty to say, ma'am. That's not my division."

Oh my God, he's serious. Change the topic, quick. She didn't want to be zapped with a mind ray gun or something.

"What are these papers?" She flipped through the stack, and a sickness settled in her stomach. On every page in front of her was information about her life. Everywhere she had lived, her neighbors, who she associated with, who they associated with and more.

"Where did you get all this information?" Her eyes went to him in disbelief.

"The Matrix."

Mia was beginning to think he didn't have a sense of humor, but his lips finally cracked into a full smile. "Is that really the name of it?"

Agent Kent looked at her as he pulled his shoulders back and straightened his posture. "We're the FBI, ma'am, that's what we do—we watch you. We believe you're in danger. Vampires have attacked you, and civilians are helping them. By signing these papers, you and your family will be protected. You now belong to us, and we will use your *skills* to help us capture the vampires."

"My mom may be in danger?" Mia's eyes snapped to Cole.

"This is all being thrown at you at once. I'd rather take you aside and tell you everything—let you absorb it." Cole glared at Agent Kent, then looked back to Mia. "I'm sorry I don't have control over this procedure. We don't know if your mom is in danger, Mia, but we'll do everything to protect her."

"If the people I associate with can be harmed, what about Cynthia? Cole, could they come for her?" Her voice rose in panic and she glanced at him.

"Yes, Mia, they could. That's why you shouldn't see her until we have the rogues in custody."

The woman who accompanied Agent Kent had been sitting quietly until now. She'd looked annoyed when she walked in, and now she looked completely put out. "Okay, this is absolutely ridiculous, and a complete waste of time. We have vampires breaking our laws and killing humans. They want her, so the solution is to use her as bait. They see her. They come for her. We capture them—Done. I have no patience for this other bullshit." There was a coldness to her voice that chilled Mia.

Cole stood so abruptly his chair flew back.

"Nancy, we are not using her for bait. If the three vampires from her visions are different from the two in the store, then we have five rogue vampires on the loose. We haven't seen such a high number of rogues in decades, and the fact that they are bringing civilians into their crimes is even more of a concern."

Nancy stood. She faced Cole with an intense look in her eyes. Mia could tell she wasn't afraid of anything. "Fine. Do it the hard way. Here's my card." She tossed her card toward Mia. "I'm the FBI agent assigned to you. Call me when you guys get your shit together." She didn't wait for anyone to speak. In a blink, she was gone.

Mia looked down at the stack of papers, signed them quickly, and gave them back to Agent Kent. He picked them up and left the room without a word.

Mia wanted everyone to leave. She'd been hoping for a better day than yesterday, but now that she knew her mom and Cynthia could be targets, her day had gone to shit.

Al turned around with a needle in his hand and a basket full of empty vials.

"I don't think so!" Mia inched back into the seat. The thought of the needle sent silent tears down her cheeks as her hands tightened around the arms of the chair.

Her pulse began to race, and the room spun as the nauseous feeling began to tug at her stomach.

Al walked over and set the basket on the table in front of her.

"Mia, we have to have your blood. It's for your own safety. Since you're not mated with a vampire or a carrier of one's blood in your veins, we need blood to give to a tracker in case you go missing."

She thought about it. It made sense, so she decided to tone down her objection. "Okay. I understand." She sighed and looked into Coles eye's begging for help. He moved his chair to sit in front of her, and then held her hands.

As Al put the elastic band around her forearm and began to tap her arm with his fingers, Cole's fangs popped. "I have an easier way of extracting the blood." Mia jumped, staring at him with tense eyes.

"Sorry." He shrugged. "No matter how hard I tried to fight it, I couldn't hold them in. It's all I think about when your blood starts racing. And if you only knew how jealous I am of those needles right now."

Al tapped her arm again, twisting it to look around at her veins. "Mia, I can see why you hate needles. You must have a hard time when someone takes your blood—you have no veins," he said, intensely staring at her arm.

"You have no idea how many times I have been poked, Al." The thought of him sticking her repeatedly was wreaking havoc on her stomach. It wasn't actually the needle. It was the penetration that made the dark memories swirl. Her grip tightened around Cole's hand.

"Mia, you have to relax or it will hurt. Relax." Cole's voice was soft and soothing as he leaned closer to her. "Is this why you have an issue with biting?"

Her fear escalated at the mere mention of her issue. She slowly shook her head. At least, it wasn't the *root* of her fear.

"Will you tell me why?"

"No." The dark memory started to climb up inside her until it choked her.

"I'm sorry, Mia. I'm going to have to stick it in the top of your hand. You really have no veins. I can't find any of them." Al sighed in defeat.

That was the worst place to be stuck with a needle. Mia dug her nails into Cole's hand, and he winced. When she looked at him, it was as if he felt the intense fear sparking out of her body. He knew it was making her physically sick.

"Al, don't put it in her hand. I can assure you, she has plenty of veins. Give me a minute." Cole pulled his chair closer to hers and turned her head to face him. He took the arm Al had chosen to draw blood from. Staring into her eyes, his fingers slowly stroked her skin, then came up to her neck to gently caress her artery.

Mia felt the energy spark from his lips as they hovered just above hers. "Let it go," he whispered.

Her breathing relaxed as she dived into the depths of his eyes. The sounds in the room became muffled in her mind except for an annoying snapping sound in the background.

"Okay. All done. Thanks, Cole." Al tapped her arm and removed the elastic band.

Cole searched her eyes. "I could stare at you forever. Every time I look deep inside you, I find more of myself—parts I thought were lost." He spoke just above a whisper before he stood.

Finally allowing herself to blink, she pulled away from Cole's stare. "I feel it too. What was that, what did you do to me?" She turned toward Al. "Did you say you're done? I didn't feel anything. Thank you for not hurting me." The sincerity in her voice made Al beam.

"Thank Cole. He's the one that distracted you and made your veins surface. Just give me a minute while I label the vials."

Mia stood. The hard chair and her tense posture stiffened her body. She began to work out the kinks, twisting and stretching her limbs. "What do you mean he made my veins surface?" She tilted her head toward Cole who was giving Al a look of warning.

"That's something you need to speak with him about."

"We will talk later." His voice was firm as she turned to him for answers, and she knew not to press the matter.

"Can I walk around and stretch? All this sitting has my legs hurting. Oh, and can I ask you some questions, Al?" Mia clasped her hands together and stretched them over her head.

"Sure, of course you can," Al replied as he pressed a label onto a tiny vial of blood.

Mia kicked her legs out to get the blood flowing and then began to walk around the room. She inspected the old photos on the walls as she walked past them, circling the room.

"How come you're not a vampire, Al? I mean, everyone else seems to have a weird aura except for you—yours is normal." She stared at one of the photos, waiting for his answer.

"I haven't proven myself yet. Once I do, they'll make me a vampire like I've asked. I have hopes. They need a scientist on their side anyway." Al halted his task, suddenly he seemed lost in a memory.

Mia turned from the picture she was staring at with an expression of bewilderment, and Cole stood in silence, leaning against the table with his arms crossed over his chest. He was relaxed, and she knew his gaze never left her as she walked around the room.

"Why would you want to be a vampire?" Her questions seemed to pain Al, and he quickly looked back down, grabbing another label to continue his task. He cleared his throat before he spoke. "I lost my wife to cancer. I pledged to her that I would find a cure so no one would have to see the people they love be eaten away by the disease. I promised her I would stop the suffering. If I become a vampire, I can live forever, and I will find a cure." His voice was distant, yet he spoke with confidence and pride for the destiny he wanted to follow. It tugged at Mia's heart. Then in a flash, a quick image played in her head of Al holding his wife's hand as she took her last breath. Mia squeezed her eyes tight and quickly shoved it out, not wanting to intrude on their private moment.

"Al, I'm sorry for your loss, and, if that's what you really want, I hope you get to become a vampire." Mia caught a glimpse of Cole. His lips twitched with a smile and he looked happy that she wanted someone to become a vampire. To become like him.

Al breathed deeply before picking up the next vial. Mia was touched by the love she still saw in him for his wife. She wondered what it would be like to love someone that much and be loved in return.

"Was that all your questions, Mia?" Al asked.

"Oh, no. How do you kill a vampire?"

Cole snapped his head toward her so fast Mia thought his head would pop off. She got the same reaction from Al.

"Why would you want to know such a thing?" Al's stunned expression was completely different from Cole's, who was glaring at her.

"Because I need to know how to protect myself. I don't like to depend on others. In my experience, they usually let you down." Cole's features softened a bit, but his face remained hard.

It was just a question. I guess he's relieved I didn't say, "Because, I want to ram a stake through Cole's heart while he's sleeping."

He shifted his stance. Mia could see she had upset him, but she still didn't fully trust him. Al looked at Cole who nodded, giving Al permission to answer. Mia rolled her eyes. This was getting ridiculous. If Al needed approval from Cole every time she asked a question, she might as well just ask Cole the damn questions. Then, she had another thought and her stomach turned. Was she being disrespectful for asking Al and not Cole? Oh, God, that's not what she intended to do.

"Cole, I'm sorry, should I be asking you these questions? I just thought this was Al's job and..."

"No. This is his job, and I'd rather you hear things from him, instead of me. Just understand he has to follow protocol. There are some things he is not permitted to tell you. This is why he's asking for permission, which I see is annoying you," he said with a wink.

"You don't miss a thing, do you, Detective?"

"Not where you're concerned, Miss Starr."

She smiled and continued walking around admiring the pictures as Al spoke. "Some things are different than how movies and literature have painted them. Sunlight will burn a vampire quickly, and if left in the sun, they will die. The sun completely drains a vampire of everything—power and blood. The vampire will look like a mummified corpse afterward. Fire—but you better make sure the vampire is completely disintegrated. A light burn will do nothing but make them mad. Silver, as you already know, makes them weak and drains their powers, plus, it burns. Wooden stakes do little, but silver through the heart will kill them, as long as you shred the heart in the process. Of course, that would probably kill a human, too. But you already know that from Art." He looked at her with a curious expression. "Mia, I was wondering—how did you know that sword would kill Art? I mean, most swords are made from steel."

"Most are made of steel, but some of the swords from the cavalry period used a Niello alloy, which uses a compound of silver. I originally put the sword in the coffin, and I could tell by its elegant silver finish that this was one of them." She smiled, proud of herself for being a wealth of useless trivia information. She lived on the History and Discovery Channels.

Both men looked impressed, especially Al.

"Mia, has anyone ever told you that you have an old soul?"

"Yes, mostly older people. It's one of the reasons I don't blend well with people my age. Is there anything else that bothers vampires?" A little laugh bellowed up from her chest.

"No, everything else is pretty much a myth."

"Al, something doesn't make sense to me. Art was set on fire, and if fire kills vampires, I don't understand why he lived."

"Unfortunately, I didn't get a chance to examine Art, so I can only speculate. It seems he was made, then burnt so he would appear dead. Someone hoped his body would be taken and placed in a dark area for a couple days while the change took place. The only sure way to kill a vampire is decapitation. If you can do that, then you don't have to worry about any of the other methods." He broke into a comforting smile.

Cole's hand cupped the back of his neck, then he tilted it from side-to-side. "Can we move on to something else? Having my woman arming herself with knowledge on how to kill me isn't the most comfortable conversation to hear."

"I'm not interested in killing you; I want to protect myself," Mia said as she inspected the fascinating photos on the wall. She glided her fingers over one of them. Old photos held a special place in her heart. They held so much history and she wondered about the events that occurred in each of them.

"Al, is it true that a vampire cannot enter a home unless they're invited inside?"

Al cleared his throat as he looked at Cole. "Yes, for the most part, it's true. You can also withdraw that invitation at any time, and they'd have to leave immediately."

"Well, good. I'm safe in my home then," she said with sigh of relief and crossed her arms at her chest.

"Yes, unless you have already invited one in." Al chuckled.

"But I have the power to take that away, right?" She couldn't help but be relieved knowing that she may have the upper-hand at some point. What if she had invited someone in and didn't realize it was a vampire. In fact, that cable guy did seem a little shifty.

"Maybe. When it comes to older vampires, they may have already been in your house before it was yours. This means they don't need to be invited in, and you don't have the power to ask them to leave. You have a fifty-fifty chance on this one."

Her eyes trailed to an eight–by-ten photo at the end of the wall. She walked over to it, trailing her fingers over the wood-grain frame. The photo was from the old west era. It depicted a sheriff with a rifle over his shoulder, dressed in all the sexy cowboy attire. She couldn't make out the other man's face with his head tilted down. His cowboy hat shielded it from her. However, his features were pleasing to her eyes. His pants seemed tailored, and they matched the black vest that slightly overlapped his belt. A small gold chain draped from inside his vest, trailing down to disappear behind the flap of a black duster. A black holster hung from his hips with a large Colt peacemaker revolver snug inside its leather, and a badge peeked out from behind his duster that hung above his heart. This man was all cowboy and Mia couldn't help but glide her tongue over her bottom lip.

The two men held another man between them, each holding one of his arms. His face glared into the camera as he was dragged by the lawmen. His eyes held the devil, and a faint resemblance of a badge hung from his chest.

Mia squinted and leaned in closer for a better look. Something was familiar in those eyes.

"You recognize the sheriff, don't you?" Al said.

The one with the shotgun must be the sheriff. Mia tilted her head and stared. "No, that's not it. There's something familiar about... Oh, fuck!" Her breath retracted into her lungs, and her eyes went wide. First, she took a step back, then she had to look again to make sure. She placed her back against the wall by the photo, placing her palms against its flat surface for balance. Both men stared at her as her fear mounted.

"What? What is it, Mia?" Al asked wide-eyed at her reaction. She lifted her hand, pointing, not wanting to look back at the picture.

"It's the man with the glowing eyes," she said with a shiver of fear.

"Oh, shit." was all she heard from Al before Cole was in front of her. His fangs were dangerously long, and his eyes glowed with rage.

"Are you sure?"

Mia swallowed hard, trying to control her breathing as Cole towered over her. An uncontrollable shake rocked her body as his hand roughly grabbed her shoulder, then ripped the photo off the wall.

Mia's eyes darted to Al who frantically dialed the phone. His actions weren't reassuring, and she now felt she was in serious danger.

Cole gripped her shoulder and held the photo up to her face. She tried to loosen his grip. He was hurting her, and pain shot down her arm.

"Are you sure?" His voice was as intimidating as a lion's roar.

"Yes, I'm sure."

Cole lifted his head to the ceiling, his growling roar vibrated the bones in her body, and then he slammed the photo through the wall leaving a gaping hole two inches from Mia's head. She froze in fear.

"I will kill him just for looking at my bride." His eyes engulfed with blind rage, and Mia had never seen him struggle so much to get himself under control. He was on the edge of going full vamp any minute, and she recognized the glazed look in his eyes from the graveyard.

Al looked to be on the verge of hysteria. "Cole, don't do it. Ca-calm down, and wait for the sheriff. Cole. Stay right here." Cole's eyes darted toward the exit. Al leapt toward the wall, flipping open a box hanging above the light switch. Without hesitation, he pushed the red button. "Cole, you made me do it. Please, calm down," Al pleaded.

Mia couldn't believe the rage erupting inside of him. If evil had a face, she was looking at it. The room started vibrating as large gates began to emerge down from the ceiling.

"Are you fucking nuts? You're sealing us in with him?" Mia shouted over the noise of the gates, and then an alarm sounded.

Cole's head followed the sound of Mia's voice. He stared at her, and followed her gaze as she looked up at the gate coming down. She was stuck between the path of the gate or a raging vampire. If she moved forward, she would be closer to Cole. She couldn't think, her heart beat wildly as tears stung her eyes.

Cole roared again, then reached out, grabbing her arm and pulled her away from the gate. He slung her past him to safety. Putting his hands on the gate, he screamed as smoke instantly billowed up from his skin.

They must have been made of silver. A piece of her wanted to comfort him, but she was static with fear, and the energy he dispensed knocked her in the gut.

Cole looked back at her. Pain and rage poured out of him, but when his eyes met her fear stricken ones, he looked devastated.

"Cole, please. Just wait for the sheriff." Al's last plea went unheard as Cole backed up and busted through the wall. The gate had only made it halfway down.

The door swooshed open, and the sheriff stopped abruptly before he ran into the silver gate that had descended half way down. "Al, put this shit back up into the wall!"

Al pressed a couple buttons on the phone and the gates stopped, then began to retract back into the ceiling.

Mia's knees collapsed, and she fell to the floor. Her hands went to her face covering her tears. Her shoulder hurt, but that wasn't what pained her—her heart was breaking. She had never felt such an intense feeling of pain before, not only from her own heart, but also from Cole's. The feeling had engulfed her to where she couldn't breathe until Cole had left the room.

The sheriff knelt down beside her. She winced in pain when he tried to help her up by her arm. He pulled her shirt off her shoulder, and his face contorted at the sight of her skin that had already begun to bruise.

"Cole did this?" His tone was laced with concern.

Mia nodded with affirmation.

He turned to Al who was still visibly shaken. "Al, round 'em up. Tell 'em we have a serious situation on our hands. See if someone can track Cole."

Without a word, Al left the room.

The sheriff extended his hand to help Mia stand. She took it and sat in the chair he offered. He looked down at her. "You know he'd never intentionally hurt you." His tone was apologetic.

"Really, John—a couple of seconds later and I would have been vampire food."

"You're a spit-fire, Mia. I like that."

She crossed her arms in front of her and sighed as he chuckled. "My heart tells me he wouldn't have hurt me, but you didn't see him..."

"It looks like you've uncovered someone Cole's been searching one hundred and twenty-nine years for—Evet Bass." He ran his fingers through his hair. His calmness relaxing her to the point her hands stopped shaking. There was something about John that made her feel safe.

"You're in that photo, John. What year was it taken?"

His eyes became distant as he drifted off into a memory. "1881. That's the year all hell broke loose with outlaws killing everything in sight. Different gangs were trying to take over and run the towns." He walked over to the hole in the wall. Bending down, he picked up the picture from the floor and stared at it as he came back to Mia.

"Evet used to be one of us. He was a lawman, sworn to protect the people. Then he bought a saloon and started getting greedy. He turned and became an outlaw, robbing and raping his way through different towns. He evaded us for a while, and then one day, just before dawn, he showed up in our town. He was tired of running and thought he was top dog. Evet called Cole out, and they faced each other in a gunfight. Cole was the faster gun and shot him. He didn't die though, and that's when this picture was taken. Evet escaped and did some unforgivable things to Cole and Cole has hunted him ever since." The pain in John's eyes wasn't there until he spoke of Cole.

Mia swallowed the lump in her throat as she hung on to every word. "What did he do?"

John looked up from the picture, pulling himself from the memory. "Mia, it's not my place to tell you. I'm sorry."

"Will he be okay, John? You'll find him, right?" He only offered her a comforting smile.

The door opened, and Al nodded to the sheriff.

"Get me an agent to get Mia home safely." John placed his hand on her shoulder and lightly squeezed as Al picked up the phone. Within seconds, a man was standing in the room waiting for instructions.

"Take Miss Starr home," the sheriff said, and then turned to Mia. "Remember... stay in your house. Don't go out to visit anyone." She now understood the urgency of this request and happily nodded her head in compliance.

Her escort drove fast and in silence. As they drove, she made up her mind—she would fight sleep tonight. She didn't want to see what might haunt her in her dreams.

EIGHTEEN

*M*ia brewed a pot of coffee. She needed something to keep her awake, and her mind was numb. She couldn't stop thinking about him. She'd seen people lose their shit before, but Cole made everyone else look like amateurs. What had tormented him for so long?

When the phone rang, Mia she snatched it from its cradle.

"Cole?"

"Do I sound like a man?" Cynthia's voice was refreshing to hear.

"Cyn? Is everything okay? It's eleven p.m."

"I have something that I've wanted to tell you, and you have been so preoccupied lately that I haven't had the chance."

"Well, what is it?" Mia asked, sliding down on the couch and thumbing its seam.

"I want to tell you in person."

"I can see you tomorrow, but you have to come here," Mia said and turned her head as the coffee pot beeped in the background.

"Yeah, okay. See you then, BFF."

Mia clicked the off button and laid the phone in her lap.

Her mom was coming for a visit in the morning and then Cynthia in the afternoon. This would be a good distraction for her, since she couldn't get Cole out of her mind. *Why?* She didn't know enough about Cole, yet he consumed most of her waking thoughts.

Walking to the sliding glass doors, she put her fingers into the notch to slide it open and paused. She could still see him—it was as if his image had been burned, leaving an impression on her patio, leaning against the glass. As she slid the door open, the memory of that night, when he sat here as she melted down inside, came back to her, vividly. She stepped out onto the balcony. A beautiful night breeze blew through her hair, lifting the strands off her neck. She closed her eyes and thought of Cole. She couldn't pull her mind away from him. Even when he wasn't near, she felt him. As much as she fought him, she felt sad. The loneliness she had buried deep down inside her for years had surfaced. As the strands of her hair stroked her neck, she felt his fingers on her skin. He was so gentle and deadly. Yes, deadly.

***

The coffee was useless, and the bed called to her. The sheets cooled her skin as she slipped under them. After pulling the covers to her neck, she hugged her extra pillow and turned on her side. The last thing she saw before surrendering to sleep was Cole's face filled with rage. She pushed away his image, and let the drums beat in his place.

This time she felt empowered over the dream, and pushed it forward to where she left off. More Indians surrounded her, chanting louder than ever before. Only one voice was clear in her head. She struggled to see whose voice was so close to her ear. Almost there...

The familiar rapping on the door slammed her thoughts back into reality. *Can't these people let me sleep?* She kicked her legs like a child and slapped the mattress with her hands as she yelled toward the door.

"Hold on!" Snatching the clock from the nightstand, she focused her hazy eyes on the time, then slammed it back down. *It's nine a.m. already?*

Her sleepy legs tripped over the rug by the door as she cracked it open, peering through the small slit. "Hey, Mama. Come in." She leaned out into the hallway, searching for Gonela. *Hmm, that's odd.*

"He's in his car. He said he'd come back when we're done."

"Who?"

"The detective out front. You have some of that sweet tea that I like, the kind that tastes like your grandma's?" her mom asked as she pulled out a chair from the kitchen table and looked around the apartment.

Mia always kept a little tea in her place, just in case her mom stopped by. Her face lit up with a smile. "Of course, I do. I'm going to make some coffee for myself and freshen up real quick." When she returned to the table, her mother was staring blankly at the empty chair in front of her.

"What have you discovered about yourself, my dear?" She always had a knack of knowing what Mia was going to say, before she said it.

The steam from her coffee danced in the air as she lifted the cup to her lips. "I think I moved Cole through the air when he was in a levitated state. I pulled him to me, and there have been some other minor things. He thinks you have the answers for me." She told her almost everything that had happened—well, mostly what happened—the other night with Cole. She left out the part of her trying to pleasure herself. Not that she was afraid to tell her mom. She was afraid of the response. Her mother has always been very open with her about everything.

Her mom took a minute to collect her thoughts. "Well, I didn't think your mind was that powerful, but if you pulled him over to you, then it is." She took a sip of tea, holding the liquid in her mouth before swallowing.

"What are you talking about?"

"Stop looking at me like I need to be wrapped in a straight jacket. You weren't named Miakoda for nothing. You have a calling, Mia, and the Native-American blood running through your veins is powerful." Sharon added another spoonful of sugar to her tea and clanked the ice against the glass as she stirred it. "There are some powerful Indians in our family tree. A witch doctor, as well as a medicine doctor, is in your blood. That's all I know." She stopped, letting it sink in before she continued.

"What are you trying to say, Mom? That, what? I have powers?" Mia rolled her eyes.

"Yes, Mia, that's what I'm saying. You have the power of the moon. You can control water, the power over someone's emotional state." Sharon's eyes lit up. "The moon moves the tides. Mia, can you imagine the power that the moon holds? You have that power, Miakoda!"

Mia's head shook in disbelief as her mom continued. "You can influence psychic energies—drive sane people psychotic and do worse for those who are already. Oh, and you can call forth and control night creatures. You are very special, Mia."

Mia's jaw dropped as she tried hard to wrap her brain around what she was hearing. She held up her hand. "Whoa. Hold up. Night creatures? What, like, raccoons?"

Her mom sat back in the chair and tapped her fingers on the table. She stared at her and inhaled a deep breath. "Mia, there is a lot more out there besides vampires. I've been trying to tell you for years, but you block it out."

"Yeah, like the time you called the airport to see if they had any special planes in the air because you swore there was an alien spaceship over the neighbor's house?" Her eyes rolled along with her sarcastic tone.

Her mom narrowed her eyes and stood abruptly. "Until you come to terms with it, Mia, I can't help you. No one can. Try to control your temper and concentrate. You'll see your power come forth. Believe in it, Mia, and you will see it surface. Embrace it. I'm going now. You're a downer." Sharon gave her a slanted smile.

"Gee, thanks, Mom." They both smiled as Mia walked her to the door.

Her mom paused at the top of the stairs and looked back at Mia. Her loving eyes held her daughter's, and then her lips drew into a tight line. She waved her hand in the air to dismiss the words she wanted to say. "It's pointless to tell you anything, you're just gonna' have to figure this out on your own." She turned and quickly descended the stairs.

Mia leaned against the open door until she heard the metal gate shut behind her. Her mom's visit was shorter than she expected. Now she needed a distraction until Cynthia arrived.

A couple of hours of cleaning did the trick, and now she actually had time to use her bathtub. She turned the water until it was steamy hot, just like she liked it—hot enough to see her skin turn red. She leaned back and closed her eyes, enjoying the sweat beading on her body. Gliding her hands on the rim of the tub, she sank deeper into the water. Her mind drifted to the people in her life. She thought about her mom's words and about what Al had said. But mostly, she thought about Cole. She tried hard to place her feelings for him. It seemed like lately everyone was telling her to relax and focus. She felt relaxed, right now.

Let's try this. What should I focus on? She kept her eyes closed and visualized Cole—his strong features and handsome face were pleasing. Just the thought of him sent her body into a shiver. Her hands itched to slip down between her legs and make the ache go away. Years of pent-up aggression bubbled inside her, combined with the brief encounters with Cole. That only intensified the urges brewing inside, urges she thought she had buried deep within her. Years had passed, and not once had she craved a man or missed anything about sex. Now, she found her mind constantly straying to him, craving his touch. *Damn.* There went her concentration.

Mia struggled with her emotions for him, and she knew she had to make a decision—end it or give herself to him. She spoke into the empty air as if she were confiding in an old friend. "I don't think I could ever let him bite me, especially after today. He was the scariest thing I have ever seen in my life. I can't imagine what he looks like before he bites someone and feeds on them."

Her body tensed with the visual, and she shook away the images. Breathing deeply, she tried to focus once again. When her mind locked onto his image, his appearance became clearer. Drawing back from Cole's face, his body came into view. Her expression softened as she watched him sleeping. More deep breaths... *Hold on to it.*

Mia felt a wave of pain sliver up from him. He was hurting, even in his sleep. She concentrated hard, pulling her focus back and resting it on his handsome face. *Deep breaths, Mia.* She visualized getting closer... closer, until she could bend down and lightly place a kiss on his lips.

My lips.

They were soft, inviting and felt so good. She allowed herself to linger, pressing harder as her hunger grew. Tiny bites of electricity rolled over her tongue as she slipped it inside and her hands slid down between her legs. A low moan escaped her.

Cole's eyelids flew open and stared directly into hers. *Holy shit!* Water spilled over the edge of the tub and splashed onto the floor as she jerked herself from the vision, her fingers flying to her mouth. She felt the energy from Cole still prickling the surface of her skin. *Did that just happen for real?*

She jumped at the knock on the door. Grabbing her wrap, she fastened it around her waist as she hurried to the door, her face still flushed as she opened it. "Hey, Cyn. Come on in. I need to get dressed. Lock all the locks behind you." Her voice was almost threatening.

Cynthia's head cocked back as she looked at her. "Aren't you a little paranoid these days?"

Oh, you have no idea.

"Why haven't you been to work, Mia?"

Mia pulled her shirt down and jumped on the couch next to Cynthia. "It's a long story." She waved her hand in the air to dismiss her question as she turned sideways and crossed her legs.

Cynthia's lips tightened. She narrowed her eyes and stared at her with suspicion. "Well, aren't you lucky that I have time for a long story? What's up with you? Does it have to do with the cop? You know, the one you know you want to be with, but for some reason you have decided to torture yourself... and for the rest of your life you will be alone, because you won't let yourself fall in love..."

It went deeper than that, but Cynthia was a hopeless romantic. She thought everything was roses. That was what happened when your boyfriend wasn't a vampire, and you could actually worry about things like picking out a china pattern.

But no, not me. She had to worry about being bitten from her un-dead boyfriend. She rubbed her hands together. Her emotions were coming to a head. If Cynthia only knew why she couldn't let herself love Cole, she wouldn't press.

For Cole, feeding while having sex was the ultimate pleasure, and she couldn't bring herself to let him bite her. It would be like telling a regular guy "Hey, I love you, but I'm never giving you head." In Mia's experience, that man will eventually go find someone that will shine his pole—even if he loves you. Cole needed blood. He needed to bite people, and it wasn't fair to him if she accepted him now and couldn't give him what he needed later.

All her thoughts compiled into a big ball of emotion and hit her head on. Her face turned red as she struggled to hold it in, and then the dam broke allowing tears to stream down her face.

Cynthia reached out and wrapped her arms around Mia. "Oh, my God. What is it? You never cry. It's him, isn't it?"

Mia stared at her hands in her lap. That was all she'd been doing—crying. She hated it. Mia wasn't this weak person she'd turned into. Her voice stuck in her throat so she nodded her head in agreement.

"Mia, do you love him? You need to be honest with yourself." Cynthia grabbed tissues from the end table, and Mia accepted them as an uncontrollable sob escaped her.

"Yes... I do." Her guarded heart knew the answer, and now she admitted what she'd been denying. Mia knew she had fallen quick, and she didn't know much about Cole, but he already had her heart. It scared her to death.

Cynthia grabbed her and rocked back and forth. "Then what's the problem? And you better not get snot on my shirt girl, it's *Coach*."

Mia burst out in laughter. She looked at Cynthia's shirt and laughed even harder. Cynthia was a walking advertisement for Coach, all the way down to her wristlet.

"We're just different; it will never work."

Cynthia drew her head back in a clockwise motion. "I'm a white woman in love with a hot, black islander. Who you gonna tell you're different to, please," she said, in a mocking tone.

"Cyn, there are things I can't tell you right now. I'm sorry. I would love to tell you everything, and I really need to tell you everything, but I can't."

"Are you in some kind of trouble?" Cynthia's face pinched with concern.

If you consider being wanted by vampires, trouble, then yes. Mia couldn't lie. Lying one of the worst qualities to have. She'd have to distort the facts. "Yes, a little trouble. There was an incident at the store the other night, and the cops think the guys might be back." Mia's gaze flicked down to Cynthia's phone as it rang.

Cynthia danced to the ring tone before she answered it. "Hey, baby. Nothing. Talking to Mia." She tilted the phone away from her mouth. "Kevin says, 'Hi.'"

Mia waved at the phone, then got up to give them privacy, making her way into the bathroom. *I can't believe I just admitted to myself that I love Cole. Can I satisfy him? Would he really be okay with a no biting relationship?* She splashed water on her face and returned to the living room.

Cynthia gathered her things and headed toward the door. "I'm sorry, he got off early, and he's home. I need to go get me some play." Her excited tone caused Mia to laugh and shake her head.

"No problem. I'm a big downer anyway. Oh, wait. What did you want to tell me?"

"Um, it was nothing. I'll tell you later."

Mia was alone once again, and she sat on the couch for hours lost in her thoughts as the sun began to set. She craved fresh air, and stepped outside, her hands sliding along the railing of the balcony as the wind stroked her skin. The moon shone in the sky. Even in the remaining daylight, a bright aura circled the orb and Mia stared at it as if it was a long lost relative.

I have some kind of connection to the moon. Like I don't feel weird enough without this knowledge. She should just sign-up with the circus and be done with it.

Looking down, Mia scanned the area and saw Detective Gonela's car. He must be lurking around somewhere because Cynthia didn't mention him being in the hallway.

The last of the sun's light vanished, and Mia stayed on the balcony, waiting, hoping to see Cole. For an hour, Mia peered into the darkness. The chill of the iron chair soaked into her skin, making her remote thoughts more focused. Mia felt confused. With her identity lost, it was time to fire up the computer and do some research.

Mia researched everything her mom and Al had told her and Google overloaded with information. She rubbed the dull aches that throbbed in her eyes and tried to focus on the computer's clock. Three a.m. glared at her. She'd managed to occupy her mind, and made a mental note to do the same tomorrow as she slipped into bed for the night, exhausted.

NINETEEN

Shortly after her eyes closed, she awoke to knocking on the door. *What the fuck, really?* "What?" she screamed toward the intrusion.

Detective Gonela's voice sounded muffled as it traveled through the wood. "Good morning, Miss Starr. I'm here if you need me." His tone was mischievous.

Has she ever needed him? Her eyes widened as a thought crossed her cloudy mind. She ran to the door, cracking it as he turned to leave. "Wait, Detective. Do you know if they found Cole?"

His strange amber-colored eyes flickered as he smiled. Did she just see that? It took a minute for her mind to register his action. "Yes, we did. Yesterday morning. Thank you for your concern." He grinned as he walked away.

"Thank you, Detective." She shut the door heading straight for the coffee. *Yesterday morning?* He hadn't come last night. Maybe he was working. She knew that crap wouldn't work. *Oh, just focus, Mia. You, have to believe.* They had her going—she really thought she had kissed him.

It took several cups of coffee, breakfast, and a shower for her to feel somewhat refreshed. It was going on five p.m., and the sun would be setting soon. She went to the balcony and waited. Seven p.m. Nothing.

Feeling like a caged animal, she needed to occupy her mind. She turned on the computer and changed while it booted up. Friggin' Windows. She could probably brew more coffee, and the thing still wouldn't be ready.

Changing into her nightclothes, Mia slipped off her shorts and slid into a tank top. She walked over to her desk and sat, propping her feet up, crossing her legs at the ankles. Leaning back in the chair, she brought her keyboard to her lap and pulled up a search engine. Tonight she was going to research something different. *Let's see what information Google brings.* First, she had to find out what they called police officers back in the old west days. She tried "Cole Barnett, Marshal." Nothing. Her eyes scanned to the bottom of the page. "Cole Barnett, Texas Ranger, 1865." Great—no picture. It was going on ten p.m., and by the looks of the information, she would be there all night before she came up with anything on Cole.

Tapping a couple more words in the search engine, she smiled when the next page loaded: Cole Barnett, 1881. She'd see if the date John gave her from the picture worked. *Yes!*

She clicked the link and read. The same picture that had hung on the wall was on the website. The caption on the picture read, "After a shoot-out, Deputy Marshall Cole Barnett and Marshall John Carr apprehended one of the most feared lawmen-turned-outlaw, Evet Bass, whom was shot by Marshal Barnett." Her eyes soaked up every letter as she scrolled down to read the article.

"Cole Barnett, a career lawman, started out as a Texas Ranger and was then a Deputy Marshal alongside Marshal John Carr. After his apprehension in 1881, Evet Bass, sent word to his gang urging them to swear allegiance to the Clanton gang, also known as "The Cowboys," who were wreaking havoc in Arizona. The gang members broke Bass out of jail, two days after he was apprehended.

"Bass took his revenge out on Barnett by taking his family away from him. He started with Barnett's fiancé who, weeks prior, had been his brother's fiancé. The

Bass gang had already killed Barnett's brother who was also a lawman. Bass killed him in a shoot-out and dragged him behind a horse, leaving his body for his fiancé to find the next morning. Out of honor for his brother, Barnett took on the responsibility of his brother's fiancé. Bass took her first. He raped and killed her, then turned his rage on Barnett's mother and sister, who also met the same fate.

"The Bass gang kept the lawmen busy in town creating a diversion while Bass took out his revenge on Barnett. When word got back to Barnett, he was devastated. After he properly buried his family, he was left with no one. He stumbled into a saloon one night, then disappeared for years. Some say he buried everything inside him and became a walking time bomb. He showed up years later as an Arizona Marshal where he swore he would hunt every one of the gangs down, until the last man was dead."

The tears burned in Mia's eyes. She swallowed hard and scrolled down more.

"This can't be. Come on. Give me a picture." Her eyes came across a tiny image. She clicked on it. "Please enlarge the thumbnail..." The photo seemed to load one pixel at a time. Her gaze locked into the eyes on the picture. It was him, but she refused to believe it. The reality of her world crumbled more every day. "Oh, my God. No. It can't be him. All that pain... It just can't be."

"It is me." The voice coming from behind her shattered the silence. Her heart jumped in her chest, and the chair fell backward. She grasped at the air to stop herself from falling.

In warp speed, Cole caught the chair before it hit the ground. He stared down at her as he held the chair, his jaw twitching as his eyes continued to burn into hers. Without pulling his gaze away, he slowly lifted her in the seat.

His heated stare burned her as he sat the chair back down on its four legs, then pulled her to her feet. The intensity in which he gazed at her made her heart beat more rapidly. His voice was low and raspy. "Miakoda, I need you." He stepped toward her, and she took a step back away from him.

"Cole, this isn't going to work. I-I can't. I can't get over the biting thing." Her heart ached for him, but her body ached even more. She yearned to reach out and help him. He stepped toward her, and she took a step back. "Cole, I may have to take your invitation into my home back if you don't back away. Please." His eyes swept over her body, lingering on her breasts, before they returned to her eyes. He stepped forward again. This time she didn't move.

"Then do it." There was a hunger in his gaze, and he devoured her with it. Her breaths came fast, sweat dampened her palms as a dangerous grin stretched across his face, and a wicked light glimmered in his eyes at her hesitation to send him away.

He closed the gap between them and put his hand on her stomach, slowly lowering his palm. Gliding his finger across her belly, he followed the path of fabric to the hem of her panties.

"May I touch you?" His lips brushed across her ear as he whispered his words. At the slightest twitch of her head, he slid his hand underneath the soft cotton fabric. She stopped breathing and locked into his gaze. The shock of his touch caused her to sway, and she grasped his arms for balance. Desire burned in his eyes as he lightly touched the fleshy part of her warmth, stifling a moan at the feel of her flesh. "I still feel on the edge and you're the only one that can calm me. I need you—now." He submerged his fingers in her wet folds, and she could feel his cock, hard as a diamond, against her. He rotated his hand inside her panties, placing his knuckles on her flesh. His seductive voice tingled in her ears. "You won't need these." He bunched the material in his hand and with one fast forward jerk, her panties were gone.

She sucked in a breath, reminding herself to breathe as he walked her backward into the living room.

Cole shed every inch of his clothing on the way to the chair.

Mia couldn't fill her lungs fast enough with air, and fear pricked at her skin.

"Cole. I can't do this. Please, this is way too fast for me."

Ignoring her words, he pulled her body to his, his cock jumped wildly against her. She gasped at the feel of his hardness against her belly.

"You were able to release some of your pain the other night. I can sense you still have some inside you, as do I, Mia. Don't deny me my pain. Let's release it together. Let go. Love me." He burned a kiss onto her lips as he continued to walk her backward until the back of her legs hit the armchair.

He grabbed the bottom of her tank top, and her hands shot up over his in protest. "No, please. Let me leave something on. I would feel more comfortable." Her cheeks flared with heat.

With a wicked grin, his hands grasped the top of her tank top. She gasped as he ripped it in half, causing it to fall open like a vest.

"There. I compromised." He lifted her, and her legs wrapped around his waist. There was no stopping him. Her heart wanted him, her body ached for him, but somewhere deep inside, she screamed *no*.

Cole knelt onto the seat cushion of the chair, and laid her body over the backrest. Her legs straddled his thighs as her toes frantically felt around, seeking leverage from the chair to lift herself away from his thick shaft.

"Cole I can't. Please, don't do this." Panic set in. He cupped the back of her head and pulled her up to meet his eyes. "Oh, God. Do it... just do it."

"I am not going to do anything until I know it's okay." His voice had a low seductive pull.

A silent tear fell down her cheek. She fought hard to keep the dark memories at bay. "I don't want you to bite me."

"Then, I won't." His eyes were full of passion as he leaned down, catching her tear with his tongue. "Are you ready?"

"Oh, God, no. I'm not." Her body began to tense as it had her entire life when it came to intimacy. *Block out the images. Block them out.*

"Mia, breathe." His thumb stroked her cheek.

"I find it hard to breathe around you, Cole."

His eyes caressed her face, and the back of his fingers stroked her cheek. "That's funny. I find it easy to breathe around you. Don't tense up on me, Mia. Please. It kills me to see you fear me." He shifted their position, easing his shaft to rest at her opening. His voice softly stroked her, as his hands lightly brushed her inner thigh.

Uneasiness tugged at her, but she knew why. And she needed to get past it—for him, and for herself. She was about to have her first orgasm that wasn't self-induced, and he hadn't done anything yet. She wanted to please him.

His hands slid across her skin, and cupped her breasts, then he lowered his head and took an erect nipple into his mouth. "Mine." He growled against her skin.

Her body tensed, but she didn't know if it was from the fear, or the unfamiliar feeling jolting through her body.

"Mia, I'm not going inside you. You will have to do that part. Relax and breathe." He strategically positioned her legs on his thighs so if she relaxed, she would slide down onto his rigid shaft, and he would be inside. She kept her legs tight.

Cole's hands slid down her stomach, past her trimmed mound, and his fingers circled her wet flesh. An unexpected moan escaped her throat. His fangs popped at her pleasure, and her body tightened.

Still, she fights me, he marveled. He trailed a line of kisses up her stomach, then tilted her head to the side. Resting his mouth on her neck, he closed his eyes, savoring the feel of her pulse beating against his lips. His fangs grew longer with need. The smell of her blood called to him. He fought hard to control the vampire urges within. *Want to bite. Need to bite.*

She trembled under his touch as he nuzzled his nose back and forth on her neck, breathing in her scent. He let out a moan. "Mmm... your blood calls to me, your body calls to me, and your soul calls to me. You are mine, Miakoda." He felt it, even without tasting her.

Her body tightened with tension as his deep voice rumbled over her skin. And then he watched as her internal defense mechanism kicked in. She was drifting away from him, running. Her expression went blank as she stared into the empty air. Cole froze and snapped her head back to meet his eyes.

"No. You will not do that to me! Look at me. It's me— no one else. Tell me to stop, but don't do that to me. Don't... leave me." His tone was pained, and the tip of his erection waited patiently to explore the warmth inside her.

"Cole, I'm... Just do it. Please. Just do it."

His face tightened, and his jaw ticked. "I will not. You have to do it. It's your fear—overcome it, my love. Miakoda, I want you to need me. I need you to want me, like I want you." His lips passionately took hers as his thumb flicked across her wetness. His fingers wiped the strands of hair from her face, and they locked eyes. *Does she know how stunning she is? How hard she makes me? Does she know what it takes for a vampire not to rip into something as beautiful as she is?*

His gaze heated Mia's very soul. *Give in to him.* She felt her pleasure rising higher and higher as he rotated his thumb below. Still, he waited at her entrance with such control. As much as she tried to block the images, they flashed through her mind. Her stomach began to ache as the blurred image cleared. *I knew it. It's a woman. Wait... it's me? He's thinking of me.*

Her legs began to relax setting herself down onto him, and she felt the tip of his hardness slide into her. He let out a desperate moan against the nape of her neck.

His voice became hoarse, pleading. "Give yourself to me."

She was on the verge of an orgasm when he moved his hand away. She whimpered in protest, relaxing more.

"You're not where I want you, yet. You'll just have to wait," he teased as he rubbed his lips on her neck. The tip of his fangs raked across her skin, and she tensed. He lowered his hand back to her wetness and rolled her hard nub between his fingers as he whispered into her ear. "I want to bite you, but I won't. Give yourself to me.

Now." Although he had no need for air, his rapid breathing matched hers.

"Cole, I do want you, and I need you." Her pulse was racing, and her voice burned with desire for him as she watched his control slip away.

She relaxed her legs more and felt his hardness slide in further, the girth already filling her. *Fuck, this was maddening.* Her whole body felt like a tongue on a nine volt battery.

Cole threw his head back and stared at the ceiling trying to hold on to his control. The need to replace one urge with the other overwhelmed him. Mia's words pushed him to the edge. She needed him, wanted him.

Need to bury myself inside her. Need to bite. Don't bite. Don't bite.

It had been years since he had touched another, felt the softness of a woman's skin. He had hardened himself toward affection, love, and now she shattered years of mastered control with just a few words. He kept one hand on the back of her neck, cradling her head in his open palm so he could lose himself in her eyes, which had masked over with an eerie blue glow.

He slid his other hand through her silkiness below and she closed her eyes, letting another moan loose as her orgasm was about to peak.

When she opened her eyes, he tilted his head sideways, staring at her with an expression he hoped she could clearly read: Sorry for what I'm about to do.

Her legs instantly tightened as his mouth opened, curling back his lips, exposing his fangs as his hunger increased. He seared a kiss onto her lips, flicking his tongue over hers. *Mine. Hungry.* The taste of her—the feel of her—was more than he could take. He was losing *control.*

Cole tilted his head back like a snake before it attacked. And like a cobra, he lunged forward and buried his fangs into his forearm resting beside Mia's head.

Her scream shattered Cole's sensitive ears. As she flipped herself backward over the chair, Cole grabbed for her but missed When he stood over Mia, she pushed her feet against the floor, retreating quickly until she hit the wall.

Cole raked his fingers through his hair, while cursing himself for losing control. Searching Mia's eyes for forgiveness, he knelt and held out his hand to her. "I'm very sorry. It's been so long. I usually don't lose control like that. This is what you do to me, Mia. I can't control anything around you."

TWENTY

*M*ia stared at his hand until the fear subsided. She moved her gaze slowly to his. "You... you almost bit me. Jesus. How are we ever going to make this work?" The intensity of his stare became too much. She looked away before it consumed her. "It's not going to work. Is it?"

Ignoring her words, Cole kept his hand extended. "I think we should talk, Mia. I have something I want to tell you."

The urge to run surfaced, her eyes darted around the room for an escape route. Jumping off the balcony was an option. A one story fall shouldn't kill her. *Shit.* He'd catch her. She needed to end this now—end the torture for both their sakes.

The words to save them both were on the verge of spilling from her lips until her gaze flicked to his perfect mouth. She stared at his lips, making her own tingle. The heat from his kiss still lingering on her skin made her body crave one thing, while her mind wanted, *needed*, to run from the dangerously handsome man. Mia slid her hand into his and took a deep breath. He needed to tell her something and she hoped to say it before he did. "Cole, sex with me could never be fulfilling for you. I felt you holding back—you bit yourself." She looked down at their hands as his thumb stroked the top of her skin, sending a shallow current of energy through her. "You said you could have sex without feeding."

Cole leaned forward and kissed her forehead, her nose, then lingered over her lips before brushing them back and forth. Electric bites shifted between them. "That's not what I wanted to tell you." His eyes darkened with a troubled look before he lowered his head. "I know you despise what I'm about to tell you, but I never want anything between us. I fed tonight, on death row." When she did nothing but stare at him, Cole continued. "And you're wrong, Mia. Just to have you would be satisfying enough. I've never bitten myself before. I'm sorry I couldn't control it."

Cole was wrong, and his words just proved her point. He bit himself, so *just having her* wasn't enough. "Cole, this is what I'm trying to tell you. It's not fair to you, and you will never be completely satisfied." She recalled the hunger in his eyes as they blackened, and how the glow intensified just before he slammed his fangs into his arm. "What if you hadn't fed on death row? And I don't know how to feel about that either. Did you feed on the same guy we saw?"

"No. I fed on all of them. I wanted to come to you, but I was too lost in my rage."

His phone rang as her jaw dropped from his admission. *All of them?* She was beginning to hate the constant interruption of his phone.

Cole slid his hands under the bends of her knees, then lifted and deposited her back into the chair. He searched his discarded clothes on the floor, pulling his phone off the clip of his belt.

Mia stared at his backside as he walked away from her, already engaged in conversation. The moonlight coming in from the window made his skin glow. He was a vision of masculinity and looked like a model ripped from the page of a magazine.

Her gaze roamed his figure, from the strong chiseled features of his back, down past his muscular ass, to his hard thighs. He looked like a sculpted god, and now she knew why Michelangelo took such pride in every inch he carved.

Cole closed the phone and walked back to her.

"Is this when you tell me you have to leave after conveniently getting a phone call? And I'm supposed to feel okay about it, because you have to go help somebody?" She tugged her knees to her chest, shielding her body from him, and emptied her face of all emotion.

He stared down at her with sadness in his eyes and shook his head. "I want to kill every man—boy —that has made you feel like this. No, Mia. This is when I take you to your bed and make our vision come true. You know... the one you wouldn't tell Al about"—he scooped her into his arms—"shame on you, lying to poor Al." Their eyes locked as he walked toward the bed. Heat rolled through her body.

"You. Are. Bad, Cole. I knew it! I knew the images weren't coming from me, which means you made me see your thoughts. So, I can—"

His lips silenced her before he laid her on the bed. She gazed at Cole, standing like a Greek god next to the bed. Her eyes trailed down to his erection and shot back up to his eyes. Cole was ready.

Mia tensed when he crawled onto the bed. She didn't move an inch as Cole maneuvered his body behind hers. Sliding his arm around her stomach, he pulled Mia to him, pressing her into his lap. His hardness jabbed into her skin making her breath catch. He held her so tight she felt like a baby in a security blanket.

Cole swept the hair from her neck, "Mm, this is the spot I yearn to bite." He stroked an across the vein on her neck then kissed it. "Sleep, my love. I have plenty of time to make you mine." His breath rolled in the shell of her ear as he spoke.

Mia felt protected in his arms and surrendered herself to sleep. Beautiful, sexual visions danced in her dreams. No death, no drum, no Indians. Just peace.

* * *

Cole awoke for the fourth time to Mia's warm backside. His cock, hard and throbbing, lay against her skin. He should have forced his blood to fill his shaft and stroked himself off earlier. His hand slid down and pinched the head of his cock—just the feel of Mia's skin had his seed threatening to spill. When his hand drifted over her thigh, wetness poured from her warmth. Her response to his touch pushed him closer to the edge. Cole brushed his lips over her ear. "Spread your legs for me." His voice husky with need.

Goosebumps blanketed her skin, sending her body into a quiver. Mia seemed to stay in a state of sleep, and the fact her mind was trying to fight even in this state made him grin. She stayed silent and still.

The throbbing pressure below made Cole painfully hard. "I have to have release, Miakoda. And you're the only one I want to touch." He lifted her thigh, pulling it over his, and then slid his engorged flesh through her wetness. A deep growl rumbled in his chest as he waited at her entrance.

Mia arched her body, pressing her backside deeper into his lap. When she stiffened, he knew the sleepy fog had lifted, and awareness took its place.

Cole rocked back and forth through her silkiness. Each time he slid through her wet folds the head of his cock massaged her clitoris. He slid his arm between her breasts, then clamped down on her shoulder as he pulled her closer to him.

The air thinned. Mia parted her lips to draw in more oxygen. With no willpower, or the energy to delay her orgasm, she would come quickly for him. She had been so close before, and for the first time in her life, she waited at the edge of ecstasy.

Cole moaned against her shoulder as her body melted into his, and she felt his lips pull into a sexy grin, hidden in the darkness. "Miakoda." His voice stroked her nipples, and they hardened to painful points.

Mia wrapped her arm around his, digging her nails into his shoulder. She was there—just seconds away from blissful pleasure.

"Mia, come for me." He gripped her tighter. His erection jumped wildly against her wetness as he inhaled deeply.

Her body stiffened. *Lost it.* "I can't, Cole."

He moved through her folds. "Your body and scent tell me differently." He groaned with a painful need and his movements became more urgent. "You're so close. I can feel it. Just let go." His breath on her skin sent waves of electricity through her, and a shallow moan escaped her lips. "Fuck. You unravel me, Mia." Grabbing her hand resting on his arm, he forced it to his throbbing cock. "Hold me tightly to you," his ragged voice urged.

She sucked in a breath and pressed his shaft between her folds. Cole's was larger than anything she had ever touched. The girth alone had her stomach knotted into a ball of nerves.

Earlier, she almost sat down on his mass, but now she gulped at his size, and questioned if she could fit her fingers completely around it.

As he slipped his length through her folds, she felt his pleasure rising with every sound he made—manly sounds, tiny moans and grunts of pleasure. Sounds for her. New emotions formed within her. She wanted to please him, wanted to give him the release he desperately needed. And *oh, God,* she wanted to come.

Cole moved with rapid thrusts between her warm, wet flesh. Cupping his girth with her hand, Mia held him tighter to her. Her breaths became rapid gasps, and Cole matched her breath for breath. When sweat beaded on her neck, Cole's tongue touched the salty liquid, licking and tasting her. Mia flinched in response. Her involuntary nerves attacked her libido, a familiar action embedded deep inside the dark chambers of her mind. *This is Cole touching me.* She reminded herself and tried hard to fight the demons swirling inside her.

"Trust me, Mia."

Her body stiffened further at the sound of his fangs jutting out. The fear of being bitten, combined with excitement, and the constant rubbing against her sensitive flesh pushed her to the edge where she teetered in agony between pleasure and fear.

Cole tightened his arm around her and rested the tips of his fangs on her neck. A low growl rolled slowly up from his throat as he gently pressed his fangs into her neck, careful not to break the skin.

Mia began to convulse in his arms. Cole gripped her tighter, holding on to every movement she made. He didn't know why his breaths mimicked hers—he had no need to breathe, but it was as if they were melting into each other. Her beautiful screams tingled through his body all the way to his cock, pushing him over the edge. His hips lunged forward as he spilled his seed onto her delicate stomach, bucking forward with each pump.

When Mia's body jerked with the aftershocks of pleasure, Cole's fangs nicked her skin. Unable to resist the scent of her blood, he leaned down and licked the bead of crimson. The tiniest taste of her blood set him on fire, his cock painfully hardened again. He wanted to bury himself inside her. The need to claim her—to slam his fangs into her—burned inside of him.

He questioned the control he'd mastered over the years, questioned if he could control himself if Mia pushed him too far. He quickly took her leg from his hip and rested it back on top of her other leg. Cole continued to slide between her legs savoring the aftermath of his pleasure, wanting desperately to be inside her.

Mia trembled in his arms, and he sensed the struggle within her. She wanted to enjoy what they shared, but conflict fought her pleasure. He gently kissed her shoulder. With her back still to him, she latched onto his arms, snuggling deeper into his body and tucked his hand underneath her side.

Cole opened his mouth to speak, but paused when hot tears seared his skin.

He stroked her arm and sighed. "Mia?"

"I've gone too far. It's not your fault. I'm angry with myself. You're just so... overwhelming. Here I lay with a magnificent man who just gave me an orgasm for the first time, and all I feel is shame."

"Mia, tell me what torments you."

"I can't open that door, Cole, it's too dark. It stays deep inside me, locked in the basement."

Although she was wrong, it came out of the basement every time he tried to touch her, he'd have to wait for her to tell him. "There is no shame in what we shared." He kissed her temple.

"This is going to hurt."

"What, my love? Tell me."

"I've fallen hard, and you're a highly sexual being. I'll never live up to your standards. Ever."

"Baby steps, Mia. Don't over think it."

"I can't let you hurt me. Don't hurt me, okay?"

Cole didn't answer, just held her tightly in the silence of his arms until she was asleep. Moving the covers off her body, he stared at her through the darkness, watching her chest rise and fall with each breath. Her perfect breasts moved in a delicate rhythm. She was everything he had ever desired, and his blood had stirred once more after having tasted a tiny drop of her. *It has to be her—she is mine.* Cole wanted desperately to crawl inside her to slay her demons but knew a woman like Mia needed to fight her own battles. Tonight, Mia trusted him. He smiled to himself. *It's a start.*

TWENTY-ONE

*M*ia stretched, yawning as she pulled herself out of a deep sleep. She sat up, pulled her knees to her chest, and looked around the room. *I didn't dream. I slept... peacefully.* Her lips arched into a smile.

She slept late. Seeing daylight was starting to be a rarity. Hunger tugged at her stomach to the point that she actually smelled food.

For the first time, she had slept naked, and she was still naked as she walked through her home. She stopped and stared at the object lying on the kitchen table, laughter gliding out of her. She picked up the note, and then ran her finger over the red square brick that was the size of a large block of cheese from the deli. She scanned the writing:

My love, I can see a piece of your heart after removing this brick last night and it beats for me. I know you won't make it easy, but I look forward to knocking down the rest of your wall. I made you breakfast, it's in the refrigerator. I don't want you to be bored with your food. You need something with more nutrition, other than cereal. I also put your box of silver by your door. P.S. You sleep like the dead. Cole.

Mia scanned the kitchen. Her grandmother's cast iron skillet was in the dish drainer along with some other utensils. When she opened the refrigerator, she found a plate with eggs, bacon, and a note attached to the bread saying "toast."

Cole was making her heart soar; she felt giggly inside. As she sat down to eat, her thoughts took over. How long would this last? She was a realist, and she had issues with some stuff, but doesn't every relationship have issues? He fed on death row. Was he as violent as the other vampires? She had to face reality—he was a vampire, and he was capable of being animalistic like the others she'd seen.

She rolled her thoughts repeatedly over in her head, trying to give solutions to the excuses she was making to run the other way. Yes, he did take a brick out last night, and now she was trying to run so he couldn't get any closer. This was going to hurt, bad. She feared she wouldn't recover from the hurt he would cause.

Tangled in her thoughts, she didn't hear the phone ring. Al's voice filled the room as the answering machine beeped.

She quickly threw on a simple skirt and blouse and was out the door. Skirts weren't her norm, but after last night, she was feeling sexy.

After making a quick stop to drop off her silver, along with the list of items she requested to her friend Derrick's house, she arrived at the FBI building at six.

Detective Gonela, who had been tailing her, stood beside her and held his secret key fob against the elevator panel. That was still so cool.

"Thanks, Detective," she smiled as the elevator began to climb. He tilted his head, returned the smile.

"Why Miss Starr, you're glowing today."

Heat quickly painted her cheeks. She wasn't innocent by any means, but he could obviously tell why she was glowing. "I guess I'll take that as a compliment. Thank you, Detective." She avoided his eyes as she spoke.

The doors opened, and she walked straight to the desk to give her name. There was a confidence in her walk that hadn't been there before. She threw her shoulders back as she greeted fake boobs from the other day. "Have a seat Miss... Starr. I'll let Al know you're here."

Guilt tugged at Mia for attacking the girl the way she had. She didn't know the woman, and she usually didn't behave like that. "Hi, I'm Mia. I'm sorry we got off to a bad start the other day." Mia held out her hand in a truce, and the woman accepted it.

"I'm Stacey. It's okay. I was out of line."

Mia shook her hand and gave her a vampire nod.

Al was at the secret door motioning for her to come in. The room looked untouched.

"Wow, hey, Al. You guys really get things fixed quickly around here." The hole in the wall was patched; even the picture frame was repaired and replaced on the wall.

"Yeah, vampires move quickly. You should see how fast the silver gate comes down now. Of course, we had to get someone else to fix that besides a vampire." They both laughed. She felt relaxed with Al. "Oh, and we added something for added safety." He nodded toward the wall by the door. Encased in glass was an ax, which she could guess was only made to look like it was for a fire. The wide shiny blade screamed decapitation.

"Anyway, let's get to it, Mia. I want to try an exercise on you before everyone gets here for the meeting. I want you to focus on this piece of metal wire. Try to bend it." When he pulled the tiny piece of wire from his lab coat, she burst into laughter.

"I'm sorry, Al, with all due respect—"

"Mia, this is very exciting. You have to believe you can do it. I believe you can do it. I believe you're the one we have been searching for."

The excitement on his face was something she couldn't deny. Although, she was exhausted with everyone's "You have to believe attitude," she gave in to

Al. But she was thinking he should get ready to be disappointed.

"Okay. Let's give it a try."

Al sat down and held out the piece of metal vertically between his fingers. Mia looked at it. She thought about bending it to the right as she focused more on the small piece of metal.

Al's expression of excitement caused her to avoid his gaze. She didn't want to let him down, but that was going to be the end result. She focused—pulling her energy up from below as she followed Al's steps—believe, visualize and do. She could do this. She visualized the metal bending to the right. I'm more powerful than this tiny piece of metal, she thought, building herself up. Tilting her head down, she narrowed her eyes at the object. You're nothing but energy, and I control you. Her eyes tunneled on the metal. Everything went away except for her and the object that challenged her.

The air charged, and the metal twitched to the right. Her wide eyes snapped to Al's. "Did you see that or was that just my imagination?"

Al stood quickly, knocking his chair to the floor. He pulled Mia to him, hugged her tightly, and then shook her by the shoulders.

"You did it, Mia. You did it! Did you see the metal jump? Oh, my... I have to go log this." He grasped his hair with both hands. "I have to... oh, my... it jumped in my hand! I'll be right back."

Al was much more excited than she was. Mia's head began to ache from the level of concentration she'd used to slightly move a piece of metal. As she waited for Al, she walked over to the photo that started Cole's rampage a couple days ago.

She stared at Glowing Eyes, a.k.a. Evet Bass. She hated him. He was an evil man, and she wanted to help catch and bring him to justice. That reminded her... what had happened to Igor from the other night?

Al returned with a pen, and as soon as his body connected with the chair, he wrote in the leather-bound journal.

A few minutes later, the sheriff, Gonela, and Nancy walked in discussing the case.

Al jumped up. "Sheriff. You are not going to believe what just happened."

Mia quickly spoke over him. "Al, please. I would rather that not be out right now. I'd like to do a little more one-on-one with you to make sure," she lied. She really didn't want anyone to know, especially vampires.

The sheriff narrowed his eyes at her then made a sound as he sucked his teeth. "I don't like secrets, Mia."

And I don't want to die, John, she thought. "It's really nothing. I meant no disrespect, sir."

The door opened once more as Russo and Cramer walked in and took a seat at the table. Russo's smile sent shivers up Mia's spine. Something was up, and her instincts nudged her to stay alert.

"Everyone, have a seat," Sheriff Carr said. "We'll get started in a minute." Tom came in next, and the sheriff didn't wait for him to get comfortable. "Do you have any information on the two other illegals that were found on the beach, down south from us?"

The door slid open again, Mia didn't have to turn her head to identify who it was. She felt him. Her pulse instantly accelerated, causing her blood to race through her veins. Her heart pounded inside her chest as Cole walked to the other side of the table and sat. She couldn't look at him, or she'd be done for.

"Cole, you're late!" The sheriff spat out his words. "You know I don't tolerate tardiness."

"He was just having a little dinner, Sheriff, and I bet she tasted good. Huh, Cole? The way I saw you holding her out in the waiting room..." Russo's words stabbed Mia in the heart.

Ouch. She knew it would hurt. Worst one yet. Mia's eyes darted to Cole, and she felt her temper rising. Her knee began to bounce uncontrollably—she was pissed. When she locked eyes with Cole, she knew Russo was telling the truth.

The lights flickered around the room drawing everyone's attention to each bulb. "Al, did they mess with the wiring when they patched things up in here?" the sheriff asked.

"Not that I know of," Al said, focusing on Mia as he answered.

She wasn't sure who to be more pissed at, Cole or Russo? *This is what he is, this is how he eats. Just relax.* Her temper boiled as she tried desperately to find understanding for his actions. She needed to go somewhere—she needed to breathe, to get control of herself—she needed to hit something. The ends of her hair felt as if she rubbed them against a balloon. She stood up. "If you guys will excuse me for a minute. Al, where's the restroom?" She kept her tone controlled.

Al pointed in the direction behind him, which meant she had to walk past Russo. He snickered as she reached his chair, and her temper snapped.

"You know, Russo, you really do need to learn when to shut your mouth." Venom seeped through her tone.

Without delay, Russo stood, towering over her. She felt the energy soar from everyone in the room.

"I don't think you need to be telling me what to do, human."

Mia stood her ground and glared back at him. "If your problem with me is that I'm human, I can accept that, but here are the facts..." Feeling the air charge with energy, she paused and looked around the room.

Cole's lips pulled back exposing his fangs, and his eyes lit with a glow. The sheriff was ready to pounce as Mia turned back and continued. "All of you could feel my pulse quicken when Cole walked in the room. All. Of. You." She glared at each one of them. "You obviously know what effect he has on me, and you know from the other night that he's protective of me. You don't care about humans, Russo, so what would you have to gain by hurting me? Nothing. I'm insignificant to you. So the information you felt compelled to share with everyone wasn't intended to hurt me, it was intended to hurt Cole, and that really pisses me off."

Cole's chest bowed, he held a look of admiration and respect as she defended him against a vampire. Russo burned holes into her with his eyes and stepped closer to her. Cole stood, backing away from the table. If Mia had any doubt before that Russo hated her, it was removed right at this moment.

"One of these days you're going to mouth off to the wrong vampire."

Her anger mounted. Disgusted by his threat, she didn't allow him to continue. Something tingled inside her; energy from deep down came forward. The lights flickered as she stepped toward him. "And then what? What, Russo? There's nothing between you and me but air and opportunity, so when you're ready, jump." Mia recalled her brother would say this exact line before a fight to intimidate his opponent, and right now, she was feeling bulletproof. She held her arms out to her sides waiting, watching his shoulders for the first sign of movement. In the next blink, she turned her head as Cole's back brushed her cheek.

His voice rumbled from his chest. "I'm sure you don't want any of this, do you Russo?" Cole was inches from his face.

"Russo, outside until I come for you." The sheriff's voice vibrated the room.

Cole turned to Mia. She couldn't meet his eyes. Laughter broke the silence that lingered in the room.

"Mia, get your butt over here, and sit down. You are the only human that I have ever known who would challenge a vampire. That just makes me laugh. I'm just thankful you're not a vampire. You're like a female Cole, and I don't need two of ya."

Mia sat. Her eyes went to Cole as she responded. "I have nothing to lose, Sheriff." She couldn't help but feel hurt. This is why she was trying to end it. He can't do without feeding, and now he has touched another woman.

The sheriff laid his hand on her shoulder as he spoke. "Let's get back to work. Tom, anything on those other two victims?"

Tom cleared his throat. "No, Sir, and we're still waiting on the blood DNA back from the Sector 13 analyst on the other three."

The sheriff nodded then looked at Nancy and Cramer. "Any luck on tracking Vincent?" They shook their heads "No." The sheriff looked around the room. "Mia needs to form a bond with a vampire." He looked at Cole, and Mia's head snapped up to look at the sheriff.

"No. I will not bond to him." She was upset and not willing to bond to someone who was sucking on other women in the hallway.

"Mia, why do you have to be so difficult?"

"I get that a lot," she responded with attitude, and the sheriff shook his head in frustration. He exchanged looks with Nancy.

"No fucking way. I don't do women." Nancy folded her arms across her chest.

The sheriff sighed and ran his hands through his hair.

"Well, Mia that leaves Tom. Cramer doesn't do blood bonds." Mia stood, swallowing hard as she faced the sheriff.

"No, I'm not bonding to any vampire."

"Mia we need to be able to track you, fast, for your safety and our need for you. You need to bond. Let Cole do it, Mia. I don't want to see you hurt." He was done battling with her and it was evident in his tone.

She looked at the sheriff and positioned herself, so no one else could see her face but him. She felt her eyes tear and cursed herself for her weakness. She was stronger than this. It was him. He was making her weak.

The sheriff took one look at her and dropped his head. "Everyone out. I need a minute with Mia, and it's not like any of you brought any fucking clues to the table."

Cole stayed behind. The sheriff raked his eyes over him. "It would seem that you disobeyed an order, Cole."

"Yes, I did, John. I had to have her, touch her. She makes me feel alive, complete." He kept his eyes on John as he spoke. "I'm sorry for today. I find it hard to control myself around her, and I knew she was called for this meeting. That's why... It's not what you think. I wanted to be able to concentrate on my job. My intentions were not to hurt or disrespect anyone. I'll leave you now."

As the door slid shut, John looked at Mia. "He's my best detective and my strongest vampire. In the matter of days, you've managed to strip him of the control others envy him for. You're like a daughter I never had, and that makes it hard for me... Dammit, Mia, he feeds on humans when the drawn blood isn't enough. This is the way of life for all of us."

She held back most of the tears, but one escaped down her cheek. John reached out, brushing it away with his thumb. She managed to meet his eyes.

"I know, John. I understand everything you have said. I just don't know if I can deal with it."

"Why don't you test yourself, Mia, and see if you can deal with it. Come on. There is work to be done."

When the doors swished open, everyone in the waiting area was silent and still.

"This meeting was as useless as tits on a bull. Let's meet back up in a couple of hours. I'll give everyone a call." The sheriff barked out orders. "Cole, take the night off. Russo, you go straight back to my office. I'll meet you there."

Mia was dizzy as she watched everyone leave the room, everyone except Cole. They stood by the elevator door, his posture straight, and his jaw tight. He turned slightly toward her as he spoke. "You're angry with me, and I have lost your trust."

She faced him. "Did you have sex with her?"

His head snapped toward her revealing narrowed eyes. "No. I did not."

She searched his dark pools, trying to find the answers that would make everything ok on the inside. "I'm not angry at you, Cole. You are what you are. I can't change that. I'm angry at myself for letting my guard down." She flicked her gaze over his frame. "Did you enjoy it, feeding from her?"

His eyes reflected pain. "It's food, Mia."

Her face tightened, making her jaw twitch. "I don't lick my steak, Cole. Did. You. Enjoy her?"

"Yes."

At least he was honest; she had to give him that. She pushed the elevator button several times as the urge to run surfaced. Her eyes shifted to the woman behind the desk, and Cole's posture stiffened. *No, fuck that. I'm not running.*

"I want to see."

His eyes widened, and his voice came out quick. "What? You want to see what?"

She stepped back, looking around him to Stacey. "Was it her? She doesn't remember, does she? Do it again—I want to watch you do it." He was still in shock as he spoke.

"No, she doesn't remember, and no, I will not do it again. Nothing good can come from this. You'll definitely hate me afterward."

"I want to see how you hold her when you feed from her. I need to see it." She narrowed her eyes as his bored into hers, the heat radiated through her. She desperately tried to keep it together as her nerves tugged, knotting her stomach. John said, she should test herself Well, here she goes. If this wasn't a sink or swim moment, she didn't know what was.

TWENTY-TWO

Cole's lips became a tight line as he narrowed his eyes at her challenging gaze. Turning his head toward Stacey, his voice was deep, demanding. "Girl, come to me."

As soon as Stacey looked up, she was caught. She walked around the desk slowly, blankly staring back at him.

Mia's lips parted in disbelief.

It was incredible, but regret instantly set in. What if he went too far, and she couldn't forgive him? Stacey stopped in front of him, and Cole laid her back as if he were dipping her in a dance. His left hand cradled her neck, while his right arm encircled her body, bringing her close.

Mia's heart raced as he put his lips next to Stacey's neck. He looked up and locked his eyes with Mia. Stacey softly moaned as he lightly brushed his lips over her neck. *Not right. Should be my neck.*

He raised his lips and hovered them just above Stacey's skin. Instantly, a blue tent appeared as the artery swelled at the surface, bringing blood forth.

The glow in his eyes began to illuminate as Mia watched his soft, gentle gaze turn predator. When his fangs darted out like a switchblade, Mia flinched. Cole pulled his lips back and raked them over Stacey's neck, glaring at Mia. He paused as if he was waiting for Mia to stop him. When she didn't, he continued down Stacey's flesh.

Mia's breathing quickened; her heart raced out of control. She should be angry at this—she should be; however, she was turned on like never before. Leaning back to rest on the wall, Mia shifted her legs as the silkiness escaped from below. Cole was the hottest thing she'd ever seen, and his power swirled in the surrounding air intensifying her excitement. Mia licked her dry lips. The glow in Cole's eyes intensified, and the beautiful amber hue zeroed in on her with an acute awareness. She gasped at the knowing look in his eyes. Cole must smell her arousal, feel her blood soaring through her veins, and he was staring at her in disbelief.

Mia watched as Stacey's nipples hardened underneath her shirt, then flicked her gaze back to Cole's. He was a vision of masculinity and a dangerous predator. A feeling of possessiveness washed over her. She had to stop this. *He's mine.*

The elevator chimed as it reached their level. Mia's voice was firm as she spoke. "Enough. Drop her." The elevator door opened on her last word.

Cole looked into Stacey's eyes. "You have to go to the restroom. When you look in the mirror, you will only remember taking your last phone message." He turned her and pushed her back toward the desk. Then he turned his deadly eyes back to Mia. His presence filled the room with hunger and desire. Intense power radiated from him and swirled around Mia, making tiny pricks of electricity that teased her skin.

She stared at him, and he looked confused. "I'm not sure if you're angry or excited, but whichever it is has your blood racing. And your eyes... I've never seen them that color, and you're emitting a level of energy I didn't know was possible for a human."

She said nothing.

"Mia..."

"Shh. Just get in the elevator." With her body awakened, Mia felt alive and her flesh crawled with raw power. The thought of his hands upon her skin made everything tingle. Mia's nipples tightened as she remembered the feel of his lips around them. She stifled a moan and wanted more of everything, now! Mia didn't want him to hold back; it wasn't fair to him, but she could no longer deny she felt something for him. It was just a matter of getting past her fears and years of mental blocks.

Her mind worked feverishly to make her body one with her thoughts. *I must please him, and there is only one way to do this—he must lose control.* A naughty plan emerged. *I'll bring him to the point where he can't control himself, and then maybe he'll take what he needs. That's the only way that I'll know I've completely satisfied him.*

Cole knew she was up to something, his gaze held a hint of caution, and that had knocked him off balance. He stared at her with an arched brow as she stood far away from him and pressed the button to the ground floor.

His glare penetrated her; it was relentless. He didn't blink, or move, just probed her with his eyes right down to her very soul.

She shifted her legs, wetness flowed between them, and her body was at the point of no return. "Cole, I... I want you *now.*"

"I've wanted to hear those words since the day we met."

Mia stared at the growing bulge below his waist, licking her lips she watched his cock twitch from the hunger in her tone. She remembered how it felt in her hand, how her fingers barely fit around the girth of his shaft as she helped stroke him to orgasm. Mia cursed herself for not taking him inside her when she had the chance. Now she ached for it.

Her plan clicked into place as she reached back and hit the red button. The elevator jerked to a stop, and she stumbled into his arms.

His eyes lit with an amber hue and blazed down at her. "Oh, baby, this is a bad idea. Not here." She slid her fingers between the buttons of his shirt. "Mia, I can't..." Feeding off the agony in his tone, she stroked his skin, and then before he could protest, she fisted the shirts material, ripping it open, the buttons ricocheted off the walls and bounced onto the floor, flying in every direction.

She reached her hand behind his neck and pulled him to her, taking his lips until they swelled with passion. Her mouth was hungry, and her body was wet.

Cole's skilled tongue danced in her mouth, bringing her excitement higher. Desire built a fire inside that began to burn out of control. Five years of pent-up sexual tension was about to explode. She glided her hand across the front of his pants. He moaned as she grabbed his throbbing erection.

"Now, Cole. Please, quickly." Her words panted out with her breath. His cock twitched beneath her hand as she pleaded for him to take her.

"Fuck, my bride wants me," he said, and the predator shone in his eyes. "Not here." He groaned, his voice deepened with need. "You hit the stop button coming from the eighteenth floor, Mia. I want to please you, but quickies are not my style and..."

As his radio beeped and voices began to hurry through call signs, she fell to her knees.

Cole hissed in a breath when he felt her tongue flick across the head of his shaft. It was like being licked by fire. The head of his erection moistened with his desire as his shaft filled with seed. It had been too long without pleasure, and the short release she gave him before was nothing compared to the need building in him right now. To have her on her knees, willingly taking him into her mouth, pleasing him, was an indescribable pleasure. She knew what he was, and he wouldn't have to erase her thoughts. Even if he tried, he couldn't erase her right away, it would take time. She was so different from anyone he'd touched in the past. She was his. He felt it more and more, but the only way to be sure was to feed from her.

He wrapped his fingers around the rail on the wall and leaned back as she licked his shaft up and down. When she looked up into his eyes, they glazed over with hunger.

He rested his head against the wall. Images of what she was doing to him, what he wanted to do to her, and where he would touch her next, flashed through his mind. *Fight it. Stop her. Not here.* The next image that flashed made his body stiffen. Mia was so relaxed and calm, that she had started projecting images, and Cole was pulling them from her unguarded mind. Her plan unfolded inside his head. A plan he didn't understand— a plan that he didn't let his mind finish. He shut his mind to the images and anger built inside him. His calm, cool demeanor shifted. *What was this? Why would she toy with me like this? Jealousy? Was she angry about Stacey? Was this how she would get back at me?* Bringing a vampire to the edge of his control and then stopping wasn't a very wise move. Maybe he should let her find out... *No.* He would play a game of his own.

"Stop!" His voice rolled out like thunder. She jumped to her feet, stumbling back into the wall as he shot her a look of warning and stuffed his cock back into his pants.

Her hands felt the wall as she slid over toward the elevator buttons. In a heartbeat, he was in front of her, pressing her against the flat surface. His narrowed eyes burned into hers, and the muscles in his jaw ticked as he grabbed her arm. *Calm. Must stay calm.* He was about to lose his cool.

She gasped as he spun her quickly. Stumbling, she stared at the wall. His deep voice rolled inside the shell of her ear. "Put your hands against the wall."

Her breath hitched as his hands cupped her elbows, placing her palms up. He skated his hands up the length of her arms and caged her hands beneath his. His cock pounded inside his pants. It took every ounce of control not to shred her clothes and bury himself inside her. The look she had given him when he peered over Stacey's neck had made him hard. She was accepting him for what he was, not judging him, wanting him. Now he was about to explode from the fire he had just seen in her. He leaned forward and pressed against her backside.

Cole placed his lips on her ear, and felt the chill roll over her body. Her breath caught in her throat as he growled, then kicked her legs apart.

"Spread your legs." Aching to be inside of her, tasting and touching, Cole lifted her skirt. He stretched an evil smile against her neck as his fingers slid through her silkiness.

Stifling more than a moan, he brushed his lips over the sensitive spot behind her ear. "You have a very bad girl inside of you, Mia."

"Cole? You've always been so gentle, what—"

He flipped his hand inside her panties and tore them from her body. Mia cried out in pleasure when his fingers stroked her soft folds. Within seconds, she teetered on the edge.

The voice on the radio grew louder, and Cole paused as they called out his name.

"No, don't stop. Please, Cole, please."

Her pleas began to strip him of his sanity and the urge to please her doused his anger. "How does it feel to bring someone to the edge and then stop?"

She gasped and turned toward him. "Did you read my thoughts?" Peering over her shoulder, Mia locked into his gaze.

"Answer me."

"It feels as I hoped it would, Cole. I'm out of control, like I had hoped you would be." She rotated her hips on his hand, shamelessly moving against him, and he began to unravel. His fangs grew longer as he rolled his finger around her sensitive spot. "Please, don't stop. Don't let me think. I'm so lost to you, I feel mindless, wild. Take what you need."

The pain in his shaft became unbearable. Reaching down he released it from his pants. The touch of his own hand sent shivers through him. He had never been this aroused. Mia had worked him into such a state that the slightest touch of his own hand almost had his seed spilling against her backside.

"Take what I need? That's a bold thing to say to a vampire. What do you want to give me, Mia?" His amused laughter caused her to shiver. Stroking his length with one hand, he flicked his finger over the fleshy tissue of her folds with the other. Mia laid her forehead against the wall and panted.

"Everything, Cole. Take it..." Her hands fisted as he worked her wet flesh, faster, coaxing her to come. When his finger entered her, her knees buckled. Cole grabbed his throbbing cock, and slid it through her legs, releasing a moan when the heat from her silky folds seared his flesh.

She arched her back and rotated her hips. Cole's fingers flexed on her hips, dug into her skin, and stopped her motion. He was breathing much more than a vampire needed to, and he could hardly catch his breath. He strained to hold the beast inside him back.

"Don't do that." He could smell the aroma of her warm blood calling to him. Like *déjà vu,* the head of his shaft rested at her entrance, and he strained not to shove it inside her.

Mia clawed at the wall as her body began to envelope the head of his shaft. His voice grew hoarse. A hungry growl filled the room. "Bare your neck to me."

He watched each strand of her hair slide back off her shoulder and sweep across her skin. As the last lock swept across her back, his control fell with it. The need to take her like an animal surfaced. Cole placed his lips on her skin and inhaled the scent of her blood. *Mine.* He would soon know for sure.

Mia rocked against his hand bringing her body closer to the edge. He pulled back his head and prepared to strike. He'd waited so long, imagining what it would feel like to have his heart beat once again. Would he feel warm instantly? How long would it beat? All the answers to his questions were seconds away, and they all relied on Mia. He tried hard not to shove into her. First, he would feed, and then he would pleasure himself inside of her. He bent down and licked her delicate skin, marking the spot he would taste.

"Are you ready, my love?" All the restraint was gone from his voice.

"Make me yours, Cole."

She had no clue what that entailed, but he had deprived himself of human emotion for so long, he couldn't comprehend what her words just did to him. And he never wanted to lose this feeling again. He pressed his lips upon her skin. His mouth watered as the aroma of the warm red liquid filtered through his senses.

Slowly. Calmly. Take her slow. Must not scare her.

Mia's emotions were still fragile, he could feel it. The struggle to hold back was harder than ever before. If he had been in this state of arousal with anyone else, his fangs and his cock would be buried inside already.

Cole positioned his fangs on her skin above her artery. As his eyes rolled back and closed, he realized he'd never been this aroused before. New desires surfaced. He wanted to take her hard, yet he held back his bite as his fangs made an indentation on her flesh threatening to penetrate her skin.

Mia cried out as the sharp points poked at her, and she clawed at the wall desperately trying to brace herself, then he felt her fear surface and her muscles tense. Her cry tingled in his ear, making the vampire he pushed down inside of him roar with excitement. Harder he pressed his fangs into her flesh, pulling it taut. The next movement would bring her blood forth. The head of his cock slickened, bloodlust was taking over. As soon as he penetrated her skin, he would spill his seed on her backside. *Waited so long. Now, I will prove she is mine.*

TWENTY THREE

*T*he radio at Cole's feet sounded an alert tone—three long beeps.

"Detective Barnett, this is the sheriff. If you're in the elevator you'd better answer, because they're about to break in. Last chance."

Cole's lids flew open, casting a blazing, light-amber glow against the wall. His jaw slackened. John's words echoed through the haze that overtook him. His thoughts were in turmoil. Painfully, he pulled his mind back as the reality of the situation penetrated the bloodlust. He opened his mouth wide, careful not to nick her with his fangs as he pulled away from her. If one drop of her blood seeped through, he would be lost. He tried hard to harness the beast that wanted to rip into her, and his mouth salivated as he licked his lips, savoring the salty taste of her skin. His fangs retracted with protest, and his body stiffened as he mastered his control.

"Fuck. Game over."

Mia rested her forehead against the wall and groaned with an ache Cole fully understood.

Cole breathed in the sweet smell of her arousal; she wasn't leaving this elevator unsatisfied, not around all the special units that will be waiting for them. He pulled his cock away from her and focused on her silky flesh. Working it back and forth with his thumb, he whispered in her ear, "Come for me."

Mia trembled as the tremendous build inside unknotted in her stomach and rushed down to the sensation between her legs. She couldn't hold her voice, crying out as her body began to convulse.

Cole swiftly reached down and grabbed the radio. "10-4 sheriff, I'm in the elevator." The radio clicked continuously with different voices, canceling other units that were in route as the elevator jerked into motion.

Cole's dark brown eyes flaked with tiny pieces of amber as he tucked his hard shaft back inside of his pants. "You are a bad girl, Mia. See all the trouble you have caused." Pulling her to him, he brushed gentle kisses over her lips, whispering onto them, "I like when you're bad." His gaze was still heated as he zipped his pants.

"You know that control we discussed? You have approximately one minute to gain it, before these doors open." A low laugh pushed through his grin.

She straightened herself, brushing her hands along her skirt. When she reached down to pick up her torn panties from the floor, Cole's fingers wrapped around them.

"Cole, give those back!"

"I should at least get a souvenir from this ride, especially since *I* didn't get any release." He teased her with his smile.

"Cole..." She reached for them, only to have him shove them in his pocket.

"If it bothers you that much, you can have them back when you make me scream your name." His eyes challenged her. With her cheeks burning, she dropped her gaze.

Buttons were scattered around the floor from Cole's shirt and it was torn beyond repair. He tried to tuck it in to make it look neat. As they reached the bottom floor, she felt her face flame. Mia pulled at the hem of her skirt. Would they know she wasn't wearing panties?

With a devilish grin, his eyes stroked her frame. "Knowing you're not wearing panties will make walking difficult." He stole a look from the corners of his eyes. "Here we go. Put your game face on." Mia rotated her shoulders, trying to shake off the moment. The elevator dinged. "I was just thinking how easy it would be to slide my tongue through your wetness without the restriction of panties."

Her mouth dropped. The doors opened, and the sheriff stood directly in front of them shaking his head.

"I already cleared the area because I thought this is what you were up to, Cole. I told you to stay away from her unless I order otherwise. Like the blood bond she just refused."

"It wasn't me." Cole jerked his head toward Mia, and her jaw dropped. She glared at him, snapping her mouth shut she turned toward the sheriff.

"You said I should test myself. I just took your advice."

"You two get out of here, and we'll call you if we need you. Mia, I may need you to look at the other two bodies that turned up." He waved a hand of dismissal then walked away, muttering under his breath. "A female Cole... Two of them. That's what I have to deal with now, dammit."

"It looks like we have the night off. If I knew pushing that button would do that, I would have pushed it a while ago." He chuckled as he rolled up his sleeves.

"With whom?" The words blurted out before she could stop them.

He arched an eyebrow. "Are you claiming me, my love?" His voice was low. He tugged on his sleeves as he stared at her in silence. "Still unsure? You have vampire tendencies, even if you won't accept it. We are very territorial, so even if you won't let me in all the way, know that I will harm anyone that comes near you. You are mine, and I have no qualms in protecting what's mine. Nor do I have shame in claiming you."

He finished with his shirt. Placing a finger under her chin, he tilted her eyes up to meet his. "What would you like to do?"

Run. Stay. Hell, after that "claiming" comment, she didn't know. What does it mean? What if she wanted to claim him—could anyone else touch him? Does it mean he was going to pee on her to mark his territory?

"I'm hungry," was the action she decided on. She couldn't remember the last time she was actually hungry.

"Dinner it is. I'll follow you to your apartment. We can drop off your car, and then go get something to eat."

Cole retrieved an extra shirt from his trunk before walking up to her apartment. Mia stopped in the doorway. Turning to him, she grabbed his shirt and met his eyes.

"Thanks for being honest with me about everything. I could never forgive you if you lied to me. The one thing I cannot tolerate is a dishonest person."

"I will never lie to you." The back of his hand caressed her cheek.

"Do you really want to go out to eat? I can always order something, and we can stay in. I would like to have you to myself, if that's okay." She stepped inside the door, pulling him by the hand.

"You've made me extra hungry, so unless you are planning on feeding me, we'll have to go out. I didn't bring any containers with me. Although, you were willing in the elevator, I could feel your hesitation then and now. I want you, Mia, in every possible way, but not if you are unsure." Cole removed his torn shirt as he spoke.

Looking at her feet, she shifted uneasily. The thought of his fangs penetrating her skin like huge needles, extracting her blood, made her stomach nauseous. Yes, she did lose herself in the moment, but now she was thinking clearly.

He wrapped her into his bare chest. She placed her head against it, closing her eyes tight in an attempt to drown out her conscious thoughts. She could never fully please him.

He squeezed her tighter, and she knew he felt something shift inside her. "What I feel for you runs much deeper than the need for the blood in your veins. I tease you, but I would never force you to do something you don't want to." Cupping her face in his hands, he placed a kiss on her forehead, nose, and lips. "Now, let's get ready to go out before I start checking on the things that I've wanted to do to your body. We'll never eat if we stay here."

TWENTY-FOUR

Cole pulled into the restaurant's parking lot, which set tucked back into a wooded area. When the name on the restaurant was in view, Mia laughed.

"*Vamppelli's?*"

"*Soprano's* was taken," he replied with a playful grin. "These are old friends of mine. We have many restaurants that are owned by vampires, and those are the only places I can eat because they carry... vampire food." He winked, and she took comfort in knowing something about him that other humans didn't. She smiled inwardly at the thought. A man greeted them at the door as they walked inside the quiet, cozy restaurant.

"Cole?" The man's tone was elevated with surprise as he continued with a thick mob-like accent. "I haven't seen you in decades. I'll let the boss know you're here. What beautiful company you keep this evening." The man reached down and kissed Mia's hand, then led them to a secluded table in the back.

Maybe they should've named the place Soprano's, she thought as he took her drink order. Before she could blink, he was back with a beer. After pouring it, he placed a wine glass and a black mug in front of Cole. He held a carafe filled with red liquid as he looked at Mia. She knew it wasn't Pinot Noir, and she knew what he was waiting for. Should he pour it into a clear glass or conceal it in the black mug? The silence thickened.

Cole's eyes traced up to Mia's as he grabbed the black mug, pushing it under the carafe. Mia quickly replaced the black mug with the wine glass, staring back at him. The man nodded in approval, smiling at her as he poured the liquid into the clear wine glass. She wanted to ask him if she won a toaster oven for passing the test.

Cole waited for him to leave before he spoke, his eyes still on her. "You didn't have to do that. I don't want you to be uncomfortable."

She leaned back, studying his face, searching her feelings as she looked into his beautiful, deep eyes.

"If this is going to work, I need to see everything. If it bothers me, I'll tell you. It's not fair to you if you're constantly hiding who you are."

She had to admit, Cole made her feel very relaxed most of the time. Even if he was drinking human blood as she ate a salad.

"Where is the vampire you brought in the other night?"

"He's below the prison; that's where we keep vampire criminals. All the cells are made of pure silver, and there's no sunlight. He'll await trial and then be punished for his crime." Cole enjoyed telling her about his world, most of it. There was still a much darker side that he'd hoped he could shield her from. But for right now, for the first time in his existence, he was telling someone about his life, his work. His being without companionship for so long, had caused him to lose a piece of himself. Now, with each word that rolled from her lips, he found himself feeling more alive.

"I find this all fascinating—crime, death, trials. Will he go through the court system?"

Cole chuckled. He ran his fingers through his hair. "Kind of. He will go through our court system. It isn't as forgiving as yours." The waiter returned, placing another beer on the table and taking her salad plate.

"Can I ask you a personal question, Cole?"

He twirled the stem of his glass, still looking into her eyes, studying her. He loved the way her mouth moved when she chewed her food, the way her eyes lit up when she was excited. "Yes, you can, but then I get to ask a question."

"Okay, I have so many questions." She laughed and her face lit with a smile. Her laughter did something to him. Something new was happening inside. After being dead and lifeless for so long, it was something he did not want to let go.

"I did the math based on what you had told me, and you were made in 1881, which is the same time as the incident with Glowing Eyes. Um, Bass. Is your maker alive?"

Cole stiffened in his seat; his face masked like a stone statue. His expression lodged a lump in her throat, and she swallowed it down as his look became cold. "I'm sorry, forget I asked. I didn't mean to make you uncomfortable." She watched the pain surface in his eyes.

Cole looked away from her. Taking a breath she knew he didn't need, then reached across the table and took her hand. He seemed to struggle as he tried to smooth his expression. "Being made is very personal, Mia. Vampires don't share this information often."

Way to go, Mia. Ruin the evening by bringing up his past, which you knew was painful. Why don't you ask him why he couldn't save his family next? His pain tugged her heart. She had to get away, breathe, anywhere but here. *Why do I feel his emotions so strongly?*

"Excuse me, I need to go to the restroom." When she stood, he looked stunned by her emotions for him. She knew he'd felt her matched pain and he grabbed her hand, pulling her back into the seat.

"No, you will not run from me. Sit down." He stared at her before continuing. "Your calculation is correct. I was made in 1881. After what happened to my family, I swore revenge. The sheriff... John, came to me. He told me what he was, which explained why he never worked in the daytime. He asked me to ride beside him, join his cause to rid the world of evil. He pointed me toward the saloon and told me to see one of the girls." He stared at the red liquid in his glass, and his voice trailed into a distant memory. "The girl's mother had been raped and killed by the Bass gang, and John had taken her in. I went to her... She made me." He paused, picking up his glass he twirled the red liquid. "Somewhere down the line, Evet was made a vampire; we are still not sure by whom. Evet found out the saloon girl was turning peacemakers, so he had someone shove a silver spike through her chest while she slept in the daytime."

Mia reached forward and grabbed his hand. She cupped it inside of hers.

"Bass made his way toward Arizona to meet up with the Clanton Gang. I've been chasing him ever since. Mia, I respect my badge and what it stands for. I want people to live in peace and not fear the place they live in."

She swallowed several gulps of her beer. The more she learned about him the more real this became, and the more she felt him dig deeper into her heart. "You will catch him. You're a good detective, Cole, and you're dedicated." She could tell her words of encouragement relaxed him. Cole looked up from her hand with a gorgeous smirk as she continued. "Did you say that Bass went to meet up with the Clanton gang?"

"Yes." His eyebrows drew together in question.

"Wow, the *Cowboys*, and all this was in 1881. The shootout at the O.K. Corral was on October 26th that same year. Were you a part of that? Were you there?" Mia couldn't help the excitement building inside her. This was the Wild West, and she loved it.

His smiled broadened, and his eyes lit with an amused adoration. "Hundreds of women, decade after decade, and none of them came close to being you." He shook his head. "No, sorry to let you down, my love. John and I were heading that way after Bass, but the shootout took place before we got there. I would have loved to have you with me back then, Mia."

A burst of laughter erupted from her throat.

"Oh, I'm sure you would have. You could have me in one of those tight corset things and a dress, at home, obeying your every command. Popping out your kids—just like most of the women back then—seen and not heard."

Cole leaned over and kissed her lips. He sat back in the chair and stretched his legs out. "That's where you're wrong. I would have wanted you riding beside me. I would love to have you in tight pants, riding boots and a gun belt wrapped around that beautiful waist of yours. And of course, a nice big smoke wagon slid into the holster. And, Mia"—she swallowed hard as his stare intensified—"I would never want to tame that wild spirit in you. In fact, I could've used it in a couple of gunfights. You're fearless at times."

"Would you like me if I were normal? If I couldn't talk to the dead and see vampires?"

He leaned forward, his face so close that he was almost touching her nose. "Mia, when I saw you in the woods, and when I pulled you over, I didn't know about your power. And yes, it is a power. That is the moment when my soul felt you. Sometimes, I wish you didn't have it. Then I wouldn't have to share you with the FBI and the sheriff. I wouldn't have to worry about you so much."

"Wait. You don't care that I'm weird?"

"My love, I'm a vampire, and we all have special traits just like you. Besides, you haven't seen weird yet. Just wait." A knowing smile bridged across his face.

When the waiter placed her dinner in front of her, she felt strange eating in front of someone that wasn't. The hunger gnawing at her stomach disagreed, and she cut into the thick, juicy piece of meat in front of her. She closed her eyes, and a tiny sound of pleasure escaped her as the flavor filled her mouth.

"Oh, my God. That is good." Her eyes opened to find Cole staring at her. "I'm sorry. Do you miss food?"

His mouth pulled into a thin smile. "I miss some food, but I have gotten used to it. I can pick up the taste of certain foods from blood."

"What do you miss the most?" she asked as she cut off another chunk of meat. His eyes looked down at her plate, then returned to her face. He twirled his glass stem between his fingers before he raised it to his lips, then paused before he took a sip.

"Steak."

She stopped chewing. Looking down at the big slab of meat on her plate, she wondered how much more torture she could put him through.

TWENTY-FIVE

*C*ole raised his brow as Mia's phone emitted a tone.

"What? It's Cyn's ring tone. She likes Eminem." She flipped open the phone. "Cole, do you mind?"

He nodded, and she answered the call.

"Hello..."

"Cyn... she's gone. Missing. I've tried everything."

"Kevin, slow down... what's wrong?" She dropped her fork and panicked. "What do you mean she's missing? Did you call the police? Did you try her cell?"

"Yes, I did all of that! I'm worried. The car was broken into, and a detective came out, and now she's missing!" Kevin spoke fast, and his words ran together. Mia had never heard him like this before; true panic in his voice.

Her eyes darted to Cole and she placed her palm over the speaker. "Can you hear him?" She whispered and Cole nodded. She turned her attention back to Kevin, "Who? What cop came over?"

"I don't know. Mia, she's gone!"

"Okay. Slow down. Kev, let me call you back."

Cole was already on alert by the time she hung up. "Cole, can you call the sheriff to see what detective came to their house? Kevin said the car was broken into, and a detective came out to take their statement around 5:30. Kevin left for work and hasn't heard from Cynthia since."

She felt her heart race as she looked at her watch. "It's going on ten p.m. This isn't like her at all. She'd never go a half-hour without talking to Kevin." Her pulse elevated. "The police told Kevin that she's an adult and hasn't been missing long enough for them to do anything."

Mia's gut told her something was wrong, and she could tell Cole had the same suspicion as he called the sheriff. He quickly ran through the story, and his face remained expressionless. He closed his phone as he motioned for the waiter to bring the check.

"Mr. Barnett, I was told to relay a message to you. The owner, he... he is in your debt. There is no charge for your visit. Please, come back again."

"Tell him I'll speak to him about this. He still has a business to run, and I will pay him the next time I'm here." The waiter bowed and disappeared before Mia's eyes. *Damn they move fast.*

Cole was calm, and she was about to lose her shit. He took her hand, and pulled her from the seat. "Sorry to cut your dinner short, but John said to come in just in case there's something to this."

His calm tone didn't stop her nerves from knotting. There was something to this. He knew something, and he wasn't telling her—she could feel it.

***

It wasn't until they arrived at the FBI building that she spoke. "Cole, did you find out who came to their house today?"

Cole glanced at her. "Yes. It was Russo."

Although she was very worried for Cynthia, she couldn't help but smile when Cole's eyes found hers in the elevator.

It was after hours, and the waiting room was dark and empty. Mia's thoughts went to Stacey and how Cole had erased her mind. Could a vampire really erase someone's memory?

They were the first ones to arrive. Mia paced the room, the nerves building inside were making her tremble. She could feel something wasn't right.

Cole sat in his usual chair with his legs stretched out. Mia couldn't help but drink him in. *Eye candy.* No matter what he wore, you could always see the contour of his muscles through his clothes. He reached his foot out, tugging the chair in front of him closer to his, and then motioned for her to sit.

Her nervous tick had her leg bouncing as soon as she connected with the seat. Cole placed his hand on her knee.

"Easy, we don't know anything yet." His voice was calm as usual. She hated that, but respected and envied it, as well. He was the guy to call when shit went down; the person you could count on to get you home safely, or help you bury a body.

She needed a diversion from her thoughts, or she was going to drive herself crazy. Her mind already had Cynthia dead and mutilated.

"Cole, what's on the 19th and 20th floor?"

"The 19th floor is sleeping quarters for our special agents and police. The 20th floor is a combination of test labs and offices."

The door slid open. Nancy, Gonela, Cramer, Russo, and the sheriff walked in and made their way to the chairs.

The sheriff walked around the room. His fingers rubbed his mouth. Mia didn't know where his mind was, but it wasn't here. Rosetta walked in next; Mia hadn't seen her since that night at the funeral home.

The sheriff rested his hands on the back of the empty chair and turned toward Mia. "What do you know about your friend's disappearance? What I mean is... Has your mind picked up anything?"

Mia shook her head.

Nancy leaned forward and tossed a couple of bags on the table labeled "Evidence." Detective Gonela stared at the sheriff, as he was adding something to the white board affixed to the wall.

"Sheriff, Mia's mother is fine. I checked on her before I came here." Gonela nodded as if he were sending a personal message to Mia that she was safe.

Mia felt a wave of negative energy. She slowly turned her head toward it, and Russo stared back at her. His eyes narrowed as she locked into his gaze and focused on his aura. A mixture of red shades and brown appeared. Just what she thought, selfish. She didn't need to see the brown to tell her that. The red was disturbing though, and the different shades of it said he was very unstable, sexually. Look at that other shade of red. *You hate me, don't you, Russo?* She wanted to blow him a kiss to see how far she could push him, but decided on a devious grin instead.

"Mia, did your friend's boyfriend try to call her?" Nancy asked, pulling Mia's attention away from Russo.

"Yes, he said everyone has tried to call her cell."

For the first time, Cole's face masked with concern as he looked at Mia. "*You* haven't tried. Give me your cell."

She took the phone from her purse and handed it to Cole.

"I'm going to put it on speaker, and you talk, okay?" Cole waited for her response as he scrolled through her address book. Once he pressed Cynthia's number, he placed the phone on the table. The instant the call was answered, Mia stopped breathing.

"Ahh... Mia. I haven't seen you since the gas station. How's your blood? Are you keeping it warm for me?" The voice was cold and calm.

Cole abruptly stood, placing his hands on each side of the phone.

The sheriff latched on to Cole's shoulder, trying to calm him. A million things were going through Mia's head. Should she play it calm, or be a bad ass? She wasn't prepared for this or trained like the others. She didn't know how to handle psychopaths, not to mention, psychopaths who were already dead. She took a deep breath before she responded, deciding to be herself.

"Glowing Eyes, how's the energy I stole from you? I see that you needed a weak human to get it back. Did I hurt you that bad?" Although fear raked her insides, her tone was as smooth as glass.

His response shook the phone, moving it on the table. "I'm gonna have fun draining you dry. But first, I want to have a little fun with you. I want those blue eyes."

Cole's grip tightened on the table, the top bowed underneath his hands. The sheriff applied more pressure to his shoulder, and squeezed. "Here, blue eyes. Someone wants to say 'hi.'" Bass's tone was nothing less than deadly.

"Mia," is all Cynthia got out before Bass came back on the phone.

"You're lucky she's still alive—the bitch stabbed me."

Mia smiled on the inside. Cyn always said, "Don't fuck with a Jersey girl, or she'll stab you." Guess she wasn't kidding.

"Bass, you hurt her, and I'll..." Cole put his hand over Mia's and gave her a look of caution.

"You'll what? If you want her to live, you'll come and give yourself to me."

Cole looked as if he was about to burst. The control he was showing was commendable, but Mia didn't know how much more he could take. She leaned over Cole's arm and put her mouth to the phone.

"Oh, I'm coming to you, Glowing Eyes. You can bank on that. And I'll drain every ounce of energy you have left. Send your men. Come and get me!" She felt an icy rage building inside her as she spoke.

Cole slammed the phone shut, and everyone looked at him as he glared at Mia. "Do you have a death wish?" He was clearly upset.

No, he was pissed.

"What? You're going to go get her right?"

When he looked away from her, her eyes widened.

"No, we are not." He turned back to her as he spoke.

Her mouth dropped in disbelief. "Cole, you're not going to save her?"

He squared his shoulders, and she glared back at him. "No, she is expendable. There is something going on that is much bigger than her and—"

"And what? Me? So, as long as you catch the big fish, it doesn't matter how many little fish get slaughtered? Is that it?"

Cole stood, pushing her back with his chest. "Now is not the time for human emotions."

She backed away from him, glancing at everyone in the room. Their expressions held the same conclusion as Cole's. Glaring back at Cole, she had a mixture of feelings wrapped so tight in her belly, she thought she would vomit. She was upset for giving into him, letting her guard down and wanting him. Now this? She didn't want anything to do with him but knew it was too late for her heart.

"Fine. I'll get her myself. If he wants me, he can have me." Before Mia reached the door, Cole stood in front of her like an unmovable barrier.

"Sit down!" His voice was a thunderous command.

The sheriff swiftly took her arm and led her back to the chair. Nancy stared at her with a grin. *What the fuck is she looking at?* Mia's thoughts were about to erupt as she jerked her arm away from the sheriff's grasp.

Rosetta's voice broke through the tension in the room. "I couldn't track the the stuff Cole left for me at the funeral home, but Gonela was able to pick up a scent. We tracked it back to a location in Lake Worth. I spoke with Tom earlier, and there was vampire blood in each of the three bodies from our cases. He's trying to gain access to the other two now."

"And we still can't locate Vincent." Nancy was still staring at Mia as she spoke.

Mia's reality finally crumbled. "You guys are vampires. Why can't you just go kill everyone and control this? This makes no sense to me. You're supposed to be these powerful creatures, but you sit here and do nothing." Her voice sounded foreign and unfriendly.

The sheriff left a trail of wind behind him as he quickly came to stand in front of Mia.

"Now that's enough, young lady. Yes, I've taken a liking to you, but that doesn't give you the right to insult my people. We are sworn peacekeepers, some for many decades. We still have to follow the law, Mia, or we would be no better than them. I understand that you're upset about your friend, but there is nothing we can do right now."

Mia fought back the tears, refusing to let them fall this time. A rage she had never felt before brewed inside, and it felt like an electric fence was hugging her.

"I understand, Sheriff. Humans are expendable to you, unless of course you need them around for food or"—she stood quickly and glanced at Cole—"to release some tension." She locked eyes with Nancy who was still grinning at her. *What is so amusing about this?* Her eyes flicked down to the table.

"Nancy, is that evidence regarding the cases?" Mia asked with a taut nod toward the bag on the table. Nancy slowly and deliberately nodded as if she were waiting for Mia to put everything together. Mia stared at the clear plastic bag, and within it was Art's pack of Reds. She glanced back at Nancy's broadening grin. Her mind clicked. Grabbing the bag, she emptied the contents onto the table. Her stomach instantly clenched. She focused, refusing to give in to the nauseous feeling. The vision quickly flashed through her mind. She held onto them, slowing them down until they seemed weightless. She froze the next image, seeing the hand Art took the pack of Reds from. Staying inside the vision, she waited. She could feel the next clue; it was so close... *Got it!*

She knew Cole felt her energy soar, swirling around him as it did before, and she didn't care. He rested his hand on her arm, his voice dissolved the images in her mind. "Mia, did you see something?"

She jerked away from his touch. "Nothing you'd be concerned about." Turning quickly, she gave Nancy a quick nod, hoping and praying she'd understand, and then walked toward the door.

Cole blocked her exit, grabbed her arm, and tightened his grip as he pulled her into him. "Whatever you're thinking, stop. What did you see?"

Mia narrowed her eyes, she felt used by all of them. Had she been a game to him? He'd been dead for a long time, maybe it was fun for him to toy with human emotions. She could come to understand many things about Cole and deal with them. However, at this moment, an evil vampire was holding her best friend, and they didn't care. She unfolded the anger inside of her and directed it toward Cole.

"I saw a vampire who couldn't get to a human mentally, so he tore down her walls and finally got to toy with her. Now he can move his cold, dead heart on to someone else." Her voice was as cold as the painful look in his eyes. Ignoring the emotion, she jerked her arm from his grip and continued to walk toward the door. Again, he blocked her exit.

She could physically see his temper mount. Curling his lips back, he exposed his fangs. "Don't push me. You may see something you don't want to see, something that may give you nightmares for the rest of your life."

Mia didn't like being intimidated. Out of impulse, she reached out to push him back. Grabbing her wrists quicker than her mind could register the touch, he slammed both of them against the wall.

"You're pushing me, Mia. Do you really want to do this, here? Let's get this biting thing out of the way."

The air charged with a powerful wave of energy radiating between them. When a vision flashed through her mind, she remembered her mission.

Knowing that Cole would hear her, she kept her voice barely audible. "You won't save her from Bass. How am I supposed to react to you? You seem so cold and heartless. I don't know you. Are you evil, Cole? Just like him? You are the walking dead—one has to think about where that energy comes from. Are you a demon like him?"

Cole's grip tightened on her wrists, and she winced in pain. "How dare you compare me to Bass." He pulled her closer to him. Glaring down into her eyes, his voice was like steel as he spoke through clenched teeth. "Everyone has a demon inside them. *Everyone.* It's how you control the demon once it's awakened that matters."

The energy in the room made her mind spin. She contemplated her next move. She didn't need him to save Cynthia or to help her. She was strong enough to do this herself. Her mind formulated a plan. She pulled away from Cole and walked back to the table where everyone stood.

"Mia, we have to follow the law—please, understand. This is the way it is. You humans have made it so the criminals have the upper hand. Vampire law is a little different, but since we have humans involved in this, we have to be careful."

Mia ignored the sheriff's words and passed the table to the back wall where the red button taunted her. She turned, and glared at everyone. Her hand hovered over the casing of the button. They stared at her, waiting for her to twitch so they could pounce. The tension in the room grew as Mia made eye contact with each one of them.

When she slowly dropped her hand away from the button, the vampires relaxed. In the next second, before Mia's hand completely dropped, she smashed the glass case concealing the brand new silver fire ax. She had it in front of her before any of them could touch her. Russo was the first to step back as she gripped the ax, her hand dripping blood from the open wound on the top of her grip. She looked at the sheriff, blowing a lock of hair from her face.

"Not this human. I'm for killing them all." She grasped the ax in her hands, loosely, with just enough room to swing. The lights above flickered as she walked past them to the door. *Decapitation anyone?* She grabbed Cole's keys as she passed the table, moving faster as fangs popped around her. Backing out of the door, she pushed the tile to shut it behind her and ran as if Hell was on her heels.

The sheriff halted Cole's forward motion. "Let her go. She's obviously delusional if she thinks she can really get away from a vampire."

Even if Cole knew the sheriff was right, his legs twitched to run after her. His mind urged him to disobey the sheriff's order. He'd never seen her so focused, so determined to complete whatever her mind had set on. This time, she wasn't running away from something, she was running straight for it. He had to go to her.

TWENTY-SIX

*M*ia could still feel Cole's eyes burning a hole through her as she pulled into the sheriff's headquarters. After trying every key on Cole's ring, the lock to the back door clicked. Figures... last one on the ring.

She descended the stairwell. With each step, her heart pounded, and adrenaline raced through her as she reached the basement door. Another small set of stairs, and the use of Cole's security key, and she was right where she wanted to be.

Her eyes darted around, the damp chill in the room making her shiver. Cole was right; there was no light pollution at all down here.

The cells shined with a silver metal luster that she admired with her hand, as she walked past each cell. One by one, the vampires inside them looked up as she went past. Coming upon the one she was looking for, she froze, staring at the vampire inside.

"Igor!" Her tone was strong. The vampire slowly turned his head to look at her.

"Aren't you dead, yet?"

"No, but you'll soon be." She pulled the ax from behind her, and his eyes widened as they locked onto the shine of the blade.

"What? Wait, you can't do that. They said I have to stand trial first," he stammered.

She began fitting the keys into the lock. As each one failed, rage built inside her. Igor was the answer. He knew how to find Cynthia.

"You will stand my trial. Where is Evet Bass?" Rage slowly crept into every fiber of her body. Her hands became clumsy as she fumbled with each key.

"No, you can't. You have to go by the law. Vampires... cops follow the law. They never break it!" He was frantic, his eyes falling to the ax resting against her leg as she worked the keys. He scurried back into the corner of the cell, avoiding her eyes.

"Well, sucks to be you. I'm not the police or a vampire, and I will ram this ax right through your neck. Tell me where he is!" She only had two keys left until Igor was hers.

"I don't know where he is. He just made me into this creature, and told me to bring you to him."

"Where? Where did he tell you to bring me?" Mia heard the key click inside the lock and felt an internal release. She paused. Could she do this? Was it right? She struggled with herself. She was about to kill a man, even if he was a vampire. Could her mind distinguish between the two after she killed him? *Can I forgive myself?* With each thought, her feet moved forward until she glared down at Igor.

She had to save Cynthia, at any cost. She raised the ax above her shoulder. Her eyes narrowed at him, trapping his power with her gaze. "Tell me where he is!"

"I don't know." He put his hands up in an attempt to block the ax as he screamed back at her.

"Wrong answer, Igor!" Her mind unraveled, everything spun through her head. She was furious with Cole. She was angry with everyone. She abandoned herself to a fit of rage and swung the ax.

In the next instant, she was flying backward through the air. She heard the cell door lock. Instantly, a figure pinned her to the floor. Her rage consumed her, and she fought until exhaustion set in. She breathed heavy on the concrete floor. When a voice whispered in her ear, she shuddered.

"It excites me when you fight—you know that. Now, stop fighting, or I'll take you right here," Cole's voice was calm, but laced with a primal lust.

"Get off of me!" She jerked her body again, trying to buck him off.

His mouth came down upon hers, hard, devouring the taste of her rage. He had no regard for her skin or bones, and her teeth cut into her lip from the pressure. The iron taste of blood flowed over her tongue as it leaked from the cut.

He took her bleeding lip into his mouth, sucking, releasing a soft moan as the taste of her flowed into him. She bucked again with more strength, trying hard to push him off.

"Mia. Stop. I'm very hungry, and you're pushing me too far. Calm your pulse." Cole lay on top of her as she struggled with her self-control. Her emotions were raw, and his expression reflected her pain and rage. With his lips close to her ear, his breath rolled across it as he spoke. "I would save you. You're the only thing that matters to me. That's why I just saved you from yourself."

Her body went limp beneath him. He was right. She wouldn't be able to live with herself if she'd decapitated Igor. Art was different. He begged her to set him free and let him go to his wife. She would have killed Igor out of hate and anger. He was obviously young and had been made a vampire under false pretenses.

Mia was on an emotional rollercoaster that was about to derail. Cynthia was missing. No one would help her. She hated the man she loved.

Mia heard noises from inside the room, but Cole didn't move.

"Cole, get off of her." The sheriff's voice echoed through the long corridor of cells.

Cole stared down at her, his eyes turning as black as the night sky. At first, his voice was a whisper. "Hate me, Mia."

"Is he going to kill Cynthia?"

"Yes." His eyes began to pull at her mind. She could feel him trying to gain control of it, and the tug was more powerful than he'd ever displayed.

Mia felt her breath as it bounced off Cole's skin. There was movement all around them as others joined the sheriff. Cole's eyes intensified, and she stared back at him.

"What if I just let go and let you win?" She searched his eyes. His face tightened, and his jaw began to twitch as he clenched his teeth.

"Don't let me win. Fight me, Mia. Wake the demon up inside you, and learn how to control it."

He knew something she didn't. She could sense it. What was he doing? Tears pooled in her eyes.

Cole pushed his body harder against her, squeezing her wrists. "No tears. Don't do that. Hate me."

"Why?"

"You won't have a chance if you show weakness. I must protect you anyway I can."

Cole quickly glanced behind him, and she peered over his shoulder to where everyone stood watching. He turned back to Mia. She felt his power grabbing her, and the familiar look of pain surfaced in his dark eyes as he spoke louder than before. "I'm done with her now. I had my fun. The sheriff has first choice if he wants her."

She narrowed her eyes at him. "You bastard. Get off of me! I *do* hate you!"

"No, it's not enough yet. You have to feel it," he whispered.

Confused, her pulse raced, and her anger built into a ball that settled in the pit of her stomach, growing with every word he spoke. She refused to let the tears stinging her eyes fall. Like a switch, she turned every emotion she was feeling into hate, and the pain she felt was so deep, her soul screamed.

"When I get up from here, I'm going to grab that ax and ram it through your dead heart, and then I'm going to cut your fucking head off."

"Yes, that's it. I can feel your demon. It wants out, Mia. Let it out. Hate me." Cole peered behind him as he spoke, with a smug and arrogant tone, "I suggest whoever gets her takes her on an elevator. She'll give you quite a ride."

Oh, that's it. I hate him now for sure. With every ounce of strength she could pull up, she rolled with him until she straddled his waist. The lights flickered in the room as her body jerked to the side, and she grabbed the ax on the floor. Cole quickly sat up, knocking it from her hand and pinned her arms behind her. She slumped forward onto his shoulder, breathless from her rage.

"Okay. Shows over! Everyone out!" The sheriff pushed everyone out the door, locking it behind them.

Cole loosened his grip on her arms. "John, was everyone here?"

"Yes, they all witnessed it."

Mia sat motionless on her knees, straddling Cole's lap. She brought her head back, brushing her cheek against his, until she met his eyes. As angry as she was, she couldn't resist his scent. It was intoxicating. *Great. I'm addicted to him, which means I'm an idiot and fucked.* She bent down in thought, brushing her lips against his neck. He stiffened under her touch. She pulled back, and then buried her teeth into his neck, licking the blood as it surfaced. Her aches instantly felt better.

Cole gasped, and grabbing her shoulders, he pushed her back to glare at her.

"That was payback for my lip. Now, let go of me." Her emotions were unguarded, and she knew he saw right through to her soul and straight into her heart.

"No, Mia. Hate me. It's over. We're done." She pulled her hands free from his grasp and straightened herself on her knees. Mia stared back at him. Her hand went to the back of his head, pulling him to her lips.

Mia now fully understood why vampires became excited in times of bedlam. He responded to her out of impulse, and she pulled away from him. With ragged breaths, she stared into his dark eyes, eyes that told her a different story than his words, deep pools that she loved and hated so deeply.

"I do hate you. I'll hate you for the rest of your existence." *And love you for the rest of mine.* She couldn't take the pain in her heart, or his eyes, any longer. She knew this was going to hurt. She stood and turned toward the sheriff. "I'm going home now. Can Nancy drive me?" Her voice was empty of emotion.

Cole stood, exchanging looks with the sheriff as they began communicating without words, or so it seemed.

"Have Nancy take her home. Tell everyone that I'll be out in a minute." For the first time, the sheriff looked weakened.

Cole turned his back to her.

She was happy for that, it made it easier to walk away from him.

Cole had stared down into the face of an angel, his perfect match, and the only woman he'd ever loved. He would rather be scorched by the sun than to see her in pain—pain that he had caused. However, when he had searched her eyes, he saw something he didn't want to see. Finally, he saw a piece of her heart, and it killed him to shatter it. He kept his back to her and tilted his head toward John once she was gone.

"At an hour before sunrise, this is the route I'll take to investigate an area where Cynthia may be. Make sure this information leaks, in case I need backup." Cole winked as he handed the sheriff a piece of paper.

John looked at him with a bewildered expression. "Are you sure?"

It would definitely flush out an inside leak, but it could also get Cole killed. "It's time to finish this." Cole saw the look in his friend's eyes. "It has to be done."

"Cole, you're going into this blind, and for what? Revenge?"

Cole ran his fingers through his hair and met John's eyes. "No, for Mia. Bass will not stop until he gets to her—you know that. The minute he spoke her name through the phone, none of the pain from the past mattered. She is mine, and I will protect what is mine."

"You don't even know that. You haven't fed from her, you could be wrong."

"I've never felt surer about anything. I can't explain it, but even without having her blood, I know. She is my fated bride, the one that is meant for me. I can't stand the thought of Bass touching her."

John placed a hand on his shoulder, sighing in defeat. "I'll come with you then. We'll ride together once again to take down Bass."

"No. Sorry, my friend. I go alone. I need you to look after her if I do not return."

"You have my word. I'll watch over her, but you know I can't control her without harming her."

Cole laughed low. "I know. She's a fighter, and if it comes to that, let her do what she needs. But watch over her."

***

Nancy pulled the key from her pocket as Mia relayed the rest of the sheriff's message. When they reached the parking lot, Mia paused.

"Nancy, can you wait one second?"

Nancy arched a brow, looking at her sideways as she stopped by Cole's car. Luckily, the doors were still unlocked from earlier. When she reached in to grab her purse, she noticed something on the floor that she couldn't wait to wrap her hands around. Shutting the door behind her, she stepped back.

"Hey, Nancy, do you guys get these department cars repaired pretty quickly?"

Nancy cocked her head, giving Mia a suspicious look. "We get a new car until the one that's broken is repaired. But Cole *really* loves this car."

Mia bit the inside of her cheek and with a wicked grin, she stepped backward. "Good. That's what I was hoping for." The beautiful, rectangular, red brick rolled out from her fingers as if she were a pitcher on a mound, shattering Cole's window.

Nancy's mouth twitched, and it almost looked like she would smile. "Hell hath no fury like a woman scorned." Nancy stopped a couple cars over, pressing the key fob to unlock the doors.

Mia whistled as she glided down in the seat, running her hands across the leather. "Nice Beamer. I take it this is not a department car?" She admired it further by looking into the back seat.

Nancy smile as she turned the key in the ignition. "Yes, it is. They give me what I want. I'm a full Sector 13 agent, whereas Cole works for the department and is on the Sector 13 Task Force."

Mia filed the information, smiling at Nancy. She had a feeling Nancy didn't give out information easily, and was honored to get the info she got.

Nancy brought the car to a stop in front of Mia's apartment.

"Thanks for the ride. Nancy, do you remember your idea? Are you still up for using me as bait?"

Nancy's eyes glowed with excitement giving them a light chocolate hue. "I'll call you tomorrow. Cole and the sheriff can't know, Mia."

"Okay. I know who's bringing the girls to Bass. I can take you there. I saw it through Art's pack of Reds."

Nancy's smile broadened. "I knew it. I was hoping you'd pick them up. That's why I placed them on the table for you to see. Hey, do you know anyone with a big truck? Something that would hold a couple of girls and provide a safe place for us to sleep?"

"Won't the FBI provide that?"

"We are alone on this, Mia. If the sheriff knows, he will stop it." Nancy's tone was firm with a touch of a threat.

"Well, if I'm going to be used, at least I can do it of my own free will. I can get us a truck. See you tomorrow." As soon as she walked into the apartment, Cole's smell filled her senses, jerking her emotions forward. She traced the scent with her eyes to the couch. His torn shirt hung over the backrest. She stared at it as if it had a heartbeat.

After a quick shower, she grabbed the shirt on the way to bed, curling herself around it. The drums beat with a thunderous boom in her head. One dream fading into another. Something was coming, something powerful.

TWENTY-SEVEN

*M*ia felt pain in her wrist—burning intense pain. A sharp stab in her back followed. It was just below her shoulder blade, and it felt as if her flesh were on fire. The pain increased, and the agony began to suffocate her.

She screamed. Jumping from the bed, her hands went to her body, searching it, inspecting herself for marks from the burns she was sure were there. Her breathing was rapid as her mind swirled, trying to make sense of which part was a dream and which was reality. She'd never felt physical pain from a dream before, and that was the strongest feeling she had ever felt. Shaken, her eyes searched the room. They landed on Cole's shirt still lying next to her pillow were she had used it as a safety blanket.

Cole.

Franticly, she pieced her thoughts together. She bolted toward the door, halting as it blasted off its hinges and landed on the floor by her feet.

"Detective Gonela!"

"Are you okay?" He scanned the apartment, his nose was in the air, and his eyes were trained on any movement.

"Cole. They have Cole. He's in pain." Silent tears streaked her face.

Gonela's features turned to stone as he picked up his radio and walked away from her. She stood in the doorway, cursing the daylight. *What time is it?*

She walked to the coffee maker, and her unsteady hand grabbed the pot. Detective Gonela grabbed her hands and slid the pot from her grip.

"Miss Starr, please, sit down, and let me get this for you. I have a car dispatched to Cole's house to see if there is any sign of him there. And I have someone coming to fix your door. I'm sorry. I heard you scream and thought you were in danger."

She stared into space as Gonela made coffee, his voice a hum in the background. She looked out the sliding glass doors to see that nightfall had just begun.

"Please, get yourself some coffee. I'm going to get dressed." She couldn't stop her hands from shaking as she pulled on a pair of jeans, boots, and a simple button down shirt.

Gonela poured a cup of coffee, pushing it toward her as she sat at the kitchen table, his radio breaking the silence. The dispatcher's voice was clear. "That's 54 on Barnett's car at his 20."

Gonela looked up, his eyes telling her everything. "Cole's car isn't at his house." His tone was apologetic.

Mia grabbed the phone, flipping Nancy's card between her fingers, she dialed. Gonela stared at her with raised brows when she finished leaving Nancy a message.

"What are you planning, Mia? These are vampire criminals. They won't think twice about ripping you to shreds." He stepped closer.

"I know. But I don't feel that it's my time to go, just yet. If Cole is in as much pain as I felt, I have to try to help him, and I have to try to find Cynthia. I've been brought into this weird alternate reality. I'm trying hard to be understanding, accept things for what they are, and... Gonela, I was dead inside before I met Cole. He woke me up and it feels great. Without him, I'm dead again anyway. So if I must die, I would rather go down fighting."

Gonela bowed his chest then placed a kiss on the top of her hand.

"Mi Querida, you are a remarkable woman. I, too, would die for the one I love. You have no idea what I would do to protect what is mine. Tell me... what do you and Nancy have planned? I will help."

"What are you?" Mia asked.

"You also have keen senses. I will reveal myself to you when the time is right. You are dealing with too much right now to even discuss it." His answer confirmed her suspicions—he wasn't human. In addition, her new friend was thoughtful enough to know when someone has had enough shit thrown at them for one day.

"I have to go pick up some items at a friend's house. Do you want to follow me, or do you want to ride together?" She grabbed her purse, heading toward the door, then paused.

"If it's a box labeled 'silver,' it's in the hallway. Some guy dropped it off earlier." Gonela picked the door up, and laid it against the frame.

Mia squeezed through the opening to retrieve the box. She shrugged at the irony of her constant imprisonment, and now, her apartment would be open for anyone to come inside, uninvited.

Excusing herself, Mia Left the room to add the new accessories her friend had made, then they'd play the waiting game. She paced the room, waiting for Nancy. Her hands fidgeted as she entwined her fingers and dug her nails into her palms. Her eyes constantly searched the room.

"Mia, you need to relax. We will do what we can." His tone held an edge of concern. Mia knew this as well and tried to control her emotions, recalling what Cole had told her. Subconsciously, she just needed to hear his calm voice in her head. She thought back to everything he had told her, like it was a training lesson.

She closed her eyes, trying to calm herself, breathing deeply as she focused on Cole. She searched for him, and her mind stumbled upon a faint vision of him wrapped in chains. His eyes popped open as she peeked into his mind. *He felt me.*

Gonela shook her arm, stealing Cole's image away from her. "Don't try to reach him. If the others find out that *you* are his weakness, it will make it worse for him."

Mia nodded. *Shit, I didn't think of that.*

"Why do you think I'm his weakness?"

"Because I have known Cole for decades, and he has never looked at anyone the way he looks at you. He has never lost control, either—until you." His gaze held her in admiration.

Mia lunged toward the phone, only half a ring sounded before she jerked it from its cradle. Nancy gave instructions on where to meet, and Mia told her where to find the guy with the illegal immigrants.

Mia kept her mind open, trying hard to pick something up, anything that would help figure out why the hell they wanted these girls. *I could see if they needed food, but why kill them? If they kept killing off their food source, they wouldn't have any food left.* She filled Gonela in on the plan and called Kevin to give him instructions.

TWENTY-EIGHT)

*M*ia stared out the window as Gonela drove west on the long stretch of Southern Boulevard. The streetlights became scarce, and farmland began to appear. Mia rolled down the window to breath in the air. It always seemed fresher out west of town. Once they passed Lion Country Safari, Gonela turned down a dirt road hidden by the overgrown grass of open fields.

Mia saw an eighteen wheeler parked next to a large gate. Kevin stepped out of the truck as they pulled behind it. He still wore his navy blue work pants and his unbuttoned light blue shirt hung open.

Mia had to admire his abs and chest. They were perfectly formed and belonged in a magazine with the way they rippled down his front. Cynthia had always said it was one of her favorite things about him. She loved him so deeply.

The thought of them losing each other, made Mia's heart ache. Kevin's dreads framed his face like a lion's mane, and his hair bounced as he reached the ground. His arms wrapped around her, hugging her tight with his fear.

When Nancy's BMW pulled up with a couple of cars behind her, Mia grabbed Kevin's hand and dragged him to the front of the truck.

"Kevin, listen, I'm about to tell you some stuff you're not going to believe, but if you want to get Cyn back, you have to trust me." Mia took a deep breath, squared her shoulders and prepared for him to freak. Kevin never was much of a talker, so he just nodded in agreement.

Nancy strolled toward them with a younger woman by her side. Mia didn't recognize her. She scanned her quickly. *A young vamp. Great, just what we need.* Mia was particularly concerned by the red and scarlet rings in her aura that screamed, "I'm in heat." She stared at Kevin as if he was an all-you-can-eat buffet.

Mia introduced Kevin to Nancy and Gonela.

"This is Scarlet." Nancy motioned toward the vamp next to her. Her hair flowed down past her shoulders in different shades of fire. She was slender with beautiful green eyes. "Let's get to work."

"Mm, if he's driving, I call shotgun." Scarlet traced the top of her lip with her tongue.

"He's taken. Back off." Mia stepped in front of Kevin.

Scarlet narrowed her eyes, and moved toward Mia. Nancy stepped between them. "I don't have time for this shit. We have to get moving." A car came to a sliding halt in front of them. "Oh, shit. We're busted." Nancy's usual cool tone held an edge of concern.

The car door swung open, and a hand grabbed the top of the doorframe. The sheriff pulled himself from the car and stared at them with an exasperated expression. He locked eyes with Mia and was in front of them before her next breath.

Kevin jumped back against the semi. "What the fu—"

"Kev, trust me. It's okay," Mia reassured him. She recalled her reaction when she had found out the things in her nightmares were real.

"Would someone like to tell me why you're all out here? Nancy. Why is a new agent that doesn't have authority to go out on cases here? And you have two human women in your car..." His voice grew louder, and his eyes began to glow.

Mia swallowed and stepped forward. "It's my fault, John. This is all my doing, and they're all here because you told them to protect me. I'm going to do this with or without anyone's help." She held her posture straight, her tone confident. She felt empowered until the sheriff stepped forward with long strides, walking her backward into a large iron gate. His eyes blazed into hers.

With a voice so low she could barely hear him, he said, "Do you know he gave himself up for you?" His words punched her in the gut. He glowered over her with elongated fangs, and he spit his next words out between clenched teeth. "He didn't want you hurt, Mia. He would rather be tortured and die, than to see you get as much as a scratch. If you think I'm going to let any of you try this rescue mission, and let him die in vain, you're mistaken."

This side of the sheriff she hadn't seen, and frankly, he was scaring the shit out of her.

Kevin began sliding down the truck, making his way to the driver's door, and the others backed away from him. Mia swallowed hard, trying to get some moisture into her suddenly dry mouth before she spoke.

"John, if you think I can just sit back and do nothing, knowing Bass has Cole, knowing what he did to his family, and that he'll win after Cole's searched for him for one hundred and twenty-nine years... then *you're* mistaken. I can't let Cole or Cynthia, die." Mia held all emotion back. Her body trembled as she suppressed everything and continued to meet John's challenging gaze. "Bass wants me for a reason. Whether it was to trap Cole, or torture him with my pain, he's going to get me. Do you honestly think he's going to stop? Bass has a plan, and he'll follow it through—just like with Cole's family. You don't have to agree to it, John, but don't stop us. I need them." She tilted her head toward Nancy and the rest of them.

He moved back, searching her eyes before he nodded. Mia knew he had come to the same conclusion. "Bass won't stop. He's organized, always has been, and one way or another, Mia, you'd be dead." He sighed heavily. "I knew this when I promised Cole I'd watch over you, but I also promised to let you do what you felt compelled to do, as long as you're protected." He yelled back behind him, still holding Mia's gaze. "Nancy!"

In vampire speed, Nancy stood beside him. "Sir." She bowed her head.

"You're in charge of this cluster fuck. There are too many humans involved in this, on both ends. Call me when you need a clean-up crew." He pushed a code on the keypad next to the gate.

Lights illuminated the area on the inside grounds, and Mia turned, staring in disbelief at the sight in front of her. If she had the log cabin clipping from the home magazine she had looked at a few days ago, she could have held it up and matched it to the one she was gazing at now. She laced her fingers through the iron gate and stuck her face in between the bars to get a closer look.

It was huge, breathtaking. Her eyes welled at the sight. The cabin filled a void inside her. She turned to John. "This is stunning. The house, the land... There's horses..." It warmed her in her time of need.

"And there is much more behind those gates." He smiled, and turned to Nancy giving her one last look, then disappeared.

"You know, he likes you—the sheriff. You remind him of Cole. I don't know what you said to him, but thanks. All the paperwork that comes with this job sucks, and I was looking forward to the excitement."

Nancy tapped her tongue against her fang. "Now, let's go get your man."

"He's not my man."

Nancy shook her head. "I'll ignore that. Whatever you need to tell yourself, human. Just please, tell me you bonded with Cole so we know where they are."

Mia nibbled her top lip and shook her head in dismay. Nancy rolled her eyes. Looking up to the sky, she said, "Great. Does anyone have a clue where to start since we can't use Mia as a GPS? Have we had *any* leads?" Nancy put her hands on her hips and by everyone's expression, they were fucked.

Two more cars pulled in behind the semi. Rosetta emerged from one, Cramer and Russo from the other.

"Nancy, what is Russo doing here? I don't trust him." Mia kept her narrowed eyes on Russo as she spoke.

"He probably came with Cramer—they've been teamed up all week for the investigation. We need all the help we can get, Mia. We're fighting other vampires, and we don't know their abilities or strength. I'll keep an eye on him." She smiled, winking at Mia.

"Funny, I didn't think you liked me much."

Nancy's smiled broadened. "For a human you're not bad. I admire your strength. It's all the human drama you let your emotions get tangled up in that I don't care for. There's no time for that in life, or in death."

Mia shook her head in concurrence. Russo slid up to her as she rested against the gate.

"Well, hello, delicious. Now that you're available, I can't wait to try you." His voice made her ill.

"Back off, Russo, or you can leave." Nancy's voice was stern as her eyes challenged him. A tiny smile curved her lips, taunting Russo to defy her.

Nancy stepped in the center of the group. "We have no clue where Cole or Mia's friend is being held. Mia didn't form a bond with Cole, and we cannot track him.

All we know is where the girls in the back of my car are supposed to be delivered, so we can start there." Nancy paced like a commanding officer planning a strategic strike.

"Russo, Gonela—I want you to follow the semi. Cramer, Rosetta, Scarlet and Mia are with me in the semi. We're going to put the girls in the back of the semi and—"

Kevin stepped forward, and Nancy paused to stare at him. "What's this bond thing I keep hearing you guys talk about?" he asked.

"If I had Cole's blood in me, I would be able to track him, to feel him more deeply. As it stands, I've only had a little taste and that's not enough. It's a vampire thing. I'll explain more, later." Mia waved her hand in the air, dismissing the topic.

"What if Cynthia has my blood in her?" Kevin asked, looking at Nancy as he spoke.

"How's that possible? Neither one of you are vampires. What need would you have drinking each other's blood... unless you're vampire posers?" Nancy arched an eyebrow and waited for a response.

Kevin's shoulders went back with pride. "Cynthia's pregnant. Will that work?"

Mia's heart sank. Kevin's expression reflected pain at the thought of losing Cynthia, and also his baby.

Nancy walked to Kevin, her hands cupped behind her back. "That would be a very strong bond, and yes, it would work, but you're not a vampire, so you wouldn't feel it."

Kevin's muscles tightened as he pulled his hair off his shoulders. "Make me one." There was no hesitation in Kevin's tone. He was serious as death. Scarlet licked her lips at the sight of him.

"This might work. I'll approve this re-birth. Who will embrace him?" Nancy looked around the group. Scarlet raced passed Mia, knocking her forward; she flung her arms around Kevin.

"No, absolutely not. Nancy, get the vamp slut away from him." Mia stepped forward to do it herself, but when Nancy snapped her fingers, Scarlet immediately retreated back to her side.

"Mia, we really have no choice, and we're running out of time."

"Can't you do it?"

Nancy blew out a burst of air, pulled her head back, and looked at Mia as if she had offered her a coke. "Denied! He's not my type, and I don't have the patience for a fledgling."

"What about one of the guys then?"

"Whoa, back up, Mia. I'm not fixing to let a man suck on my neck. No way. I don't play that." Kevin's expression was set firm.

"No worries, Kevin, most of them feel the same way about you. Blood tastes different from a male to a female, but some of us have no preference. Scarlet let's get to work—embrace him." With Nancy's command, Scarlet went to Kevin and began to rub his neck.

"No sex," Mia blurted out. Scarlet looked over at her as if she just threw silver on her. Mia glared at Nancy, waiting for her to speak.

"Agreed, no sex." Nancy flicked her hand toward Kevin, trying to move things along.

"Oh, come on. Where's the fun in that?" Scarlet stomped her foot like a child.

"Do it. Now! You're wasting time." Nancy's tone was impatience. "My reputation is riding on the success of this mission, and I've never failed before. I won't have your childish behavior jeopardizing this operation."

Scarlet's fangs slid out as she pushed Kevin to his knees. Walking around him until she was at his back, she pulled him into her.

"Kevin, are you sure about this?" Mia asked one last time.

"Mia, if something happens to her and my baby, I would die inside. Yes, I want to do this." Although his words were strong, fear gleamed in his eyes.

Scarlet wrapped her arms around his chest, parted her lips, and placed them on his neck. Her tongue licked where she would bite. She pulled her head back briefly before striking like a bolt of lightning and sinking her fangs into his flesh.

Mia's pulse quickened and Nancy slowly turned to her. "If I didn't know any better, Mia, I could swear you were a vampire by the way you get excited in times like this." A slow grin emerged through her smug tone.

Heat crept into Mia's cheeks. She turned her back on the scene before her. *I am excited. Why, what is the matter with me?* "How long is this going to take?" she asked, avoiding her thoughts.

"She'll have him drained in about thirty seconds, and then she has to keep him awake while he drinks her blood. His human body will then die, some parts quicker than others, and he will rise as a vampire in a couple of hours. His body is very strong, so he'll probably rise sooner than others. It usually takes days to control the bloodlust, though. That's the hard part. Did you get the coffins?" Nancy reached out, smacking a mosquito on Mia's arm. Her lips twitched as Mia stared at her. "What? Cole wouldn't be happy if I let anything else suck on you. Coffins—did you get them?"

"Yes, Kevin stopped by the funeral home first. I wasn't counting on Scarlet or Kevin. Someone can borrow my coffin, but we are still short one," Mia said, brushing the legs of the smashed bug from her flesh.

"Your coffin?" Nancy asked with an amused tone.

"Yes. I had Kevin pick up my favorite coffin for Cole, in case we needed it."

Nancy burst out in laughter. "You are a strange human, Mia, and you make me laugh. Just to be on the safe side, we should get another coffin."

Nancy turned to Gonela. "Can you get Cole's coffin? The last I remember, he kept it in the barn."

Mia's lips parted in surprise as Gonela walked toward the iron gates, punched a code on the key pad, and the gates glided open.

Nancy looked over her shoulder as she walked through the entrance. "Yes, Mia, it's Cole's place." Then her aura left a trail like a comet as she zoomed through the gate after Gonela.

Why didn't he tell me when I was looking at the picture?

Kevin hung limp in Scarlet's arms as death wrapped around him. She carried him toward Cramer who opened the large back door of the semi. When she reached the back of the truck, she jumped in as if she was attached to a wire and laid Kevin inside a coffin.

Mia peeked in the back. The two girls from the back of Nancy's car sat motionless against the side panel, their eyes glazed over and their faces blank. She could only assume Nancy had put them in a state of reverie.

"Okay, who can drive a semi?" Nancy asked as the iron gates to Cole's estate began to close behind her. Gonela raised his hand and headed toward the truck.

"Rosetta, that puts you with Russo. Let's get going, we're burning the night hours. Cramer, put Cole's coffin in the back before you close up back there." Nancy barked out her orders, then jumped in the passenger seat with Cramer and Mia sitting behind her.

"We're heading south. The two girls were to be delivered down in Homestead." Nancy nodded toward Gonela who started the truck.

"Near the Everglades?" Mia asked.

"Yes, why? Did you see something?"

Mia shook her head and leaned back. *I don't know who to trust.* She wasn't going to tell anyone that she felt Cole, and he was there. Gonela pushed the semi into gear, and the truck jerked into motion.

TWENTY-NINE

*T*he constant hum of the wheels against the asphalt had Mia drifting off within minutes. Emotionally wiped out, her mind drifted to Cole, and she heard his voice in her mind. *No Mia, hate me.* She jerked awake, elbowing Cramer in the arm. Cole's voice was so strong in her head. *Why can I feel him better than anyone else?*

"You okay, Mia?" Cramer asked. "You were thinking of Cole, weren't you? You must be worried about him."

"Nope, I hate him. I'm worried about my friend that got pulled into this world of the undead because of me."

Nancy looked back at her, narrowing her eyes. She knew Mia was lying. Mia averted her gaze. Although she could read a vampire's aura, they were hard to read, and vampires masked themselves well. No one was to be trusted, and she couldn't give anything away— especially her concern for Cole.

They pulled into a gas station that appeared abandoned with two old pumps in desperate need of painting. Nancy insisted Mia get something to eat to keep her energy up.

It was very late. They were already into the wee hours of the next morning, and the sun would be up in a couple of hours. Mia came out of the little store with a bag of chips, a Reese's Cup, and a Diet Coke. *The breakfast of champions.*

The vampires were coming out of the back of the semi. Nancy wiped the back of her hand on her mouth, and Mia could see the red stain of blood on her hand.

After seeing Cole with Stacy, she knew the girls in the back would remember nothing unless they wanted them to. Mia still struggled with what was right and wrong. She knew if they had brought their containers, they would be drinking from those instead of using the two humans. At least, she hoped they would. Based on what Cole had told her, vampire cops are here to protect people, not use them as a buffet.

When Nancy jumped back into the truck, her skin was darker, fuller.

"Did you check on Kevin while you were back there?" Mia asked.

"He's fine. He's with his maker in one of the coffins." Nancy flipped through a magazine, and although she appeared calm, Mia could tell she was excited. No one flips through a magazine that fast. She may as well just use it as a fan and be done with it.

"Oh, crap! He's bonded to his maker, right? Cynthia is going to kill me."

"I said no sex, and she will not disobey me. Remember, this was his choice. He did this to save his love. You shouldn't feel bad."

Mia understood what Nancy was saying, but it didn't make her feel any better.

The semi turned onto a desolate road badly in need of repair. Weeds broke through the cracks of the asphalt, and patches of grass scattered along the sides of the road.

"Where are we?" By the looks of the road, Mia was thinking they might be lost.

"We have to get the others in the coffins. Daylight is coming." Gonela pointed to the approaching horizon.

"I'm a little tired myself. Can we rest, too?"

"Yes, Mia." Gonela's smile comforted her as she climbed out of the truck to stretch her legs.

Russo and Cramer parked the car behind the semi and walked to the back. Cramer swung the handle up, pulled the rod from its hole and opened the doors. Once everyone jumped in the back, Nancy glanced at Mia, a reassuring smile appeared on her face. "Are we just going to sit here until nightfall?" Mia's nerves started to swirl in her stomach. As daylight began to peek through the eastern sky, Rosetta slumped against the passenger side door. Her eyes slowly drifted shut.

"No, but we're going to rest. We need to reserve our energy." Gonela pulled himself up on the side step of the rig.

"You take the back, Mia. I'll rest in the front."

"Thanks. Do you have a first name, or do you want me to keep calling you Gonela?"

"Raul is my first name, but you can call me Gonela if you would like." His eyes lit with a tiny glow, and a smile stretched across his face. Mia laughed, quickly covering her mouth with her hand.

"Something funny about my name?" he asked with an arched eyebrow.

"Sorry, no. It's just that you look and talk like the guy who played Gomez in the Adams Family movie, without the mustache, of course. And you're a lot bigger than he was. The actors' real name was Raul—it struck me as funny. I didn't mean to offend you."

His eyes were as dark as the night, and then a flash of gold appeared, dissipating so quickly that if Mia wasn't looking directly at them, she would have missed it.

"Well, then—you, my dear, may call me Gomez." He bowed at the waist, and then held his hand out to help her into the truck.

Mia jumped in the back and stretched out on the small bed, hoping her mind would allow her to get some rest before they went any further. She had no idea what to expect.

She could feel the vibration of energy caused by the combined anticipation in the air. All of them were ready to fight and eager for blood. The energy she felt was overwhelming at times. She didn't fully trust any of them.

She quickly drifted off, clearing her mind beforehand, trying to avoid any dreams. Her hopes for a peaceful sleep were shattered as Cole's image appeared to her.

Men surrounded him, taunting him with something she couldn't hear. Pulling on the chains around his arms, he yelled back at them. Blood dripped down his arms from cuts that weren't healing. She followed the trail of red down as it dropped into a small puddle forming on the ground.

She jerked herself awake so fast, she smashed her head on the ceiling of the truck. "Fuck." She winced as she rubbed her head.

Gonela and Rosetta became alert as her head hit the metal.

"What? What is it?" Rosetta asked.

Tears formed in Mia's eyes. She pushed them back, anger and pain replacing her sadness. "He's bleeding, badly, and his wounds aren't healing." Her words seethed out between clenched teeth. They exchanged a look, and Mia knew she had made a mistake. She revealed her feelings.

Gonela looked at his watch. "We slept way too long, let's get going. Does anyone have to go to the bathroom?" He kept his tone calm, but Mia could feel his energy spike.

"Yes, and I can use some fresh air after seeing that." Mia climbed over Gonela, not caring that she had to sit on his lap to get out of the truck. She needed air, now, and she needed to empty her bladder.

She walked over to a large patch of palmettos and concealed herself behind them. She closed her eyes as a small breeze blew through the air swaying the pine trees. The rustling of the leaves and bushes calmed her as if they spoke to her, soothing her. She took deep breaths, relaxing.

Negative energy blew on the wind, and it was coming in a big way.

Mia froze. It was coming from all around her. If it'd been night, she could call the night creatures her mom talked about. A couple of rabid raccoons could help attack whatever approached. She closed her eyes and gave it a shot anyway. When she opened them, she laughed. She was going mad, and was going to die trying to call raccoons to help her.

Rosetta jumped over the palmettos causing Mia to stumble back, tripping on a root from one of the pine trees. Gonela caught her before she hit the ground.

"I'm sorry. I didn't mean to scare you. You called me?" Rosetta's eyes flashed with a familiar light.

Mia stared at them both as Gonela pulled her to her feet.

"I heard you calling me, too. Are you okay?" Gonela released her arm, his face was full of concern and confusion.

Mia stared at them, her eyes wide as thoughts tumbled through her mind. *Okay, what is going on? They're definitely bigger than raccoons.*

"I don't know what just happened, but there's something here with us. I can feel it. There's bad energy all around."

"Get back to the truck, now." Gonela took her arm in that familiar cop grip and walked her swiftly to the truck. He opened the passenger door and motioned for her to get in as he walked back into the open field where Rosetta stood.

Mia's hand landed on a piece of paper on the floor mat of the truck. She grabbed it. It was Cynthia's police report from the other night. She paused as her fingers went to release the paper. Flipping it back around, her eyes stared at the officer's signature.

"Oh, shit! Gonela! I need to tell you something." The door slammed shut, pinning her legs, and she screamed as the metal cut into her upper thighs. She shoved the police report in her front pocket and pushed back as hard as she could. The door flew open causing her to fall back and land on the ground with a man standing over her.

"Got her." The man's voice was menacing. Mia cocked her head toward Gonela and Rosetta who stood in the middle of the field. Gonela's head tilted down, his eyes fell upon Mia's, and she watched as they masked over in a color of vibrant gold.

Rosetta ran toward the palmetto patch, diving into its center. The man in front of Mia bent down and flipped her to her stomach. He pulled her arms back, crossed her wrists, and secured them with his large arm.

Her wide-eyed gaze still held Gonela's, her breathing increased as his energy soared. His shirt formed a hairline tear at the shoulders and the bones in his face shifted right before her eyes. Just when she thought he couldn't get any bigger, the image transforming before her proved otherwise. He fell to his knees as hair fought its way out of his clothing, tearing the rest of his shirt. His thighs ripped through his pants, and in seconds his transformation was complete. A massive werewolf stood before them, deadly and pissed off.

"What the fuck is that?" The young man holding her let go, running the other way. Mia stared at Gonela in fascination. When she was little, she heard the tales about him, the ones that her grandmother wrote in a journal and passed down through her Indian heritage.

Mia tore her gaze from the werewolf and focused on the loud roar coming from the palmettos. A beautiful leopard leapt from them and stood beside Gonela.

"You guys are skinwalkers?" Her words still hung in the air, as she turned. Off road ATVs raced into view. Rosetta made the first move, leaping toward one of the men on an ATV. She landed gracefully on the other side with the man's throat in her teeth. Shoving him to the ground, she put her large paw on his chest, and then went back down for the kill.

A roar shattered the air and everyone froze. Gonela looked around sizing up each of the men as Mia ran to the back of the truck. The two girls were gone and the door hung open leaving the coffins exposed. She jumped up, grabbed the lever on the door and put the bolt back in place, securing the door shut.

Arms circled her waist from behind, and she fell to the ground. Pulling her arm up, she slammed her elbow down into to the ribcage of her attacker. She sprang to her feet and ran toward Gonela.

Rosetta took another man down. But as she headed toward her third victim, a net came down, knocking her to the ground.

Mia's retreat toward Gonela halted as she fell to the ground, tackled from behind. Her mouth filled with dirt, she lifted her head to spit, and two massive, hairy legs stood on each side of her head. Horrible crunching sounds from above, followed by wetness on her back, made her glad she was on her stomach. Blood poured onto the sand next to her face, followed by the head of her attacker.

She stared at the head. The eyes were still open and last minute twitches from the brain made the facial muscles jump. The spinal cord peeked out below the torn, bloody flesh. She flinched as the man's body dropped next to his head. Glancing over her shoulder she saw a massive hairy claw reach down, pushing the rest of the body off her so she could stand.

Rosetta fought against the net. "Gonela, save her." Mia reached out and touched his blood-stained, hairy arm. He looked at her touch in his changed state. Mia could still see part of him in the wild beast that stood before her. As Gonela bolted toward Rosetta, Mia ran to the truck, remembering Kevin carried a hand gun for safety. When she reached the passenger door, a gunshot echoed through the air.

Turning toward the sound, she watched Gonela drop to his knees. She ran to him, and as the man pulled the rifle up and took aim, she threw herself on top of the werewolf.

"Oh, bloody hell. Move aside. This rifle is strong enough to send the bullet through you both. Being that it's silver, it'll kill your friend, love. I was told to bring you back alive, but no one said I couldn't hurt you." His tone was full of malice and laced with an Australian accent.

Mia followed the deep scar on the man's chin to his left eye, then locked into his challenging gaze. She shivered at what she saw. He wasn't lying. He would hurt her—he wanted to hurt her, would enjoy hurting her.

Her eyes trailed to Rosetta who lay wounded under the net. A patch of her human self began to appear.

Mia stood, facing the man with the scar—the man they were calling Leo. "Take me, but leave them. He'll die anyway. He can't get a silver bullet out by himself and no one knows we're here." She stared at Leo, hoping he would believe her. He tilted his head as if she was mocking him. "The leopard will also die without help. Both of them will have a slow painful death. Isn't that what you want?" Mia kept her eyes locked on his. *C'mon, take the bait. I have to get them away so they can heal.*

"Yes, that's what I want. You gonna fight?" His grin was pure criminal.

Mia shook her head and looked down at Gonela. Blood streamed from his chest with the rhythm of his heavy breaths. As she moved toward Leo, he handed the rifle to the guy behind him.

"Can I go to the bathroom first?" Mia asked.

In one long stride, he stood in front of her. "What are you trying to pull?" He stared at her as if she was a mystery.

"I have to pee! Can you honestly tell me what you just saw didn't scare the piss out of you?"

He smiled, looked behind him, and then jerked his head toward the palmettos. "Follow her. Remember, mates, no one touches her."

Two men accompanied her toward the palmettos. When she passed Gonela, she winked at him. His human form slowly began to appear and soon the men would see his identity along with Rosetta's. She didn't care if he gave her an unpleasant look when she winked, because she wouldn't be able to live with herself if all these people died because of her.

She walked behind the palmettos. "Privacy please." Mia held up her hand as the men tried to follow her.

Once hidden behind the palmettos, Mia reached her hands inside them, quietly searching. *Come on. I know it's here.* Finally, her hands came across Rosetta's clothes, with her radio still attached to her pants. Mia turned the volume down, then pushed the orange button, hoping it would send a panic alert out.

She dug the police report out of her pocket and placed it under the radio. Reaching in her boot, she pulled out her Swiss army knife keychain and sliced the palm of her hand just enough to drop a couple drops of blood on the report. When she stood, the voices on the radio started going nuts.

Mia left her clue behind, praying Nancy would understand her message. "Let's go do this thing." Mia wiped the nervous sweat from her palms and slowly breathed.

They approached the open area where everyone waited. The man to Mia's right smacked a large hand on her ass and squeezed. Mia stopped abruptly. The man grinned with a nasty expression and bad teeth. *Great. I'm surrounded by deviants.*

She knew her fate was sealed, but she didn't have to go quietly. She took her open palm and smashed it into his nose. Blood poured out as he lunged for her. If Mia knew how to do one thing in life, it was fight. She stepped to the side and he slammed into the man in front of them.

"All of you *wankers* better knock it off!" Leo shouted as he walked over to Mia, grabbing her face so tight that her teeth cut her lips. He squeezed hard, watching the blood surface, then licked it from her lips.

"I'm not a vampire, but I love blood. Do I have to tie you up, or are you going to behave?"

Leo was evil—straight out of hell—but she couldn't let her fear show.

"Tell your men to keep their hands off me, and I'll behave." Mia challenged him with her gaze.

"No one touches her again, or you'll answer to me." He pushed her face back as he released her. She refused to rub her jaw, which ached from his bullish grip.

"She broke my fucking nose. I'm not letting that go." The man lunged at her again, and this time he landed on her, bringing her to the ground.

Lifting her knee, she cracked him where it counts. Arms circled her from behind and Leo stepped in front of her.

He bent down, pulling the man on the ground to his feet, and then shoved a large knife into his stomach, twisting it as his hand met the man's flesh through his torn shirt.

"Anyone else want to disobey me? Throw a bag over her and put her in the truck."

A large burlap sack covered her to her knees. With careless intentions, the men dragged her and threw her into the back of the truck.

Her head slammed against a solid surface. She fought to stay conscious as the blood from her head streaked her face. Her eyes closed, and everything went black.

THIRTY

*T*he dull hum in her mind pulled her back into a conscious state and became louder as she cracked her eyelids. A tiny hole in the bag allowed her to peek through to her surroundings. The sky hazed over in a dim light as the sun began to set. Cattails and tall saw-grass separated as the airboat carrying her moved through the water, creating a path of shimmery light as the cattails broke apart and glistened in the sunset.

Mia's head rested on the front of the boat by the edge. She caught a quick movement to the left and watched as a gator swam away from the boat, then another. The waters were infested with them. She counted at least twenty before the motor stopped and the boat coasted to the shore. Her heart pounded. A large gator slithered into the water as the boat ascended the dirt bank. Getting eaten by an alligator was not on her "How I would like to die" list.

She stayed motionless, keeping her body limp as she was slung over a shoulder and carried like a sack of sand. A couple of minutes later, she recognized the voice of the person who carried her—Leo.

Mia's head throbbed from the blow she had received earlier. The wetness from the blood had stopped, but she felt pain from other cuts and scrapes on her body that were still bleeding. She probably needed a doctor.

Leo threw her to the ground. She heard other voices around her, and she felt hands tugging on the rope around the burlap sack. A loud growl shook the room.

"What the fuck was that, Leo?" A shaken voice asked from Mia's right.

"No telling with these vampires. They'll be up soon. You blokes can head out. I'll be there in a minute. Hey, leave some of that moonshine by the front." Leo's voice sent chills through her.

"I'm out of here. I don't want to have another run-in with one of those hairy things."

She heard footsteps fading in the distance, then the bag lifted off her head.

Leo reached down and grabbed her mouth. Mia knew without a doubt, he wanted to break her jaw. He pulled her to her knees and squatted in front of her.

"Hallo, hallo. Remember me? I'm going to bid on you tonight. I think I may want your blood more than the vampire does. I want you to run from me, and I can't wait to catch you. That's what we do here, you know?" Leo took his knife and swirled it into the air, pointing out the surroundings to her. He bent back down and licked the blood off her lips. "Yes, that's what we do here. We hunt. Now, I'm going to have some whiskey and get rotten, then I'm coming back to win you." He reached down, grabbing his manhood, and laid his large knife on her face as he spoke. "I'm just not sure what I want to do first with you, get naughty with you or cut you. Maybe I'll cut you, while I'm getting naughty with you. I'll have to think about it. G'day, love."

Blood beaded on her lower lip as he squeezed her flesh against her teeth, then he bent down to lick the blood. He froze as another growl rattled the air.

He stood and looked behind him before leaving. Mia sat in the middle of an area about the size of the gas station. Dirt covered the ground. Her gaze went to a wood-planked wall and followed it up to an area covered in glass. It reminded her of the special VIP seating you would see in a sport arena. A small light lit the inside of the glassed area.

Behind her, woods traveled back as far as she could see. The mixture of pine trees, melaleuca, and palmettos, made the area look wild and uninhabited. A long, tall fence disappeared into the woods on each side of her, fencing her in. She looked back toward the direction Leo had vanished. *That's my exit.*

Her eyes scanned the area like a search light. To the right, the wall descended back into the darkness where a faint whimper carried on the wind. She jumped to her feet and slowly walked toward the sound, stopping abruptly at an old-fashioned aluminum tub filled with water. She stared into it and visions of a girl being held there flashed in her mind. Mia felt the sting in her nose as the water took over the girl's body. This is where she had met death.

Mia jerked her head toward another whimper, which quickly turned to sobs, and the sound of scrapping against cement. She took a deep breath and continued toward the sounds, further descending into the darkness until two figures came into sight.

Mia's gaze fell upon Cynthia first, laying on the ground and wrapped in a ball at Cole's feet. Two hooks in the cement above Cole held the chains that draped down and wrapped around his spread arms. His flesh seeped through the chain holes like thick chunks of grated cheese and meshed with the burning silver. A small pool of blood formed at his feet.

Mia ran to them. "Cyn, it's me."

Cynthia lashed out, ready to fight and Mia grabbed her, pulling her into her arms, bumping Cole's leg beside her.

"Mia. I'm so happy to see you, and if I get out of here alive, I'm kicking your ass." She spoke in exhausted breaths.

Mia smiled. *Good, she wants to hurt me. She's okay.*

"I'm sorry. I didn't mean for you to get wrapped up in this." Mia brushed the hair from Cynthia's dirty forehead.

"You could have told me you were dating Dracula!" Cynthia kicked at her as she spoke.

"Shhh... keep your voice down. Just like you told me you got married, and you're pregnant. What was I supposed to do—text you a smiley face with fangs?" Mia filled with relief. Her best friend was alive and arguing with her as they usually did.

"I am so hungry, Mia," Cynthia sobbed.

"Well, lucky for you I brought you two Reese's Cups." Mia smiled, reaching into her boot. Cynthia ripped the wrappers off before they left Mia's hand. "Cyn, there's something I need to tell you about Kevin."

"Oh, my God. Is he dead?" Cynthia stared at her, wide-eyed with chocolate smudged across her lips.

"Well, kind of. You're going to get out of here, okay?" Mia inspected Cynthia's chains. Her eyes followed them up the wall to see where they were attached. "I want you to tell my mom that she was right about everything, and I love her. Oh, and take Bela. Here are my keys. I'm going to put them in your pocket." Mia's thoughts ran so fast she couldn't keep up with them. A plan brewed in her mind.

"Mia, what are you talking about? *We're* getting out of here, right?"

Mia grabbed the chain wrapped around Cynthia's arms.

"Oh, sweet! Cyn, your chains aren't silver." Mia jiggled them in her hand.

"I'm fucking glad you're excited. Are you going to answer me?"

"Be still, I'm going to switch your chains with Cole's. I have to move fast, the others are coming back soon."

Mia removed one of the chain links from the hook on the wall, removing Cynthia's chains as fast as she could. The chains were looped around her wrists several times, then hooked back on the wall to secure her hands.

"Mia, answer me. You're scaring me. Let's just go, okay. You're coming with me, right?"

"Cyn, listen to me. I'm going to tie you back up, loosely, but don't move until I have everyone distracted." She yanked at the chain on her arm. "I'm hoping the others will come find us, but I'm not counting on it." Mia dropped the last chain, freeing Cynthia's binds.

"Mia! Answer me! You're coming, right?" Cynthia's tone rattled with fear.

"No, Cyn. There's no way around the fight that's coming." Cynthia's eyes widened.

Cole finally moved, lifting his head as Mia stood to start working on his chains. She took in a deep breath, reached above him, and tried not to focus on his torn flesh, which looked as if it was grated like a block of cheese through the holes of the chain. She grabbed his arm to start unraveling the chains. His head slumped onto her shoulder, the extra weight making her movements difficult.

Cole felt the pull from their closeness. When she leaned into him, he knew she felt it too. He lifted his head, his breath rolled in her ear, and she shivered against him. "Why are you here?"

"This is going to hurt, Cole. Your skin is in the chain, and I have to pull it."

He dropped his head onto her shoulder as she continued to unwrap the first chain, the links brushing against untouched flesh. His body tightened as she peeled the metal from his skin, and smoke slithered up as the fresh flesh burned. His fangs pressed into her neck as the pain shot through his body. Mia's pulse raced as she dropped the first chain to the ground and started on the second.

Cole felt his fangs on her skin and fought the urge to sink them in deeper. His mind tempted him with thoughts of the wonderful popping sound her flesh would make. He thought of her skin wrapped tight around his fangs and the first taste of blood that would pool under his lips. The thoughts played in his mind, driving him to the edge of his sanity. *Hungry.* He was weak, and his instincts wanted her, badly, urgently. *Not like this, I must fight it.*

"Why are you here?" Cole asked again, this time his voice held more power.

She pulled on the second chain, but it didn't move. His flesh had embedded through the holes of the links almost to the bone. With a deep breath, she yanked hard, and the remainder of the chain fell to the ground with a slinky sound.

Cole let out a cry of pain into the small of her neck, cutting her skin with his fangs. He was still weak, and he knew his wounds weren't closing. She looped her arm under his and rested her hand on the back of his shoulder, clinging to him tightly.

"Go ahead, bite. You need blood to heal, right?"

"Why... why are you here?" He brushed his cheek against hers as he attempted to lift his head.

Mia pulled his head back, looking into his eyes as she cupped his face. "Because I hate you." She quickly broke away from his gaze, but not before he caught her lie. She worked diligently until she had the two sets of chains swapped.

Cole held his head up, watching her every move. "Mia, I need to feed or I'll never heal. I lost a lot of blood."

She pushed up on her toes, pressing her body against him. She stared into his eyes, pulling her hair back to expose her neck.

"No. I'll rip you apart. Please, move away from me." His tone was deep and hoarse. He quickly turned his head, struggling with his desire.

"If this is what you need, take it. I might not make it out of here alive tonight, so it's your last chance to taste me." She stood still against him.

Cole pulled his head back, narrowing his eyes. "You torture me more than the silver that was wrapped around me. Please. Move. I can't hold back much longer." He pleaded with his eyes.

THIRTY-ONE

Even now when he needs it most, he doesn't want me? She stepped back, her eyes searching around for answers until they fell upon the two girls from the semi, slumped against the wall, in a trance-like state. She ran to them, pulled one to her feet, and walked her over to Cole. She felt like a prison guard taking an inmate to his final death. Her stomach knotted, and she turned the girl around to face Cole.

How am I going to do this? It would be easier if she hadn't chained his arms back to the wall, but she didn't know she'd be feeding a human to *her* vampire. *That's me. If I can't deliver your human in thirty minutes or less, they're free.*

Cole's eyes bored into Mia's as she pushed the girl against his body. The girl was short—very short. Using the weight of her body, Mia pressed against her, lifting and holding her against Cole. She wrapped her hands around the chains, pulling hard, squishing all of them against the wall.

Cole hesitated, and then slammed his fangs into the girl's neck with such force that blood splattered and speckled across Mia. He moved his head from side-to-side like a starved, wild animal. The girl screamed, and Mia clamped a hand over her mouth, muffling her sounds of terror.

"Shh. It's okay. Oh, Jesus, please forgive me. I'm so sorry. Shh. Please, be quiet," Mia whispered trying to sooth them both. Tears pooled in her eyes as the girl's body began to go limp.

Cole's eyes stayed locked with Mia's as he continued to feed.

"Stop. Cole... stop!"

He was consumed with hunger, his eyes were lost to the bloodlust, and the girl's pulse slowed in Mia's arms. She took her hand from the girl's mouth and grabbed Cole's hair, pulling hard, repeatedly trying to dislodge his mouth from her neck until he finally released her. *And he wants to do this to me? Yeah, this looks romantic.*

"More... I need more." His voice was rough, demanding, as his eyes burned with hunger.

"Lick her wounds, and I'll go get you the other one" *This is it—I have turned into a psychopath!* Mia leaned the next girl against Cole's chest, pushing her body into him. Before she could steady her, he sank his fangs in, and the screams began, louder than the first. Mia covered the girl's mouth, holding her tight with both hands to muffle out her pleas. She closed her eyes, squeezing a tear from them.

"Look at me." Cole's voice was stronger than before. Mia opened her eyes, locking them into his as he glided his fangs back into the girl, sucking hard on the surfacing red fluid.

Mia felt a surge of power as she stared into his eyes, and she hated to admit it, but she found her strength within them. The girl's body began to sag. "Stop!" she demanded.

He instantly halted, standing straight up. She felt his stare as she put the second girl back. When she returned to Cole, Cynthia stared at her in disbelief, but she knew better than to say anything.

"Come to me." Cole's voice was infused with power, sex—death. It held everything she should run from, yet it called to her.

Mia stood in front of him. Turning her hand over inside his shirt, she wiped his face. If anyone became aware he'd fed, they'd die a lot quicker than she'd anticipated. She stood on her toes, straining to reach around to the left side of his back.

"I forgot about this." She wrapped her fingers around the knife and pulled it out from under his shoulder blade.

"How did you know?" His eyes searched hers.

"It was in my dream. I felt the knife going in and the burning pain from the silver." She lowered her eyes. "I felt all of that without having a blood connection with you. I can't imagine what it would've felt like if I had one."

"You felt pain? *My* pain?" His expression was remorseful as if he'd hurt her himself. Mia turned his arm over, inspecting the wounds. They'd started to heal, and the blood had stopped dripping into the puddle.

"Well, ain't that nice. A little lover's reunion." Evet Bass's voice sounded in the distance and raked over them. Cole's body stiffened at the sound of it.

"Mia, do what you do best—run. I'm going for him." Anger rode out on Cole's words.

"No. I'm not running. You're not healed, and he'll kill us all. Let me see if I can buy us some time." For the first time, she felt calm and focused.

The corner of his mouth hinted at a grin, and his eyes began to glow as he looked at her. "Your beautiful eyes are glazed with an eerie blue again. I do believe I see a little demon twinkling in those blue eyes."

"You wanted a shootout with me, and now, you've got one. It's high noon, baby." Mia leaned forward and kissed him.

"Are you fucking kidding me? Who are you? We're all going to die, Mia. At least you could have told him you love him!" Cynthia's voice held all the attitude of the state of New Jersey.

The thought of death felt liberating. Mia was almost giggly as she spoke. "I love you, Cyn. And I don't have to tell him how I feel—he knows."

"Say it to me." Cole's voice was deep, challenging, and the longing trailing over his words took her off guard.

Didn't he feel it? Didn't he know? Ironically, she realized she didn't know how he really felt about her, either. What she *did* feel was something deeper than her interpretation of love.

She pulled his head down to her shoulder. When she brushed her lips on his ear, his body shivered under her touch. "You have hurt me, deeply, but I love you with every piece of my existence. I'm telling you this because I'm not dumb. I know what the odds are tonight, but it's okay, Cole, because I don't know how to make this work between us. So in your own words, it's over."

Her breath left as his fangs snapped out. He brushed his cheek against hers and rested his lips on her ear, returning the whisper. "If you think I've worked this hard to knock that wall down around your heart, just to let you die, you're mistaken." Cole lifted his head, his eyes glanced past her and then came back to lock with hers. "If you can just calm down..."

"Oh, so this is about you? Don't be so sure you knocked the wall down. You weren't so concerned about *the wall* when you had me pinned to the jailhouse floor, adding your own bricks, telling everyone about us in the elevator and offering me to your friends as if I were a piece of fruit in a gift basket." Mia stepped away from him.

"You're kidding. I mean, really? Are you two fighting? Maybe I was misinformed about your relationship," Evet's voice was closer. They were both so focused on each other, they forgot about Bass.

"The demon shines bright in your eyes when you're angry. Don't let it control you, you need to control it." Cole smirked, his fangs glistening in the dim light as the glow intensified in his eyes.

"You want to see a demon? I'll show you a fucking demon. And don't you touch me if I'm dying, Detective. I've seen enough to know I don't want to feed on death row or turn into something like Vincent." She shuddered. "If you really love me, just let me die." Mia turned away from him and faced Bass.

"Woman, come to me." Bass's voice lowered as he commanded her. Mia stared at Bass, and then briefly looked back at Cole.

"Ooh... look, honey. Evet is using his *big boy voice*." Mia felt so different. Something changed inside her once she embraced the fact she might die. Now nothing seemed to scare her.

Evet's eyes went wide as she openly mocked him, and then he narrowed his gaze. In a blink, he stood in front of her. Knocking her to the ground, he grabbed a handful of her hair and then dragged her toward the center of the area where she was first dumped.

Mia put her hands over his and pulled her body up to lessen the strain on her scalp. Others started coming into the arena, and soon they surrounded her. Evet pulled her to her knees, holding her arms straight out to each side.

"Allow me, mate." Leo came to stand between her and Evet.

Leo grabbed her arm, clasping it between his legs, then made a shallow cut in her arm from its bend, all the way to her wrist. The cut was just deep enough to draw blood to the surface. She looked away, focused on the growl coming out of the darkness. She could feel

Cole's rage building, and she prayed he'd stay where he was until fully healed.

Leo repeated the same cut on her other arm, then backed away. Fangs slid out all around her. *Oh, shit. Being a vampire buffet isn't on my death list either.*

A heavyset vampire came to stand in front of her. He lifted her head, tilting it from side-to-side before looking into her eyes. He bent down, licking the blood on her arm.

"Mmm. Oh, Evet. What a treat you have for us tonight. We have grown tired of the same boring girls you bring us. She is beautiful. I'll start the bidding at one hundred thousand dollars." Snickers and sounds of displeasure filled the air.

Mia kept her head down, avoiding their eyes and trying to keep focused. Her mind played out what may happen next and what she should do. *Damn. I forgot to tell Cynthia I want to be cremated.*

Her stomach sank as several tongues pressed against her skin, tasting her blood. Her mouth watered profusely, she swallowed hard, fighting off the urge to vomit.

"She doesn't cry or scream like the others," a tall, slender vampire said. "That's odd for a human. I'm not sure she'll be much fun for me to hunt. I'm going to pass on this one. She gives me a bad feeling." He walked toward the exit with his long, black hair shining in the floodlight.

Mia stayed very still, quiet, and focused on her breathing, keeping her pulse low.

"I'd like to bid tonight, mate. I already tasted her blood earlier, and I want to hunt her—five hundred thousand." Leo's price caused a reaction of gasps and stares.

Jesus, that's it? I'm worth at least a million. I mean, if you're just going to kill me. Great, I'm bidding on myself. I'm losing it. Her mind spun. Squeezing her eyes tight, she pushed out all thoughts.

"That's absurd! No human has gone for that much in this club. I'm out, Evet." The heavyset man that opened the bid walked toward the exit, and two other vampires followed him.

"I've called in my assistant because I'm bidding tonight. My bid is one million dollars." Evet's actions caused an uproar as his assistant stepped forward out of the darkness. Mia stared at him, and her fear surfaced as GQ licked his fang. She quickly shoved it back down as the vampires began bickering.

"Evet, you've gone mad! You can't bid at your own club." The opposing vampire came to stand in front of Mia.

She looked up for the first time, her eyes widening, and her heart skipping a beat. "Vincent." The name slipped from her mouth with a sound of shock. When everyone's head snapped toward her, she immediately realized her error. So did Cole, who shifted in the darkness.

Vincent took a step closer to Evet. "What's the meaning of this? How does she know my name? Your records are supposed to be private."

Evet's eyebrows rose in surprise. The remaining vampires quickly walked toward the exit, staring him down as they passed. Evet jerked his head toward Mia, and GQ grabbed her by the hair, pulling her to her feet. "I assure you, Vincent, all the records are private." Evet glared at Mia as he spoke.

"Hey, babe. Remember me?" GQ licked her neck.

"Yeah. You remember me?" Mia took a quick step back, grabbing his arm as she brought her weight forward, falling to her knees and launching him over her shoulder to the ground.

Hmm... must still be wet behind the fangs for letting me get the jump on him. She assumed Evet liked keeping young ones around since he had control issues.

GQ jumped to his feet and wrapped his hands around Mia's neck before she could blink.

"Adam, release her at once." Evet's tone was stern, and Adam did exactly as told.

Vincent's gaze raked over Mia's frame. "Now, that was interesting. She has fire. I think I do want her—one million five."

Shit, the last thing I want is Vincent's attention.

"Two million." Leo spoke from the back, walking forward to stand next to the last two bidders.

"Three million." Evet stood tall with his offer.

"No. You can't bid at your own club. This is unacceptable!" Vincent's anger shadowed his expression, and a glow illuminated in the back of his eyes.

Evet slightly bowed his head. Vincent stood tall, proud at his victory. *Oh, no fucking way! I'm not going to be bait for Vincent.* Mia panicked as she remembered the monster he changed into. A laugh escaped her.

"Oh, I get it, Evet. Vincent's older, and if you don't do what he says, he'll kick your ass." Mia's hopes of pissing Evet off worked—maybe too well. He grabbed the hair at the base of her skull, yanking her head back.

"You have no idea how much pleasure I'm gonna get out of draining you while Cole watches. I've waited a long time for this." Evet turned to the others. "Can anyone beat my bid? If not she is mine."

"This is an outrage. We need to discuss this, Evet." Vincent turned, walking toward the exit. Evet motioned to the others to leave, glaring back at her as he reached the exit. She knew at that moment, her death would not be pretty.

As soon as the last person disappeared into the darkness, Mia ran to Cole. His arms were better, but he was healing slowly.

"Why aren't you healing faster?" Her eyes searched his.

"There's a silver chain around both of my legs. See, it's anchored into the wall on each side. I didn't feel it before, but when I tried to come to you earlier, the chain ripped through my pants and..."

"Okay, shh... I'll get it." When she knelt down something knocked her into Cole from behind, and Cynthia screamed. Mia's attention snapped toward Cynthia. *This is it.*

THIRTY-TWO

*M*ia's eyes focused on the figure that knocked her over. "Oh, thank God. What took you so long, Kev? Are the others here?"

Kevin's new fangs protruded out, making him look like a magnificent beast. "They'll be here. Let me get my woman out, and I'll come back for you." Kevin's voice was strong. He was a vision of strength, and Cynthia's expression indicated she was seeing her man in a completely new way.

"Don't worry about me. Take her to safety, and then stay away. This is my fault. I couldn't live with myself if something happened to either of you." She smiled, touching Cynthia's face.

Kevin nodded, which convinced Mia it was a mannerism embedded in the vampire re-birthing process. He bent down, lovingly scooping Cynthia in his arms, and in a flash, he was gone. Mia immediately continued her work on the chain wrapped around Cole's legs.

"I should be able to free my own arms." He looked concerned. "I need more blood. If you loosen my arms, I can get the silver chain off, and then I'll go feed again."

Mia stood, wiping her palms on her pants as the familiar nervous tug rolled in her stomach. She didn't know if it was because she knew he would kill one of the girls if he fed on them again, or the feeling that something unseen was in the room with them.

He held her with his eyes, trapping her in his dark pools, pulling her into him. "Kiss me—set me on fire with your touch. Let me feel the heat from your lips."

Mia couldn't resist his plea, leaning forward she slid her hand around to the back of his head and pulled his lips to hers. This could be their last kiss, and she put everything she had into it. A deep moan escaped his throat. He pulled on the chains, and the cement wall began to crumble around the hooks holding them.

"I must have you." His teeth clenched, and she could see the pain and bloodlust emerging in his eyes.

Mia felt a sudden wetness on her arm. Following the drops of blood up to Cole's arm, her lips parted in awe. He pulled so hard on the chains, they cut into his skin again.

Evet reappeared in the open area and walked toward them, breaking their enthrallment. Her pulse raced. With Cole still chained by silver, Evet had the upper hand.

"I have to go. If he gets any closer, he'll see that Cyn is gone, and I don't want him to see your chains have been switched."

Cole pulled on the chains, causing them to cut deeper into his arms. The silver on his legs started to smoke as it cut into his flesh.

"Cole, stop. Please, try to heal. You know if I don't go, he'll come over here and kill us both."

With his jaw clenched and lips tight, he nodded. "Okay, but I don't like this at all. I feel helpless and I need to protect you."

"You have protected me, Cole. You saved my life." She smiled, "Now It's time for me to return the favor." Mia turned and walked to Evet.

"Mmm... Marshal Barnett, that kiss looked *good*. Now, I'll taste what's yours—again." Evet grabbed the back of her head, spinning her toward Cole. Pulling her head back, he stared at Cole as he brought his lips roughly over Mia's. She knew better than to fight him. It'd only excite him more.

She could hear Cole pulling on the chains as she bit down on Evet's lip. When he threw her to the ground, she spat his taste out of her mouth.

Mia looked up. Locking eyes with Cole, she wiped Evet's kiss from her lips. Cole's eyes illuminated, and she saw the rage flowing through his body. She noticed one of the chains was embedded so deeply in his arm, it would soon reach bone.

"I thought you were a smart girl. I guess not." Evet's hand slammed against her cheek, knocking her to the side. Her hands fisted in the dirt as the feeling in the pit of her stomach began. Something was coming, and it filled the air with a strong emotional energy—angry energy.

"Now, I'm going to do you like I did your lawman's family. But this time, I do it as a vampire. I'll take your blood, too, and that's going to make it so much better." Evet grabbed her hair, pulling her to her knees.

Cole's growl rattled the air as he pulled on the chains with renewed strength. Mia became delirious with visions as they flashed through her mind. Energy pelted her from every direction. Laughter billowed up from her throat as she straightened her spine. Evet's eyes went wide, her laughter taking him off guard.

"You're a fraud, Evet. The famous outlaw Evet Bass... Is. A. Fraud." Mia could see Evet's rage building with each word. The feeling in her stomach was more than she could take. She leaned over and threw up.

"How dare you speak to me like that?" Evet pulled her head backward, flinging her to her back. With a bent knee, she quickly stuck her leg up as he came at her. The item in her boot caught her eyes.

Forgot about those! She was suddenly very thankful for her blacksmith friend who had made her such wonderful things out of her grandmother's old silver. At that moment, she felt like Batman with her wonderful toys. Her laughter increased.

"Stop laughing!"

Being that Evet was a vampire, and they're supposed to keep their cool, his frustration amused Mia. He's nothing like Cole. In fact, he was the complete opposite. *Maybe if you're an asshole as a human, then you're an asshole as a vampire.*

"I'm sorry, Evet, I can't... You see... It's the irony of this revenge thing. I have a couple people here with me, Evet, and they've been showing me such sights." For the first time in her life, she reveled in the visions.

Evet's expression held confusion. He straightened, stood in front of her and narrowed his eyes.

Mia turned toward Cole, her gaze brushed over his before she focused on the chains around his legs.

Concentrating on the metal, she began bending it back and forth. "Cole, honey, you've been lied to. And you've carried guilt and shame all of these years because of it. Evet didn't kill your brother in a shootout. Your brother challenged him like a man, but Evet had his gang distract him. Once your brother turned toward the distraction, Evet shot him in the back." As she spoke, she watched the metal give on one side of the chain link, and she began to focus on the other side.

Cole let out a thunderous growl, pulling harder on the chains.

Evet reached down, pulling at her shirt. "I don't know how you know that, but I've had enough. I'm taking you right now." He ripped her shirt open. The silver-mesh teddy that her friend had made shined in the light. Evet's hand burned as it touched the metal. With a scream, he yanked it back, rubbing the burned skin. She relished his expression. *Chainmail teddy, complements of World of Warcraft—warrior geekdom. Now, all I need are some rage points, and I'll have this vamp defeated.*

"You bitch! Take it off."

"Why? Oh, yeah. You want to do to me what you did to the women in Cole's life," she mocked.

"Shut your mouth. I don't need to touch the top of your body, anyway." Evet clawed at her pants.

Mia kicked her legs, dropping the silver weapon from her boot. She scurried forward, concealing it under her hand. Her fingers rubbed the beautiful, smooth metal of the sterling silver asp. The design, similar to what the police have, had two special additions.

Evet ripped the front pocket of her jeans, exposing more of the metal mesh. He rocked back on his knees, roaring in anger, and brought his hand down, delivering a blow to the side of her face.

A scream ripped from her chest, and then with a fierce concentration, she focused on the chain around Cole's legs. Her mind bending the other half of the link, back and forth, as Evet pulled her toward him, sliding her through the dirt.

"Take it off!" he shouted. Clawing at her jean covered legs, she could hear the cement crumbling from Cole's power.

"Cole, you know why Evet is so pissed right now? It's because he doesn't want me to tell you that he couldn't get it up before he was a vampire. He never raped your mother, your sister, or Emma. He took them all into a room and made his men *think* he did. He's a fake." Mia took her eyes off the chain and looked up at Cole—the predator had taken over. His eyes were as black as night with a glow set behind them, like an eclipse of the moon. She returned her focus to the chain.

"Woman, you die, now! Look at me. Come to me," Evet commanded.

Mia brought herself to her feet, glaring at Evet as she concealed the weapon behind her and concentrated on the chain.

"Come to me." A wicked grin surfaced as Mia walked toward him. With his arm protected from the silver by her shirt, Evet leaned her back. Mia's arm dangled, and she palmed the asp. Evet turned her face toward Cole whose head tilted down, glaring at him with his fangs fully extended.

Once more, she grabbed Cole's chain with her mind, and after two bends, the chain dropped. She smiled at Cole's wide-eyed expression. Thankfully, Evet was lost in his rage and didn't realize what she had done.

"You ready, lawman? Now I take what is yours." A perverted smirk smeared across his face.

"Why don't you take this instead?" Evet's eyes went wide as she pushed the button on the asp and impaled the stake through his stomach, bringing him to his knees. His flesh sizzled as the silver rod began to burn his skin.

"You missed my heart." He chuckled. "Take it out, and try again." His hands burned as they wrapped around the silver shaft, attempting to remove the stake, and it was then Mia saw the realization in his eyes that he was weakening.

"Let me get that for you." Mia smiled down at him, her voice calm and smooth with her demon awake and controlled. She was careful not to hit the second button, which would spike the end of the asp and lacerate his insides.

"You don't have it in you to drive a stake through my heart, human." His eyes challenged her.

"Oh, I have it in me, Evet, but there's someone else that's been waiting a long time to kill you, and it's his day of reckoning. He's not a coward like you. He likes a fair fight." Mia pulled the stake out the instant Cole grabbed the back of Evet's head.

Blood dripped from Cole's arms as his wounds started to close. His fangs extended longer than she'd ever seen them.

"Turn away from me. Don't look. Go. Now!" His demanding tone was rough, laced with pain and rage.

She lowered her eyes. Turning away from him, she walked toward the woods, squeezing her eyes shut at the horrifying sounds behind her—gruesome sounds, like a den of lions feeding on a fresh animal. Regret washed over her as soon as she looked back. Cole had ripped Evet's head off with his bare hands. She quickly looked away and fell to her knees.

"Hey, Mia, isn't this exciting?" Nancy appeared without warning. "I'm so riled up right now. There are people running everywhere screaming, and we have permission to use deadly force. Damn, I love this job." Nancy patted her on the shoulder, and then tackled one of the guys off in the distance.

Mia surveyed her surroundings. Vampires and humans were being chased from the front toward where she stood in the back. Mia spotted Vincent staring at her from the private viewing box above the hunting area.

She looked toward Cole and the pile of carnage. There wasn't one piece of Evet still attached to his torso. Cole had ripped him to shreds, literally. He stood above the pile, a vision of power, covered in blood. He looked like a king claiming victory over a battle. His eyes scanned the area looking for more prey and settled on Mia. As fast as lightning strikes, he was in front of her, forcing her back into a tree with nothing but predator shining in his eyes.

"I'll eat you next, and I'm sure you'll taste much better than he did." Cole opened his mouth, extending his fangs, and Mia pushed on his chest. He pressed her harder against the tree. "Yes... fight. I like that."

"Cole, please. It's me. Cole!" Ignoring her pleas, his hands went to her breasts. Hissing, he shook his head and jumped back as the silver singed his flesh. "I frightened you. I-I lost control. I'm sorry." His eyes softened as he tried to shake the frenzy he was in.

"You would have just killed me had the silver not been there!" Mia had never been more freaked out in her life, and the realization of what Cole was came full circle. She felt a strong surge of energy pull at her. She looked past him. "Vincent."

Cole turned, following her line of sight, and in an instant, Vincent was gone. "I'm going to have some more fun. You stay here." Cole headed toward Vincent.

Mia momentarily stilled after he left, convinced an indentation of her body would be embedded in the tree when she moved.

"Mia, you had better find somewhere, and stay put before you get hurt," Nancy yelled, perched in a tree to the right of her, with blood trickling down the sides of her mouth.

"How come you're not all sexed up like the rest of them?" Mia asked.

"I am, but I'm still a woman. I'm a little more... *selective* than most male vamps." Nancy jumped from the tree as two men appeared in front of them. Mia recognized them as part of the gang that had jumped them on the road. "Well, hello boys. Want to play?" Nancy licked her lips and bared her fangs.

"Oh, shit. She's one of them!" one of them yelled, and the men ran with Nancy in hot pursuit.

Mia stepped back into the woods, slowly backing herself inside the safety of darkness. She kept her eyes forward on the bloodbath in front of her. The dirt in the open area had turned red, and everyone seemed out of control. She guided herself backward until she felt a tree.

Reaching her hand back, she felt a sharp sting in her palm, followed by pain. The pain grew as her skin separated from something slicing it open. She released the object and was yanked backward, a heavy object slammed down onto her left shoulder, hitting her face. She sucked in a breath as something sharp jabbed into her lower back.

"Hallo, hallo, love." In a whisper, hot breath blew against her ear. She arched her back, trying to pull away from the pain poking at her.

"Leo..." Her heart raced at the realization.

"Aww, you remembered me? Now, let's have some fun. You see this high-powered rifle resting on your shoulder? There's a big, silver bullet in the chamber, and it's pointed right at your boyfriend's heart." She felt his smile against her cheek. "First, I'm going to slowly penetrate your skin with my knife, and when I'm half way in, I'm going to blow your boyfriend into a million pieces. Have you ever seen a vampire explode? It is quite amazing." Leo pulled his lips away from her ear, licking her cheek.

She fought her fear. Leo frightened her more than Vincent did. And the images of Cole blown to pieces made her sick.

No time for fear. Her thoughts went blank as Leo pushed his thick knife past the soft metal of the silver chainmail, breaking the skin. Mia flinched from the pain of the cold steal sliding into her flesh. Images of Leo's past flooded her mind. He was sick, and she had no doubt he would do everything he'd threatened. His finger tightened on the trigger.

Mia bit into her bottom lip, trying hard to hold her emotions in. *Don't scream.* "Wait. You can't see my face. Isn't that what you want?" She quickly picked through his mind. "Don't you want to see my face while you slide the knife through my body? You got so much joy watching that girl's face the other night. You liked it when her eyes went wide, and she begged you to stop."

Leo's body stiffened. He lowered the gun to his side and grabbed her arm. "Bloody hell, how do you know that?" He shoved his knife deeper inside her.

Mia fought to keep herself from fainting. She felt the blood draining from her body, tasted the iron on her tongue. If she could just keep it together, keep her mind sharp. "What I want to know, Leo, is how do you know how it feels? You can only assume what the blade feels like—don't you want to feel it? Only then will you truly know what the others felt when you killed them."

Leo withdrew his blade. She almost collapsed as he spun her in his arms, glaring into her eyes.

The blood dripped from her back. *I have to hold on.* When their eyes locked, she remembered what her mother had told her. *You can drive a person mad.* She wrapped her hand around him to balance herself, and he gasped from her touch. "Bring the knife up here. I want to watch your face as you slide it into your skin. You can stab me again, and then we will both know for sure how it feels." Mia reached down, grabbing Leo's hand. She placed the tip of the knife to his skin, right at his heart.

"I want you. I've never been this excited before. Bloody hell, my cock is so rigid I could..." His psychotic eyes became glossy.

"Shh... don't speak. Do you feel the tip on your skin?" Mia pushed, and he gasped, falling back into the tree, taking her with him. She could feel his sick arousal on her leg. Her knees were about to buckle. *Stay focused.*

She began to lose her grasp on his mind, his energy was slipping out of her control. "Look at me, Leo. Tell me—is it what you thought?" Mia pushed again, knowing the thrust she just delivered had met with his heart.

He began taking short breaths, staring into her eyes. "Yes, it's everything I thought it would be. Tell me—how did it feel for, you?" he asked with fading breaths as he pulled another knife from behind and shoved it into Mia's side.

She gasped, praying the knife didn't hit any major organs. In less than a minute, the front of her pants became saturated, matching the back. She knew she lost a lot of blood, and it was only a matter of time. Unable to sustain her own weight, her knees gave in, and she leaned against Leo, her breaths matched his. "It felt great, Leo. You know why? You didn't shoot Cole, and I'm dying. I don't have to live with the horrible images of the only man I've ever loved ripping people apart like an animal."

THIRTY-THREE

*L*eo fell first. With haze-covered eyes, Mia focused on the tree in front of her. She had to laugh at the irony as the tree's energy filled her mind with images. It was the same tree Vincent had used to kill the girl from the morgue.

Drums began to beat loudly in her head, calling to her. She placed her palms on the tree, the feeling of the rough bark becoming faint as numbness took over her body. The rhythm of the drums lulled her into the darkness.

Her dream carried her once again as the moon was shining down on her face. The vision got clearer with each fading breath she took: A man carried her, the baby cried and then she fell.

Her eyes fluttered open, and the tree bark ripped off in her hands as she collapsed back into a set of arms. She faded in and out of consciousness.

"Shit. Cole!" Nancy's voice pulled her back, and she peeked out between the slits of her eyelids.

Cole bent over her. "Nancy, get John. Call for a medic, now!" His eyes frantically searched her body, trying to find all of her injuries. When he slightly turned her to her side, she cried out in pain.

"Just give her your blood, Cole," Nancy said, matter-of-factly. "Heal her, or turn her."

"No, I promised her I'd... I would let her die. She's had enough pain caused by me."

"You're one stubborn-ass human, Mia. Have it your way. I'll get the medics. Good luck healing the human way." Nancy looked up as a light rain-shower began to sprinkle down out of the clear night sky. "Where the hell did that come from?"

Mia felt herself fading. She couldn't feel the raindrops on her skin, but she knew her skin was wet. Her eyes slowly blinked, and each time they stayed closed longer.

"No, you stay with me. I've been around enough dying people to know that closing your eyes is not good." Cole shook her shoulders. She found the strength to lift her lids, and as she locked onto his gaze, the pain from his internal struggle was evident. He wanted to break his promise, she could see it as his eyes searched hers, waiting, wanting some sign that he could do this for her. She flinched as he bent toward her face. Images from the night flashed through her mind, and she couldn't hide her fear.

"I just wanted to kiss you. It pains me that you're afraid of me. You think I'm a monster for what I've done. You think I'm evil, Mia."

The only thing she knew for certain was that she grew up tonight. She was no longer naive to the reality before her. She faced it and was still torn between loving him and fearing him. Her chest rose as she took a deep breath and lifted her hand in an attempt to touch his face. It wasn't her place to judge him. He'd been a cop for over one hundred and forty-six years, had faced unspeakable pain and had seen such hatred and destruction. Yet, he tried his hardest to control the beast within him. A lesser man would have turned, like Evet Bass.

Cole helped bring her hand to his face.

"You frighten me, and I'm afraid of you, Cole, but I don't think you're evil. Blessed are the peacemakers for they shall be called the children of God, and God has a purpose for everything—at least, that's what my mom says. I'm still undecided on that, because really, I'm fucking dying, and where is the purpose in that?" She winced through a painful smile, and he tightened his hand around hers as she forced herself to continue. "Maybe there is more evil out there than I know, and that's why you're here. I'm not going to judge you, you're a vampire. I fully understand that now, and this is who you are. Now, how about that kiss?" With her strength exhausted, her hand fell, and her eyes closed.

She could still hear muffled voices discussing a plan when the drums started to beat.

"Cole, we need to get her out front to the medic's so they can take her to Sector 13." The sheriff spoke in a consoling voice.

"That means we have to carry her, and she's wrapped herself in silver," Nancy said.

"I'll carry her. She is mine." Cole stood with Mia draped in his arms, the sound of his flesh burning echoed through her body. Her eyes fluttered open to see the anguish in his face.

After a couple of feet, the sheriff stepped in front of Cole. "She's going to be one of us soon. Let me carry her, Cole."

Mia's thoughts ran with his words. *What did he mean by one of them?* The vampires formed a line, and one–by–one they handed her off until she reached the rescue truck. The pain from the silver was marked in their murmuring voices. As Cole gently laid her down onto the gurney, she felt the wetness from her back.

"Why isn't this fucking truck moving yet?" Cole's anger flared. One of the men jumped from the back, and he growled at the other one, "Get out! Leave us."

"But... what if something goes wrong, and she needs attention?" The medic's voice was sympathetic.

"Stay, but over there." He pointed to the corner of the truck, and the medic moved away from him after attaching Mia to machines and IVs.

"Her heartbeat is very faint. Are you prepared for her not to make it to the hospital?"

Cole glared at him. "Are *you* prepared not to make it to the hospital?"

Mia's eyes flickered fast as she floated quickly toward the sound of the drums.

She was laying on the ground, feeling the dirt under her skin as a scream rattled in her ear. The people who chased her now stood over her, looking down into her eyes and chanting. A hand touched her head, speaking to her. Although it was in his Native-American tongue, she understood his words. "Forgive me my child. I will right what I have wronged, and you will lift the shame that I have brought to my people."

His hand slipped off of her. The beam of light from the moon captured her eyes, pulling at her spirit. She floated up toward the moon, and when she looked toward the ground, she saw herself wrapped in an animal-skin blanket. I'm the baby?

"She's flat-lining! I need to use the defibrillator."

Mia was stuck in her vision and a bolt of lightning struck out, running through her infant self.

The man yelled clear, and Mia jerked on the gurney, her eyes opened as the monitor beeped again. Cole turned and looked at him. Noting the man's reaction, he knew how he must look, his fangs were fully extended, and his eyes were at a full glow.

"Damn it, Mia." Cole tore into his arm like a savage, not caring about his promise any longer. He had been emotionally alone all these years—unfulfilled, lonely. Now that he'd found her, he couldn't let go. He grabbed the back of her neck and put his arm in front of her lips. "Drink it!"

She turned her head, her eyes telling him no. He growled, flipping her to her side, and it was then, in the light of the truck, that he could see her wound. Rage engulfed him. *I should have been there for her.* "If you don't drink it, I'll pour it over your wound—every last drop I have in me until you're healed."

With a shocked expression, Cole stared in disbelief as his blood beaded off of her like rain on a waxed car. He gently flipped her back over and stared into her eyes. "Why, Mia? You could do so much good in this world." His blood was useless unless he poured it down her throat.

She reached for his torn shirt and tugged. "Don't want to be a vampire. I'm trying to... have an idea. I don't know." Mia's voice was shallow as her words ran together. "Cole, the moon—I need the moon."

His chest welled at the sound of her voice. *She wants to fight.* He lunged at the top of the truck, bowing the metal out. The truck swerved, the force of his blow knocking them to the side. He looked down at Mia. The beam from the moon was tiny and weak. As he pealed back the metal, a jagged piece cut into his skin and blood poured from his arms and his hands. A finger dropped to the floor, and Mia gasped.

"It will grow back." He couldn't care less about his finger. He would gladly give up all ten just to know that she'd be okay. He looked down as the beautiful blue beam cast across her. He lifted her side and peeked at the wound.

"Mia, what did you hope this would do?" His tone was defeated.

"Save me... thanks for trying."

THIRTY-FOUR

*M*ia floated between a conscious and subconscious realm. She could hear voices, feel kisses on her cheek and a touch on her hand. The voices grew louder.

"You can just leave the paperwork, and I'll talk to her about it when she awakes." The sheriff's voice triggered a memory in her head. *She'll be one of us soon.* Her eyes were heavy, but she managed to open them and gaze around the room. The sheriff stood at the door talking to a man in a black suit.

She felt weak, and her throat hurt. When she tried to move, pain shot through her. She looked down at her arm to see an IV pumping red fluid. In a panic, she jumped, and the sheriff spun around as she yanked out the IV, spilling blood across the sheets. Confused, she tried to make sense of everything.

Her voice was scratchy, and her throat yearned for something to drink. "Whose blood is this? I don't want to be one of you. He lied to me. I don't want to be a—"

"Shh... Mia, it's okay. Look at the monitor—you have a heartbeat. You're getting a transfusion because of your injuries. You lost a lot of blood. Lay still, and I'll get the nurse to hook you back up."

The sheriff pushed a button, and instantly a nurse came running in to re-attach the IV. Mia looked around the room, trying to find a calendar or a clock—something that would ground her to reality. The nurse re-attached all the hoses.

Mia grabbed her arm. "How long have I been out?"

The nurse snapped the IV back in place. "The year is 2029, and the earth is ruled by apes."

You mean vampires. Mia thought as a faint smile pulled on the nurse's face. She tucked Mia's covers underneath her. "I'm sure you are thirsty. Can I get you anything else besides water?"

"No. Thank you, Dr. Zaius." *Don't mess with me on Planet of the Apes movie lines.* The nurse laughed and left the room.

"You've been out for a week," John said, pulling a chair next to the bed and laying the contents from a manila envelope on her chest.

"What's this?" Ignoring the ID card, Mia ran her thumb over the cold metal of the badge. Suddenly, her heart fell. Next of kin or loved ones receive the badge of a fallen officer. She tried to pull herself up.

"Relax, Mia. Cole is fine. These are yours." He smiled as he pulled a piece a paper out of the stack and clicked the back of the pen.

"I don't understand." She stared at her name on the ID.

"You're one of us now. Well, unofficially. I'm putting you through the academy, but until then, this is your temporary badge and ID. I just need you to sign some papers."

Her mind spun, and she was relieved when the nurse brought in a pitcher of water. John pushed the button on the bed, bringing Mia to an upright position, and then she poured herself a glass of water.

"What if I don't want to be one of you?" she asked, taking a sip of water.

"I expected as much." John leaned back in the chair. "Mia, a couple things have come to light while you've been out. This is the safest choice for you and your family. Plus, you'd be great at this. Trust me, I'm good at picking great investigators." He plucked a piece of lint from his pants and continued. "We want you to stay on at the funeral home until you get called."

"What things? Is my family okay?" She nervously thumbed the badge.

"Yes, everyone is fine. In fact, your friend is meeting with Al as we speak just a couple doors down. He's going to assist in delivering her baby, when it's time. We also gave Kevin a job driving. Since he can't drive during the day, he had to quit his job. Oh, and Rosetta and Gonela sent you the big bouquet over on the dresser. They're healing well over at Lion Country Safari. That's where our shifters go to heal since they have no control over their being when they're injured." He poured her another glass of water.

"Mia, the blood Al took from you is missing, which means someone can track you. We still can't find Vincent, and we think he may know, or feel, you're special. If the elders find out that you can pick them out of a crowd, you—and everyone you know—are dead."

"How did you know that?" She shifted her eyes as the nurse came in to check the monitor. John waited until she left to speak.

"Cole told me. He told me everything that happened. How you saved him—again. He has no reason not to trust me, Mia, and neither do you." He laid the pen on the stack of papers, then leaned back in the chair.

"My blood is missing, so it's an inside job. Did you get my clue that I left behind the palmettos?"

"Yes. This proves my point as to why you would be good at this. We would have never suspected Cramer until you pieced it together with Cynthia's police report. Sadly, he's missing as well."

"I'm still in danger." She rested her head on the pillow and stared at the ceiling.

"We'll protect you when you need it."

"John, I can't live like this. And I'm not sure that Cole..." *Speak of the devil.* Her words stopped and hung in the air as he framed the doorway. His face lightened when he saw she was awake.

She quickly glanced at him, then avoided his gaze. Two nurses ran into the room, pushing past him.

"What is it?" John jumped to his feet as the nurses went straight for the monitors.

"Her heart monitor jumped several beats, and her rate is elevated," the nurse said as she inspected the tape she pulled from the machine.

"I think she's fine," John said, casting Cole a look. He sat back down.

Mia kept her face toward the ceiling. She felt her cheeks heat as the red colored her skin.

"Who are you?" Cole's voice rumbled at the door.

"I was sent by her mother. Let me pass."

Mia's head snapped toward the Native American accent. "I know you. I mean, I've seen you. Please, come in." Her brows drew together as she watched the Indian step past Cole, whose face tightened in disapproval. The Indian stood at the end of her bed, dressed in jeans and a white button-down shirt. His bronze skin and long black hair accentuated the turquoise necklace adorning his neck. Its design was simple: a pendant of a hand with a swirl in its palm. It was the same swirl on the vampire's black containers.

"Your pendant—I've seen that symbol in the center before. What does it mean to you?" Mia sipped her water, her eyes flicked over the man in front of her—in the flesh, not in her dream.

"The swirl is the eye in hand. It represents a mystic or all-seeing hand. It represents the presence of the Great Spirit in man." There was pride in his voice as he spoke.

"Do you know about me?"

"We all know about you, Miakoda."

She shifted uneasily, and Cole took a step closer to her.

The man continued, laying a piece of cloth on the bed at her feet. "This is the blanket that you were wrapped in when your spirit first fell."

Mia sat straight up in the bed and stared at the blanket with wide-eyes. Her fingers twitched to take it, but her mind was too weak for the images that might come.

The Indian looked into her eyes. "You can see it all later, Miakoda. Now, you must rest. I will tell you the things you want to know, then you can dig deeper." He pointed to the chair beside him. "May I?"

He sat down after she nodded and began his tale. "Miakoda, you are very special to us. We have been watching you, making sure you don't turn like the true spirit of your father." He turned to Cole. "*You* carry his blood, Detective, and we are amazed that you have not turned to the side of evil. It must be a struggle for you to control such a beast inside. The woman who made you was made from evil, like Miakoda's spirit."

"Mia is *not* evil." Cole stood tall, his fangs barred as he defended her.

"We know, but like you, she will struggle to stay that way. Now that you have helped her awaken her true self, she will continue to grow with a great spirit inside of her, one that will bring peace to our people and others. But she can easily turn... if not loved." He touched his necklace, rubbed the center, and closed his eyes.

"Can you please tell me what you're talking about? I can turn? Turn into what?"

"Let me start from the beginning. You come from a very bad choice made by a Medicine Man and healer. What they did was most forbidden. He was stricken from grief—many nights he prayed unto the great sprits to give him a child, to make his barren wife pregnant. But, the Great Spirit turned a deaf ear to his plea. Many moons passed, and his wife grew old and soon it would be too late for her to conceive. He turned to the dark spirits and opened a portal by the use of magic. A powerful, dark spirit entered—the spirit of the vampires. The spirit dominated the medicine man's soul, overtaking his body, feeding on the village's people, drinking their blood, raping their women. Most of them died, and those who didn't, became pregnant. The tribe could take no more and sent messengers to nearby villages, to learn the ancient methods for the vampire's destruction. He could not be killed as a mortal man could be killed. They returned after several months to find the medicine man's wife large with child. The child was brought into the world, and its mother died shortly after. After the dark spirit drained her body of its blood, he took the child and escaped the village. The braves had formed a plan to kill him. They chased him down, and soon found him in a feeding frenzy, lost to his bloodlust.

"He grabbed the baby and ran as he heard them approach. The villagers chased him, chanting the magic that would kill the dark spirit. A hatchet hit the back of his body, and he and the baby fell to the ground. They chanted until the dark spirit rose out of the body and was destroyed by the magic given to the hunters to kill him.

"The Medicine man's spirit returned to his body. He laid a dying hand on the baby and chanted, using his last breaths to weave a Shaman's web of spiritual good. This was a force to be reckoned with. As he chanted, a bolt of lightning struck the infant, and then he gazed into his baby's eyes as a good man, with a good spirit. Then they took their last breaths together."

"Legend says they saw the moon lift the baby's spirit, to hold in its power. *You,* Miakoda, were the baby."

"I'm the baby? That's a lot to take in." Silent tears rolled down Mia's face.

The Indian stood, walked to the edge of her bed, and regarded each one of them before returning his focus to Mia.

"Have you looked at your wounds? Have any of you seen her wounds?"

They all shook their heads, and he walked to the side of her bed. "May I?" He motioned toward her bandage.

She nodded and he turned her gently to the side. Cole leaned in, as well as John, and stared as the Indian peeled back the bandage.

"I haven't had a reason to smile in a week," Cole said as his lips curved.

"Well, ain't that some shit," John said as he sat back in the chair.

"What? What is it? I can't see my back. Hello?" Mia stretched her neck, straining to see her backside.

John shook his head in disbelief. "Your skin has closed, and it's smooth. I've never seen a human heal like that. And I've seen a lot of creatures in my day but none like you, Mia."

"Great. It's true." She wiped the falling tears from her eyes. "This is just great." She placed the items John had laid on top of her down on the table.

"Why are you so upset about this?" John asked.

"*Why?* Before I was just a weird girl that worked in a funeral home. And now, I'm this embodied spirit thing that people want to kill. Also, this Indian just informed me that the man that I've been *kissing* is kind of my relative."

"Miakoda, you and the vampire are not related. You embodied the spirit, and he carries the blood. I didn't come here to upset you. I will go." The Indian turned to leave as a nurse rushed in with a shot. Mia's eyes went wide as she stared at the needle.

"This is just to calm you down. You're getting too upset."

Mia jerked away from her. John and Cole came to each side of the bed. The Indian went to her feet as she thrashed. "No! You are *not* sticking me with that." Mia kicked, and they all grabbed her limbs.

"Miss Starr, it's for your own safety. You're going to hurt yourself." The nurse flipped the cap off the needle, and Mia felt the anger build inside.

"I. Said. No!" She stared down at the needle. With wide eyes, everyone stared in awe as the needle bent into a u-shape. She was released, and they stepped back.

"Nurse, go and don't come back in unless we call you." John grabbed her arm and moved her away from Mia. She scurried out of the room.

The Indian smiled at her. "I'm proud to have witnessed some of your power. After feeling your energy surge, I can't wait to see what else will come forth inside you. Miakoda, you will make my people proud... as long as you stay on the side of good."

He patted her leg, walked to the door, then paused in the doorway. "Miakoda, open your soul and listen to your spirit. If you stray away from your destiny, the great spirits will guide your path. Open your mind to the paths."

"Can I find you if I want to talk?" she asked.

"That is not wise. There are still people that would like to see your spirit destroyed. Some to make sure you don't turn. Others are afraid that you will destroy them. I will find you if you need me." He turned to leave. "Oh, and don't fear the bite. It will complete you." He disappeared out the door.

Mia stared at Cole. He looked tired and hungry, his face paler than she had ever seen it. Mia grabbed the pen and began to sign the forms John handed her. She laid them on the table, one-by-one, as she finished reading and signing. "John, can I talk to you in private?"

"If it concerns me, you can say it in front of me. I have my big vampire pants on today." Cole's tone was exhausted.

"Okay. John, if I do this... I want to do it alone."

John sighed as he rubbed his hand through his hair. She saw his eyes trail to Cole's as he winced.

Cole straightened his spine and narrowed his eyes. "I don't have the strength to battle you today. If that's what you want, so be it." She blinked and Cole was gone.

"He's hungry, he hasn't eaten in days, and he's been staying awake past sunrise. Mia, he cares for you, and he's been sick with worry. Why do you turn him away?" John leaned up in the chair, placing his forearms on his legs.

"I need time. I love him. God help me, I love him. But all I see when I look at him is a fully enraged vampire, ripping the head off another, drinking his blood for revenge, then turning his rage on others. He could have killed me, John." She slouched down in the bed as exhaustion set in.

"Is that what you think he killed Evet for—revenge?" John stood, grabbing his coat that lay across the chair. "Mia, you need to think hard about what you want. I told you once, if you don't want him, cut him loose." He walked to the door.

"I do want him. I'm scared. Just keep him away from me, John, please. I need to figure out how to make all this work." She turned to her side, hugging the pillow.

"I'll try, Mia. Your classes begin next week. I'll call you to give you your schedule. After the academy for regular police procedures, you'll need to be trained by a vampire for the other stuff." He patted the doorframe with his hand, opened his mouth to say something, then closed it and walked away.

As she started drifting off, Cole's hurtful gaze haunted her. When she woke, she'd try to figure all this out. She'd seen him at his worst, hadn't she? What if he attacked her and she couldn't bring him back like before? Oh, God. Could she even cut him loose if she had too? She realized that even when she was in a room full of people, she still felt alone until Cole looked at her. That was when she felt alive.

THIRTY-FIVE

*M*ia gazed at the clear sky blanketed with stars and a bright full moon. She was sitting on her favorite bench at the funeral home eating dinner.

She had started schooling at the academy. It was more paperwork and tactics than anything. John assured her that she would have extensive training in vampire combat, and since she was staying away from Cole, John would be training her himself. John called her out for her first case a couple of days ago, and she was delighted to go alone. Three weeks had passed since she last saw Cole. She didn't need a man to define her, but she did come to realize that she wanted one to love her.

Mia bit into her leftover steak, ignoring the background noises. She still had detectives watching over her, so she was accustomed to the noise coming from the front parking lot.

The hair on the back of her neck suddenly stood, and her pulse began to race as an electric current washed over her. *Cole.* She stood, looking around her, then froze as her eyes fell upon him. She backed into the tree and swallowed the piece of food in her mouth. His body almost glowed in the moonlight as he strolled toward her, his eyes fixed onto hers.

As he got closer, her hands grabbed at the tree, steadying her legs. He still looked weak, hungry, and tired, but deadly gorgeous. She tipped her head back to keep her eyes on his as he stood in front of her. "Miakoda, you have enthralled me like the moon that captured your spirit. I cannot eat or sleep. Nothing has meaning without you." His eyes searched hers.

"You need to eat, Cole."

"I'm not concerned with food, Mia. Tell me to stay with you. Tell me you want me." His eyes fell to her lips, and her breath hitched.

She stayed silent, unable to speak. Her mind spun with words, but she didn't know what she should say.

"Mia, if you let me leave, I won't come back. I will not play games."

Still no words fell from her lips as she stared back at him. He twitched his head into a quick nod, drew his lips into a thin line, and turned away from her, walking slowly back across the graveyard.

Her body shut down, nothing would respond as she watched him walk away from her. *Forever*. She knew he would be a man of his word and push her out of his mind. *Say something!* She begged her lips to move as her mind screamed his name.

In the distance Cole stilled, lifting his gaze from the ground, with his palm out as tiny rain drops Mia pulled from the sky fell upon his skin. He remained still, silent, as if waiting for a deeper affirmation from her. She sent an electric current through the air and watched his fingers twitch when it rode by him on the wind. When Cole sagged his head, Mia whispered his name and knew the instant her call slithered by him.

He twirled around, locked into her gaze, then was against her, pressing her into the tree before her next breath. His hands reached toward her face then dropped back to his sides. Wetting his lips, Cole stared at her mouth, his hunger and need so acute it was near tangible, but he held back. With the tiniest twitch of her lips Mia attempted a smile, and it seemed to be the sign Cole needed.

Cole cupped her face, and like a match, his lips brushed against hers, lighting a fire inside her. He was the spark that ignited her passion.

Reaching up, she grabbed the back of his neck, pulling him into her and deepening the kiss.

His fangs instantly jutted out, and he moaned.

She pulled away. She'd given this a lot of thought. If she was going to do this, she needed to feel like she pleased him—completely.

He stared at her, his eyes flicking back to her lips. "What, Mia? What's wrong?" He rested his forehead against hers, stroking the side of her cheeks with his thumbs.

When she slid out of her shoes and pushed him back, he stared at her with a stunned expression. "There's only one way I know for certain to make this work, and you're not where I want you yet." She licked her lips as her mind ran wild with her plan.

"Mia, I haven't fed in a while. I'm very hungry. Please, do not toy with me." His tone was strained.

"Well, that means your strength is down. That's good. You'll be slower than normal."

"Why would you say such a thing?" He looked at her with a puzzled expression.

"Because if you want me, you'll have to hunt me," she said as she moved to the side, slipping out of his grasp.

"Mia, no! I'm too deprived. I'll lose—"

Mia bolted into the graveyard.

Cole looked down at the bench, saw what was left of her steak, and licked his lips before he began the chase.

Slowly, he stalked his prey. He grew hungrier as he hunted, the vampire within him surfacing. His fangs grew longer, and his mouth salivated with need. *Must take her now.*

Cole watched her slide behind a large stone tablet, peeling her jeans off. He could see the anticipation in her face. And as she ran to the next stone, he could see her pulse pounding inside her skin. Her eyes changed, and he saw the beast inside her had surfaced.

"Take me the way you want to," she whispered as she moved to the next stone.

Cole paused behind the granite block she had just left, bending down as her scent engulfed his senses. He picked up her discarded jeans and bra, then growled at the thought of her running through the graveyard with no pants on. Running from him. He turned. The moonlight cast her silhouette against a stone in the distance. His lips parted as he gazed at her image, and, in a blink, he was there, fully intending to take her the way he wanted.

"Too bad you can't feel me as well as I can you." His voice was hot with desire, his cock throbbing in his pants as he stood on the other side of the stone.

"You haven't caught me yet." She escaped into the open field, running at top speed.

His growl echoed through the night and he watched it vibrate through Mia's body. Her toes grabbed at the grass as she strived for more leverage but it was too late. He grabbed her around the waist, lifted her into the air, and twisted as he brought her to the ground. His beast surfaced as she squirmed under him, trying to free herself from his grasp, and he battled against it.

"Mia, stop struggling. God, stop." He grabbed her wrists, holding them above her head and burned a kiss onto her lips, pressing his hard length into her leg.

She moaned against him, sending his body into a shiver. When she rotated her hips touching his pulsing hardness, he couldn't take much more. He ached to be inside her, to feel her warmth wrap around him. He tried hard not to frighten her, but her game had pushed him too far.

She gulped as he pushed her back, devouring her with his eyes. Cole hunched over her. Looping his arms under her legs, he kissed her stomach, then fisted her panties. He yanked hard as he pulled himself to his knees, taking her with him and shredding her thin cotton panties. She grew still when his fangs raked across her inner thigh, and then she cried out as he buried his face into her wetness. He lapped at her folds, then flicked across her sensitive flesh. Mia threw her arms out to the side and raked the grass with her nails. "You're right on the edge," Cole growled against her flesh, and she panted into the night air.

Her taste was sweeter than he had envisioned. It consumed him with the need to make her convulse against his tongue. As her juices grew thick with each whip of his tongue, his thoughts ran wild. He explored her skin with his hands as each one of his desires flipped through his mind. His cock jumped with excitement, the head slick with desire. He reached down, squeezing the hood of his shaft, depriving it from release as his seed filled his length. So long he had been without, and he couldn't take this much longer. He needed to bury himself deep inside her until he completely disappeared.

His fingers plunged inside, preparing her for his engorged flesh. She moaned, and her breaths became shallow and fast as he flicked her sensitive spot with his tongue.

A flash of light caught his eyes, and they darted up toward the sky. As he lapped at her, he watched the street lights around the perimeter flicker with her movements, pulsing with her heartbeat. He knew it—knew it'd been her causing the electric pulse in the lights before, and now her energy was alive, making the lights dance to her pleasure.

He growled as his tongue ruthlessly pleasured her, his fingers gently stroking her warmth. "Come for me."

Her muscles went taut against his arms, and her body arched as she balanced on her shoulders. Her body jolted with pleasure, and she erupted in an explosion of ecstasy.

As she shook in his arms, her muscles grabbed at his buried fingers, making his cock painfully hard. He needed more of her, all of her. Placing her breathless body on the ground, he trailed kisses up her stomach, rolling her shirt up until he found an erect nipple. He pulled it into his mouth, sucking until it swelled from his touch.

Leaning down on his elbow, his shaft waited at her entrance as he placed his forehead between her breasts, pausing, trying hard to hold back the beast.

* * *

Mia threaded her fingers through his hair and held his head to her chest. She could feel his struggle and lifted her hips in admission. The head of his shaft slipped into her warmth.

They had been this far before, and each time she felt her body stretching around his girth, she'd tense and her arousal would fade. Not tonight. She was on fire with need, wanting more of him. All of him. Yet he still held back. She moved again, and he stilled as more of him slipped inside.

"Mia, don't do that." His voice strained through the ragged breaths blowing against her chest. His hands shot out, grasping the grass next to her, and then he began to withdraw, keeping his forehead to her chest.

She wrapped her legs around his waist, jerking upward again and again, inching his shaft into her tight sheath. With each movement, she saw him unravel.

Cole growled against her chest.

Mia gasped at the sharpness of his fangs against her breast. She fought her past. Fought the darkness threatening to wedge its way between them. "Cole, take me," she panted out the words.

"You have broken me, Mia. I can't control my urges. Can't hold back. I'm so hungry for you. Forgive me." His breath rolled inside of her ear, decorating her skin with goose bumps. When he rolled his hips, her blood shot through her veins like a jet, and she watched as the sudden surge of her blood shattered the last of his restraint.

Jerking his head up, Cole gazed at her. His eyes glowed bright with a faint amber hue, the desire in them almost palpable, and his fangs extended with need. The predator had taken over. When Mia gulped at the sight of him, his shaft jumped inside her, growing, along with his fangs.

Devouring her with his eyes, he went to his knees, grabbing her hips as he yanked her down onto him, burying himself deep inside of her.

Mia screamed into the night as she took his full length. He continued to drive into her, relentlessly taking her. The sound of her pleasure seemed to drive him to the edge of ecstasy, and she felt him expand inside her. He reached down, ripping the shirt from her body. Grabbing her arms, he pulled her into his lap.

"You once offered to give me your blood. After all you have seen—do you accept me now?"

Flooded with emotions, her hands shot out to wrap around his head and pull his lips to hers. His response was instant. His hands roamed her bare back, crushing her against his chest. She felt her hard nipples rake across his skin, ripping a moan from his throat.

He pulled away and searched her eyes. "Bare your neck to me."

She momentarily froze. Her body went rigid as the dark memories crept up her spine.

"Look at me, Mia. Eyes open, on me." When Mia swallowed hard and locked into his gaze, he knew he had dragged her back to him. He tilted his head and eyed her delicate fingers as she swept the hair off her shoulder. She leaned back in his arms and exposed her neck.

He rolled his hips once more, plunging inside her. His eyes narrowed as they flicked across her neck. Like a bolt of lightning, he lunged forward, burying his fangs into her flesh and holding his prey with a tight possession.

Mia's arms flung outward, her head fell back and she screamed to the sky, convulsing with a crushing orgasm. Her muscles grabbed at him, milking his shaft into submission.

His eyes flickered open as the lights burst around them. Tiny particles sparkled in the night as each light exploded. He paused in awe of her power—power she didn't fully understand. Nothing could top this. She came from his bite and created a magnificent light show from the pleasure he had given her. He teetered on the razor's edge.

They moved in unison until he was rocked into ecstasy and his seed shot inside her. Waves of pleasure pulsated throughout his body, each shot of his seed sending him into a new realm of pleasure.

He felt her skin tightly-wrapped around his fangs, his bloodlust soaring as he latched his lips around the wound, and for the first time, sucked hard against her skin.

Mia cradled his head as he savored her warm red liquid, each pull binding them. He could feel her and relished the heated waves of pleasure rolling through her body. The bliss she felt from Cole drinking her blood was unexpected and he almost laughed when he felt her chaotic emotions. He stilled and his body stiffened, something else was happening.

Mia stared at him under the blanket of the moon. "Cole"—her fingertips stroked his back—"your skin tone is changing and... you feel warmer."

Cole's pulse beat so loudly in his ears that he could hardly move. He fell forward, holding her and bracing their fall with his arm. His eyes widened, confusion swept over him, and his breath rushed out of his body as electric pricks surged through him. Like a raging river, his blood soared through his veins, his heart pounded in his chest. *She's mine.*

"Cole, your heart is beating." Mia pulled him down, placing her ear to his chest.

"Only for you, Mia. It will only beat for you." He sliced his tongue on a fang and licked the marks he made. He felt alive as he brushed kisses across her face. How long would it last? He pondered the question, knowing the heart beats when her blood is inside of him. His body would surely absorb her liquid, and then it would stop. He smiled against her lips. *Then I will take her again—my bride.*

They lay next to each other under the moon. Mia stroked his chest with her fingers, watching it rise and fall with each breath he took. His body warmed under her touch with each unstable beat of his heart.

The sound of the phone shattered their silence. She sighed, pulling herself up on her elbow to stare down at him. "Cole, I really do hate your work phone." Her lips stretched into a smile.

He pulled her to him, kissing her with rejuvenated warmth. "That's not my phone. It's yours, Agent Starr." His hand searched the ground for her jeans, and her cell dropped to the ground. She lay on top of him, straddling him as she reached for the phone.

John's voice came over the two-way speaker. "Mia, we have a report of a power outage by the funeral home. Are you okay?"

They both laughed as she pushed the transmit button. "I'm okay, John. Just testing out my new skills." She winked at Cole, and he grew hard underneath her, ready to take her again.

"Good. We have a lead on Cramer. Report to headquarters. You can't work this one alone, so I'll find someone to work the case with you. Our chances of finding him are slim."

She stared down at Cole. His hands roamed her stomach and then cupped her breast. "Ride with me, Mia, we'd make a good team."

"I know." She stared down into his eyes, then clicked the phone. "John, I have a partner. We'll be there soon, and don't worry, we'll catch him. And if not, the hunt will be fun." She turned the phone off and tossed it to the ground, then rubbed against his shaft, causing him to stifle a moan.

He grabbed his pants, pulling out her torn underwear from the elevator and dangled them in front of her.

"You made me scream your name. They're all yours. And so am I."

"How about I ride you first, before we go catch the bad guys?" Her eyes challenged him, and he grabbed her hips, securing her body to his.

"You're a bad girl, Miakoda." He stroked her cheek with his hand as he gazed at her.

"Only for you, Cole."

He laughed low as he slid back into her warmth. "I hope you remember that you love me when I train you in vampire defense. There's a lot I need to teach you, and I won't be easy on you."

Mia bent down, kissing him deeply. "I'll accept that challenge, Detective. And you remember you love me when I'm kicking your ass."

"Mia, you need to take my blood. Bite me so I can mix with you." His movements stopped, and his tone turned serious. "It's for your safety, in case something happens."

"Not tonight, I just want to love you. Besides, what could happen when I have you to protect me?" She sealed her words with a deep kiss, wiping his worries away.

In memory of my loving father-n-law,
Carmine Cappelli.
Vamppelli's is my dedication to you. You will never
be forgotten.

I support the Choroideremia Research Foundation.
To help make sure everyone that is going blind from
this disease has the chance to read books the way they
want to, with their eyes. www.CureCHM.org

Books by Tina Carreiro

Power of the Moon
Covet the Moon
Rearranged

Tina Carreiro currently lives in Florida with her two children and her extremely patient, and loving husband. She started reading her mother's unguarded romance novels at a young age and her love for writing romance began. She holds a degree in computer programming and is a jack-of-all-trades, working in many industries from automotive to pizza since the age of thirteen. The passion for writing never died and now she's fulfilling her dream to write and share her love for reading with others. Feel free to visit her Facebook page or her website at www.tinacarreiro.com or follow her on Twitter.

Made in the USA
Columbia, SC
28 August 2024

41252241R00233